BLADE OF THE DESTROYER

The Last Bucelarii: Book 1

ANDY PELOQUIN

To Harrison,
"May the Watcher
have mercy on you!"

Edited by: J. Ellington Ashton Press Staff
Cover Art by: **Marie Story**

J. Ellington Ashton Press

http://jellingtonashton.com/

Acknowledgements

To Peter J. Story, who unknowingly inspired me to take up writing fiction once again, and without whom I would never have published my first book.

To Vicki, Rosi, Sam, Marie, and E.J., my fearless friends who never hesitated to say it like it was, and without whom this book would have been a disaster.

A man often meets his destiny on the road he took to avoid it -- Jean de La Fontaine

Chapter One

Eyes the color of night watched Lord Damuria's body plunge to the forest floor. The wind seemed to hold the nobleman suspended in the air for a moment before slowly releasing his body to the grasping clutches of gravity.

The hard, dark face of the Hunter showed no sign of pity as the body landed with a loud *thud* at his feet.

It is no more than he deserves, he thought.

The Hunter had no idea *why* Lord Damuria deserved death, nor did he care. He had been paid, and that was all that mattered.

He felt no remorse as he watched the broken man fight for his last pitiful, agonizing breaths. Not given to mercy, the fear in Lord Damuria's eyes meant nothing.

Soot and mud stained the nobleman's robes, his bright crimson blood contrasting sharply with the white blond of his hair. Where Damuria's hands had once been, only stumps remained. The Hunter's broad-headed crossbow bolts had sliced through bone and tendon, severing the man's hands at the wrist. The bolts were buried deep in the stone of the cliff, still stained with Damuria's blood.

The nobleman struggled to speak, made difficult by the quarrel puncturing his lungs. The Hunter bent close to hear the whispered words.

"Do...it...you...bastard." Lord Damuria's eyes closed as he awaited the inevitable.

The Hunter moved with precision and speed, drawing the dagger from his belt and plunging it deep into the dying man's chest. The thrust snapped ribs and sliced through smooth heart muscle. Damuria's screams echoed in the silence of the forest, an eerie sound tinged with desperation and terror.

The screams of his victims always remained with him long after their deaths. They played over and over in his mind, accompanied by the vision of their dying faces.

Bright ruby light flared from the gem set in the hilt of the dagger, and power rushed through the blade. The Hunter gasped as the voice in his mind screamed its pleasure. The familiar pain flared along his back, but he was accustomed to it. This pain was the price he paid for the power.

This, he thought, reveling in the sensations flooding through him, *this is why I do it.*

A final shudder ran through the broken body before him, and the cries of agony faded into a gentle whisper. "Fucking...Hunter..." Damuria cursed with his dying breath.

Silence reigned in the forest, broken only by the sound of the wind whistling through the trees. After the thrill of the chase, the stillness hung like a weight on the Hunter's mind. A tremble ran through his calloused hands as he gripped the worn hilt of the knife embedded in his latest kill, his long, lean muscles bulging in his effort to wrench the blade free. The knife was caught on the dead man's ribs, and pulling it free required a surprising amount of effort, even with the Hunter's immense strength.

Blood glistened on the blade, and the Hunter watched it soak into the steel. The bright red light leaking from the gem slowly dimmed, and the stone became translucent and colorless once more.

The dagger has been sated. He no longer heard the insistent voice in his head urging him to kill. *It will remain silent, for now.*

The Hunter sheathed his blade and stooped to kneel over the lifeless form of his prey. Placing one hand on the man's head and the other on his now-silent heart, he bowed his head.

"May the Long Keeper take your body; your soul is forfeit," the Hunter intoned. His voice was rich and deep with a hint of gravel. A hard voice, reciting a final ritual for fallen prey. A ritual from a past he could no longer remember.

He stared down at the broken body lying at his feet.

This one was surprisingly difficult to track down.

Green blood now oozed from the dead man's severed wrists, staining the forest canopy a sickly color. The scent of poisoned flesh hung in the air—the effects of the venomous argam with which he coated the bolts, the Hunter knew.

A fit creature for the hunt. A sense of satisfaction flooded him. *Another contract fulfilled.*

He had killed all manner of men. Big men, little men, strong men, weak men. Cowards, and brave fools. Heroes, villains, rich men, beggars.

He was the Hunter, and all men were his prey.

Climbing to his feet, the Hunter turned his back on the corpse and strode toward the cliff. He climbed the craggy face with ease, taking care to avoid the blood-soaked rocks marking Lord Damuria's fatal path. His powerful muscles made the ascent easy, and he soon stood at the top of the cliff, showing no signs of exhaustion.

The Hunter stared at the city sprawling across the plain and along the ocean's edge.

Voramis. My city.

Thick walls towered high, the massive city gates open to allow the traffic to flow at a steady pace. Temple spires reached for the clouds, while the blocky Palace of Justice watched over the sprawling metropolis in its shadow. Upper Voramis, jewel of the city, straddled the hilltop upon which the city had been built, looking down protectively over Lower Voramis. To the west, the cloudy blue waters of the Endless Sea stretched farther than the eye could see.

The Hunter studied the position of the sun—already well into its descent toward the horizon. Night would have fallen by the time he reached Voramis. It was always easier to move through the city streets after dark; he wouldn't attract undue attention—either from the Heresiarchs guarding the city gate, or from the gangs of thugs roaming the Merchant's Quarter.

With a sigh for his road-weary feet, the Hunter began the long walk back to the city.

* * *

The streets of Lower Voramis came alive after dark. Light spilled from the numerous brothels, taverns, and gambling houses, along Reveler's Lane, illuminating Voramis' busiest and least-reputable thoroughfare. The Blackfall District served as the hub for every vice and crime created by men and women with more money than good sense.

Burly men wearing the uniform of hired muscle guarded the doors to their establishments with fierce pride, their watchful eyes never straying from the drunken revelers stumbling between alehouses and whorehouses in various stages of inebriation.

The working classes inhabiting the run-down districts spent their meager coin on drink, gambling, and cheap whores. Unwary visitors to the district often woke up with an aching head and an empty purse, not to mention a host of persistent diseases on body parts better kept free of infection.

The Hunter hated the Blackfall District, but his home in the Beggar's Quarter lay on the far side of the city, leaving him no choice but to traverse it.

He groaned at his untimely ill-fortune as three drunken men stumbled from The Cock and Bull—an inn known for cheap beer and cheaper women—belting out a bawdy tune. Two of the lushes clung to each other for support, barely managing to keep their feet as they wended their unsteady way down Reveler's Lane.

The third, a man with a forehead like a rock and a nose flattened by too many beatings, crushed his pewter tankard in his massive hands. His arms looked hewn from rock—a very hairy, very tattooed rock.

"*And then me love, a lovely lass,*" sang the two drunkards, their voices rising above the din of revelry around them, "*she kissed me face, I poked her-*"

"Won't you two shut the frozen hell up?" their companion muttered. "Drunken idiots, ya can't even get the song right!"

"You're jush jealoush becaush ya don't have me fine singin' voice, Rifter," one slurred at him.

"Oh, get stuffed, Emon," Rifter said with a glare. "If ya weren't so Minstrel-damned drunk, you'd know that ya sound worse than a pair of ruttin' cats in a laundry press."

"And that'sh why yer jealoush, Rifter," said the second drunk. "Your shingin' shoundsh like it's coming from the Watcher'sh own arsehole."

"Which is why, Eld," Rifter snarled, "I know to keep me mouth shut instead of singin' at the top of me lungs when I've had too many ales."

Something about the tension in Rifter's shoulders, coupled with the flattened nose, shouted of the man's desire to fight. In an effort to avoid a confrontation, the Hunter slipped down a darkened side street and into an alley.

The Bloody Hand kept discipline in the Blackfall District, but they failed to maintain even a moderate standard of cleanliness. Just one street away from Reveler's Lane, the stench of waste was such that the Hunter had to cover his face with his cloak to quell the urge to add the contents of his stomach to the filth. Men and women lay scattered in varying states of drunkenness and drug-induced stupor, many of them wallowing in their own filth. Debris and litter clogged the gutters, the refuse spilling out into the street.

Picking up his pace, the Hunter hurried through the streets, keeping his breaths shallow to avoid filling his lungs with the noxious air.

"Evenin', gents." A woman's voice drifted from around the next corner. "Can I offer either of ye a good time? Only four bits, and I promise I'll be gentle with ye."

"What'sh a pretty lady like you," a male voice hiccupped in her direction, "doin' in a place like this?"

The Hunter's heart sank as he recognized the voice of one of the three drunks he had tried to avoid. He was faced with a choice: backtrack and go around the men to avoid a fight, or walk past them and hope his ragged cloak would deflect their attention. With a shrug of resignation, he hunched his shoulders, bent his back, and began to shuffle forward, mimicking the slow gait of a tired old beggar.

The drunken attempts of the two lushes to accept the painted doxy's invitation seemed to have the opposite of the desired effect.

The whore stared at them for a moment, as if weighing up her options, before waving them away dismissively. "The pair of ye's looks too drunk to handle me. As for you, big boy," she said, staring up at Rifter, "I reckon ye'll split me right in half. And that's with me on top, eh?" She patted his arm provocatively, but he pulled it away.

"I'm not much in the mood for company tonight, back-bedder," Rifter spat.

Her face contorted, showing clear distaste at his words. "Well, I've no mind to bed any of ye," she protested. "I'm sure it won't be hard to find men of a *far better* stock than you sorry lot, anyways."

Rifter's expression darkened and he ground his teeth as he watched her mince away. He clenched his fists, his massive arms flexing in anger.

His gaze fell on the Hunter shambling toward him and a malicious gleam flashed in the man's eyes. The other two men saw the Hunter as well, and a grin creased the face of the one called Emon.

"Let's see if we can't have a bit of fun, eh, Rifter?" he asked, chuckling softly as he pointed down the darkened alley in the direction of the Hunter.

Eld released his hold on Emon, and stumbled towards the harmless looking beggar.

"I say there, friend," he said, struggling to imitate a member of the upper class, "it's time for you to move out of the street and make way for your betters." Emon clapped his hands on the Hunter's shoulders and shoved hard.

The Hunter had no intention of allowing himself to be pushed into the filth of the gutter. From it rose the strong, repulsive odor of human refuse mixed with the gods-knew-what else, resulting in the type of stench that seeped into the pores of a man's skin and reeked even after weeks of regular washing. He stood firm, and the drunken man sprawled into the muck.

Emon gagged as his mouth filled with the slime, and he retched—adding his vomit to the ordure staining his face. His companion, no less drunk, stared down at his friend for a long moment before reacting.

"Say there," Eld protested, "that's down…down…right rude of you, friend, to knock Emon over."

The Hunter attempted to step around Emon's fallen form, but Eld moved to block his way. Opting for retreat, the Hunter found the hulking form of Rifter cutting off his escape.

"My friend speaks the truth, wretch," Rifter growled, his breath heavy with alcohol and anger. "You owe him an apology, and an imperial for his clothing."

Emon's clothing was clearly worth far less than an imperial—an entire year's wages for a day laborer—but the Hunter could see Rifter was spoiling for a fight.

"Apologies, good sirs," said the Hunter, adopting the quavering voice of an old man. "It was clumsy of me not to see where you were walking. Alas, I have naught to give you."

"Nothing, beggar?" Rifter's voice had a hard edge.

"No, good masters. A poor man like myself can barely scrounge together two bits, much less a whole imperial. Please, I beg you to let me pass, and the gods will bless you for your generosity."

The Hunter attempted to move once more, but Rifter's hand on his arm was firm, holding him in place. "If you don't have an imperial to spare, beggar," the big brute said, "we'll just have to take what you have and be content."

Rifter reached out to pull back the hood, but the Hunter twisted away, his speed clearly surprising the hulking Rifter. The big man had still managed to close his sausage fingers around the Hunter's robe, ripping it from the beggar's shoulders.

"Let's see what this has to..." Rifter's words trailed off in disbelief.

The Hunter straightened, his eyes now level with his enemy. Rifter frowned as he took in the features of the handsome face of the Hunter; the sculpted nose, high cheekbones, and strong chin were not the features of a penniless beggar. His dark hair, its color near-black in the dark alley, was pulled back into a tight tail. His unadorned leather armor, clearly worn and well-used, revealed a lean, lithe form.

The Hunter's eyes, a color somehow darker than the starless night above, held no fear. He glared at Rifter with quiet calm, taking in the huge man's features, and his expression showed nothing but contempt and resignation.

Rifter's eyes dropped to the sword at the Hunter's waist, and the Hunter knew the man's dull mind was struggling to keep up. Only Heresiarchs were permitted to carry swords, but the Hunter cared little for the laws of the city.

"Hey," shouted Emon from the ground, spitting foul muck and wiping black slime from his mouth, "he's not old! What's going on here?"

"Last chance," the Hunter said in a voice filled with menace. "Walk away."

In their befuddled state, Emon and Eld tried to comprehend the gravity of their situation. The Hunter saw the momentary flash of good sense in Rifter's eyes, as his brain screamed for him to run away, but the anger in the big man caused it to go unheeded.

"Sorry, boyo," Rifter said, lapsing back into his usual brogue. He bared his teeth in an evil grin and balled his enormous fists. "You've insulted me mates, and now it turns out you've got somethin' valuable beneath that ratty cloak of yours."

"You've been warned," replied the Hunter, "and now you've seen my face."

He stepped back as the foul-smelling Emon struggled to his feet. His hand dropped to the sword hanging from his belt, and he stared down into the drunk's befuddled eyes.

"That's mine now!" Emon stumbled forward and reached for the sword.

The Hunter stepped forward, the blade seeming to appear in his hand.

It took Emon's befuddled brain a few seconds to register the fact that his hands were no longer attached to his arms. He didn't even scream as he fell to his knees, blood spurting from the stumps of his forearms.

"Emon!" Eld lashed out with a wild swing at the Hunter, who took a single contemptuous step back to avoid the drunken blow.

Eld stumbled off balance, and before he could recover, the Hunter slammed the hard edge of his calloused hand into the soft tissue of Eld's throat. Eld fell to the floor, clutching at his ruined windpipe.

Rifter had not moved in the seconds it had taken the Hunter to dispatch his friends. He remained rooted to the spot, eyes wide. A flicker of fear flashed through his befuddled mind.

"Two down, *friend*," the Hunter rasped, his depthless eyes burning as he stared at Rifter.

The harsh voice wrenched the big man from his stupor, and rage bubbled in his chest. "You cunt-eating bastard," Rifter growled at the dark figure. "You'll pay for that."

He carried no sword, but the long dagger he drew from his coat was razor sharp. His huge fists dwarfed the blade, and he wielded it with familiar ease.

Iron.

The Hunter's eyes flicked to the dagger in Rifter's hands for a second, and something akin to hesitance flashed across his dark, handsome face.

"Now let's see how you fare, you dim-witted fuck," Rifter said, his voice low and filled with rage.

The Hunter's burning black eyes stared back at Rifter, locking gazes with the big man. Fear flashed through Rifter once more. He saw death written in the Hunter's expression.

Rifter stepped forward, slashing with short, quick strokes meant to slice open the Hunter's intestines. His attacks lacked sophistication, yet there was brute force behind the blade's cruel edge.

The Hunter avoided Rifter's attacks with ease, not even bothering to block the blows. A dagger appeared in his free hand. Longer than Rifter's weapon, the blade had a single razor edge and a slight curve—perfect for both stabbing and slicing. A small, transparent gem was set into its hilt, and the stone caught the light of the moon in its facets. Something about it made Rifter hesitate for a moment, but that was more than enough.

In the time it took Rifter to swallow his terror, the Hunter's sword cut him to shreds. Blood flowed from a gash in the big man's neck, and he fell to his knees, grasping at the coils of his intestines spilling onto the streets.

"I warned you, *friend*," the Hunter snarled, his voice quiet, "but you refused to heed. You are not my prey this night, yet you made the mistake of seeing my *true* face."

He held up the wicked-looking dagger. "Your life is forfeit, but I leave your soul to the Long Keeper's embrace."

The Hunter slid the blade smoothly into its sheath and gripped his sword with both hands. Moonlight glinted off the flashing steel as the

Hunter struck. Rifter's blocky head fell from its place on the man's sloped shoulders, landing in the muck alongside Emon's bleeding body. His huge, decapitated torso slumped to the ground next to the convulsing figure of Eld, who somehow still lived, fighting for each breath.

The Hunter surveyed his handiwork without remorse. He stooped over the dying man, keeping well away from the iron dagger gripped uselessly in Rifter's hand.

"May the Long Keeper have mercy on your soul, *friend*," the Hunter whispered in the man's ears.

Eld's eyes closed, and his struggles weakened. The dying man voiced no protest as the Hunter wiped his long blade on his clothes.

Shaking his head in disgust at the foolishness of these men who had thought to accost him, the Hunter stooped, recovered his cloak, and donned the disguise of the old man once more.

With slow, measured steps, he shambled away, leaving death in the street behind him.

* * *

The Hunter tossed and turned in his bed, unable to sleep. His blankets suffocated him, but chills shook his body when he kicked them off. He had no idea how much time had passed since he had climbed into bed. It could have been hours or days, but he cared little. The musty scent of unwashed bed linens hung thick in the air, ignored.

While he hunted, the thrill of the kill sent shivers of pleasure down his spine. He could stalk his quarry for days on end without sleep or food, as the inner voice urged him on.

Disgusting mortals, it would whisper in his thoughts. *So weak, so easy to kill.*

But once his prey lay dead at his feet, the absence of the voice echoed like a void in his head. The death of Lord Damuria had silenced the insistent chatter, filling his head with a numb, dull ache that pressed inward and muddled his thoughts.

The end of the hunt brought on a weariness that days of sleep could not ease. He would lie in bed, staring up into the darkness or idly watching the movement of the sun through his windows. He could sleep for days and wake up exhausted, or he wouldn't sleep at all. He had no appetite; the power of the kill fed his body, yet it felt as if every death ate away another piece of his soul.

He tried to ignore the gnawing in his chest. His blade, Soulhunger, remained silent, the kill temporarily sating its bloodlust. He hated the silence more than anything else in the world. In these moments, his mind would replay memories of the hunt. The faces of his victims would float before him, their empty eyes accusing.

He absentmindedly watched dust motes dance in the rays of sun filtering through his window, all the while reliving the gruesome deaths at his hands.

As their lifeless faces danced through his head, he drifted in and out of a fitful sleep, his thoughts filled with hate. He could discern irrationality from logic, but at times like this, he didn't care. He despised every single one of the humans around him, and the voice in his head echoed his ire. He could ignore the voice and its hatred of humanity when he surrounded himself with others, but when alone, the hate bubbled within him like a cauldron of vitriol.

Hours passed, time moving at a snail's pace yet flashing by in the space of a few heartbeats.

The light filtering through his window weakened, doing little to illuminate his bedroom. Peering outside, he saw the sun had begun its plunge into the Endless Sea. The ache in his head subsided, replaced by the voice whispering its renewed bloodlust.

Feed me, it said. Fighting the profound weariness tempting him to remain in bed, he forced himself to climb to his feet. He shook his head to clear the languor, to push back the gloom filling his mind.

It is enough. Time to get up.

His clothes lay piled on the floor, and he sorted through them in search of an unsoiled garment.

Let's see what new victims await me in this new day, what sport I can find to distract myself from this aching.

* * *

A chill hung in the night air, and sweat dripped down the nameless nobleman's back, soaking his thick tunic. He clenched his fists to still his shaking hands. His nondescript clothing blended with the rough crowd of the Blackfall District, and yet he felt eyes upon him, following his every step.

He cast anxious glances around the darkened alleyway, searching for a sign of…what?

By Derelana, why do I fear so?

Perhaps it was the terror of a moonless night, or the instinctive fear dredged up at the thought of meeting the legendary Hunter of Voramis.

He chided himself. *Fuck me for a jumpy little princess!*

He would rather be somewhere else, anywhere else, but here. He had no desire to face the creature the mothers of Voramis used to threaten their children into behaving. His mother had used those legends to frighten him, and he had developed a healthy fear.

Get it together. You have a job to do. Get in, get it done, and get the fiery hell out of there!

The doors to the dilapidated tavern swung shut behind, but none of the handful of patrons at the tables paid him any heed. He slipped a pair of copper bits into the bartender's hand.

"Top of the stairs, door at the end of the hall," the portly pub landlord drawled as he made the coins disappear.

The stairs creaked dangerously as the noble climbed, but he forced himself to place one foot in front of the other. The smell of mold filled his nostrils and threatened to make him sneeze. Swallowing hard, he stared at the door at the end of the darkened hall. It looked like something out of his nightmares, and it made his blood run cold.

"Hello?" he called in a weak voice as he entered the room.

He saw no one in the gloomy darkness, and breathed a sigh of relief as he closed the door behind him. Believing himself alone, the noble took deep, calming breaths.

"What brings you to the underbelly of Voramis, little man?" The voice sounded far too close for the nobleman's liking.

He leapt backward, a feminine squeak bursting from his mouth. His back slammed against the door, knocking the breath from his lungs.

Fucking Hunter!

The nobleman struggled to regain his composure, trying to ignore the thick drops of sweat rolling down his face and coating his palms.

"I-I-I h-have a c-c-commission for you, er, Hunter, sir," he managed to stutter.

"Tell me more," the Hunter said in a rough voice. He stepped forward, pulling back his hood.

Scars crisscrossed the dark face, twisting his upper lip into a perpetual sneer. Heavy brows hooded his dark eyes, and his crooked nose had been broken and badly set. A scarlet ribbon bound his midnight black hair, which hung in long, greasy strands.

Bloody twisted hell, no wonder he hides himself. I would too if I looked like that!

The nobleman realized his mouth hung open, and snapped it shut. He belatedly tried to hide his revulsion at seeing the Hunter's grim visage, but knew it had shown through.

The dark figure with the horrible face waited in silence, clearly unaffected by the nobleman's disdain.

"My, er, master," stuttered the shaken man, gulping as he spoke, "requests your services in a matter of a…er… *delicate* nature."

The Hunter raised an eyebrow. "Your master understands that *delicate* situations cost more?"

"Of course, sir, er, Hunter. I have more than enough to c-cover any extras beyond your usual fees." The nobleman removed a leather purse from his cloak. His hand trembled as he passed it to the Hunter, who balanced it in a burn-scarred hand.

"Good. It will suffice." The purse disappeared into the Hunter's cloak with a movement that caused the noble to jump. His cheeks burned with shame, and he saw mockery in the Hunter's cold eyes. "You have the other item?" the Hunter demanded.

"Of-of course," the noble stammered. He fished around in his robes for a moment before producing a handkerchief. His fingers brushed dangerously close to the Hunter's hand as the assassin took the kerchief, and the aristocrat's skin crawled.

"I-I hope it is enough," the noble whispered, the fear in his voice audible. "It was all my master could procure."

The Hunter's rough fingers traced the initials embroidered in one corner of the delicate cloth. *G.D.*

"It will do," the Hunter rasped.

"So you will take the job? You'll make the coward pay for his affront to my master? The swine—"

The Hunter cut him off. "I care little for your master's reasons *why*, as long as his coin is good. The job will be done." He pulled the hood up, obscuring all but his mouth from the nobleman's view. "Does your master have any special requests?"

"No," the noble replied. "He simply wishes for the job to be done before the Feast of the Mistress, and would prefer the target die in his own home. It is to send a message, you see, to all the nobles of Voramis that—"

"No details, fool," the Hunter growled, interrupting him. "They matter not."

The nobleman stiffened, offended at the Hunter's interruption. The muscles in his back went rigid, and he somehow summoned up the courage to glare at the Hunter. One look into the dark hood, however, and his pride deflated.

"Good." The Hunter's mouth twisted into a horrifying semblance of a grin. "I will contact you when the job is complete."

Shuffling nervously from foot to foot, the noble called upon all of his limited courage and limitless self-importance to stand tall, when he wanted nothing more than to flee. He thought he detected a smile twitch the corner of the Hunter's lips.

"Have the rest of the sum at hand," the Hunter grated. "I will expect it once I have carried out the contract."

"Of-of course," the noble said, "I will…"

He trailed off as he found himself talking to an empty room. The Hunter had simply disappeared, startling him and leaving him feeling like a fool.

Long moments passed before the noble regained his shattered composure. The darkness of the room haunted him, and his eyes darted around as if expecting to see the Hunter standing there once more. His breath came in ragged gasps, and every muscle in his body tensed in fear.

"Fucking Hunter," he cursed in a quiet voice.

He wiped sweaty palms on his fine robes, and his hands shook as he reached for the doorknob. His fear diminished with each shaky step toward the dim light of the stairwell, his relief growing as he stepped into the smoky alehouse taproom. Ignoring the few patrons sitting and drinking, he stumbled into the cool Voramis night.

He breathed deep, filling his lungs with the foul-smelling air and letting the chill calm his nerves.

"Fucking Hunter," he repeated. The curse helped to restore some of his shaken confidence.

His sweat-sodden robes clung to his body, causing him to shudder and pull his cloak tighter. The heavy garment offered some protection from the cold, but the noble knew it would be hours before he would be able to sit without feeling a stab of panic.

With his attention consumed by his desire to leave the stinking alehouse and the horrific memory of the Hunter's scarred visage behind, the terrified man failed to notice the dark figure sitting on the inn rooftop. Midnight black eyes followed the noble's steps, and a scarlet ribbon fluttered in the breeze.

Chapter Two

The Hunter slipped into the abandoned building in which he lived. The massive structure looked on the verge of collapse, but the façade only ran skin deep. He had shored up the timbers of the building, ensuring it would continue to stand, even through the tremors that occasionally shook the city.

He had taken great pains to ensure the construction remained as unattractive and unwelcoming as possible on the outside, even allowing beggars and lepers to occupy sections of the structure. After all, he reasoned, no one would look for anything more than the refuse of humanity in a place like this. The smells of offal and filth alone would dissuade even the most curious potential visitors.

But the beggars were there for more than just disguise...

On the rare days when they found somewhere else to spend the night, the emptiness of the building haunted him. He had begun to leave bundles of food and clothing out in the hope of attracting even a few looking for shelter from the night air. Something about having companionship—even that of filthy beggars and lepers—made him feel less alone when he lay in the silent darkness. They made him feel needed, and he had come to see himself as their protector.

He strode past the forms of men and women huddled under their blankets, nodding to the ones he recognized. Jak the Thumb and Twelve-Fingers Karrl sat playing with a deck of ancient, frayed cards, gambling for scraps of who knew what. Jak stole a look at Karrl's cards as Twelve-Fingers waved at the Hunter.

Passing Old Nan's tent, he scanned the mound of tattered cloth that marked her shelter.

"You'll need more blankets soon," he said, crouching in front of the old woman. "Winter's not far off."

"Aye," she wheezed, "don't I know it? These old bones feel the chill comin' on." She coughed, a horrendous, wet thing that set her frail shoulders shaking. Hacking up a foul green gob of phlegm, she shivered and pulled her ratty bundle of assorted cloths tighter.

She's not long for this world, the Hunter thought, studying the old woman's face—twisted and hideous from some unknown acid—and her liver-spotted skin, gnarled fingers, and stringy hair. She was almost too thin to be alive, and yet fire burned in her eyes. A stubborn determination to live kept Old Nan from the Keeper's embrace, but the Hunter knew she couldn't escape for much longer.

The winter will be harsh on her.

Sorrow flashed through him at the thought. He resolved to leave blankets and one of Graeme's healing potions the next time he returned.

He felt oddly protective of the beggars who lived just beyond his door. They were outcasts from society, just as he was. He would not call them his friends, but it was as close to friendship as he came. It felt…good to do something for someone else, even poor, miserable wretches like Old Nan.

With a gentle pat on Old Nan's shoulder, he picked his way toward the door of his apartment.

A toddler wobbled toward him on unsteady legs, interrupting his progress. The child, losing his balance, grasped the hem of the Hunter's cloak for support. The boy's pursuing mother shot an apologetic glance at the Hunter.

"Arlo's walking quickly, I see."

"That he is," replied Ellinor, a girl the Hunter guessed to be barely into her adolescence. Dark circles framed her bright green eyes, and she looked exhausted.

The Hunter studied the sores and blisters covering the boy's arms, legs, and face. Graeme had told him they were the result of the lad's body burning him from the inside out. The slightest friction would cause the lad's skin to slough off, causing pain and festering wounds. It hurt to see Arlo, yet the lad always appeared happy despite the constant pain.

Ellinor had no money for bandages or poultices to manage the lad's pain, so the Hunter left them in her small makeshift shelter whenever she was out. Even in her poverty, she fought to retain her dignity.

"You'll want to keep a closer eye on him," the Hunter told her. "You never know where he'll disappear to the minute you turn your back."

Arlo tugged on the Hunter's dark robe, and a smile played at the corner of the Hunter's mouth. The smile disappeared when the lad wiped a long trail of snot from his nose on a corner of the Hunter's cloak.

"Back to your mother, lad," said the Hunter, giving Arlo a gentle nudge with his boot. The toddler waddled away, and Ellinor followed in the boy's wake without a backward glance at the Hunter.

A bit of food for the growing lad wouldn't go amiss. He made a mental note to visit Graeme for bandages before the week's end.

The voice in his head begged for blood as he slipped past the beggars, but he ignored its pleading.

Not here. Not them. Once I've found my target, then you will be fed.

Soulhunger's insistence remained a pounding headache in the back of his mind. It craved death, and he could only stave off its urges for so long.

At the heart of the building, past the unpleasant odors emanating from the unwashed mass of bodies, lay his private rooms. A door constructed of bloodwood—one of the densest trees found on the face of Einan—guarded his room, with locks so complex they could only have been designed by an Illusionist Cleric.

The mechanisms worked like a puzzle, requiring precise placing of each piece of the lock. With dozens of moving parts, thousands of possible combinations existed.

Placing his tired fingers on the mechanisms, he let muscle memory guide him.

This one up, that to the right, twist this knob, pull that lever, push these together.

The door swung open on well-oiled hinges, and the Hunter slipped into his home—the only place in the city where he could escape the watchful eyes of the Bloody Hand and the Dark Heresy. Only here could he remove his disguises and show his true face. Not even those poor wretches out there could be allowed to see the real him.

The false flesh required less than a minute to remove. A specially prepared unguent softened the now-rigid molding clay forming the "scar tissue" on the Hunter's face, making it easy for him to wipe away. The greasy black hair pulled free, and it joined the scarlet ribbon in the concealed wardrobe where the Hunter stored all of his alchemical disguises.

Looking out the window, he saw the last vestiges of night had begun to fade.

The sun will rise in an hour. I'll have plenty of time to rest once the ritual is complete.

A face stared back at him in the mirror—his face. It had grown unfamiliar of late, and he found himself uncomfortable staring at his true features. His disguises felt like a part of him.

Who are you? His face mocked him. *Who is the Hunter?*

His changing identity added another element of mystique to the legend. No one could see his true face and live, though few knew the real reason why. He preferred to keep his identity a secret—it would make it easier to hide should he ever have occasion to do so.

He craned his neck, peering over his shoulder at his latest scar. It joined the multitude etched into his back, chest, and shoulders like raw marks on a fleshy chalkboard.

One scar for every life Soulhunger takes. How many are there now? He had no desire to count them, to remember each soul his blade had consumed.

Casting a glance toward the dagger where it hung in his sword belt, he recalled the final moments of the hunt for Lord Damuria.

He nearly escaped, but in the end, the Hunter always gets his prey.

He couldn't remember where the name "the Hunter" originated. Truth be told, he didn't care. He only cared that mention of the name drove fear into the populace of Voramis.

'Where the Hunter goes,' they say, 'death follows in his footsteps.'

He smiled at the thought. *I like that.*

The Hunter encouraged the fear his reputation bred. The more the people of the city feared him, the more willing they were to pay the high price he demanded for his services.

A smile touched his lips as he recalled his brief encounter with the terrified noble earlier that night. He remembered the man's scent—the reek of fresh lace, perfume and pomposity drowned out by the stench of fear.

The foolish little lordling meeting the Hunter on behalf of his employer. His grin turned mocking. *Pissed himself, that one did. Long on money, short on brains and courage. If only he knew how easily I can track him and his master down, thanks to that purse he gave me.*

He threw himself into a plush armchair and reached for a pitcher of wine. Exhaustion overwhelmed his body, but his mind still ached for the thrill of the hunt.

As he drank, his thoughts meandered. The wine was good, but he barely tasted its fruity notes. He studied his room, taking in the soft bed, the plush carpets, and the luxurious pillows. The Hunter had simple tastes, but he loved comfort.

A collection of exotic weaponry hanging on the wall, his one compromise to luxury. He had paid a small fortune for the pieces, many of which had belonged to ancient races long dead. The simple stone, bone, and wooden weapons looked primitive and odd, but he felt a sense of kinship with the artifacts. He was out of place in Voramis, just as these adornments were.

This is my palace, he thought. *These are my treasures.*

His thoughts turned melancholy, so he pushed them aside and forced himself to stand. He strode over to his sword belt hanging on its peg. The blade slipped free of its oiled sheath with a whisper.

She is beautiful. The Hunter couldn't help admiring the way the light glinted off the watered steel. *She has served me well for so long.*

He fell into a relaxed stance, extending the sword in a classic fencing pose. Tension drained from his body, and he moved slowly through a basic sword form he had learned…*how long ago?*

Ragged gaps in his memory left him uncertain of his age, where he had been, or even what he truly was.

He remembered nothing of his life before arriving in Voramis, as if a wall blocked him from recalling details of his past—his birth, childhood, his parents, anything. His earliest recollection was of walking through the city gates. Before that, nothing.

No human lives as long as I have. Voramis had been his home for at least three decades. *Or is it four?*

His missing past had stopped bothering him long ago, but occasionally he found himself wondering who he had been before arriving in Voramis. He had ignored the question for so long the answer no longer mattered.

Sweat broke out on the Hunter's lithe body as he moved faster and faster through the forms, his muscles rippling with each thrust and cut. His mind grew clear, and the aching in his chest diminished with every step. His movements blurred, his sword whistling as it sliced through the air.

The Hunter relished the way his mind detached itself from his body. Muscle memory kept his motions consistent and quick, and he allowed his mind to wander. It served as preparation for what was to come, helped him to block out the voices in his head. As his heart beat faster, the sound of his blood ringing in his ears would drown out Soulhunger's lust. For a few short minutes, he found peace in motion.

With a final cut and thrust, he completed the form. Panting, dripping with sweat, and flushed with exertion, he was ready for the ritual.

The sword slid home in its sheath, and the Hunter's hands closed around the hilt of the dagger.

Soulhunger, we have work to do.

Yes, the voice greeted him eagerly. *We must kill!*

The Hunter lowered himself to the ground, sitting in a comfortable cross-legged position. He let his mind drift, and, closing his eyes, felt the blood rush through his body. At one with the world around him, the Hunter commenced his ritual of seeking.

Soulhunger's razor edge sliced a shallow wound into his palm. The Hunter clenched his fist, squeezing out a few crimson drops onto the knife's blade. The dagger's voice screamed in pleasure, setting his head pounding as it tasted blood.

Removing a whetstone from his pocket, he stroked it along the blade. Soulhunger never needed sharpening, but the activity helped the Hunter clear his head in preparation for what came next.

Pulling out the handkerchief with the initials *G.D.* embroidered into it, the Hunter used it to wipe the blade clean. The contact of the cloth bonded it with the blade, and through the blade to him. The bond would remain until Soulhunger drank deeply of the man's lifeblood.

His subconscious mind sought out the man to whom the handkerchief would link him. He saw a picture of the cloth's owner in his mind's eye, inhaled the scent of the man. His senses surpassed those of a bloodhound once he had located his target.

Parchment, ink, and steel.

He had the scent, and it would lead him to his prey. Soulhunger served as his divining rod, searching out his targets and leading him to them. The weapon amplified his own unique abilities, and without him, the weapon would be just another dagger sitting lifeless in a jeweler's case. The bond between man and weapon made it possible for the Hunter to do what he did.

Long moments passed in silence, the Hunter breathing in a steady rhythm. His mind cast about the city of Voramis for his target, searching for the essence found in the handkerchief.

There! A heartbeat echoed in his mind. *I've found you now!*

We will feed, the voice of the dagger whispered.

The Hunter knew Soulhunger would be drawn ever closer to that heartbeat until it finally sated itself. His target's heart would act as a beacon, and the Hunter would simply have to locate the man.

Together, we are the Hunter.

Truthfully, he had no idea how it worked. He didn't know if his abilities were sorcerous or pure animal instinct. But he didn't care. All that mattered was that it worked.

With care, the Hunter replaced Soulhunger in its sheath. Even with the weapon encased in leather and steel, he could hear it beckoning for him, aching to find its target and drink its heart's blood.

Kill! The voice shouted. *Feed!*

He pushed the insistent voice to the back of his mind.

For now, I need rest. I will deal with the matter of locating my target later.

He slept through most days, preferring to do his work under the cover of darkness. In the shadows, the risk of anyone seeing through his disguises diminished.

Faceless, nameless, and yet with countless names and faces, the Hunter walks among the people. A grim pleasure filled him.

He opened his wardrobe and rummaged through its contents in search of a suitable disguise. His evening plans included a visit to a rougher part of Voramis, and he required a face that would allow him to blend in.

Holding up a mask of alchemical flesh—complete with false hair—he smiled.

This will be perfect for tonight's activities.

Chapter Three

Business was brisk at The Iron Arms tonight, though most nights found the tavern well patronized. Thanks to its proximity to the docks, the alehouse saw a steady stream of day laborers, roughnecks, and roustabouts eager to quench their thirst at the end of a long day.

Drunken tradesmen and merchants filled the tables. Tired dockhands sat at the bar, nursing tankards overflowing with frothy ale. The smell of sawdust, peanut shells, and stale sweat permeated the tavern, and the sounds of clinking glasses, shouting patrons, and loud conversations filled the air.

Barmaids wended their way through the crowd, delivering drinks with a hearty laugh and a hard slap to roving hands. Their tight bodices often looked in danger of spilling their luscious contents, a possibility that kept the men they served entertained and eager to buy more ale. Indeed, the wenches found themselves fending off advances from all sides, though occasionally one would hustle up the creaking stairs with a customer willing and able to pay for 'additional services'.

The man who entered The Iron Arms looked just like any other day laborer scattered around the bar, though he carried himself with more confidence than the slouching roustabouts. His heavy features gave him a vicious look, his huge arms banded with thick muscle. Those sitting at the bar gave him a wide berth as he sat down.

The Hunter had donned the disguise of a rough working man for tonight's activities, and he played the part well.

"Well, aren't you a big lad?" teased one of the barmaids flitting past. Her garment left little to the Hunter's imagination, her ample charms visible and appealing.

"Tankard of ale," he grunted.

"Aye," the wench smiled at him, "I'll have it right up for ye. You sure ye don't want to finish it upstairs? I know a good place beneath the roof where we can explore the things we have in common, and"—she threw him a lascivious wink—"the things we don't."

He studied the woman appreciatively, allowing his eyes to follow the curvature of her body. He couldn't deny that she was attractive, though her eyes were tired and hard. Desire filled him, the voice in his head whispering of carnal desire, lusting for passion, and begging for death. It took a considerable amount of effort to ignore it.

I'm not here for that, he thought. He might have allowed himself the luxury of a distraction another night, but he had a purpose for being here this night.

"Sorry, darlin', I'm fresh out of coin or I'd take you up on that." He gave her bottom a pinch, which evoked a delighted squeal from her. "I don't get paid 'til the ship leaves tomorrow, and I'll be sailin' out with it. Next time I'm in Voramis, though…" he trailed off, a suggestive look on his face.

The wench, though disappointed, gave him a small smile, and promised to make herself available next time he was in port.

"And ye'd better have a full purse," she reminded him. With a saucy look over her shoulder, she walked away, the exaggerated roll of her hips intended to show him what he was missing.

The Hunter had spent his fair share of time in the company of whores and courtesans, but he always left their company feeling repulsed—not by them, but by himself and his desires.

The weakness of the flesh. The urge always came more strongly immediately following a kill. It would remain in the back of his mind until he satisfied it.

He eyed the woman as she minced away, swaying through the crowd. The men of the tavern called out for her, their language rough.

Animals. He felt disgust at their crude nature—a nature he saw reflected in his own lustful desires.

Soulhunger throbbed in his mind, agreeing with his disdain for the men around him. The weapon—hidden beneath his clothing—radiated its loathing for the noisy, sweaty, drunken crowd.

The bartender placed a giant mug of frothy ale before the Hunter, who drained it quickly in an effort to distract himself. He gestured for another, turning his attention to the conversations around him. His ears strained to pick out the various threads of conversation woven into the hubbub of the bar.

"I heard his body was found at the bottom of Dead Man's Cliff," said a rough voice a few seats along the bar to his right.

"Some say it was the Hunter's work," whispered a man at a table behind him. "His hands were sliced clean off, oozing blood the color of vomit."

Word of Lord Damuria's demise has spread quickly.

A feeling of elation ran through him as he relived Damuria's final moments. Even now, he could feel Soulhunger plunging into the noble's chest, the blood warm on his hands, the power coursing through his body.

A fleeting smile touched his lips, hidden by the tankard of ale he held in front of his face.

"I've heard tell," said the man to the Hunter's left, "that one look in the bastard's eyes and you drop dead from fear. He's a demon, is what he is!"

"He's no demon," shouted the man's companion, "but a ghost of the Swordsman come back to punish the wicked."

"Idiot," cursed the man next to the Hunter. "You can't believe everything you hear. No one knows who he is," he dropped his voice to a conspiratorial whisper, "or *what* he is."

What am I, indeed? The Hunter found the question ringing in his mind. *How many times have I asked myself that question, yet found no answer?*

We are death, a quiet voice whispered in his mind.

At times like this, with liquor coursing through his veins, he would sift through the few memories that remained to him.

His memory stretched back to the time immediately before he arrived in Voramis. He could remember traveling from a nearby city—*Horranz, I think it was called*—but prior to that, nothing but ragged gaps and empty voids filled his mind.

But the memories of death will always remain.

The faces of every man and woman who had died at the end of Soulhunger's wicked blade were etched into his memory.

Those faces never leave.

We fed well, his inner voice crowed.

The dagger's bloodlust rose within him and begged for death. He needed a distraction, and quickly.

At a gesture, the pub landlord brought him another tankard, and he set to work draining his third mug of ale.

Focus on the conversations around you, he told himself.

"Found three bodies near Reveler's Lane a few nights ago, they did." This voice belonged to a drunken man stumbling towards the door, hanging on to his marginally less inebriated friend for support. "Deader'n my Aunt Ilfred."

"But," protested his friend, "it can't be the work of the Hunter. He's only s'posed to kill when he's paid to."

It seems my exploits are the talk of the tavern. It's always good to know one's handiwork is appreciated.

One conversation in particular interested him.

"I heard copper's the thing to kill the Hunter," insisted one man in a loud, drunken voice. "They say it turns his blood to solid metal."

"No, no, you fool," retorted his friend, "you're thinkin' of silver. It's why I always carry me lucky half-drake with me."

A steady stream of patrons moved through the taproom. His ears remained attentive to the conversations around him, and he listened to the chatter with interest. Conversations ebbed and flowed around the Hunter, but he was content to simply sit and listen. The volume within the bar increased as the night wore on and the tavern filled.

After all, listening is always the best source of information.

Their conversations were so mundane, so blissfully unaware of reality.

Fools! The voice in his mind echoed his contempt. *So content in their ignorance. If only they knew who sat among them this night.*

A glazed window behind the bartender cast his reflection back at him. The face he wore tonight bore heavy, dull features— nothing like the handsome face he called his own.

He stared at the reflection of the face he wore—an unfamiliar one—peering back at him over a large tankard of ale, and for a moment, he wondered who the man really was.

What is this big brute's story? Does he have a family, a wife, someone to care for him?

The men who filled the bar had friends, companions to share their tables, or people waiting at home for them, but here he sat, alone. Even in the middle of this bustle and commotion, he was alone.

I prefer to be alone, he told himself. *It is easier than having to worry about being stabbed in the back, or being betrayed by a 'friend'.*

Someone slid onto the stool to his right, jostling him gently. He ignored the newcomer, preferring to drink his ale and listen to the conversation in the tavern.

"Slumming it, milord?" A silky voice purred beside him, breaking into his stream of thoughts mid-flow. Uncertain if the voice addressed him, the Hunter ignored the question.

A hand touched his arm gently, which got his attention. He turned to see a diminutive woman sitting on the stool next to him. Dark eyes stared back at him, a mischievous smile playing at the corners of full lips. Her features hinted at something more hidden beneath the rough exterior.

It's those silky locks that really make her stand out.

Raven hair fell to her shoulders in gentle waves, and the Hunter caught the scent of a delightful blend of oils and herbs.

She wore simple clothing, which fought to hide her curves. *Trying to avoid attracting too much attention.* The Hunter sized her up. *She looks as if she can hold her own in a fight* and *between the sheets.*

"What's that you say, miss?" he asked, confused.

"I said, 'Slumming it, *my lord?*'" She emphasized the last two words.

Her question surprised him. He wore rough clothing and an even rougher disguise, meant to blend in at The Iron Arms.

"Do I look like a lord, lass?"

"Not at all," she replied with a smile. "Your clothing certainly *does* give you the appearance of nothing more than a simple dockhand."

"But…?" the Hunter asked, raising an eyebrow.

"Look around you." She motioned to the crowd filling the tavern. "We are surrounded by rough, hard men burned by the sun, their hands calloused. They stink of a full day's work." Her gaze returned to him. "*That* is the sign of a true laborer, not just some rough clothing. Plus, you smell like old leather rather than old sweat, and you sit with a straight back while everyone else slouches over their drink."

"And this makes me a lord?" he asked.

She graced him with another smile.

"I've been watching you for a while. You addressed the serving girl with respect, and only your eyes wandered—your hands stayed on your tankard. I've not seen you shout once at a passing patron, even though you've been bumped a handful of times."

She is good, the Hunter thought, at a loss for words.

"Don't bother to deny it, my lord," she cut him off before he could protest. "I know it has become a popular pastime among the lesser nobility of the city to dress in lower class clothing and experience 'life on the underside', as they say. Hence my original question, 'Slumming it, my lord?'"

"Quite the eye for details," the Hunter said, shrugging by way of acceptance. "What did you say your name was?"

"I didn't," she responded with a sly smile. "Buy me a drink first, and we'll see if I feel like giving it to you."

For reasons he couldn't explain, the Hunter found himself intrigued by this woman. Something about her pulled him from his solitude, and he felt the desire to know more about her.

He signaled for the pub landlord, who deposited two fresh tankards of ale in front of them before bustling away to attend to his other customers. The voice within him whispered lustful thoughts, which he ignored.

"So," said the Hunter, "I guess you can say I'm guilty of 'slumming it', as you say." He adopted the role of a noble lord in disguise with ease. "It *is* good to get away from the perfumes, the too-sweet wines, the annoyingly slow waltzes—"

"The lavish banquets," she cut him off, "the comfortable carriages, the luxurious homes."

The Hunter shrugged. "It's not *all* bad, truth be told. Life isn't all suffering," he said with a grin.

"What makes it awful," she glared at him, clearly finding no humor in his words, "is that you treat our lives like a novel experience, something to be enjoyed. It's just another thrill for you, but this is how we have to live every day. Lower Voramis is a rough place, especially for those of us without a fancy mansion to return home to once we've had enough cheap ale and sluts."

Her anger surprised him. "I apologize if my lifestyle offends you, lady, but—"

She cut him off with an angry glare. "I'm no lady! Just as you're no dockhand."

What a woman! He thought. He watched her out of the corner of his eye, though he tried to be unobtrusive about his interest.

She downed the contents of her tankard and gestured for the bartender to bring her another. The Hunter motioned for a refill as well.

When the tavern keeper finally replaced the Hunter's pewter mug with a fresh, full one, it was accompanied by an almost imperceptible nod. The Hunter's fingers closed around the small piece of parchment folded beneath the cup, and he slipped it surreptitiously into his pocket.

I have what I came for, he thought.

Turning to face the woman once again, he slipped back into character. "Well, miss, I've got to get back to the ship. Shame I'm sleepin' on board," he said with a wink filled with veiled meaning.

The Hunter half-expected her to take offense at his forthrightness, but his mysterious companion simply ignored him. Shrugging, he said, "Goodnight, miss…?"

"Goodnight," she responded, her voice icy with disdain.

The Hunter stood and pushed his stool back from the bar. A spluttering sound came from behind him, and he turned to find a huge man staring down at him.

Sloped shoulders and a square jaw were the man's best features. An oversized nose, cauliflower ears, and far too few teeth gave him a bestial look. Beer dripped down the man's beard and shirt, and anger filled his dull eyes.

"Watch it, idiot," the big men yelled at him, grabbing the Hunter's arm in huge hands.

"Excuse me. My mistake," apologized the Hunter. He made to move away, but the large hands remained firmly wrapped around his bicep.

"I think you should buy me a drink," the big man said. "S'only fair." He gestured to his beer-soaked tunic.

The man's face was far too close for comfort, and the Hunter struggled to keep down the contents of his stomach as the man's noxious breath filled his nostrils.

Blood rushed to his face, and the urge to break this man with his hands nearly overwhelmed him. He took a deep breath, determined to swallow the anger flooding him.

With a nod, the Hunter signaled the bartender to bring the big man another drink. He tried once again to leave, but the man's massive hand continued to hold him in place.

"Maybe," said the big man, "you should also buy my friends here a drink."

"Come on, Garlin," said one of the men sitting at the table, "he already paid for your drink."

Garlin's friend clearly had better sense, or was at least less inebriated than his hulking companion.

"I said," spittle accompanied Garlin's words, "*my friends* need a drink." The big man stared into the Hunter's face, his eyes daring him to argue.

The Hunter stared back for a tense moment, clenching his jaw and grinding his teeth. He was tempted to listen to the voice telling him to drive his dagger deep into the man's eye.

Let me feed, the dagger begged. It took every shred of his rapidly diminishing self-control to ignore the voice.

At a nod from the Hunter, the pub landlord filled tankards for Garlin's three drinking companions. The Hunter tossed a silver drake to the tavern keeper, who caught it in deft fingers. The coin would cover the cost of the Hunter's drinks, as well as the ale consumed by the mysterious woman at the bar, the massive Garlin, and Garlin's friends.

"Now might be a good time to take your hand off me," said the Hunter in an even tone.

Garlin studied him through ale-soaked eyes for a moment, smiled, and unclenched his sausage fingers. "Aye, you've paid off your debts, boyo, so you can scurry away now."

The big man stepped around the Hunter, moving toward the woman sitting at the bar. He draped a muscled arm around her shoulder, and spoke without taking his eyes off her.

"Now that you're leaving, let's see if this little lady doesn't fancy the company of a *real* man, eh?"

Whatever Garlin whispered into the woman's ear made her shudder in revulsion. Her face twisted with disgust.

"Forget it," she spat, "not even if your shriveled cock was made of pure gold."

The big man's eyes narrowed, his face flushing with anger.

"I wasn't askin', girly," his voice turned ugly, with more than a hint of menace. "Time for you to play nice and come upstairs with me. If you need a bit of...encouragement, I can always bring me mates along."

Before he realized what he was doing, the Hunter stepped toward Garlin.

"I believe the lady said something about wanting to leave the alehouse without a drunken gorilla clinging to her arm." A dangerous light glittered in the Hunter's eyes. "Might want to get back to that ale, *friend*."

He gripped Garlin's arm, and the drunken man found himself being steered away from the bar.

"Bugger off, you little pissant," Garlin hissed at the Hunter, wrenching his arm free from the vice grip. "The little lady and me are gonna have some fun, aren't we, my sweet tickle-tail?" Spittle flew as he leered at the woman. She glared back at him, wiping her face in obvious disgust.

The Hunter's patience with the drunk had run out. "I said *enough.*"

He accompanied his words with a short, sharp punch to the man's solar plexus. The force of the blow knocked the wind from the big man's lungs with a loud *whoosh*. Garlin's legs buckled, and the Hunter brought his knee up hard. It connected with the man's jaw, rocking his head back. His huge frame slumped unconscious toward the floor, crashing through a bar table and a pair of stools before finally hitting the sawdust with a loud thump.

A tankard slammed down on the table next to him, and the Hunter turned to see Garlin's enraged friends charging him. He kicked high, his heel catching a man in the temple. The assailant dropped to the floor without a sound.

A hand grabbed his shoulder from behind. The Hunter lashed out with his elbow, and he heard a satisfying *crunch* from the man's nose. Hot blood spattered his arm.

Adrenaline surged through the Hunter's veins, an eager smile crossing his face. Soulhunger, hidden in its sheath beneath his clothes, sensed blood and the voice pounded in his head, begging to be fed.

Another of Garlin's friends swung a meaty fist toward him. The Hunter caught it in mid-air. A quick twist of the man's hand sent the assailant to his knees, and the Hunter delivered a sharp blow to the man's thick wrist with the edge of his hand.

The sound of cracking bones echoed in the bar, a sound soon replaced by the man's agonized screams.

"Oh gods, me wrist! He broke me fuckin' wrist!"

His blood pounding, his heart racing, the Hunter reveled in the thrill of the fight.

There should be one more. He might—

He heard a heavy *thunk* behind him, followed by a groan of pain. The sound caused him to spin around, preparing for another assault.

The last member of Garlin's party had crept around behind the Hunter, a pewter tankard raised high overhead. Before he could bring it crashing down on the Hunter's head, the drunken man had found himself caught in an arm-lock by the diminutive woman. His nose bled freely into the shattered pewter mug embedded in his face, and the pressure she applied to his fingers had him begging for mercy.

The tavern had fallen silent, though the encounter had lasted for little more than a minute. The Hunter saw the heavy-set bouncers wending their way through the crowd, and knew he had outlasted his welcome.

No matter. I got what I came for.

The Hunter flipped a gold imperial to the bartender. "For the mess."

The portly pub landlord nodded and motioned for the crowd to resume drinking. When the bouncers laid rough hands on the Hunter, he waved the thugs away. "He's leavin'." He shot an ominous glare at the Hunter.

Silent stares followed the Hunter as he strode to the door, the din of conversation only resuming after he had stepped out of the doors of The Iron Arms.

He breathed deeply, enjoying the cool night after the cloying heat of the bar. A miasma of scents hung in the air, but he found them much more enjoyable than the smell of old sweat, crusted vomit, and cheap beer.

It smells the way a city should.

His steps quickened, and the noise of the tavern faded as he strode down the cobbled street.

"Hey!" A voice rang out behind him, calling after him. "Hey, you!"

The Hunter turned and found the woman from the bar chasing him down the street. She glared at him, her face flushed with anger.

"Why in the empty hell did you do that?" she raged. "I had the situation in hand."

This took the Hunter by surprise. "I did nothing any other man of class wouldn't do. I saw a lady in an untenable situation, and I thought—"

"You thought *wrong*! I'm no delicate lady. I can take care of myself."

"I can see that," the Hunter responded with a grin.

"Good, and remember it, stranger." Her eyes glittered with anger, but she no longer yelled at him. "I'm not some painting to be hung on a wall and protected; I'm more than capable of handling anything and anyone."

"Consider it a lesson learned," the Hunter said with all the grace expected of a lordling, bowing to complete the façade. He turned and strode off into the night, but he had only walked a few steps when her voice called out to him once more.

"It's Celicia, by the way."

The Hunter turned to reply, but the woman had disappeared.

Who is this mysterious woman? Intrigued, the Hunter let his imagination wander.

She saw through my disguise easily enough, though she mistook me for a lord rather than realizing who I really am. Perhaps…

He refused to voice the thought, but deep in his mind, he continued to ponder the question.

Soulhunger's voice throbbed in his head, returning him to the present. With an effort, he shook the image of Celicia away.

Enough. I have a mission to accomplish.

Closing his eyes, he cast out his senses. Soulhunger, attuned to the unique scent of its quarry, sought the life force of the man—or woman—he had been hired to kill.

There you are.

He sensed the direction in which he would find his target. A slow smile of anticipation spread across his face.

Let's find out what brings you to the port so late.

Chapter Four

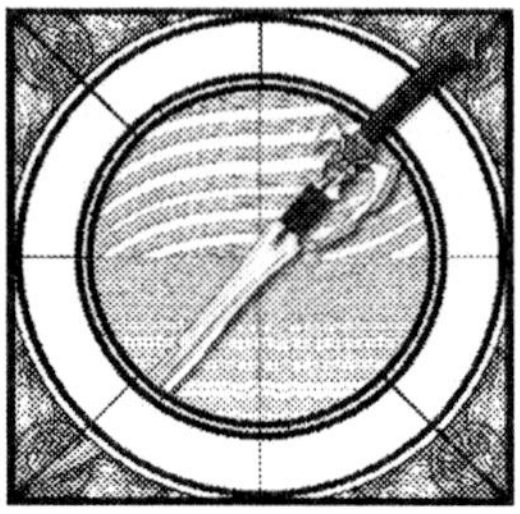

"Watcher's balls, it's cold!"

Two men stood in the near-darkness of the Port of Voramis, the pitiful flame of a single torch struggling to ward off the night. The flickering light did little to keep out the cold, and both men shivered and pulled their ragged cloaks tighter around their blocky frames.

"Aye, that it is," echoed the second man. "And just to make matters worse, it looks like rain."

A chill wind swept through the darkened port, setting chains rattling and canvas billowing with an ominous echo. The sound of creaking timbers accentuated the emptiness of the port at night, and the noise of scurrying feet indicated the passage of numerous rodents. The stench of rotted fish permeated the air as it rose to the heavens.

"The gods mock us tonight, Sor," the first man whined. "Why'd you have to go and lose that wager to Harkin? We could've been back in Blackfall with the rest of the lads, drinking at The Cock and Bulls. Instead, we're stuck out here in the middle of the bloody port, freezin' our cullions and waitin' for some pompous lord."

He glared at his friend, but the expression was lost on Sor, who stared out into the empty night.

"Well," began Sor, "I knew I had a—" His words were cut off as his friend smacked him on the back of his head. "Ow! What in the flooded hell was that for, Yim?"

"That's for wagerin' our duties on a pair of rods, and forgettin' Harkin had been sittin' on triple spires all night long," Yim muttered.

"It's not my fault you forgot the code to tell me what he was holdin', Yim. Next time—"

Yim cut him off sharply. "There won't be a next time, Sor. Watcher knows, I've made the mistake of playin' cards with you one time too many. Wherever you go, hell's own luck is sure to follow. If I want to go home with more than a pair of bits to spend on a cheap cunny, I'll be sure to always gamble against you."

Sor protested. "Yim, you know full well that I always win in the—"

His words died, and his eyes went wide with terror as he stared into the night.

"Did you see that?" He pointed into the darkness.

"There's nothing to see, Sor," Yim said in exasperation. "Every time we get stuck workin' after dark, you get jumpier than a one-legged man in a foot race."

"I swear it, Yim," Sor insisted, "I saw somethin'. A dark shape movin' in the darkness."

"And there's no chance your eyes are playin' tricks on you?" Yim was tired of putting up with Sor and his eternal paranoia. "Don't tell me you're scared of the dark, Sor."

"Not of the dark, Yim, but of what's out there at night." The man's voice filled with terror. "They say the Hunter can move through the night like a serpent, strike, and disappear before you see him."

"Aye, and I've heard tell that he shits scorpions and pisses venom. We've all heard the tales," Yim sighed, "and they're nothin' more than that."

"But—" Sor began, but he cut off again, spinning around and pointing into the night. "There! There he goes!"

Yim felt a very real moment of fear as he saw the shape moving through the darkness towards them. His heart rose to his throat, and he gripped the cudgel at his belt with whitening fingers.

"Halt!" he called to the figure. "Who goes?"

"It's me, you fools." The voice from the darkness held a tone of disdain. "You're expecting me, I believe?"

Relief flooded through the brutish Yim as the approaching figure pulled back the hood of his cloak.

"Ah, Lord Dann—"

The nobleman cut him off with a sharp gesture.

"No names, you fool. And lower your voice. You don't want every drunken sot on the docks to hear us, do you? Mistress knows what eyes and ears lurk in the dark." The aristocrat's expression showed his disdain at having to do business with these two louts.

"Of course, sir," Sor touched his forehead in a sign of respect. "We're both just a tad jumpy tonight, what with stories of Lord Damuria's grisly end floating about the city."

"You're fools to believe the rumors. The Hunter is nothing for you to fear. After all, your masters have this city firmly under their control, do they not?"

His look of utter confidence rallied the men's limited courage, and they nodded at him.

"Very good," the noble said, his voice haughty and imperious. "Now, if you don't mind, I'd like to inspect the merchandise."

"Of course, m'lord."

Sor turned to the crate they had been guarding. He fumbled at his belt for a moment, his fingers numb from the cold.

"Aha!" He produced the key. "The merchandise, sir."

With a loud *clang*, the padlock snapped open. Sor moved to unlatch the chain, and pulled the door open with a grunt.

The nobleman stepped forward, rubbing his hands together in eagerness. "Let us discover what the good ship Aeremor has brought us this evening."

Moonlight shone on the pale faces of the women huddled in the container. A horrifying stench of fecal matter and too many bodies cramped into too small a space wafted from the wooden box, and both of the thugs had to stifle a gag. The nobleman appeared unaffected, peering into the darkness.

"The torch?" he demanded impatiently, holding out his hand to Sor.

"Of course, m'lord."

Sor handed the aristocrat the torch, and the nobleman held it aloft. More than a score of young women—*girls younger than thirteen or fourteen, if I don't miss my guess,* thought Sor—sat in the container, a listless expression on their grimy faces. They shielded their eyes with their hands as the torch cast its meager light on their filthy, rotting rags.

The noble stared at the contents of the container for a long moment, then, with a nod of satisfaction, gestured for the two men to close the doors. A gentle murmur of protest ran through the women, but the lack of food and water left them too feeble to do more. As Yim chained and locked the wooden doors, the nobleman barked terse orders.

"Make sure they are delivered to Mistress Croquembouche at The Arms of Heaven—after they are bathed, of course. And keep your filthy hands off them. They are to arrive unspoiled and untouched by"—he looked at their rough hands and faces with disgust—"those of your ilk. It is part of their…unique *charms*, after all."

"Very good, m'lord," Yim nodded. "Anythin' else?"

"That will be all, I believe." The aristocrat waved in dismissal as he turned to return the way he had come. "Your master knows where to find me."

"Yes, m'lord," Sor called after the nobleman's retreating back, but the man showed no sign he'd heard them. Within a moment, the man had disappeared into the night.

"Watcher-damned nobles," growled Yim as he pulled the cloak tighter around his shivering frame. "Leaving us workin' stiffs in the cold to wait."

"Aye, but at least we're here by the torchlight," Sor reminded him, "and not walkin'out there in the dark…. where *He* is."

"We don't even know *He* is—"

Sor cut Yim's words off mid-sentence. "Oh, there's no doubt about it, *He* is out there. I can feel him…"

* * *

The voices of the thugs arguing behind him faded as the Hunter followed his target away from the container of unfortunate captives.

A fresh crop of virgins for the nobility of Voramis to deflower.

A flash of pity ran through him as he imagined their fate.

He knew Lord Dannaros earned his money in less-than legitimate fashion, but he was surprised to find the noble dealing in this particular commodity.

You don't get to be the second richest noble in Voramis just by marrying the daughter of a Duke.

The thought of the flesh trade repulsed him, but he shrugged and dismissed the subject.

Who am I to judge how a man earns a living?

Lord Dannaros strode through the darkness, confidence in his steps. He clutched his cloak tight to ward off the cold, but his dark hair fluttered free in the wind that whistled through the empty port. The Hunter couldn't make out his features in the darkness, but he didn't need to. His nostrils filled with the man's scent even from this distance.

Lord Dannaros, it has been a long time since we have seen each other. I have a feeling we will come face to face once again very soon.

Dannaros' heartbeat called to Soulhunger. The knife throbbed with urgency, demanding to draw closer to its prey.

Let me feed, it begged. *Let me kill!*

Easy, Soulhunger. Soon enough.

The weapon's insistence faded, but the blade would only be truly silenced once it had drunk the blood of its victim.

The Hunter slipped through the darkness, confident in his dark grey cloak's ability to keep him hidden. His quarry moved ahead of him, completely unaware that death padded silently in his wake.

The Hunter called to mind a map of the port, tracing Lord Dannaros' route to ascertain the place where the noble's carriage awaited him. Slipping ahead, he found the vehicle waiting in a deserted alley adjacent to the docks.

Midnight eyes watched Lord Dannaros scurry towards his coach, darting nervous glances in every direction.

At last, his fear shows through his mask of calm.

The carriage door slammed shut behind the noble. "Take me home, Ari," Dannaros' voice rang out in the silence of the deserted streets.

The Hunter smiled and watched the chaise clatter away into the darkness of Lower Voramis. He had until the Feast of the Mistress—yet a week away—to complete his mission, but he planned to carry out the contract well before then.

Until we meet again, my lord.

Chapter Five

The light of a new day filtered through gauzy curtains, chasing away the shadows of night. Shirtless and weaponless, the Hunter stared at his reflection in the full-length mirror hanging on the wall of his bedroom in The Golden Sunrise.

The face staring back at him belonged to Lord Anglion, a wealthy noble from the neighboring city of Praamis, a week's ride to the east. Lord Anglion made occasional appearances in Voramis, but only when the Hunter needed a persona that allowed him to mingle in high society. He had spent years cultivating the disguise as a means to gain access to the wealthy nobles and merchants he was often contracted to kill.

Lord Anglion had a nose most would call prominent rather than long, high cheekbones, a weak jaw, and an angular chin. His blond hair hung to his shoulders in perfect ringlets, though the vain young lord preferred to tie it back with a bright green ribbon.

"Brings out my eyes," he loved to say.

The Hunter despised the character of Lord Anglion, and avoided it often as he could. Unfortunately, to carry out this contract, he must adopt the disguise of the overweening, primping aristocrat.

He wore the young nobleman's face, but the hard, lean body reflected in the mirror could never belong to an over-indulgent member of the Praamian aristocracy. Years of killing had shaped the Hunter's frame.

What stood out most, however, were the scars. The Hunter no longer tried to count them, but he guessed they numbered in the hundreds. They looked like tally marks, and served as a grisly reminder of the cost of Soulhunger's power—and the price of taking a life.

Odd how these marks remain while all others fade. His body healed from the most grievous wounds, but not these scars.

As he ran his fingers over the scars, memories flashed through his head. He could see a face for every mark on his body, haunting him with their lifeless, accusing eyes.

Such maudlin thoughts.

A rueful grin split Lord Anglion's pompous face. Soulhunger's desire to kill pounded in his mind, and he blocked it out.

Today is a feast day, a day of celebration. He returned his attention to the looking glass, running the fine-toothed comb through Lord Anglion's blond hair.

The Hunter strode to the massive wardrobe standing opposite the mirror. Opening the heavy doors, he scanned the expensive garments hanging within.

Lord Anglion would wear green on a feast day.

He selected the outfit he deemed best suited for the occasion, donned it, and checked his reflection in the mirror one last time. Not a wrinkle showed, not a ruffle looked out of place. The Hunter nodded, satisfied.

The disguise of Lord Anglion is complete.

He stared at the room around him, marveling at the wasteful opulence. A set of elaborate couches occupied the antechamber in which he stood, and a massive four-post bed dominated the adjacent room. A walk-in wardrobe held Lord Anglion's fine clothing. Running water flowed in the marble sink, a rare luxury in Voramis.

His rooms at The Golden Sunrise cost a small fortune, but he considered it a worthy investment. The inn's proprietor received a generous stipend from the 'young noble' to keep his rooms available at all times.

It is necessary to play the part of the visiting noble for the Lord Anglion disguise. No aristocrat in his right mind would stay anywhere but the Golden Sunrise.

The doors to his room shut behind him with an audible *click* as he strode into the lavishly carpeted hall. Turning the key in the lock, he heard the deadbolt slide home with a satisfying *thunk*. He had insisted upon the extra security for his room, and a heavy purse of gold imperials had guaranteed acquiescence to the eccentric client's demands.

Descending the stairs to the elegant foyer of the inn, the Hunter nodded to the rotund figure of his host. Portly Master Aramon returned his greeting with a smile.

"Welcome to Voramis, my lord," he said, his voice cheery.

"My thanks, good Aramon." The Hunter forced a pleasant smile, as expected of Lord Anglion. "It is always good to visit, particularly during the Season of Plenty."

"My lord always comes to Voramis for the feast days," the fat proprietor said with an unctuous smile.

"Of course," the Hunter replied. "When my good friend Lord Dannaros throws a party, it is in one's best interest to be in attendance. Besides," he lowered his voice in a conspiratorial whisper, "I hear the Lady

Dannaros is looking particularly ravishing this year."

A grin split Aramon's face. "Indeed, my lord. I hear that she has had every tailor and seamstress within a hundred leagues to her home. In search of the perfect dress, they say."

"Well, tonight we shall see the fruits of her labors. Now, if you will excuse me, I must see Voramis in all its beauty."

"Of course, my lord. With the Snowblossom trees in full bloom, you'll find the city is more radiant than ever."

A voice called from behind Aramon, drawing his attention away from the Hunter.

"Apologies, my lord," the fat proprietor said, "but business calls me elsewhere. Safe journeys." With a bow, he hurried away.

"Until tonight, Aramon," the Hunter called after the man's retreating back.

The front doors of The Golden Sunrise stood open, the midday sun shining beyond. The Hunter shaded his eyes as he strolled into the open air, letting them adjust to the brightness.

He basked in the glorious sights and sounds of Upper Voramis during the Season of Plenty. These were the final weeks before winter's chill gripped Voramis, a time when the city was at its most beautiful.

The lords and ladies of Voramis spent vast sums of money in an attempt to make their parties the event of the season. Their excesses served to remind the commoners of Lower Voramis just how little they had.

At least some of the coin finds its way into the hands of the honest working merchant.

A team of horses clattered past, pulling wagons laden with casks, boxes, and sacks filled with food and drink for the evening's festivities. The merchant sitting atop the lead wagon tipped his hat to the Hunter, who nodded in return.

The Hunter might hate the disguise of Lord Anglion, but he loved the freedom it provided. He could mingle with the wealthy nobles and merchants strolling leisurely through the guarded streets of Upper Voramis without calling attention to himself.

Best of all, he could explore Maiden's Fields—the breathtaking gardens sprawled across a quarter of the upper city. It held a special place in his heart, especially during the Season of Plenty.

Flowering trees thrust their multi-hued branches into the sky, the colorful blooms paving the walkways in a vivid carpet of petals. Marbled walkways twisted and turned through the manicured lawns of Maiden's Fields. Roses, lilies, and gardenias filled the air with their intoxicating scents, each unique and yet all blending into a harmony of fragrance.

Being in the park during the Season of Plenty made him feel less alone. He loved to sit and watch the trees sway in the breeze. Their gnarled branches, rippling leaves, and bright petals always made him feel welcome.

The nobles strolling the gardens wore colors nearly as bright as the plants around them. The latest fashion—*a ridiculous one, in my opinion*—

demanded the wealthy dress in the oddest combination of garish hues. A mixture of yellow, purple, and a dull grey were in style this season.

Men and women held hands, whispering to each other in the hushed voices of lovers. One young couple strolled through the Snowblossom trees, arms linked. The man whispered into the woman's ear, and she giggled in response.

Fools, he thought with disgust, *if only you knew that your love is nothing more than a lie.* Soulhunger's voice in his head echoed his disdain.

You think you will find meaning in your life by joining it with that of another, but in the end, you'll die alone.

All of the men and women he had killed had died alone, screaming, crying, or cursing him and their gods. None of them had cried out for their husband or wife.

He saw an elderly, obese lord wearing robes of a garish red and green checked pattern. The old noble's arm was wrapped protectively around a woman decades his junior, who listened to him speak with a look of boredom on her face.

I wonder what lies she tells herself as she sleeps beside him at night. It's not so bad, she no doubt says, better than poverty and loneliness. Likely he lies and tells himself that she loves him for who he is, not for his wealth.

It is all a lie, the voice of Soulhunger shouted in his head. *You can trust no one, for all will lie to you.*

The Hunter believed this more and more with every life he took. He had seen the myriad secrets his victims had fought to keep hidden from their so-called 'loved ones'; with every death, his abhorrence for his prey grew.

"Flower, my lord?" The weak, shy voice of a young girl came from his elbow.

The corners of his mouth turned up into a smile as he saw the familiar child beside him.

Only the innocence of a child is beyond reproach.

She had long, dark eyelashes, and piercing green eyes set above a smiling mouth. Rough clothing hung loosely on her thin shoulders, but she had grown since he saw her last. She stood nearly as tall as his chest, but her gaunt cheeks and pale skin made her look far older than her eight years.

"Of course, child," the Hunter beamed at the waif. "Two of your finest roses, if you would be so kind."

The little girl produced two long-stemmed roses, and the Hunter made a show of inhaling the flowers' scent.

"These *must* be your best, child, for they smell so beautiful." The little girl smiled up at him. "I say, do you have a knife?"

The girl he knew as Farida fumbled around in her cart for a minute before producing a small cutting blade. The Hunter trimmed the stems from the roses and tucked them in his lapel. "What do you think?"

"Very elegant, m'lord," the girl responded shyly.

"Wonderful." With a smile, the Hunter reached into his purse. "For you, my dear," he said, placing the imperial in her hand.

The girl's eyes widened at the sight of the gold coin.

"But, m'lord," she protested, "it is too—"

"Nonsense," he cut her off with a wave. "It will cover the cost of these two beautiful roses, and the dozen you will deliver to the house of Dannaros on my behalf."

"Of course, m'lord," the child said, pocketing the coin.

"Thank you, dear. Make sure that they are delivered with the compliments of Lord Anglion."

"Of course, m'lord," she repeated.

"Good. I *will* see you again when next I visit Voramis, won't I?"

"Yes, sir. I love the Maiden's Fields, so I come here as often as I can." She stared at the gardens, a wistful expression in her eyes. "Though the Heresiarchs don't let me in much anymore."

She probably wants nothing more than to run and play, like the child of a noble family. But she must work to eat.

"Until next time, then." He waved her away, dismissing her as Lord Anglion would. The wheels of her cart clacked loudly on the cobbled stones as she pushed it in the direction of Lord Dannaros' palatial mansion.

There is no lie in that one, no half-truths or distrust. At least not yet, not until this world sinks its claws into her. This life will sully her, poison her mind, and twist her until she is as deceitful as everyone else in this city. Life on the street is harsh, particularly to children like Farida.

The Hunter had found the girl as a babe, abandoned in one of the many unnamed slums of Lower Voramis, lying next to the frozen corpses of her parents. He had no hope of raising her, but his effort to track down any living relatives proved fruitless. Only the Beggar Priests—servants of the Beggar God—would take her in. They had raised her as one of their Beggared.

The red-robed Heresiarchs patrolling the city turned a blind eye to Farida and the other Beggared children whenever possible, and the coins she earned selling flowers from her small cart bought the meager food and clothing shared among the children living in the House of Need.

For some unexplained reason, he found an excuse to visit her often, albeit always in disguise. He told himself it was a weakness he could ill-afford, but he found himself growing fonder of her with each passing year. No matter how hard he tried to keep his distance—*for her protection,* he insisted—his visits had grown more frequent in recent months. He made sure to give her a few extra coins every time one of his disguises paid her a visit.

Suppressing a smile, the Hunter returned his attention to the gardens around him.

Ah, Maiden's Fields, you truly are beautiful. He stopped to smell a flower—*something I expect an empty-headed noble like Lord Anglion would do*—before resuming his stroll.

The Snowblossom trees were in full bloom at this time of year. Delicate white and pink blossoms drifted slowly to the floor like a lazy velvet snowfall, their sweet scent filling Maiden's Fields with a heady aroma.

Every flower, bush, and tree came into bloom during the Season of Plenty, nature's final farewell to the summer. Winter would soon descend upon the city, but not before the people of Voramis celebrated life with feasts and festivals in honor of the gods. It was the last hurrah before the harsh winter winds and snows caused the temperature to plummet.

From his vantage point on the hills of Maiden's Fields, he stared out over the city sprawling below. The skyline sloped sharply downwards from Upper Voramis, and few of the buildings in Lower Voramis rose higher than two or three stories. Only the massive structures of the Temple District rose to the level of the mansions of Upper Voramis. Indeed, the obelisk that honored the Swordsman stood nearly as tall as the imposing Palace of Justice itself.

His destination lay beyond Maiden's Field, but he knew he had hours before night fell and the festivities began.

I think it is time Lord Anglion is seen in public. Perhaps eating a fine lunch at Volieri's.

The Hunter hated to leave the park and the beautiful Snowblossom trees behind, but he had a mission to complete. Part of it was playing the part of Lord Anglion.

Time to act like a spoiled lord of Praamis.

Chapter Six

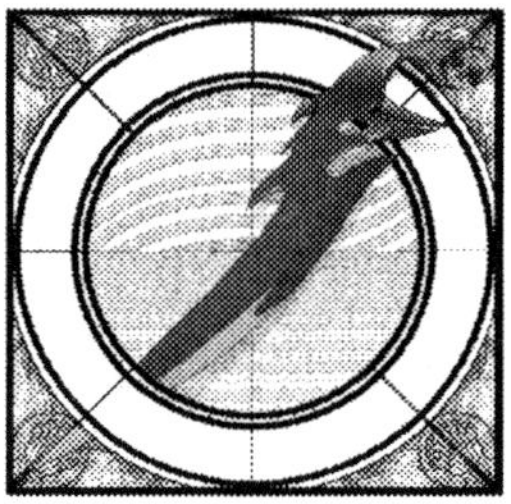

A crescent moon stared down on the busy avenues of Upper Voramis, but the myriad lamps and torches casting a soft glow on the streets outshone the stars twinkling above.

Truly, thought the Hunter, staring out the window of his carriage, *nightfall transforms Upper Voramis into a magical place.*

Upper Voramis was home to only the richest nobles of the city. Their palatial mansions towered high, offering peerless, breathtaking views of the city below and the plains beyond. With the Season of Plenty in full swing, every manor sported festive decorations, colored lamps casting multi-hued light, and garlands made from aromatic blossoms. Only the Palace of Justice outshone the houses of Voramis' wealthiest.

Tonight—and every night for the coming week—parties, balls, and gala events distracted the lords and ladies of Voramis. This evening's festivities celebrated the Illusionist, the god of coin, success, and madness.

Carriages clattered through the cobbled streets, the rattling of their wheels echoing in time with the gentle clopping of horses' hooves. Teams of horses clattered in and out of the mansion of Lord Geddellan Dannaros, host to the gala soiree that was the envy of the city. Friends of Lord Dannaros counted themselves fortunate to receive an invitation, as only the most affluent members of the peerage attended this event on Illusionist's Night.

Heresiarchs—the guardians of the city—strolled the streets in crimson dress uniforms reserved for formal occasions. A few of the wealthier guards sported lace and ruffles at their wrists and neck, an attempt at opulence complemented by gilt-worked scabbards—though the swords within were plain, utilitarian things. The uniforms were a pale imitation of the garments worn by the nobles, but those fortunate few felt pride at being a part of the festivities, even if only as spectators. Only Heresiarchs with the right family connections received a posting to the wealthy district.

The bright red uniforms of the Heresiarchs looked almost threadbare compared to the elegant gowns and tunics worn by the nobility of Voramis. Gold and silver jewelry adorned noble necks, wrists, and fingers, and precious stones glittered in the light of torches and lamps.

The Hunter's carriage slowed as it neared the entrance to the House of Dannaros, pulling to a halt at the magnificent marble walkway leading to the main doors of the mansion.

As he dismounted, the Hunter tried not to stare at the men and women emerging from the carriages around him. They wore bright clothing cut to the latest fashion, and he guessed many of the outfits cost more than a working man earned in half a year of hard labor.

The Hunter couldn't help but marvel at the breathtaking opulence of the Dannaros mansion as he walked through the huge double doors. He stared at the room around him, struggling to keep his mouth from hanging open.

Light flooded the hall, shining with such brilliance that the torches burning on the wall were as candles by comparison. An enormous gold-worked chandelier hung from the ceiling, adorned with hundreds of sparkling crystals. Music floated up from the enormous ballroom below, where hundreds of elaborately dressed aristocrats whirled around the dance floor.

Some whispered that Lord Dannaros' wealth exceeded the king's. Judging by the sheer elegance of the man's home, the Hunter guessed the rumors might not be far off.

It seems the flesh trade is highly lucrative. Disgust filled him, but he took care to keep it from his face—the face of Lord Anglion.

The bright, lace-festooned garment popular in Voramis this season chafed, rubbed, and constricted in all the wrong places. The pompous, pretentious nobles around him looked all too comfortable in their lace and tight outfits, but sweat drenched the Hunter's undergarments.

"Presenting the Lord and Lady of Brightkeep," the Dannaros' herald bellowed. "The Lady Muniset of Heredos, and Lord Anglion of Praamis."

The Hunter descended the stairs, his senses reeling from the display of wealth. The plush carpet covering the marble staircase made the Hunter feel as if he walked on a cloud, and he knew the bloodwood railing beneath his hand cost a fortune.

Gods how I hate this disguise, the Hunter thought. He fought to restrain himself from tugging and adjusting the stuffy, intolerable clothing. Unfortunately, Lord Anglion's face had to remain a mask of utter delight. He attended the gala event of the year, and his hosts awaited him at the foot of the staircase.

"My Lord Anglion," Lady Dannaros purred, "how good it is to see you again!"

Lady Dannaros was considered one of Voramis' great beauties, and the Hunter found the reputation well deserved. Dazzling green eyes sparkled above a perfectly shaped nose, and her luscious lips spoke a word of greeting that was drowned out by the noise of the crowd around him. Her golden hair hung in tight ringlets, adorned tastefully with golden pins set with jewels.

Perfect dress indeed, the Hunter thought. *Master Aramon spoke the truth.*

The woman's gown plunged at the neckline, revealing her ample curves in a display that would have tempted the Hunter's imagination had she been any other woman. Lady Dannaros had a reputation for being fiercely loyal to her husband, and Lord Dannaros' defense of his wife's honor had sent dozens of men to early graves. Out of respect for his hosts, the Hunter kept his eyes on the lady's face.

"My Lady Dannaros." The Hunter bowed low, giving her hand a reverent kiss while inhaling the heady scent of her perfume. "It does my heart good to gaze upon your beauty once more. How long has it been since my last visit?"

"Almost a year to the day," Lord Dannaros said from the stair below his wife. Reaching up, he grasped the forearm of the man he knew as Lord Anglion. "You had me worried, Harrenth. We thought you might not arrive in time for the festivities. I know the Windy Plains are rough at this time of year."

The Hunter could only think of the word 'strong' to describe Lord Dannaros. Piercing eyes stared out from beneath heavy brows, and the man had a handsome nose, a well-defined jaw, and a masculine chin. The Hunter felt tight sinews on Dannaros' forearms, and there was power in the noble's firm grip and calloused hands.

Soulhunger whispered to the Hunter as he stared at the man he had been hired to kill.

Later. He pushed the blade's voice to the back of his mind.

"Ahh, good Lord Dannaros," the Hunter said, with a forced smile he hoped appeared genuine, "you know nothing could stop me from celebrating the Season of Plenty in Voramis. Praamis is such a dull city at this time of year, and I absolutely *had* to see the Snowblossom trees in bloom. Besides, when I heard that my friend Lord Dannaros had planned a gala event, the matter was immediately decided."

"Good, good. It is well that you have joined us, my Lord Anglion." Something behind the Hunter caught Lord Dannaros' eye. "If you will excuse me, my friend, I see that Lord Ravell has arrived."

"Of course," the Hunter replied.

He and Lord Dannaros exchanged bows, and the Hunter watched the noble stride off in the direction of an aging lord approaching from across the ballroom floor.

"My Lord Anglion," said Lady Dannaros, drawing the Hunter's attention once more. "I notice you have not brought a companion along with you. I take it this means you are still one of the most eligible bachelors in Praamis?"

"Yes, my lady," replied the Hunter. "Curse my ill luck, but I have yet to meet the lady who can match *your* charm and grace." This elicited a dazzling smile from Lady Dannaros. "Had the good Lord Dannaros not laid eyes on you first, I believe I might very well be wed this day."

Lady Dannaros' laughter rang out, turning the heads of those around her. "Ever the golden tongue on you, my lord." She laid a slim hand on his arm. "Now, if you will excuse me, my lord husband calls."

She motioned for a passing servant, who handed the Hunter a glass filled with bubbling wine.

"Drink this down, Anglion, and we'll see if one of the ladies of Voramis can't spark your interest tonight. Until later, my lord." With a smile and a nod for the Hunter, Lady Dannaros minced away in a flurry of ribbon, lace, silk, and soft curves.

The chilled wine had a light, airy flavor reminiscent of spring berries, with a scent mimicking the fragrance of Snowblossom trees.

Damn, that's good. I must get more of that wine.

He scanned the ballroom until he found a tray-laden servant. The attendant slid through the crowd toward the Hunter, who nodded his thanks as he took a fresh goblet.

Drink in hand, the Hunter surveyed the party. Hundreds of guests whirled around the dance floor, and those along the walls had already found their way into various stages of inebriation. One florid-faced man clung to a marble column for support, struggling to stay upright as he emptied the flagon clutched in his sausage fingers.

A miasma of perfume-laden scents hung heavy in the air, flooding his nostrils and overpowering his senses. He hugged the wall in an attempt to escape the smell, preferring to be alone in the multitude of the pomposity filling the mansion.

The Hunter felt disgusted by those around him. He had no desire to join the figures moving around the massive ballroom. In fact, the longer he remained, the stronger his repugnance grew. He found himself wishing for the simpler company of Old Nan, Jak the Thumb, and even the perpetually screaming, eternally snot-producing Arlo.

How can I be so morose when surrounded by the wealthiest lords and ladies of Einan? I should be happy, enjoying myself. Why am I even here?

Truth be told, he knew he could have carried out his mission of killing Lord Dannaros without attending the soiree. Something had compelled him to attend—perhaps to find his place among the people around him.

Here, the persona of Lord Anglion would fit in among the noble and wealthy of Voramis. The Hunter beneath, however, felt as alone as ever.

The ache within his chest had not diminished since his arrival, even though he stood surrounded by a sea of people.

I know none of these people, and none of them knows me beyond the occasional exchange of words.

He was as isolated as he had been in The Iron Arms, except here the scent of perfume filled his nostrils instead of the smells of vomit, piss, and cheap ale. His eyes drank in the opulence around him, as well as the men and women floating through the room.

Smug, arrogant bastards, each with their secrets.

He saw men who had paid him to kill, and the family members of those he had killed.

I may be the only one in disguise, but all wear masks this night.

Soulhunger's pounding intensified beyond his ability to ignore. The blade sensed the presence of so many victims dancing around him.

An intoxicating scent wafted toward him, accompanied a moment later by a voice he recognized.

"I see my lord is singularly unaccompanied this evening."

The Hunter felt a delicate touch on his arm. A tingle ran through him as the hand traced his muscles toward his shoulder.

Disdain or no, I find myself ever drawn to creatures like this. The frailties of being a man.

"My Lady Damuria," he said, turning to the woman and giving her a deep bow. "You look absolutely ravishing." He kissed her hand, lingering for a suggestive moment. "Your dress is truly a masterpiece."

"This old thing? Do you like it?" She blushed at his compliment and gave him a demure smile.

Lady Damuria wore a dress cut far lower than was common in the fashion of the season. The material was a thread away from being sheer, though small pieces of cloth covered the more intimate parts of her ravishing form. He might have found the dress repulsive, but his knowledge of what lay beneath the gauzy fabric inflamed his imagination.

And yet, she is married…

He forced his eyes upwards, taking in the full lips, the button nose, the long black lashes curled to perfection, and the deep blue eyes staring back at him with a hint of amusement. For one moment—this moment—the ache in his chest was all but forgotten in the presence of the creature before him.

Was married, he corrected himself.

"Forgive me, my lady," the Hunter managed to stammer out. "I must admit, the beauty of that dress has boggled my mind and rendered me an ill-mannered boor."

"Then it has served its purpose, Lord Anglion," she replied, giving him a smile filled with innuendo and temptation.

"I can say, without a doubt, it is a garment quite unlike any of the others in this ballroom."

"I knew you would like it, my lord. When Lord Dannaros invited me to his party, I knew you would be here. It felt like the perfect dress for the occasion."

"It truly does your beauty justice, my lady. I see your hand is empty, a situation I must immediately remedy."

The Hunter motioned for a passing servant, retrieving two glasses and handing one to Lady Damuria.

"My thanks, Lord Anglion. Ever the gentleman." She took a delicate sip from her glass.

"And your lord husband, my lady?"

Lady Damuria's face registered a flash of annoyance, but her features softened quickly.

"My lord was called away from the city on business of an urgent nature. He is due to return any day."

Of course he is, the Hunter thought. *Do you even know where he is? Do you know that he lies rotting at the foot of Dead Man's Cliff?*

Aloud, he said, "It is his misfortune that he is not here, but I consider it my own good fortune to see you wearing this marvelous gown."

"Lord Anglion, you are too kind," she replied with a provocative smile.

The Hunter held out a hand. "My lady, in lieu of your husband, I would be honored to take a turn around the dance floor with you."

"Of course, my lord."

Her hand felt soft and warm in his as he led her into the center of the ballroom. He marveled at the sensuality of her movements, the way her hips swayed with every step. She turned to face him as they began to dance, her eyes teasing him.

The Hunter was fully conscious of his hand nestled in the soft hollow of her back, and she pressed against him as they moved in time to the music. He fought to keep his body from responding to the sensations flooding through him. A sly smile flitted across Lady Damuria's lips as he lost the struggle.

"My lord," she said in mock surprise, her voice breathy and seductive.

Damn it, he thought. *Like a schoolboy peeking into a bathhouse.*

He whirled her around the ballroom, fighting to control his desire. The trilling music, the flurry of elaborate, colorful dresses, the intoxicating effect of the wine, and the feeling of warm flesh in his hands set the Hunter's head spinning. He found enjoyment dancing with this beautiful creature in his arms, who responded so well to his every touch.

It felt like an eternity had passed before the song ended and the sound of applause filled the room.

An insistent pounding in the back of his mind brought him back to reality.

Feed me, Soulhunger whispered, hidden in its sheath beneath his clothing.

I'm not here to dance, he reminded himself. *Can't let myself get distracted.*

Lady Damuria clung to the Hunter's arm as they walked to a nearby table. He deposited her in a chair but remained standing.

"I apologize for leaving you, my lady, but business beckons. I must speak with Lord Argenes before he gets too far into his cup of wine. My father's interests must be attended to."

A look of mock anger flashed across her face. "You men! You can't stop doing business even when trying to enjoy a bit of *pleasure*." The Hunter heard the emphasis placed on the last word.

"My lady, it pains me to leave your side even for a moment, but I must." He pointed to Lord Argenes, a sinewy white-haired noble with flushed cheeks and a glassy stare. "As you can see, that good gentleman is one drink away from losing his battle with gravity."

"Very well, Lord Anglion. I will grant you this indulgence." She stood and extended her hand to him.

"My thanks, my lady." The Hunter kissed her hand. "If I am able and you are willing, I must have another dance with you before the evening is through."

She graced him with a teasing smile. "I make no promises that I will be free during the soiree, my lord."

Before he could respond, she pulled him close, pressing her warm body into his. She stood on her tiptoes and whispered, "But I will be free once it is done. Tonight, in my tower."

The Hunter was keenly aware of the swell of her breasts and hips pressing into him. Her hot breath on his ear sent a shiver of anticipation coursing through his body. His nostrils filled with the scent of her desire. For a moment, his temptation warred with disgust at his own needs, but the outcome was inevitable.

At a loss for words and finding his mouth suddenly dry, the Hunter nodded.

Lady Damuria smiled and disengaged her body from his. "Good. I will be expecting you," she said in a low voice.

"U-Until later, my lady," the Hunter managed to stammer.

"Do seek me out, *my lord*." The emphasis on those last words made her intentions plain.

With a final innuendo-laden smile, she turned and glided away.

By the Mistress, thought the Hunter, admiring her retreating figure, *what a distraction!*

He shook his head to clear the lingering thoughts of the intoxicating woman.

But enough—there is work to be done.

Chapter Seven

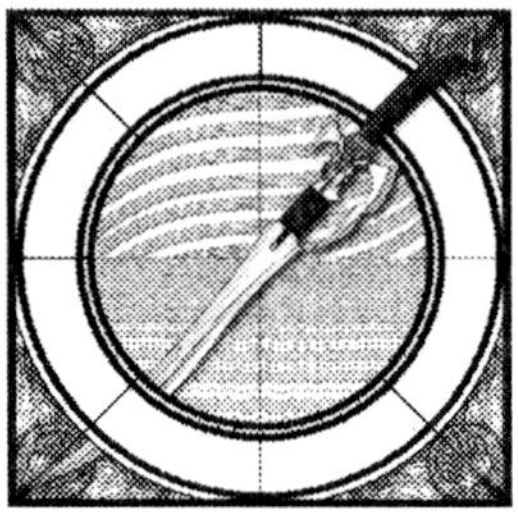

Thank the gods, thought the Hunter, holding his hand over his nose.

He stared down at the snoring form of Lord Argenes, passed out in a pool of his own vomit. He had dreaded speaking to the drunken lord, but it was a necessary part of the Lord Anglion disguise.

No need for that boring chore now. I can escape without pretending to enjoy listening to that old fool drone on about wheat tariffs.

He strode through the mingling guests, his eyes tracking Lord Dannaros' movements.

The noble made polite conversation, but his eyes darted repeatedly in the direction of a darkened corridor adjoining the ballroom. A strange expression flitted across Dannaros' face as he stared toward the hallway, but the Hunter could see nothing from where he stood.

He sidled closer to his target, arriving in time to hear Lord Dannaros excuse himself. "Urgent business, my dear."

Lady Dannaros interrupted her conversation with a tow-headed countess to smile up at her husband.

"Of course, my lord. But hurry back."

With a nod, Dannaros kissed his wife, turned on his heel, and strode away. The Hunter watched him push rapidly through the crowd between him and the corridor. From his past visits to the Dannaros mansion, he knew it led to Lord Dannaros' private office.

Perfect, he thought. *He will be alone.*

And we will feed, Soulhunger's voice echoed in his mind.

Yes.

The Hunter moved through the throng of revelers, pushing toward Lady Dannaros. He tapped her shoulder, and she turned to face him, a smile wreathing her face.

"My lady," the Hunter said with a deep bow to Lady Dannaros. "I must excuse myself."

"Lord Anglion, are you well?" she replied. Concern filled her eyes and her smile faltered.

"I fear the stresses of the journey are doing my stomach an injustice. I apologize for my early departure, but I must rest."

"Of course, my lord," Lady Dannaros replied. She extended her hand to the Hunter, who bowed low and kissed it. "Do feel better. I look forward to seeing more of you during this Season of Plenty."

"Precisely why I must rest," the Hunter said with an apologetic smile. "Please convey my apologies to your lord husband."

"I shall, my lord."

With a final bow to his host, the Hunter took his leave.

The night beckoned to him, but he made an effort to climb the stairs at a dignified pace. He was sick of the perfume-laden air, and his sensitive nostrils complained with every breath. It was with great relief that he stepped through the huge front doors, grateful for the crisp freshness of the air outside the mansion.

He strolled with casual ease down the long marble walkway. There were few people outside, as most were within the mansion enjoying the party.

Good, thought the Hunter, glancing around, *the path is empty.*

Torches smoked in the night air, offering little in the way of illumination as the wind buffeted their meager flames. Thick hedges bordered the path, but the Hunter had found a section where the branches thinned. With a quick glance around to confirm he was alone, he slipped through the hedge and into the darkened gardens beyond.

The tall hedge cast shadows across the dark lawn, but he preferred the darkness. It provided him with cover as he moved silently toward the walls of the mansion.

The scent of wet earth filled the garden, as well as a hint of fragrances from the delicate flowers for which the Dannaros estate was famous. He stepped over flowering trees and bushes, but his heavy elaborate garments weighed him down and caught on branches as he ran.

Stupid costume. Gods damn Lord Anglion and his accursed fancy clothing.

The heavy outfit did have a single redeeming quality: it allowed him to smuggle a slim sword past the guards.

And Soulhunger. The dagger pressed against him, its voice whispering in his mind.

Soon enough, he thought through the throbbing ache in his head. He found himself longing for peace, for the insistent voice to fall silent.

The Hunter raced through the night, moving along the wall of the towering mansion.

There it is! A grim smile played on his face.

Light streamed through a large window set in the second floor of the building. The window to Lord Dannaros' office.

* * *

The clacking of Lord Dannaros' boots echoed in the silence of the darkened corridor. His apprehension increased as he reached the heavy bloodwood doors to his office, and he hesitated a moment before pushing the doors open. They closed behind him with a *click* that sounded ominously loud in the quiet room.

Waiting in tense silence, unwilling to speak first, Lord Dannaros studied the figure standing beside the fire. A dark cloak hid the man's features from view, but the firelight glowed off the myriad scars crisscrossing the man's rough hands.

The Fifth, thought Lord Dannaros. Sweat rolled down his back, and his heart thundered. The man before him set his nerves on edge. *What in the fiery hell is he doing here?*

"My master has...concerns," said the man, not turning to face Dannaros. "After your failure to deliver the promised goods—"

"The failure was not mine," spat Dannaros, his eyes flashing. "Lord Damuria was charged with the task, and it is he who has failed to arrive in time."

"Damuria is dead," said the man, simply. The Fifth turned to face Lord Dannaros, and the aristocrat shrank back from the intensity in the man's gaze. "You and he were given the task, and you have failed. My master—"

"Will be pleased to know that I have found an alternative," Dannaros said hurriedly. "The first shipment arrived last night, and another is on the way."

"You would do well to inform him in person," said the Fifth, turning back to the fire.

"I will compose a letter immediately. You can take it to him."

"I am no messenger," the Fifth snarled.

"O-Of course," Dannaros stammered. "I will arrange for it to be delivered."

"Good." The man turned to face the sweating aristocrat. "See that you do." His voice held an edge of steel, chilling Lord Dannaros to the bone. Sweat broke out on the nobleman's palms.

The grim figure walked to the huge doors through which Lord Dannaros had entered. "I can show myself out, *my lord.*"

The door shut behind the Fifth with a loud click, plunging the office into silence. The shadows pressed in on Dannaros, and his pulse raced. He breathed deeply, struggling to master his fear.

He hurried to his massive desk, throwing himself into his plush chair. His desk drawer held a feather pen and inkpot. He ignored the shaking of his hand as he began to write furiously.

His pen flew across the page, ink dribbling from the nib. In his hurry to pen the letter, he abandoned elegance in favor of speed. He knew the one who would read his missive wouldn't care what the words looked like, provided the contents of the message satisfied him.

Sweat dripped from Dannaros' forehead onto the parchment, and the sound of his quick breathing matched the hurried scratching of pen on paper.

Finally, it was done. He stared at the contents of the letter, reading over every word. He hoped it would placate the man who had sent the Fifth.

Lord Dannaros removed a small seal and a pot of wax from the desk drawer. He had just removed the stopper when a harsh, grating voice rang out in the silence of the office.

"Lord Dannaros, your day of reckoning has come."

Chapter Eight

Startled, Lord Dannaros dropped both wax and seal. He squinted up at the figure standing at the far end of the room, hidden by shadow and beyond the reach of the firelight.

"Who—?"

The unfamiliar voice had startled Dannaros, but he thought he recognized the face beneath the dark hood.

"Harrenth? Is that you, Anglion?" He stared wide-eyed at the figure. "What are you doing h—?"

"The man you know as Anglion does not exist," the figure rasped. "He is simply the tool I used to bring about your destruction tonight."

Lord Anglion pulled back his hood and stepped forward into the firelight. His hands went up to his face, and Lord Dannaros gasped as his friend peeled the skin from his own face. Beneath the false flesh, a hard, unfamiliar face stared back at the gaping man. The green of Anglion's eyes came off with the disguise, revealing the depthless black ones beneath.

A shudder ran through Dannaros, as he stared into the burning eyes. His blood turned to ice. "The Hunter," he breathed. "B-But…"

His words trailed off as steel whispered from a sheath. Firelight played across the Hunter's face in an eerie pattern. The grim smile that touched the assassin's lips sent chills down Lord Dannaros' spine, and fear overwhelmed his arrogance. He stared in horror at the jewel-hilted dagger gripped in the Hunter's hand.

He knew what its presence promised.

A sudden temptation to try to reason with the Hunter seized him, and he opened his mouth to offer the assassin gold, jewels, and women; anything he wanted if the man would spare him.

No, thought the terrified lord, *none of that will sway him. He won't stop coming for me until I am dead. Or he is.*

"For your sins, Lord Dannaros, the Long Keeper calls you this night." The Hunter's voice rang with an ominous tone of finality. "May the gods have mercy on you."

Something snapped within Lord Dannaros as the Hunter spoke his pronouncement. His fear faded, the terror in his veins replaced with resolve. He clenched his jaw, and anger burned within him.

I will not be sent to the Long Keeper with empty hands.

"You'll find me far less helpless than your usual victims, you bastard!"

Dannaros' fingers fumbled beneath his desk, and he smiled as he felt the hilt of the slim fencing sword hidden there. He drew the long blade, holding it before him unwaveringly. The edge of the blade gleamed in the firelight, and the feel of solid steel in his hand restored some of Lord Dannaros' confidence. He strode around the desk, coming to stand face to face with the Hunter.

I refuse to cower. I will fight!

"So," said the Hunter, a savage grimness in his voice, "you have a sword, but all I have is this dagger." The assassin tossed his blade from hand to hand, and a mocking smile spread across his face.

Lord Dannaros watched the Hunter, his eyes following the movements of the wicked blade. In the moment when the Hunter released the blade from his right hand, the aristocrat made his move.

Lightning fast, he lunged forward—a motion that had skewered dozens of rivals in the past. Shocked surprise flashed briefly across the Hunter's face, and Dannaros knew he had caught the assassin off guard.

The Hunter leapt backwards, just managing to block Dannaros' thrust with his dagger. The noble pressed his momentary advantage, unleashing a flurry of blows in an attempt to overwhelm the Hunter's defense. If his longer weapon could hit something vital, he had a chance.

After a flurry of blows, Lord Dannaros disengaged, his breath coming hard. His efforts to break through the Hunter's guard failed, but a few of his desperate strikes had found their target. The assassin bled from a pair of wounds, but showed no sign of slowing. Instead, he stalked toward the panting nobleman with feline grace, the wicked smile still on his lips. Fear once again flashed through him as he saw the implacable intensity burning in the Hunter's eyes.

"They say Lord Dannaros has the fastest sword in the city," the Hunter said, his voice as cruel as his smile. "Let's put that to a real test."

The Hunter reached within his dark robes and drew a sword of his own. The blade matched Lord Dannaros' sword in length and weight, and the assassin gripped it with casual ease. Lord Dannaros' eyes widened in desperation, a sinking feeling in his stomach. He now faced two weapons, and a foe clearly skilled in their use.

With a salute of his thin sword, the Hunter attacked. His strikes came quick and hard, yet the desperate Dannaros found them easy to counter. They exchanged dozens of cuts, thrusts, and parries in the space of a minute, the clang of steel loud in the silence of the office.

The doors are too thick for the guards to hear us, thought Lord Dannaros, his panic rising. No matter how many times he batted away the Hunter's lightning sword strokes, the assassin followed up with two more. Dannaros bled from a handful of shallow cuts, but the Hunter's movements remained unhindered.

But I wounded him, Lord Dannaros' mind protested. *He should be slowing down, unless...*

"So it's true what they say, Hunter," Lord Dannaros spat out, contempt in his voice. "You truly are the devil incarnate."

The Hunter raised an eyebrow. "Lord Dannaros, you wound me. If only words could kill, my lord..." He trailed off, a mocking smile on his face.

"What must it be like, being what you are?" The noble's voice filled with anger, but confusion flashed on the Hunter's face.

"You know nothing about me, Dannaros," the Hunter snarled.

"More than you'd think," Dannaros mocked him. "I know you are the last of the accursed Bucelarii."

From the puzzled look on the Hunter's face, the assassin had never heard the name before. This struck Dannaros as odd.

"If you kill me," he told the Hunter, "you'll never know the—"

The Hunter launched his attack, taking Dannaros by surprise and cutting off his words. The assassin pressed the noble hard, and Lord Dannaros fell back beneath the onslaught. The assassin didn't bother to use the blade in his left hand; the long sword in the Hunter's right hand cut through Dannaros' guard with ease.

A crushing feeling of dread filled the noble, and with a sinking gut Lord Dannaros realized the Hunter had been toying with him. He disengaged once more, breathing hard, and edged backwards, moving around the heavy desk in a desperate attempt to escape the Hunter for a few moments more.

"You are as skilled as they say," Lord Dannaros said. "Now let's see if the...GUARDS!" He had to believe the guards in the corridor could hear his cries through the thick door.

Panic rose in him as the Hunter attacked, implacable, inexorable, ruthless. Lord Dannaros saw death written in the depthless eyes of the Hunter, and he wondered if the assassin could sense his fear.

The Hunter's slim sword was everywhere, and all of Dannaros' skill failed to stop the blade from finding flesh. With a stubborn tenacity, the aristocrat fought on, struggling to prevent his panic from overwhelming his mind. He was outmatched, he knew, yet he refused to yield. His primal instinct to fight—to survive—kept him from fleeing a battle he had no hope of winning.

The Hunter's blade scored his face, his forearm, and his leg in rapid succession. Blood dripped from a piercing wound in Dannaros' shoulder, slowing his movements. Sweat trickled into his eyes, and his lungs burned.

"Guards!" he yelled in desperation. "GUARDS!"

The expressionless face of the Hunter stared back at him. " Scream all you want, Lord Dannaros. No one will arrive in time to save you from the fate you have earned this night."

* * *

Soulhunger shouted its insistence in the Hunter's mind, pulsing in time with the rapid beat of Lord Dannaros' heart. His nose filled with the scent of Lord Dannaros' fear, blending with the smell of the smoking fire and old parchment. A thrill of pleasure ran through him as he fought. Lord Dannaros' parries came slower, his movements more pronounced as he flagged.

I can feel his terror, the blade whispered to him. *Let me feed.*

The Hunter's face creased into a grim smile.

I have toyed with him enough, thought the Hunter. *Time to put an end to this.*

His blade flashed in the firelight, moving faster than Lord Dannaros could follow. The razor tip bit deep into the noble's inner thigh. Dannaros screamed in pain, and clutched at the wound in a vain attempt to quench the torrent of blood pouring from the major artery in his leg. His knees buckled, and he slumped to the floor.

Defiant to the end, the noble's right hand scrabbled in the widening pool of blood. His sword lay just beyond his reach, but that didn't stop him reaching for it. The Hunter's boots crunched down hard on his fingers, shattering them. Soulhunger's triumphant laughter echoed in his mind.

The Hunter stared at the struggling man on the floor, adrenaline coursing through his veins. Soulhunger throbbed in his left hand, lusting for the blood dripping onto the floor.

Feed me, it pleaded.

The Hunter wiped his sword on the fallen noble's clothing, grinning at the look of outrage crossing Dannaros' face. Lord Dannaros struggled to sit up, but was too weak from blood loss to do more than glare at the Hunter.

"I curse you, Hunter," said the nobleman, venom dripping from every word. "May all you love turn to ash, and may the gods shit on your corpse as you scream in the flames of the fiery hell."

The Hunter smiled the pitiless grin of a predator. "Keep a place warm for me, Lord Dannaros."

His sword slammed home in its sheath with a ring. He knelt over the dying nobleman and passed the dagger to his right hand. Soulhunger twinkled in the firelight. Fear fill Dannaros' gaze as the noble watched the blade rise and fall.

The Hunter's powerful muscles drove the jewel-hilted blade deep into Lord Dannaros' chest. Ribs broke beneath the force of the blow. The

Hunter felt Soulhunger's point enter the nobleman's heart, heard the dagger cry out its ecstasy as it fed. Dannaros' scream echoed loud in the silence of the darkened room. It held a note of abject terror—a man dying with the knowledge that Hell came for him.

Pain racked the Hunter's body as the blade in his hand drank deep of Lord Dannaros' soul. Fire flared beneath the Hunter's skin, and his chest burned as a new scar was forever etched into his body.

And still the dagger fed, pulling more and more of Dannaros' being into itself. The weapon didn't simply kill: it gathered the essence of its victims and transferred it to the Hunter. Power flooded his body from another life stolen by Soulhunger's wicked blade.

Crimson light flared from the gem set in Soulhunger's hilt, illuminating the dark office. The Hunter stared at the long blade of the dagger, watching the steel absorb the blood. He thrilled at the sensation coursing through him.

This is better than any drug, he thought. Closing his eyes, the Hunter savored the moment. Raw power surged in his veins. He no longer needed food or drink; all he wanted was the life flooding his body. The intoxication of the hunt warred with the pleasure of Soulhunger's feeding. The coppery smell of fresh blood filled his senses.

The light in the room slowly diminished, and the Hunter opened his eyes as Soulhunger's gemstone faded to a dull, clear stone once more. His fingers still clutched the dagger tightly, his forearms aching from the strain. Slowly, he unclenched his fingers.

The Hunter took deep, calming breaths, reveling in the rush that followed the kill. He slipped Soulhunger into its sheath. The blade had fallen silent. Blood pooled at his feet, soaking into the plush carpet.

He stared down at the lifeless body of Lord Dannaros, a man he had befriended while in the disguise of Lord Anglion. He studied the man's corpse, looking at the still, slack features that were so familiar. He knew he should feel anguish at the man's death, but he felt nothing. No sorrow, no remorse.

Lord Dannaros was always just another tool to be used.

The Hunter placed one hand on Dannaros' head, the other over his heart. "May the Long Keeper take your body," he intoned. "Your soul is forfeit."

It was a simple ritual, but one that served as a final kindness to those who would never know the bliss of the Long Keeper's final embrace.

Death is nothing to Soulhunger's victims. It is simply the first step in the endless torture they face in the hells to which all the soulless dead are sent.

The stillness felt eerie after the furious struggle. The absence of Soulhunger's cries in his head amplified the unnerving quiet. His eyes took in the details of Lord Dannaros' office, studying the room around him.

For the first time, the Hunter noticed the seal that had fallen from the noble's hand and rolled beneath the desk. He stooped to retrieve it and held it up to the firelight to make out the details. What he saw chilled him to the bone.

"Shit!"

He stared at the etching on the seal: a five-fingered hand tipped with sharp, bestial claws. He knew what it was.

The symbol of the Bloody Hand.

"By the Watcher," he cursed aloud.

What in the twisted hell was Lord Dannaros doing in bed with The Bloody Hand? How deeply involved was he? Could he be one of the Five?

The Bloody Hand—or the Hand, as most people called it—ruled Voramis with near-absolute power. Only the king wielded more authority than the Hand, and some whispered that even the king answered to the vile criminal organization. They had a hand in every murder, kidnapping, and strong-arm operation in the city, and dealt in every form of illegal trade. If a coin could be made, the Bloody Hand had already found a way to get their hands on it.

And now it appears Lord Dannaros is involved in The Hand's business. They are an enemy I can ill-afford, but it is too late for that now.

He imagined scores of Hand thugs storming his home and safe houses in vengeance for Lord Dannaros' death.

Let them come, he thought with a smile. *We will see whose hands are bloodier.*

For a moment, he forgot that he still stood in Lord Dannaros' study, that the dead noble's body lay just a few paces away. His mind filled with visions of Soulhunger carving through the ranks of the Hand, flooding him with the power the blade—and *he*, truth be told—so desperately craved.

The sound of booted feet clattering down the hall ripped the Hunter's attention back to the present.

Someone actually heard Lord Dannaros' cries for help. though far too late for them to help the poor bastard.

Shouts sounded outside the door, followed by the thud of something heavy slamming against the thick wood.

He faced two choices: fight or flee. He chose the latter. He had been paid to kill *only* Lord Dannaros. There was no point wasting the lives of guards merely doing their jobs.

The Hunter turned on his heel and sprinted from the room, into the private room adjoining the study, where a window stood open—the window through which he had gained access to Lord Dannaros' study. He raced towards it and leapt, his powerful legs propelling him through the air.

His hands closed around a thick branch, and he swung himself toward the trunk of the tree. The foliage of the tree was thick enough to hide him from the sight of those below, but not so thick that it impeded his descent.

His eyes scanned the darkness, searching for the bag he had hidden earlier. A smile touched his lips as he saw it nestled in the crook of a thick branch. He pulled the strap over his head, feeling the comforting weight of the bag.

Time to disappear.

The Hunter swung from branch to branch with the dexterity of an acrobat, descending quickly.

I only have a minute or two before—

"There he is!" A shout rang out above his head. "Get him!"

He cast a glance over his shoulder, and a quiet curse burst from his lips. A guard stood at the open window, pointing a crossbow at him.

Watcher be damned!

The Hunter leapt to a lower branch, desperate to evade the hurtling bolt. With a loud *thunk*, the projectile buried itself in the trunk of the tree, less than a hand's breadth from his head.

"He went out the window," the guard at the window shouted. "Get some guards into the garden, now!"

Desperation filled the Hunter. He grasped his bag tightly and launched himself into the air. Branches snapped and cracked as he collided with the trunk of a nearby tree. The impact knocked the wind from his lungs.

"Gods…damn…," he gasped, fighting for breath.

The Hunter slid down the barren trunk of the tree, landing hard on the soft grass below. His powerful legs absorbed most of the shock, but he felt muscle fibers straining. Ignoring his protesting leg muscles, he sprinted through the darkened garden. His body would heal from any minor injuries long before his pursuers caught up.

Crossbow bolts flew through the air, but the Hunter knew the archers fired blind. His dark grey robes blended with the shadows, just one more patch of darkness in the night. Still, he made it a point to weave between the trees. He couldn't risk one crossbowman getting off a lucky—

"Argh!"

A crossbow bolt slammed into his shoulder, sending him stumbling. He barely managed to keep his feet.

Gotta find cover.

A massive oak tree towered in the darkness ahead, and he rushed toward it. Pain raced through his upper body with each step, but he gritted his teeth and pushed on. He threw himself behind the tree just as the air filled with more humming bolts.

At least I have a minute or so before the bastards reload.

He growled in rage and ripped the bolt from his shoulder. He knew it would heal in a matter of minutes, but that didn't make it hurt any less.

I fucking hate *crossbows!*

Breathing deep, he struggled to take his mind off the agony. His body mended, and slowly the pain receded. He risked a glance towards the mansion and cursed as he saw Lord Dannaros' guards racing in his direction.

Four crossbows among them, he thought. The pain in his shoulder made him wince. *Need a bit longer to heal.*

He drew two handheld crossbows from his bag. The arms of the small crossbows snapped out from within their compartments in the stock of the bow, and the string pulled taut with a *twang*. Designed with an intricate system of springs that self-loaded the weapons, each crossbow could release two bolts in quick succession.

Let's see how you like this, you bastards.

He leapt from behind the tree, turning to face the onrushing guards. His right shoulder still aching, he raised his arms and gripped the triggers.

Four bolts sped into the night, and three screams echoed through the gardens. *Got you!*

The Hunter thumbed a mechanism on the stock of the crossbows. This released the arms, allowing him to fold them up once more. He slid the weapons into the bag and retrieved a brace of throwing daggers.

He moved his right arm, testing his wounded shoulder once more. His healing muscles still protested, but he could move without too much pain.

By the time I reach the outer wall, it should be healed. With their crossbows out of commission for the moment, I have a minute to—

"Release the hounds," came the shout.

Fuck, thought the Hunter. *As if things aren't bad enough, now they have to bring the dogs into it.*

Rumor had it Lord Dannaros had brought his dogs from beyond the Great Dividing Sea. They were called bear hounds, a name given not because of their ability to hunt, but due to their sheer size. The beasts stood nearly as tall as a man, and moved far faster. They guarded his sprawling estate with a fierce loyalty.

The Hunter had heard tales of intruders ripped limb from limb by the powerful jaws of the massive canines. He had no desire to see their work firsthand.

Guards shouted in fear as the sound of howling filled the air, rumbling from huge lungs in heavy chests. Massive dark shapes pounded towards him, with eyes glowing red and teeth shining white in the darkness of the gardens. With paws the size of a man's head and fangs nearly as long as the Hunter's knives, they were a fearsome sight.

The Hunter cast around in desperation. He drew a dagger from his brace, being careful not to touch the thick black tar coating the blade. A forked tree provided him with the closest thing to cover he would find, and he slipped behind it.

Let's see how you beasts handle a bit of argam.

He ignored the pain in his arm long enough to release the first of the daggers. Steel flashed through the air, and the weapon buried itself to the hilt in the massive shoulder of the dog. The creature yelped in pain, but its momentum didn't slow.

He cursed, drawing another dagger and launching it even as he scrambled to draw a third. The weapon found its mark in canine flesh, and two more knives flew in quick succession.

The first dog staggered and slowed. Dark green blood leaked down its forelegs. It dropped to its belly, whimpering in agony and writhing as the argam flooded its body. By the time the first bear hound stopped convulsing, the other three dogs lay twitching on the grass beside their dead companion. The scent of poisoned blood wafted to him, a sickening stench heavy with rot and decay.

Good riddance.

The Hunter resumed his sprint, hoping he would find the wall surrounding the Dannaros property soon. Heavy footfalls sounded behind him, but the Hunter knew he could outrun the guards coming from the mansion.

If I can just get to that wall...

From the garden ahead stepped four guards. They spread out quickly to, cutting off his escape and forcing him to skid to a halt.

Swordsman damn them!

The men wore leather armor and moved with the familiar ease of trained professionals. Their heavy military swords looked to be well-used, yet kept in excellent condition. The scent of their terror filled the Hunter's nostrils, accompanied by the odor of stale wine and sweat. Their faces showed no fear, however, only rage. With determined expressions, they closed in around him, preparing to attack.

Can't risk breaking my own sword. Better help myself to one of these fellows' blades.

He lunged forward, and his sudden charge caught the guard in front of him unprepared. Before the man knew what had happened, the Hunter slammed his fist into the man's throat. The guard dropped to the ground, gasping and struggling for breath. He dropped the sword to clutch at his throat, and the Hunter scooped up the blade before it hit the grass.

With a smile, the Hunter turned to face the remaining three guards, holding the stolen sword in his right hand. With his left, he drew a long, notched blade from the bag he carried. The guards eyed the blade with nervous respect. They knew the razor edge of the swordbreaker could slice through even leather armor.

"No use trying to talk you lads out of this, is there?"

His jovial tone did little to dissuade the three men in front of him from attacking. Two of the guards charged him together. One thrust for the Hunter's stomach while the other aimed a slashing blow at his head.

The Hunter twisted out of the way of the thrust and caught the high cut with his sword. He continued moving, dancing to his left. His movement placed one guard between him and his companion, buying him precious seconds. The Hunter's stolen sword disemboweled the first guard before the other two could react.

The third guard joined the fight, slashing at the Hunter's knees. The Hunter simply stepped back, moving toward the second guard. He chopped his sword in an overhand blow, and the guard blocked high as expected. The swordbreaker in the Hunter's left hand found the man's exposed neck.

He left the notched blade embedded in the guard's throat, unable to wrench it free before the remaining guard attacked. The man rained heavy blows on him, trying to use his superior strength and size to overpower the

Hunter.

The guard made the fatal mistake of putting too much force into one of his strokes, and his heavy sword whistled through empty air as the Hunter dodged. That was all the opening the Hunter needed.

The Hunter's stolen sword lashed out before the guard could react and the guard's skull gave a wet *crunch* as the Hunter's sword sliced into his temple. Brain matter leaked from the wound, and the guard died with a wordless scream.

Not a pleasant way to kick it.

The grooved swordbreaker resisted his efforts to rip it from the fallen guard's neck, the blade's notches catching on the gristle of the man's throat. He pulled it free with effort, and cleaned it on the man's cloak before sheathing it.

The Hunter's eyes darted through the darkened gardens around him, searching for a new foe. No more guards rushed out at him, but he could see flickering torchlight coming from the manor.

The Hunter resumed his easy lope through the garden. The wall towered high above his head, but he scaled it with practiced ease. His powerful fingers dug into the fissures and cracks between the heavy stones. Within seconds, he had reached the top.

The sounds of pursuit echoed in the gardens below, the guards shouting in confusion.

"Where is he?"

"I heard something over there!"

"Keeper take you fools! Don't let him get away, you c—"

The darkness of Upper Voramis swallowed the Hunter as he leapt from the wall and into the shadows beyond.

Chapter Nine

Count Eilenn sat alone in his darkened office, writing by the flickering light of the logs blazing in the fireplace. The office held a plush couch, but the count favored his heavy wooden desk when working.

He loved this time of night. No one else moved around the Palace of Justice, and he had the place to himself. He did his best work in this little room—*my kingdom,* he thought—and he found comfort in every small luxury added to the sparse office.

It is peaceful, calm, he thought, dotting an *i* with a flourish.

Count Eilenn took great pride in his work—both his official duties and the tasks he carried out for Lord Jahel.

The early morning hours offer the perfect silence and privacy to write out orders for—

"The hour grows late and still the messenger scribbles into the night."

The harsh voice from Eilenn's nightmare sounded from within the shadows at the far end of the room. A figure stood just out of reach of the firelight, a hood pulled far forward to hide his features.

"Frozen fucking hell!" yelped the terrified noble. His heart raced and he cowered behind the massive wooden desk, afraid of the man in the hood.

That voice, thought Count Eilenn with a shudder, *it's Him!*

"My-my lord…er…s-sir Hunter," he stammered, unsure of how to address the assassin. "You…er…startled me."

Count Eilenn thought the shadowed face split into a grin, but he could not be certain.

"Tell your master the contract is completed," the Hunter said. "He will be pleased to know Lord Dannaros will trouble him no longer."

To Count Eilenn, the Hunter's deep voice seemed to echo in the dead silence of the Palace of Justice. He had felt so safe in the privacy of his office a moment ago, and yet now the room felt more like the interior of a coffin.

"But..." He tried to form a coherent sentence, but his tongue refused to form words. His heart raced, beating with such force that he worried it might rip free from his chest.

He's going to kill me. The thought repeated itself in his head as he stared at the unmoving figure in shadow.

"You have the rest of the payment?" The Hunter extended a hand. Eilenn noted the calluses, the strong fingers, the thick wrist, the absence of jewelry. The hands of a killer.

Payment, his mind repeated the last word the Hunter had said. Like an automaton, Count Eilenn opened the top drawer of his desk and withdrew a heavy leather purse.

"Here," he croaked, all but flinging it at the man.

The Hunter caught the purse with a deft movement, and it disappeared into the folds of his robe.

"My thanks, Count Eilenn," came the grating voice again. The Hunter took a step forward, and the light of the fire reflected off the impossibly dark eyes beneath his hood.

Count Eilenn flinched at the movement. He opened his mouth to speak, but, again, no words came forth. Something warm and wet trickled down his leg.

"Your end of the contract is fulfilled, Count Eilenn."

Hearing his name terrified Eilenn even more. *He knows who I am.*

"Should your master have need of my services, he knows how to contact me." The Hunter's eyes held Eilenn's for a long minute, and the count's heart seemed to stop.

A sound from the hallway caused the count to look away for a moment. When he turned back, the Hunter had disappeared.

The silence filling the room was deafening, almost sinister. Count Eilenn's eyes scanned the shadows, as if expecting the Hunter to leap out at him once more. For a long minute, Count Eilenn struggled to control his breathing and the rapid beating of his heart.

Bloody Minstrel, he cursed. *How in the empty hell did he get into the Palace of Justice? And into* this *wing no less! I must tell Lord Jahel of it immediately. He'll want to know, both about Lord Dannaros and the Hunter's—*

A knock at the door set his heart pounding again, but only the placid face of Raska, his servant, peered around the door.

"My lord?" the man said, a puzzled look on his face. "Were you talking to someone in here?"

"No, I was not talking to anyone," Count Eilenn snapped. "I was alone and silent. You might want to visit a physicker and have your hearing checked."

He knew the servant didn't deserve to be the object of his anger, but he didn't care.

"Yes, my lord," Raska replied, with the patience of an underling who has been on the receiving end of many a tirade.

"Now, Raska, I believe I will need a fresh tunic. I've gone and spilled tea on myself."

Funny, thought Raska as he left the office, *I didn't see any tea…*

* * *

From his perch atop the roof of the Palace of Justice, the Hunter watched the red-robed Heresiarchs bustling far below. The Hunter's vantage point allowed him full view of the Palace courtyard, and he saw only a handful of the city guard on watch within the Palace this night.

They must have been called out to the Dannaros mansion to investigate the murder, he thought. *It's a good thing, too, or I might not have been able to slip in and out of Eilenn's window unseen.*

A smile played on his lips as he recalled the man's terror.

The fool even pissed his breeches. Once more, the reputation of the Hunter at work...

Soulhunger had tracked Count Eilenn to the Palace. *He might not have given me that purse of his had he known I could use it to hunt him down.*

The realization of where he was hit the Hunter.

So the Palace of Justice hired me to kill Lord Dannaros. Dannaros is—was, he corrected himself—*dealing in something much more secretive and illegal, if someone in the Palace wanted him dead badly enough to hire me.*

An image of the seal in Lord Dannaros' office flashed through his head.

Our dear Lord Dannaros was in league with The Bloody Hand, it seems. What could a noble of Voramis be doing working with those criminals? And why was I hired to kill the man?

This brought the Hunter's mind back to the man whom he had taken such pleasure in terrifying this evening.

Count Eilenn is the perfect middle man. Who would want the position of "Proctor of the Royal Post"? Such a useless title. No, that foolish little man is part of something much greater than just organizing the delivery of mail.

The Hunter had heard whispers running through Voramis, rumors of a group of Heresiarchs plying a darker trade than their counterparts patrolling the streets. A secret trade of blood, torture, and the gathering of secrets.

The name of the Dark Heresy inspired the same fear as mention of the Bloody Hand—or the Hunter.

If the Dark Heresy wanted Lord Dannaros' secret trade stopped, he must have been more than just a rich, spoiled lord. He must have been an instrumental member in The Bloody Hand. Could he be one of the Five Fingers?

"Shit," the Hunter muttered aloud. *Now both the Heresiarchs and The Hand will be interested in my actions. Things are about to get interesting.*

A stiff breeze rustled his cloak, and the Hunter closed his eyes to enjoy the cool night air and its fresh scents.

This high up, the air is clean, free of the stench of the city.

Looking out over the city below, he marveled at the beauty of Voramis after nightfall. When darkness hid the squalor of the lower city, the myriad lights twinkling in the night enchanted his senses. The voice in his head had fallen silent, and he reveled in the peace.

Power still coursed through his body, filling him with desire. He ached for release after the kill, and his body responded to the urge. He felt the need to be with a woman, but his desire for companionship had little to do with loneliness. For him, it was raw, primal lust.

Thoughts of heights brought a beautiful face to mind.

Ah, yes.

He smiled at the picture he saw behind his closed eyelids.

I have somewhere I need to be...

* * *

A sound in the darkness startled Lady Damuria from her dreams. Her eyes darted around her room, taking in every detail, searching for the source of the noise.

"My lord?" she questioned. "Have you returned, husband?"

The man who stepped from the shadows of the room's balcony and into the moonlight was taller and broader than the man she called husband.

"No, my lady. It is I."

Dark green eyes and the smiling face of Lord Anglion stared down at her.

"My Lord Anglion," she said, sitting up. "I am *surprised* to see you." Her words held a tone of reproof. "When Lady Dannaros told me you had retired early for the night, I feared you had found another to warm your bed."

Lord Anglion moved toward her, removing his heavy cloak and dropping it to the floor behind him.

"I could not wait to visit you this evening," he said. "I slipped away early from the party to finish some urgent business. This way I will not be disturbed in the morning."

"I see." Lady Damuria gave him a smile, one laden with promise.

She pulled back the covers, climbing to her feet to stand before him. Nothing but a thin gown hid her flesh from the night air. The gauzy fabric revealed her perfectly curved body, and Lord Anglion's eyes dropped to examine every bit of soft flesh.

"The night is ours, then."

"Yes," said Lord Anglion. He took her hand in his and kissed it gently. "My servant believes I am abed, wearied from the long journey."

He encircled Lady Damuria in his arms, pulling her close to him.

"We can do as we please," he whispered, his breath hot on her ears.

"You're certain your husband will not return?"

"My lord has sent no word of his return," she whispered back as her hands traced the firm contours of his hard-muscled body. "And should he arrive while you are here," her fingers traveled over his chest, "Barchai will be certain to alert me."

"You trust Barchai?"

"With my life," Lady Damuria said.

"And your secrets?"

She replied with a mysterious smile, then turned her attention to the familiar scars etched into his chest. "More scars, Anglion?"

"It has been a good year, my lady," Lord Anglion said with a shrug. "The gods demand their due, and these marks are simply the price I pay for good fortune." He smiled at her. "It is a price I would gladly pay to be in your company once again. I can think of a few things we can do to pass the night in more pleasant ways."

She turned her face up to meet his and she saw her desire for him reflected in his eyes.

* * *

She looks ravishing, the Hunter thought, staring at her full curves through the gown.

Lady Damuria let out a little gasp of delight. "My *lord!*" she smiled, feeling his desire for her through the thin robe.

He kissed her then, a kiss burning with the heat of his passion. The thrill of the kill burned in his veins, melding with his lust for the gorgeous woman standing in front of him.

For long minutes, neither of them spoke—nor had any desire to speak. Instead, their bodies entwined in the timeless embrace of a man and woman seeking to fulfill a raw, primal need. Fire burned in the Hunter as he took her, making no attempt to be gentle.

She seemed not to mind.

* * *

By the Long Keeper she took a long time to fall asleep, thought the Hunter. Lady Damuria's dark curls spilled across his muscled chest, her rhythmic breath hot on his skin. *I was certain I had exhausted her, but the Lady Damuria's...appetites truly are as boundless as the rumors say.*

Her skin was soft on his, and the gentle curve of her breasts against his side nearly aroused his desire once more. Her fragrance filled his senses, her scent as intoxicating as their lovemaking had been. However, the exertions of the day caught up to him, fatigue numbing his mind and pulling him inexorably towards slumber.

He basked in the cool darkness of the night, the feeling of the soft blankets covering their bodies. The thrill of the hunt had died, and with it, the heat of his passion. The fearsome Hunter of Voramis fell victim to the same exhaustion that claimed every mortal man.

The face of Lord Damuria—husband to the woman whose bed he shared—filled his vision. The Hunter saw Damuria's horror-filled expression as his lifeblood fed Soulhunger's thirst. The weapon throbbed in the back of his mind.

Sleep overtook the Hunter, pulling him deep into its dream-filled depths.

* * *

He awoke at dawn, covered in sweat, breathing hard. He fought to remember, to retain his grasp on the sensations lingering from his dreams.

Her scent.

"Don't leave," he whispered, desperate to cling to the final traces of *Her,* whoever *She* was.

Every morning, a raging inferno burned holes in the Hunter's mind. The delicate essence of his mystery woman left him gasping for breath, aching to fill the gaps in his memory. Why *She* mattered, he knew not. All he knew what that *She* was important to him, somehow.

The one prey who eludes me still, like Snowblossom petals drifting on the breeze.

She haunted his dreams, taunting him with a face he could never recall. Yet when morning dawned, the memory faded away like a phantasm.

The soft warmth of Lady Damuria next to him reminded him of where he was. He ran his hands along the gentle curves of her body, and breathed deep of the woman's fragrance.

Honey, jasmine, and passionflower. Beautiful, but not Her.

He pulled back the heavy covers and slipped from the massive canopied bed without a sound. He simply stood, staring down at the woman sleeping in the bed.

How could she do this? She is a married woman, and yet she consorts with men freely. Why would she betray her husband thus?

Contempt flooded him, but it was the evidence of his own base nature that served as the true source of his anger.

Are my desires so out of my own control that I can do things like this? That I must spend the night with whores like Lady Damuria? He fought to push down his self-loathing, stifling the emotion as he would a yawn.

The Hunter ignored the colorful tapestries on the wall, taking little note of the room as he moved to the heavy wooden table. A metal basin of water sat upon the table, and he splashed the freezing water on his face to wash away the night's sleep.

He studied his face in the mirror hanging on the wall above the basin. The alchemical flesh of Lord Anglion's face had begun to slip, the clay adhesive holding the disguise in place dissolving.

It is time for Lord Anglion to make his escape.

He reached for the clothing he had discarded last night, dressing quickly.

Lady Damuria stirred, pulled from pleasant dreams by the sound of her lover's movements. But by the time she opened her eyes, the tower room was empty.

Chapter Ten

Courier Balgos slunk through the slums of Beggars Row, gagging at the stench of the litter-strewn streets. He wore the simple robes of a messenger, but even his humble clothing contrasted sharply with the staggering poverty around him.

The smell of refuse, ordure, and death rose from myriad piles of the-gods-knew-what, hanging in a miasma so thick he could almost taste it.

By the gods, if only there was some way to block out this stench.

He placed his feet with care, studying the ground as he walked.

I hope I don't step in—

"Shit!" he cursed aloud. Warm wetness filled his boot, causing him to gag.

Thank the Illusionist I didn't have breakfast, or it might join the rest of the fragrances in this horrible place.

Two days had passed since the Feast of Illusionist's Night, and Balgos still struggled with the after-effects of too much strong drink. His head had stopped pounding, but his stomach still recoiled at the thought of food.

"Please, sir," a voice warbled from a nearby pile of rags, "a coin?"

From the heap emerged a scarred, pox-ridden face. The man's mouth held few teeth, and a wart protruded from his broken nose. The eyes stared at him with a dull, listless expression. A grubby hand reached towards the courier, gnarled fingers covered in a thick crust of grime. Flaking flesh fell from the beggar's arms and hands.

"Get away from me, filth!" Balgos yelled at the leper, his eyes growing wide in horror. The messenger made the warding sign of the Maiden and hurried away.

I have to get the frozen hell out of here before I catch something!

The messenger muttered oaths under his breath, cursing the Hunter and his need for secrecy. He desperately wanted to flee Beggar's Row, but he had a task to complete first.

He scanned the street, searching for the sign of The Rusted Dangle. Relief flooded him as he rounded a corner in the street and spotted the inn.

I just have to deliver my message and I can take a very *long bath!*

The Rusted Dangle stood—*barely,* he thought—at the end of the lane. It appeared to be a nail away from collapsing. Its roof slanted at a dangerous angle, and far too many hastily constructed support beams held up the building.

Rust had worn away the phallic sign depicting the inn's name, suspended on a rope so frayed that a light breeze could blow it down. The inn's front doors hung from hinges older than Voramis itself, and Balgos feared he would rip them out of the wall if he pushed too hard.

The interior of the inn matched its dilapidated exterior. The furniture consisted of tables and chairs cobbled together from scraps of wood that had no right being used for construction.

Behind the bar, stood a balding innkeeper that looked as old as the inn itself. "What can I get you, lad?" the man asked, his tone pleasant.

I must be his first paying customer in years, thought Balgos.

The messenger strode toward the bar, opening his mouth to answer. A raconteur in bright clothing bumped into him, almost knocking him over.

"Watch where you're going, fuckwit!" Balgos yelled at the man.

The traveling entertainer muttered something in response, and the courier gagged at the man's putrid breath.

That swill he drinks must be brewed in a latrine, he thought, pushing the man away.

The drunk hardly noticed the insult and the shove, simply stumbling toward an ancient-looking table in a darkened corner of the bar.

Balgos wiped his hands on his tunic in disgust, trying to scrub away the filth from the raconteur's clothing.

"Room four," he demanded of the bartender.

The balding innkeeper waved a pudgy hand towards the hall at the opposite end of the tavern. "Right that way, sir. But first, might I offer you something to eat or drink?"

The courier summoned every shred of etiquette he possessed. "Another time, perhaps," he replied with a forced smile as he turned away from the bar.

A quiet "ahem" sounded behind the courier. He turned back to see the pub landlord wearing an apologetic smile on his face, his hand held out expectantly.

"Two coppers for use of the room, sir," the bald proprietor said with an oily smile.

Balgos rolled his eyes and fished a pair of copper bits from his purse. He deposited the coins in the innkeeper's hand with a scowl, but the man appeared not to notice. The coins disappeared into a purse beneath his clothing, and he returned to his futile task of wiping the filthy bar with an even filthier cloth.

The floorboards of the dark hallway creaked beneath Balgos' feet, and the scent of year-old unwashed sheets filled his nose.

No wonder the Hunter likes this place, he thought. *No one in his right mind would* ever *stay the night here.*

The door stood unlocked, and he hesitantly pushed it open. The room beyond was dark, the window covered with thick oilcloth to block out the light.

Balgos closed the door and waited in silence, trying not to inhale the foul scents of the darkened room.

"I hear you're looking for me." The deep voice echoed in the stillness.

"Keeper's icy balls!" Balgos cursed, startled. The courier jerked back, instinctively moving away from the threatening figure materializing before him.

I didn't even see him enter the room!

"What the f—?"

"You came for a reason, I assume," the Hunter cut him off.

Balgos snapped his mouth shut, fighting to calm his racing heart. The Hunter towered over him, his silhouette framed against the dim light filtering through the covered window. Balgos couldn't see the assassin's face, nor did he want to.

"Sir Hunter," he said, struggling to keep his voice calm, "I come with an unusual request."

The Hunter could have been made of stone for all the response he gave. The silence unnerved the courier and set his hands trembling.

"Right," Balgos stammered, "er…um…well…right." He drew in a deep breath before continuing. "My…er…master requests that you visit him in his home. He—"

"I don't make house calls," the harsh voice of the Hunter interrupted.

"I know, sir, but I believe you will want to make an exception. My master is—"

"I don't care who your master is. If he wants to meet me, he will do so on my terms. The door is behind you."

"My master is unable to move around the city, or else he *would* meet with you in person."

Silence answered him.

"But," Balgos burst out in desperation, "my master will pay your normal fee just to hear what he has to say, and double if you agree to take the contract."

The room remained silent.

Has he gone? Am I talking to an empty room?

"He-hello?"

"I am considering your master's offer," the Hunter intoned, his voice thoughtful.

Balgos' heart pounded in his chest, and sweat trickled down his back as he waited for the assassin's answer.

"Very well," came the voice from the darkness. "The payment?"

Balgos removed a heavy purse from within his robes, extending it towards the Hunter. The Hunter roughly plucked it from his hands, and the courier heard coins clinking in the darkness.

"Tell your master I will call upon him tonight," came the rough voice of the Hunter.

"Thank you!" Balgos gasped in relief. "My master will be pleased to hear it."

"Where would your master like me to meet him?"

"At the Villa Camoralia, in the—"

"I know the place," the harsh voice interrupted.

"Excellent! I will pass your message along to him, then. He will be pleased to hear it."

"Now go."

Without a backward glance, Balgos fled.

He rushed through the dim taproom and pushed through the front doors without even a nod to the bartender. In his haste, he failed to notice the fact that the inebriated raconteur in his outrageous bright clothing no longer sat at his table.

The foul streets of Beggar's Row rushed by, yet still he ran, heedless of the voices crying out for coin, food, or drink. Only when he reached the Merchant's Quarter did he slow.

"Fucking Hunter," he cursed, turning his steps toward Upper Voramis and the Villa Camoralia.

* * *

The Hunter slid the wooden wall panel shut without a sound, emerging from the secret passage connecting the taproom of The Rusty Dangle with Room Four. He made no noise as he moved from the darkened booth at the back of the taproom, and the occupants of the bar were far too drunk to notice him.

I love this inn, he thought. *The food and ale may be terrible and the smells worse, but this passage is sheer brilliance. I can slip in and out of Room Four unseen and unheard. It's also bloody entertaining to see people's reactions to the Hunter "appearing" in front of them, as if from thin air.*

The Hunter enjoyed putting the fear of the gods—or fear of him—into those seeking out his services. People who believed the Hunter could appear out of thin air tried harder to avoid angering him.

Perhaps the rumors of my superhuman powers are *a bit exaggerated, but they're worth every coin.* It cost him a small fortune to spread whispers through the city, but it was a necessary investment.

The Hunter nodded to Eliryo—the owner of the run-down establishment—and tossed him a silver drake. He had paid the fat innkeeper more than enough to own the room, but an extra coin would keep the man amenable to their arrangement—not to mention discreet.

He strode through the taproom, pushing through the front doors. His face—the face of the drunken raconteur—twisted in disgust as he inhaled the foul odors wafting through the streets of Beggars' Row.

I have time for a few preparations before tonight's meeting.

His curiosity had been piqued by the mysterious client—a man willing to pay double his high fees.

It seems I will soon find the truth behind one of the best-kept secrets in the city.

Chapter Eleven

A cool breeze wafted through Upper Voramis, bringing with it the sweet scent of Snowblossom trees from the distant Maiden's Fields. Stars twinkled overhead, and the moon shone down bright on the dark figure crouching atop the high walls of Villa Camoralia.

The Hunter's vantage point allowed him a clear view of the dark grounds within the mansion. He saw no guards on patrol. Not a soul moved in the darkness, and he could detect no human scents on the air.

They must all be inside, he thought.

A wall twenty paces high surrounded the Villa Camoralia, and scaling it had been no easy task, even with the Hunter's superhuman strength to aid him.

The legendary Hunter, winded like a fat butcher chasing a stray pig.

The thought brought a smile to his face as he rested, regaining his strength.

Tonight I meet the mysterious occupant of the Villa Camoralia.

None knew who lived within the massive, fortified mansion, but rumors spread among the citizens of Voramis like a plague.

Whispers had spread the name of a long-dead sorcerer around the city, while others claimed that King Gavril the Conqueror had wakened from his six thousand-year slumber to reclaim the throne of Voramis.

Some speculated that the Demon of Voramis—the reclusive commander of the Dark Heresy—resided here. Others insisted—always with hushed tones and terrified glances—that the Bloody Hand held court behind its towering walls and iron gates.

He dismissed this last rumor as unlikely.

I doubt the Bloody Hand would extend a polite invitation to me after what I did to Lord Dannaros.

Either way, he placed little faith in the rumors. They were the way of the ignorant, and he dealt only in facts.

Tonight, I will put the rumors to rest once and for all.

He strode along the top of the wall, moving in total silence. His dark grey cloak blended with the shadows as he descended into the gardens of the Villa Camoralia.

He wore no armor—even oiled leather made noise as he moved—but the padded jerkin beneath his tunic would suffice. His long sword, a thick, heavy blade with a vicious edge, hung from his back. Soulhunger sat on his belt, its sheath wrapped in dark cloth to prevent the weapon from clanking.

Tonight he wore the disguise he preferred when meeting new clients for the first time. A heavy jaw with a strong chin, a thick scar running across his flattened nose, dark eyes, and hair of an unremarkable length and style allowed him to blend in with the hired muscle of Lower Voramis.

His rough features would stand out in Upper Voramis, but he had no need to walk the streets. The rooftops of Voramis served as his private highway, allowing him to traverse the city unseen. Only the man inside the mansion would see his face this night.

The mansion rose hundreds of paces into the night sky, and he relished the challenge of climbing its vaulted heights. Sculptures of mythical creatures—long ago eradicated from the face of Einan—adorned the walls of the mansion. The horrifying figures provided perfect handholds for climbing, and he leapt from statue to statue with the ease of a jungle primate.

He climbed at a steady pace, moving toward a balcony half a dozen stories above the ground. It provided a breathtaking view of the sprawling city below, and the Hunter paused to look out over his city. He breathed deep, basking in the fresh breeze blowing across his face.

Huge windowed doors stood locked behind him, held shut by a simple latch. A dagger inserted between the doorframes allowed him to unhook the latch with ease. The room within was dark, but a door on the far end of the room stood ajar—revealing a hall filled with flickering torchlight.

The Hunter slipped through the open window and into the empty room. He peered into the illuminated hallway, taking in the details of the mansion's interior. He searched for any indication of where to find his mysterious client, and his eyes settled on two men standing at the far end of the corridor. They had the look of thugs, with their thick necks, flattened noses, cauliflowered ears, protruding brows, and fists the size of hams.

It looks as if they were cut from the same unthinking, dim-witted mold. The guards smelled of leather, sweat, and lard.

The men stood before a pair of huge double doors, which looked to be made of heavy bloodwood—all but impossible to break, with a natural imperviousness to fire. The doors would have cost less had they been made of solid gold. The Hunter knew they would only be used to guard something—or someone—valuable.

He crept from shadow to shadow, taking care to move in absolute silence. Thick columns lined the hallway, and he kept the pillars between himself and the guards. When he finally stepped from behind the last pillar, he stood no more than a handful of paces from the guards.

"Your master is expecting me," the Hunter rasped.

His words startled both guards. They fumbled for the thick cudgels at their belts, and one nearly dropped his in his haste to draw it. Their violent reaction to his presence made it hard for him to maintain a straight face. With impressive self-control, the Hunter managed to keep his stare impassive and disdainful.

"Who the fuck are you?" one guard demanded, waving his club menacingly at the Hunter. "And where in the tormented hell did you come from?"

I've wounded their pride, the Hunter thought. *Good.* The corners of his mouth twitched into a small smile, but the shadows of his hooded cloak obscured it from the view of the thugs. He eyed the thick wooden cudgel in the man's hand.

"I wouldn't do anything foolish, if I were you," he said aloud.

The guard opened his mouth to speak, but a feeble voice called out from the room beyond before he could form coherent words.

"Let him enter, Targ."

Targ gripped the handle of his club even tighter, clenching his jaw in anger. He looked ready to protest, but the voice came again, this time with an edge of steel in it.

"Unmolested, mind you. He is my guest."

Targ and his companion loosened their grip on their weapons and reluctantly moved out of the way of the door. The Hunter pulled back his hood, and the two guards jerked back as if struck. With a mocking smile for the thugs, the Hunter strode through the huge double doors.

The room beyond was dimly lit, though a fire blazed in the hearth. Eerie shadows danced in the darkness of the room, and the Hunter's nostrils filled with the scent of wood smoke. He took in the sparse comfort of the room—a sitting room, he guessed.

A frail-looking man sat in a wheeled chair—his mysterious client, he assumed. Scars contorted his mouth into a horrible grimace, and thick ridges of scar tissue covered the place where his nose should have been. The old man's hair hung in long white wisps down to his shoulder, and a thin beard covered his weak chin and scarred cheeks with uneven stubble.

Those scars could only have come from the claws of a northern bloodbear, thought the Hunter, studying the four parallel scars crisscrossing the man's face. *Definitely a story there.*

A blanket covered the man's slender legs, and a heavy cloak lay draped across his shoulders. The man emanated a powerful stench of decay.

Soulhunger pounded in his head, a note of joy filling the dagger's bloodthirsty voice. The Hunter ignored the blade, pushing its voice to the back of his mind.

"Take a good look, Hunter," the old man spoke. His words slurred from between ruined, twisted lips. He turned his face to the side, exposing the scars running down his neck and disappearing beneath his thin shirt.

The man gave him a weak smile. "I wager it has been years since you've seen something this twisted and mangled. Though I hear our good Lord Damuria's body was found in a...similar state."

The Hunter said nothing. His attention shifted from the marred features of the old man to the hulking figure standing behind the wheeled chair. The scars on his arms were a testament to the knife fights he had survived. His massive hands rested easily on the handles of the wheeled chair, his forearms heavily banded with muscle.

How many men have those hands broken or killed? The Hunter thought.

The huge man gazed calmly back at the Hunter from beneath heavy brows, but intelligence burned in his dark eyes. The Hunter knew those eyes were taking his measure.

Judging by his expression, I must not be what he was expecting.

The man's scent held a hint of acrid bile, mixed with the overpowering smells of steel and the copper of dried blood.

One thing is for sure, he is no mere attendant. A bodyguard, perhaps.

The old man spoke, breaking the tense silence in the room.

"I know the Hunter only meets at the time and place of his own choosing. Visits to old men in their homes usually ends with a dagger in an aging heart, but I thank you for...restraining yourself." A thrust of his chin indicated the two slabs of muscle standing guard at the door.

The Hunter held his tongue. Years of experience had taught him that remaining silent encouraged people to speak more freely. Loose tongues often spilled more information than their owners realized.

"My...condition being what it is," the old man waved a bony, wrinkled arm toward his legs, "I cannot get out much. I therefore greatly appreciate your coming here. Truth be told, I would trust this matter to no other, for it is of a delicate nature."

"I understand," the Hunter said, his voice deep and harsh. "What would you have of me, lord...?"

The old man gave him a mysterious smile. "You can call me Lord Cyrannius." He waved his hand in a dismissive gesture. "Yes, you and I both know that no 'Lord Cyrannius' exists among the noble houses of Voramis. We both have our secrets to maintain, good Hunter."

"Fair enough. Now, I will hear you out. Be warned, however, I reserve the right to refuse your contract should I choose to."

"And, should you choose to, you will leave the mansion unharmed," the old man said.

The Hunter raised an eyebrow, and the aging Lord Cyrannius gave a gentle laugh. "Yes, I do see the irony in the statement."

Cyrannius steepled his long, slim fingers, studying the cloaked figure of the Hunter.

"You have a reputation as a peerless fighter and I have no doubt you would cut through my men"—he nodded towards his guards again—"with little difficulty."

The Hunter gave a small nod of assent.

"However," Cyrannius continued, "I do have an awful lot of men, and they may present an...inconvenience that you might wish to avoid. Suffice it to say, if you choose to decline my request, none of my men will throw themselves on your blade in an attempt to keep my secrets."

"A wise choice, my lord," the Hunter said. A predatory smile touched his lips, but Cyrannius—and the giant standing behind him—seemed not to notice.

"I know that you care little for details, provided that your services are paid for in full. However, I would like to lay out my reasons for contracting you, nonetheless."

"It is your right, Lord Cyrannius," the Hunter said, "though I dare say they will do little to influence my decision regarding whether or not to accept the contract."

"Fair enough, fair enough."

The man fell silent for a moment, as if collecting his thoughts. When he finally spoke, his words emerged slowly and with hesitation.

"I have a matter that requires your unique...abilities. First off, let me assure you that I have vast resources at my disposal, as you can see by my humble home."

Lord Cyrannius gave the Hunter a deprecating smile, but the Hunter's face could have been carved from stone, for all the reaction he gave.

"To say my fortune rivals that of the Crown would not be a boast, and I have access to wealth beyond anything you could imagine. However," the old man's eyes filled with sorrow and he swallowed hard, "the one thing I am in short supply of... is family."

The Hunter raised an eyebrow, prompting Cyrannius to continue.

"Before my...misfortunes," he waved at his covered legs and scar-twisted face, "the gods saw fit to grace me with a daughter, my only child. She was the light of my life, and when she married, she gave birth to a daughter of her own. This young girl—my granddaughter—was the light of her parents' eyes, and the one good thing a broken old man had in this world."

Had? Were?

"You speak of her as if she belongs to the past," the Hunter said.

"It pains me still to talk about this, though it happened what feels like a lifetime ago. The young girl came of age last year, and demanded her freedom to celebrate the Season of Plenty with her friends. During the Maiden's Harvest celebration, she met a young man. This young man took certain...liberties with her. To speak plainly, he violated her." Rage flared across Cyrannius' face.

The Hunter said nothing, and the old man appeared not to notice. "When we approached the man, he vehemently denied his actions and swore upon the gods that he had not laid a finger on my Eliesse. We could find no proof beyond her words, and the laws of Voramis were on the side of this, this,"—he fished for the word—"monster."

"He walked free, Hunter. The man who defiled my beautiful grandchild escaped punishment because I could not prove he had done anything."

Fire blazed in the old man's eyes, his voice growing thick and deep in his rage. For a moment, the Hunter thought he could see a hint of the man Lord Cyrannius must have once been.

"My granddaughter never fully recovered,"—the old lord's words tumbled out now—"and she spent every moment locked in her room. She refused to eat or drink, and soon began to waste away."

His voice cracked, and a tear threatened at the corner of one eye.

"We found her in her room one day, a gash in each wrist. Before we could summon the physickers to her aid, my beautiful Eliesse's lifeblood emptied onto the cold stone floor of her bedroom."

Tears rolled down his weathered cheeks, and he covered his face with his hands as silent sobs racked his feeble body. The huge attendant simply stood there, impassive, his eyes never leaving the Hunter.

Finally, with a supreme effort of will, Lord Cyrannius managed to recover sufficiently to speak once more.

"To make matters worse," he continued, swallowing hard, "my daughter, her mother, followed her a few days later into the Long Keeper's embrace. I believe she couldn't live with what had happened to her beloved child, and so she took her own life as well."

"And that, good Hunter, is why I have requested your presence here tonight. I want you to be the vengeful hand of the Watcher for me. I want you to seek justice and retribution for the death of my beloved child and grandchild."

Lord Cyrannius' voice dropped to a harsh whisper, one filled with hatred and loathing.

"Neither of them deserved the fate they received at the hands of this monster. I want you to mete out a fate far worse than death to the man who took them away from me."

The man's vehemence surprised the Hunter. "Do you know what you are asking, Lord Cyrannius?"

"Of course I do, Hunter," the old lord scoffed. "I make it my business to gather information, and I know as much about you as anyone else in Voramis—or on the face of Einan itself, for that matter."

Lord Cyrannius stared at the dagger hanging on the Hunter's belt, and the Hunter saw a curious expression cross the man's face

Is that desire I see in the old man's eyes?

Soulhunger throbbed in his mind, and the Hunter fought to keep the weapon's urges from overwhelming his thoughts.

"Oh, yes, Hunter," Lord Cyrannius said, giving him a knowing smile. "I know all about that blade and what it can do. They say it brings a fate worse than death, that it steals the soul of its victims from the Long Keeper's grasp and sends them straight to the darkest depths of the forgotten hell."

"I see you have indeed done your research, my lord."

The old man's knowledge of the weapon's ability surprised the Hunter.

It's no secret what Soulhunger can do, he thought, *but neither is it a commonly known fact. Who is this Lord Cyrannius?*

"Of course I have." The old man's voice turned patronizing. "Which is why I know full well what I am paying you to do. I also know that your services are worth every gold imperial." Cyrannius' eyes blazed with an inner fire. "It is the fate that man deserves, and you are the only one who can fulfill an old man's request."

The Hunter remained silent for a moment, pondering.

Is it worth it to take the contract, even though I know nothing about this mysterious man?

Something he couldn't put into words compelled him to nod his assent.

"I will accept your contract, Lord Cyrannius."

"Good, good," the old nobleman beamed, clapping his frail hands together in delight. For a moment, the Hunter thought the firelight played tricks with the old lord's twisted features. The face staring at him contorted, looking like a horrible creature preparing to feast on its victim.

"You know what I require?" the Hunter asked, dismissing what he had seen as nothing more than the room's dim lighting.

"Of course, Hunter. I have had it readied in the hope that you would accept my offer. Tane," he spoke to the huge man holding his wheeled chair, "would you bring the case from the next room?"

With a grunt and a nod, Tane released the handles of the old lord's chair and stalked through the open door behind him.

The Hunter couldn't help admiring the huge man's grace and fluidity. Tane walked on the balls of his feet with ease, stepping with the unconscious grace of a predator.

He walks like a Yathi Dancer, but those arms look as if they belong in a Hradari beast pit. He'd put the fear of the gods into me, *if such a thing were possible.*

The huge bodyguard disappeared into the room beyond, returning a moment later carrying a small black box.

Bloodwood, the Hunter thought, noticing the unique whorls of the wood fiber. *That box alone could cover the cost of the contract.*

Tane held the box before his master, opening the lid with a huge hand. A simple white cloth lay folded within, a fat purse sitting next to it.

"As you can see, Hunter," the old man said, "the case contains the item you require, along with the payment for your services." Lord Cyrannius' voice grew feeble now that his fit of rage had passed, but fire still blazed behind his dark eyes.

The Hunter said nothing, simply slipping the white square of cloth into the pocket of his dark grey robes.

"I can't say I quite understand why you requested that cloth, Hunter," Lord Cyrannius said, his voice probing.

It is a safeguard, thought the Hunter. *It allows me to track you down should you try to double-cross me.* He kept his expression impassive as he stared at the aging man and his hulking attendant.

One greedy client had tried to cheat him out of a payment nearly a decade ago. When the primping noble's body had been discovered, only his signet ring had allowed the Justiciars to identify the mangled, broken corpse. Since that day, those hiring the Hunter made certain to pay in full and with alacrity.

When the Hunter said nothing, the old man shrugged his frail shoulders. "No matter. I trust everything is in order?"

"Your courier mentioned double the usual fee due to the...special nature of this contract?" The Hunter hefted the purse in his hands, hearing the satisfying clink of coins.

"It's all there. Count it, if you wish." The old man gave him a sly smile.

"No need, Lord Cyrannius," the Hunter said, tucking the purse into the folds of his robe. "Expect me to find you and...*discuss* the matter, should there be any missing."

The Hunter's voice held no threat, but the old man's smile wavered for a moment as he locked gazes with the assassin.

Surprise flashed through the Hunter as he stared at Lord Cyrannius.

Something within those eyes is somehow...familiar.

The huge bodyguard bristled, his hands flexing with dangerous strength. The wooden handles of the wheeled chair creaked in his grip, but the old lord held up a weak hand to forestall any aggression.

"Peace, Tane," Lord Cyrannius said without taking his gaze from the Hunter. "Never fear, Hunter, it is there."

"Good," the Hunter grunted. "If that is all—"

"I would request," the old lord interrupted, "that you carry out the task quickly. You have a reputation for being thorough in your task, but I would prefer that it be carried out with haste. Should you complete the contract before the end of the Season of Plenty, I will be willing to pay you triple your fee."

Three days, mused the Hunter in silence. *That's cutting it a bit close. But for triple...?*

"I know it is a lot to ask, but I trust my coin will more than cover the inconvenience." Lord Cyrannius leaned forward, fury burning in eyes. "My attempts to locate and...*deal* with the man have been unsuccessful to date, but I trust that you will do the subject justice."

"You will receive your coin's worth, Lord Cyrannius," the Hunter replied, his deep voice edged with steel.

"Make him suffer," the old lord said in a harsh whisper. "By the all-seeing eyes of the Long Keeper, make the bastard scream."

The Hunter nodded.

Three days to complete the task, he thought. *Should be more than enough.*

With a wary glance at Tane, the Hunter turned and strode from the room. He glanced over his shoulder as he walked through the door, and for the span of a heartbeat, he could have sworn the firelight once more cast sinister shadows across the twisted, scarred face of the old Lord Cyrannius.

Chapter Twelve

The first signs of dawn had crept over the rooftops of Voramis by the time the Hunter slipped through the doors of his home. His body felt the call of his bed, but he forced all thoughts of sleep from his mind.

No time for rest, he thought, rubbing his tired eyes.

He slipped from the dark grey clothing he'd worn that night, stripping down to a simple pair of breeches. Shirtless, he strode to the nearby window, opening it to let the fresh morning breeze wash over him. He ignored the scent of decay wafting up from the ocean to the west, and closed his eyes. For a long moment he simply stood, allowing his body to feel fatigue.

His calm was broken by the throbbing voice of Soulhunger whispering in his mind. A dull ache spread through his head as the blade again demanded death.

More than anything else, the Hunter hated the way Soulhunger's voice would grow insistent when too much time elapsed between kills. The weapon's desire would nearly overwhelm him, urging him on until he finally gave in. Killing was the only way to silence the voice.

I may need to kill, but I only bring death to those who deserve it, he told himself. *No matter who they are, they deserve their fate. They are all filthy, disgusting creatures hiding behind the mask of civility. When you open them up and see their true selves, you see what repulsive beasts they've become.*

But what does that say about you? A small voice inside him questioned. *You hide behind a mask of your own. How are you any better than they are?*

Enough, he thought, snapping his eyes open. *Time to get to work.*

He strode to his sword belt hanging on its peg, fighting to push back his languor as he moved. His fingers closed around the worn leather hilt of his long sword, and the blade pulled free of its sheath with a hiss of steel.

A smile spread across his face at the familiar weight. It felt good in his hands, as if it belonged.

It may be no match for the quality of Soulhunger's artisanship, but it is a worthy weapon in its own right.

Made of bright watered steel, the single edge of the blade held its razor sharpness with ease. It tapered with a gentle curve to a slim point, perfect for stabbing through flesh and armor. The hilt curved slightly, long enough to grip with one or both hands. Its pommel held a sharp spike, perfecting the beautiful sword's balance.

The weapon's weight rested near the crossguard, allowing for lightning fast strikes. The crossguard sported a short blade running parallel to the sword's long edge. This not only provided the Hunter with a trap in which to catch an opponent's sword, but also an additional weapon.

The feel of the weapon sent a thrill of anticipation coursing through his body. He held the hilt in a loose grip and, with slow precision, began to move through his sword forms.

These forms allowed him to sharpen his reflexes and hone his muscles, but they were so much more. The world around him disappeared in a blur of steel and sweat. While his body moved, his mind was at peace.

He pushed himself to greater speeds, the blade singing with every step. One misstep or wrong move could prove fatal, yet each thrust, cut, and slash of the sword fell with the accuracy of a blademaster. For a moment, everything in the world ceased to be, and only he and the beautifully crafted weapon in his hands existed.

With sudden speed, he executed the final motion of the final form—arm extended, blade buried in the eye of an imaginary enemy. Sweat dripped down his body and his breath burned in his lungs, but the Hunter felt no fatigue, no anxiety…nothing. Mind devoid of thoughts, blood rushing through his veins, he simply *was.*

It was time for the ritual.

His mind calm and clear, the Hunter sheathed the sword with a ring of steel. He gripped Soulhunger in sweaty hands, the dagger's insistence throbbing in time with his heartbeat. Its voice filled his mind with a lust for death.

Find your victim, he told the blade.

I will feed, it whispered.

The Hunter sat, closing his eyes and casting his mind adrift. The dagger's edge bit into the palm of his hand, but he felt no pain as crimson dripped from the wound. His whetstone grated across the blade's edge, and the familiar sensation of stone grinding on metal filled his senses. The ritual calmed him, allowing him to attune his mind to Soulhunger's voice.

The small square of white cloth given him by Lord Cyrannius lay on the floor, and he reached for it. The rough material absorbed the blood falling from the Hunter's wound, which had already begun to heal.

In the back of his mind, the Hunter felt oddly unnerved by his meeting with the old man. He had thought to find answers, but he had only more questions. Something told him that the mystery of Lord Cyrannius had yet to be resolved.

He pushed thoughts of the mysterious old man from his mind and inhaled deeply, letting his senses roam the city. The beat of his heart grew slow and steady, but blood still pounded in his ears. He sought the man who had condemned an innocent young woman to die.

Where are you? You cannot hide from me.

A new rhythm filled his mind—the beating of his quarry's heart. His nostrils filled with the unique scent of the man.

Moldy cloth. Damp stone. Iron.

We have found him, the voice told him.

All I need do now is follow you until you lead me to our victim, the Hunter thought. *The hunt awaits.*

The Hunter's eyes felt heavy as he opened them, but he smiled at the sight of his rooms filled with the golden rays of the morning's light. Dust danced in the air, and the scent of fresh-baked bread wafted in from the nearby Confectioner's Lane. His stomach growled, reminding him he had not eaten since the previous morning.

But first, some food.

Soulhunger slipped into its sheath with a final pulse, and the Hunter turned to the closet in which hung his myriad disguises.

Something nagged at the back of his mind as he applied the adhesive clay to his face. He had caught the barest hint of a familiar scent on the wind as he left the Villa Camoralia. It had been too faint for him to make out clearly, but it had reminded him of the woman he had met at The Iron Arms.

He lost himself in pleasant reminiscence for a moment, allowing his mind to recall every detail of their encounter.

Celicia, she said her name was.

He remembered her stubborn insistence that she could take care of herself, remembered her fierce pride. The woman exhibited a strength of will that refused to be dominated.

There is something about her; something the soft, feminine charms of Lady Damuria cannot offer.

His hands applied the alchemical clay without direction from his mind, and when he finally focused on his face in the mirror, he saw it bore a fiery red beard contrasting with dark black hair. One eye had been colored green, the other a deep blue.

Damn it, he thought. *I cannot allow these thoughts to distract me.*

The alchemical clay sloughed off his skin with ease, revealing his true face beneath. He studied the features in the mirror.

Now, who shall I be today?

Chapter Thirteen

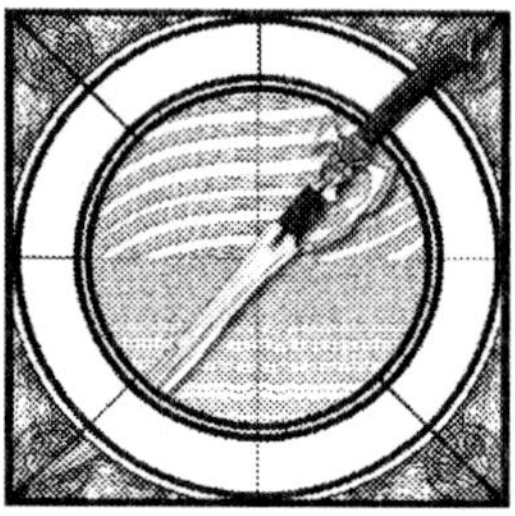

"Danther? Is that you?" The childish voice rang out in the busy streets of the Merchant's Quarter.

A bearded man in the dull clothes of a tailor turned around, and a smile broke out across his face as he saw the little girl charging towards him. She wrapped her arms around his generous waist.

"Farida, child!" he exclaimed, returning her fierce hug. "How wonderful to see you! It has been a while, hasn't it?"

"Of course not, silly," she gave him a look of childish exasperation. "You stopped by just a few weeks ago, don't you remember?"

The tailor shrugged his shoulders. "I guess my memory is slipping again, Fari dear." He looked sad for a moment, but a sly grin crept across his face. "But you don't think I'd forget about your nameday, do you?"

He produced a small toy from within his robes and held it up for the child to see.

The little girl's eyes went wide. "Oh, Danther! A doll? For me?"

"Aye, child. I had the missus put it together from a few of the scraps lying around the house." Danther handed the ragged cloth doll to the girl, who clutched it to her chest with a fierce protectiveness. "I know your nameday is still a few days off, but I will be busy. I just knew I had to give you your gift now."

"Oh, thank you, Danther." The girl's eyes sparkled with delight and she clasped him in a hug once more.

"My, child," he exclaimed, pushing her out to arm's length and studying her, "you *have* grown since I last saw you."

"Yes," she said, excitement in her voice, "Father Penitence says I'm growing like a weed. He says I'll soon be able to sing in the choir with the others, once I'm old enough."

"Did he? And have you been practicing?"

"Yes," Farida replied with a nod. "Every day, like you told me."

"Wonderful. I promise I will be sitting in the front row on your first day in the choir."

"Oh, yes, please," the child begged. "I would love that!"

Danther smiled down at the girl, noticing her thin cheeks and pallid skin. "Are you hungry, Fari?" he asked. At her nod, he searched the market for one of the many stalls selling foodstuffs.

Within a few moments, the bearded man and the little girl sat on the edge of a small fountain. The sticky buns in their hands were hot and sweet, and Farida bit into hers with delight.

"How are things in the Temple District, Fari?" He took a small bite of the pastry, enjoying the soft freshness of the bun. "Are the brothers treating you well?"

"Yes, Danther," Farida said, speaking through a mouth filled with sticky bun. "Father Penitence makes me write out my verses every day." She swallowed, wiping her mouth with the back of a dirty hand. A cloud passed over her face as she took another bite of her bun. "Brother Mendicatus has been teaching me to play the lyre, but my fingers are too small to play the strings. See." She held out her delicate child hands, covered with sugary syrup and grime from the city's streets.

"Don't worry, child," Danther replied. "Your hands will grow in time, and you'll have no trouble playing the lyre." He stuffed the rest of his bun into his mouth to silence the growling in his stomach.

"But Brother Mendicatus says I'll have to practice three hours a day," she complained.

"Well, at least you won't have to be out here peddling flowers," Danther said. The little girl eyed the uneaten sticky bun in his hand, and he passed it to her—his stomach protesting.

"I know," said Farida, biting off a large chunk of the bun before continuing, "but it's not so bad out here. I don't like the Merchant's Quarter much, but I love being near Maiden's Field. The gardens and the fountains are so beautiful, and I can always see my friends—like you." She smiled at him, her cheeks bulging with sticky bun and her lips covered in syrup.

"But—"

"Wait a minute, Danther."

A small crowd had gathered around her cart, and the girl hurried to swallow the last of her bun. She scampered off to attend to them, wiping her mouth with her sleeve.

The Hunter leaned his elbows on his knees, watching Farida scamper away. He wore the disguise of the bearded Danther, a face that was familiar to Farida. She liked the rotund tailor, as he always left her gifts and bought her treats.

I hate seeing the child on the streets like this, thought the Hunter. *Thankfully, I won't have to watch over her much longer.*

The priestesses of the Maiden took in those few Beggared children fortunate enough to show musical talent. Once she entered the Heart of the Maiden, he knew he would not see her for many years—until she emerged a full priestess. He hated to admit it, but he would miss the little girl and her bright, cheery smile.

But she will be safe, he told himself, *and that is more important. It will be a better life for her.*

He contented himself to sit and watch the girl chatter with the men and women buying flowers from her.

Such a happy child, so innocent. If only she knew what the world is really like.

Nearly an hour passed before Farida's last customer left. By then, the Lady's Bell had rung the midday chimes.

"I'm so sorry, Danther," the girl said, disappointment etched on her face, "but I have to go. I wanted to talk some more, but Brother Humility is going to give me a switching if I return late to the temple. I have to get back before the first afternoon bell rings, and I still have to sell these last few flowers."

"Of course, Fari." His big bearded face creased into a big smile. "I know! I'll buy the last flowers from you so you can return now."

"But, Danther," Farida protested, "you—"

"No buts, Fari," he interrupted her. "I just had a big order from the palace for more bed linens, so I can afford it." He drew a purse from within his robes. "Here. This should more than cover it."

The coins clinked as they dropped into her grubby hand—a silver drake and a few copper bits. Farida opened her mouth to protest, but the Hunter shook his head.

"Thank you so much, Danther," she said, hugging him again.

"But," the Hunter said, holding up an admonishing finger, "I'm not doing you a favor. I'm buying these flowers from you in exchange for a promise."

"A promise?" Confusion showed plainly on Farida's face.

"I want you to promise that you will practice singing every day, and the lyre, like Brother Mendicatus says."

"But, Danther—" the little girl whined.

"Do we have a deal, Fari?" the Hunter interrupted. He raised an eyebrow expectantly.

"Fine," she said, her voice petulant. "I'll practice, but you'll be sorry when you see my fingers all sore from those stupid strings."

"If you practice, I will take you to eat at Franiero's after your first performance."

Farida's eyes widened. "Franiero's? You mean the place that serves all the pastries you can eat?"

"Until you've stuffed yourself silly, child." The Hunter smiled at her expression of delight.

"You promise, Danther?"

"On the Maiden's honor. But only if you do your part."

"Then," the child said, her voice resolute, "I will practice for *four* hours every day, even if my fingers *do* bleed."

"Good," the Hunter said with a chuckle, "then we have a deal." He took her little hand in his own, and they shook.

An odd sense of pride rushed through the Hunter as he stared down at the child, who had grown so much in the last few years.

"Now," the Hunter said, standing, "you need to get back to the temple, and I'm heading in that direction. Shall we walk together?"

"I'd like that." Farida smiled up at him. "Just let me put my cart away, and we'll be on our way."

She pushed her cart toward a butcher's shop and disappeared within. When she emerged a moment later, her hands were empty but a wide grin wreathed her face. "Let's go."

Together they strolled toward the Temple District, the child trotting in an effort to keep up with the Hunter's long steps. The sun shone down bright and hot, but a cool breeze wafted through the city streets. The Hunter found himself laughing and enjoying the company of the little girl, and for a few heartbeats, his true purpose was forgotten.

All too soon they entered the Temple District, and the throbbing of Soulhunger's bloodlust filled the Hunter's mind.

Our quarry is near, he thought. *Time to be off.*

"Fari, child," the Hunter said, turning to the girl beside him, "I have to see a client in the Temple of the Bright Lady, so here is where we part. Will you be all right going back to the temple alone?"

"Of course, Danther," she said. "I'm perfectly fine here in the Temple District; it's supposed to be the safest place in the city, you know."

"Are you sure?" the Hunter said, unconvinced.

"Yes, silly," Farida said with a careless laugh, "I'll be fine. I walk these streets alone all the time. Besides, the temple is not far from here."

"Very well," he agreed. "Next week I'll be making a robe for Lord Ardinos, and I'll need some rose petals. Will I find you by the fountains of Maiden's Field?"

"I'll be there, Danther." The child wrapped her arms around the Hunter's waist, hugging him tightly.

He hugged her back. "Be safe, child. And practice, as we agreed."

"I will," she said, releasing him. "See you in a few days." With a final wave to him, she turned and skipped through the crowds of the Temple District.

The Hunter watched the child go, but soon lost her among the throngs surging through the busy streets. Concern for her wellbeing flashed through him, but Soulhunger's voice returned his thoughts to his mission.

He cleared his mind, allowing the insistent chatter of the weapon to fill his senses. The dagger, hidden in a sheath below his padded belly, pulsed in time with the heartbeat of the man he sought.

The disguise of Danther served more than just as a means of interacting with Farida. It allowed him to blend with the crowds milling through the Merchant's Quarter and Temple District, and it gave him a means of carrying the tools of his craft. Voramian law forbade any but the Heresiarchs from carrying steel on the streets, but the tailor's ample girth allowed him to conceal his weapons beneath heavy wool padding.

Soulhunger reached out its senses, searching for the heart with which it had bonded. Its eagerness to feed pulsed in the Hunter's mind.

It had found its quarry.

He followed the dagger's directions, moving through the bustling crowd. Soulhunger pulled him toward Divinity Square, the massive plaza at the heart of the Temple District.

There will be a crowd gathering around the Fountain of Piety, offering prayers to their gods, he thought.

Too many people milling around could make finding his quarry difficult.

Still, what choice do I have but to follow Soulhunger's lead?

The Hunter cursed as a passerby jostled against him. His bulging midsection not only made pushing through the crowded streets difficult, but he had begun to sweat beneath the wood.

Cursed Danther disguise.

As the Hunter strode toward Divinity Square, the dagger pulled him away from the crowds filling the plaza. Instead, it led him toward the Temple of the Apprentice.

The throbbing at his hip grew stronger, more forceful. The voice in his head whispered its desire to feed, the unyielding pressure in his mind making his head ache.

Where is he? He asked the blade.

He stopped outside of the temple, eyes darting in every direction, searching for his prey.

He is the one.

His eyes fell upon a figure emerging from the Temple of the Apprentice, and the echo of Soulhunger's joy in his mind told him this was his target.

The man had a plain face, and his features were completely unremarkable. He looked like one of the many thousands of tradesmen in the city, and only the shabby grey robes on his back marked him as a priest. The scent of freshly baked bread wafted from beneath a cloth-covered wicker basket the priest carried on his hip.

It seems the miserly Coin Counters in the Temple of the Apprentice find some generosity during the Season of Plenty.

The priest hardly spared a glance for the paunchy tailor standing on the steps, moving past the Hunter without showing any sign he'd noticed him. Soulhunger shouted in the Hunter's mind as he continued to watch the man from the corners of his eyes.

This, then, is the one I am to kill, thought the Hunter. *A priest of the Beggar God.*

The Hunter's eyes followed the man as he pushed his way through the crowded square. He guessed the priest was on a mission to collect donations from the other orders, judging by the basket beneath his arm. Beggar Priests were renowned for their piety and their efforts to help those in need.

He stared up at the temple from which the man had just emerged. The priests within this magnificent structure worshipped Garridos, the Apprentice, god of ventures. Marble arches supported flying buttresses hundreds of paces above the streets, and the stark white stone of the temple's exterior screamed of the wealth that flowed through the Temple of the Apprentice. Merchants of Voramis made regular offerings to their god, hoping the deity would smile down on their enterprise.

The Hunter returned his attention to his quarry once more, following at a discreet distance in order to avoid notice. He watched the priest move around the side of the huge temple. Peering around the corner, he found the priest distributing bread among the beggars filling the alley.

Filth and refuse filled the muddy lane, along with makeshift hovels and shelters. Dozens of homeless men and women crowded around the priest, emptying the wicker basket within the space of a few minutes.

It's a wonder the Heresiarchs or the temple guards don't drive them off, the Hunter thought.

His basket empty, the priest made his apologies to the beggars and strode once more toward the mouth of the alley. The Hunter ducked out of sight, turning to study the elaborate carvings of the Temple of the Apprentice. He waited until the priest had passed him before following him once more.

The priest turned away from the Temple of the Apprentice, and his steps now led him toward the Master's Temple.

All in Voramis worshipped Kiro, the Master, god of virtue and nobility. The Master ruled above the other gods, but his temple had been built without the adornments and decorations dominating the other houses of worship. Free of statuary, carvings, and depictions of any sort, the squat building held a place of prominence in the Temple District. Everyone, from the King of Voramis to the poorest mendicant, came to the Master's Temple to pay homage to the Father of the gods.

The priest disappeared into the temple, but the Hunter chose not to pursue him.

If he's doing the collection rounds, he'll be back soon.

Sure enough, the man emerged from the temple moments later, a small pouch clutched in his hands. A mass of beggars clustered around the Fountain of Piety, raising their voices in a noisy din and clamoring for alms. After tossing a few copper bits into the fountain as a tribute to the Master, the priest distributed the rest among the beggars.

From the fountain, the priest turned toward the Temple of Deralana, Lady of Vengeance. This temple stood in stark contrast to the simplicity of the Master's Temple. Dozens of statues adorned the temple's entrance, each paying tribute to the greatest warriors of Voramian history.

King Gavril the Conqueror—Voramis' founder and first ruler—watched the city from behind granite eyes.

The priest rushed from the Temple of Derelana mere moments after he had entered. A man wearing the heavy armor and clerical robes of the Warrior Priests chased him, shouting angry words and threats. The priests of Derelana were renowned for their skill in battle, as well as their disdain for the followers of the Beggar God.

Priestesses of the Maiden welcomed the Beggar Priest warmly, ushering him into the pristine white halls of their temple. They spoke in lilting, melodious voices, which marked them as worshippers of the Maiden, goddess of purity, devotion, and festivities. The sound of singing floated from within the hallowed Heart of the Maiden, the voices of the Choir of Purity rising into the air in perfect harmony with the bustling crowds outside. Serenity washed over him as he listened to the music, drowning out the impatient voice of Soulhunger in his mind.

Farida will soon join the priestesses. Perhaps I will return another time to visit her.

The Beggar Priest soon strode from the Heart of the Maiden, a peaceful smile on his face and a pile of used clothing in his arms. He distributed the garments to those sitting on the steps of the temple, basking in the warm glow of the sun and the soft singing of the choir. All were welcome at the Heart of the Maiden.

The priest strode through the front doors of the Temple of Prosperity, home to the Illusionist, god of coin, success, and madness. A jangling, dissonant song filled the air from myriad musical instruments within, grating on the Hunter's nerves. The temple's construction jarred the senses, and the elegant façade of the building—while beautiful from afar—strained his eyes and set his head spinning as he studied its patterns, a testament to the Illusionist's true nature.

A handful of clerics emerged from the Temple of Prosperity, each walking, dancing, and leaping in strange, chaotic rhythms.

Fools, he thought. *Gods alone know what they're doing, much less why.*

The god delighted in spreading madness among his followers, and only a select few of the most insane were chosen to be Illusionist Clerics. They dedicated their lives to the study of the Theory of Illusion, a theological treatise on the science of the mind.

With effort, the Hunter forced his eyes away from the cavorting clerics, turning his attention to the figure of the priest emerging from the mind-boggling temple. The Beggar Priest removed the cloth from his basket, revealing an assortment of mechanical and wire puzzles, trick boxes, and other maddening toys. He called out to the children of the beggars crowding around the Fountain of Piety, placing the small knickknacks into the grubby hands of those brave enough to leave their parents' sides.

The Sanctuary stood next to the Temple of Prosperity. Home to the Bright Lady, goddess of healing, the temple provided healing to all in need. The injured, lame, and leprous crowded its steps. The Hunter shuddered at the sight of dozens with open sores, wounds weeping pus, and withered limbs in obvious need of amputation. The nauseating stench of festering rot, disease, and decay filled his nostrils and twisted his stomach.

White-robed priestesses moved among them, offering what healing they could, along with a kind word and a gentle touch.

No wonder Voramis worships the Bright Lady so, thought the Hunter.

The Beggar Priest emerged a quarter of an hour after entering. Flecks of blood spattered his grey robe, but his basket was laden with salves, bandages, and other supplies the Beggar Priests would need when ministering to those turned away from The Sanctuary.

Priests of the Swordsman—god of war, heroism, and metal-smithing—worshipped in the Temple of Heroes. An obelisk thrust into the sky, standing taller than any other building in the city—save for the Palace of Justice. It was said the bones of the Swordsman, hero of the War of Gods at the creation of the world, lay within the obelisk.

When the Beggar Priest exited the Temple of Heroes, children from around the plaza raced toward him, clamoring to receive one of the wooden swords and shields stacked in his arms. Rumor held that any child who received both sword and shield as a gift from the Temple of Heroes would one day join the ranks of the Legion of Heroes, Voramis' standing army.

The priest made a warding gesture as he passed the shrine to the Long Keeper, god of death. The doleful deity had no priesthood, received no offerings. His only presence in the city was this small onyx altar, barely as high as a man's waist and an arm's length across. The superstitious Voramians preferred to avoid attracting the attention of the sleepless god. Where the Long Keeper walked, he left only death in his wake.

The Secret Keepers said not a word as the Beggar Priest entered the Temple of Whispers, home to the Mistress, goddess of trysts and whispered truths. It was common belief that Secret Keepers had their tongues ripped out upon joining the order. The silent, somber robes of the priests matched the dull brown of the vault-like temple.

Ribbons and garlands of blue and purple filled the Beggar Priest's arms, the gift of the Mistress. The Hunter's quarry handed his load to another Beggar Priest before continuing his rounds.

With that armload of ribbons, thought the Hunter, *the priests could earn more than enough to keep Farida and the other Beggared off the street for a few weeks at least.*

Wealthier citizens of Voramis would purchase these ribbons from the Beggared children. The garlands were hung on Snowblossom trees during the Inamorata, the debauchery-filled festival of lovers.

The Beggar Priest hesitated a moment before entering The Hall of the Cruori, home to the Bloody Minstrel, god of sickness, plague, and horrible music. Dark red bloodstone covered the temple façade, and to the Hunter it seemed the wall dripped blood. He knew it was just the appearance of the stone, but it made his skin crawl nonetheless.

The man exited the temple carrying dozens of bloodstone amulets for his fellow priests to distribute among the poor of Lower Voramis. Priests of the Bloody Minstrel insisted that the amulets prevented the spread of plague. Voramis had not seen plagues in the Hunter's memory, which lent credence to the priest's belief in the power of the stone.

The Watcher in the Dark held sway over the night, but he also served as the god of justice. The Palace of Justice provided his worshippers—the law-keeping Judiciars and their enforcers, the crimson-robed Heresiarchs—with a place to pay homage to their god. A monument to the Watcher stood in the Temple District, but time and the elements had faded the stone to a smooth, faceless lump.

Justice has no face, thought the Hunter, *but it is timeless and undying.*

The Fountain of Piety dominated the heart of Divinity Square. Superstitious worshippers dropped coins into its watery depths, hoping to attract the favor of their particular god through their offering.

The Beggar Priest turned away from the fountain and Divinity Square, his steps leading toward a small street. The Hunter followed at a distance, guessing his quarry moved toward the two small temples built away from the main thoroughfares of the Temple District.

Farther from the temple, there will be fewer people. He smiled. *He's making this too easy.*

Flagstones paved the streets of Divinity Square, but all who approached the House of Tears walked through the mud. Home to The Lonely Goddess, goddess of orphans and broken hearts, the temple was small, simple. The dark stone of the building gave off the appearance of perpetual gloom, and water wept from the walls of the temple.

They say the water is poisonous. The Hunter took care to avoid stepping in the murky puddles.

It was said the Lonely Goddess wept for her lover, lost in the War of Gods. Those with sorrows frequented the House of Tears, where they could join the Weeping Sisters in perpetual mourning. The keening chant rising from the temple set the Hunter's nerves on edge, reminding him of a Praamian funeral procession.

The building adjacent to the House of Tears appeared to be one strong gust of wind away from collapsing. The House of Need, home to the priests of the Beggar God, rarely received visitors. In fact, few Voramians even knew that a thirteenth god existed. Most considered the Beggar God unworthy of being a deity.

Only by the limited generosity of the other temples did the House of Need still stand, as well as the fact that they produced the best singers and musicians in Voramis. The other temples gave aid in an attempt to secure a child prodigy for their choirs, and any of the Beggared children who showed an aptitude for music had a chance for a better life in one of the other orders.

Together, the Beggar Priests and Weeping Sisters cared for the abandoned and orphaned children of Voramis, as well as those turned away by the healers at the Sanctuary.

Theirs is a miserable existence, the Hunter thought, watching the Beggar Priest enter the House of Need, *but the fools actually seem happy to help others.*

Soulhunger protested at the disappearance of its target, but the Hunter silenced the voice in his mind.

I can't go into that temple looking like this. *My tailor's outfit is more suited for prayer at the Temple of the Apprentice, but I will stand out among the wretched creatures in there.*

A procession of beggars, lepers, and assorted vagabonds streamed in and out of the temple, a neverending flow of human refuse. Their scents mixed with the detritus piled high around the empty houses surrounding the temple.

The Hunter took up position in a doorway. A pile of refuse hid him from casual glances, yet he could see all passersby entering the House of Need. His muscles protested as he sat, but he ignored them. He hugged his knees to his chest, settling in for a long wait.

The wait allowed his mind time to roam, and he mulled over his assignment. The thought of killing a Beggar Priest felt strange.

It is a bit odd to find a violator among the priests, he thought. *Though considering the practices of some of the orders, I guess I shouldn't be too surprised. Besides, I have been paid, so the contract must be carried out.*

He shrugged off the thought, focusing his attention on watching the streets around him.

Strains of beautiful music wafted from the decaying temple, filling his head with tranquility and blocking out Soulhunger's voice. The singing soothed him, relaxing his tired muscles, and he found himself struggling to stay awake.

No, he told himself, *you cannot sleep now.*

But his attempts to fight the lulling effect of the music failed. He drifted along with the gorgeous melody, the heat of the day and a night without rest taking its toll on his body.

His eyelids grew heavy and slowly closed of their own accord as the music carried him into the realm of peaceful sleep.

Chapter Fourteen

Wake up!

The voice shouting in the Hunter's thoughts sent a spike of pain through his head. He jerked upright, his eyes snapping open. His mind, still heavy with sleep, struggled to recognize his unfamiliar surroundings.

Where in the twisted hell am I?

He took in the details around him: the stinking pile of refuse, a painfully uncomfortable doorway, beggars, lepers, and vagabonds wandering around. When he saw the House of Need in the distance, everything clicked into place.

Of course! The Beggar Priest. I followed him here.

He scrubbed at his tired eyes, stifling an errant yawn.

I can't believe I fell asleep.

Beautiful strains of singing and instruments still wafted from the nearby temple of the Beggar God, hanging in the afternoon air and soothing him.

No wonder. It's the fault of that bloody music.

He climbed to his feet with effort, his back stiff from sitting on hard stone for…*could it have been hours?* He squinted up at the afternoon sun. *Three, four hours past midday. Good. I didn't waste too much time sleeping.*

A dull ache in his head brought his thoughts into focus. Soulhunger's insistence grew louder and more painful, and the weapon quivered in its sheath. It only acted this way when its quarry was near.

The Hunter flattened himself into the darkness of a nearby doorway as the Beggar Priest emerged from the House of Need. His target still carried the covered basket under his arms, but the Hunter smelled the scent of refuse wafting from beneath the cloth.

Good, he thought, a smile touching his lips. *That smell will make it very easy to follow him.*

The priest chose only back streets and alleys, taking care to keep the malodorous basket away from the masses thronging to the Temple District. The Hunter slipped along behind him, staying out of sight. The priest had seen him back in Divinity Square, and the Hunter couldn't risk the man recognizing him. There was no telling what the priest would do if he realized he was being followed.

Thankfully, I don't need to see *him to follow him.*

Soulhunger pounded in the Hunter's mind, begging to feed. The blade would lead him to his quarry, and he only needed to follow its voice. He was in no hurry to run the man down; patience would be his ally in this hunt.

As he followed the Beggar Priest, the Hunter realized the man's path led towards the Midden. A gaping void in the heart of the city, the Midden provided Voramians with a place to throw their offal and refuse. Carters hauled scraps and garbage from around Voramis, dumping it into the eternally hungry depths.

None knew how far down the Midden went, and the histories failed to record a purpose for the hole's existence. It had simply always *been.*

The cavernous maw stretched for hundreds of paces in every direction. Even from where he stood, the Hunter felt the gloom radiating from the dark, bottomless pit, sending a shudder running through him. He was glad he had no need to approach the gaping void, content to watch the priest from a distance.

The priest emptied his basket into the Midden, taking care not to let the refuse touch his robes. He stooped over a nearby trough to wash his hands and splash water on his face and neck. When he straightened, he stretched his arms in the air as if to work the kinks from a strained back.

Something about the movement caused the Hunter to duck out of sight. It was the way the man's eyes darted through the empty streets, as if searching for unseen dangers. The shadows of a fallen awning provided the Hunter with cover, and he waited for the man to move.

Soulhunger whispered in the back of his mind. Glancing around the corner, the Hunter saw a flash of dirty grey disappear around a corner. The weapon's insistence grew louder and more persistent as it sensed its quarry escaping.

The Hunter rushed to the intersection where the Beggar Priest had disappeared. He risked a glance at the street beyond, and relief flooded him as he saw his target. The man moved at an easy pace, seemingly unhurried and unaware that the Hunter followed him. His steps led him away from the Temple District.

Pious bastard, probably off on some new mission of mercy.

An ache in his shoulders caused the Hunter to look down at his bulging belly. It was time to lose the disguise, getting rid of the dead weight of the false paunch.

There's no need for this disguise, anyway. The priest is headed into Lower Voramis. It will be easy to stay out of sight once we leave the Temple District.

A nearby hovel caught the Hunter's attention, and he pushed through the rotting front doors. He neither saw nor heard any signs of life within.

The Hunter was greatly relieved to remove the disguise of Danther the tailor. He discarded the heavy beard, dark wig, and simple clothing. He sighed gratefully as he emptied the wool from the dark cloak that served as his bulging paunch. The cloak slipped on over the simple brown tunic he wore, hiding the weapons on his belt. The mottled brown garment would enable him to hide in the muddy streets of Lower Voramis.

He had grown tired of traipsing through the streets. Not only was he forced to walk through the mud, but there was also a greater risk of being seen by his target. Instead, the Hunter decided to take to the roofs.

Sunlight filtered through large holes in the hovel's thatched roof, and the Hunter saw beautiful blue sky above. He grasped one of the roof beams and swung his body through an opening.

He loved the Voramis rooftops. The open sky above, the stench of the city far below, and none but the birds to share the space with. The scents of sunbaked tiles and withered hay filled his nostrils. The beam beneath his feet felt as if it would crack at any moment, so he leapt to the tiled roof of the next house over. A few tiles crunched under his weight, but the roof itself felt solid enough.

Much better. Now, Soulhunger, tell me where to go.

The weapon's voice pounded in his head, its pull guiding him in the direction of his quarry.

I can't lose him.

The Hunter leapt from rooftop to rooftop, reveling in the cooling breeze and the warming sunlight. It might have almost been peaceful had Soulhunger's voice not continuously chattered in his head.

His eyes scanned the streets below, searching for the man he hunted. *There he is. Strolling as if he hasn't a care in the world.*

He crouched atop a slanted roof, studying the man.

Beggar Priests wore simple grey robes, with a stripe around the collar to denote their rank. This cleric's robe had a single faded blue stripe around the collar, marking him a minor cleric in service to the Beggar God.

He appears as ordinary as any priest can be.

The priest appeared at ease, strolling through the city without an apparent destination. He stooped to help a child from the mud, giving the urchin a smile and a pat on the head as he moved on. When he encountered an old woman struggling to fill a cracked clay pot in a nearby well, the priest offered his assistance. After filling the pot, he insisted on carrying her heavy burden home.

Not for the first time today, the Hunter found himself questioning Lord Cyrannius' story.

Where would this simple priest have the opportunity to interact with anyone from the houses of the nobility, much less assault and violate one? He looks harmless; I find it hard to believe he could have done such a thing.

It wasn't the way the man looked, nor the fact that he was a priest. The Hunter knew that piety did not preclude men from temptation. The lust of the flesh could overcome even the strongest willpower. In his years living in Voramis, he had seen the worst side of humanity. He knew what men and women were capable of when motivated by greed, anger, or fear. In his mind, every one of them deserved the death he was paid to bring.

No one is free of sin, not even that priest below.

But the priest's actions struck him as odd. The rapists and violators he had hunted tended to be violent, angry, and hateful creatures. This man showed none of those traits.

He seems to actually care about those around him.

Another thought struck him.

Don't priests of the Beggar God have their manhood removed? If that's true, how could he have raped that young woman?

Things just didn't fit.

Enough.

He shook the thoughts from his head. He had made a living out of not asking questions. The contract had to be carried out, no matter who his target was.

Deep within, he told himself, *hidden well out of sight, there is something deserving of death. I am simply the hand that delivers the punishment for his sins.*

Something nagged at the back of the Hunter's mind. The priest looked like an ordinary man, giving off the appearance of taking a casual stroll. Yet the man moved with confidence, walking with an inherent gracefulness. His eyes seemed to track the movement of every person he passed.

The Hunter had no time to ponder this, for the priest chose that moment to cross a busy thoroughfare. The wide street below forced the Hunter to search for a way to cross to the rooftops beyond, pulling his attention away from his quarry.

When his eyes returned to the streets below, the Beggar Priest had disappeared.

"Shit," he cursed aloud. He scanned up and down the bustling avenue, but saw no sign of the man.

He can't have just vanished.

The Hunter closed his eyes, breathing deeply and letting the tension drain from his muscles. He attuned his mind with Soulhunger's insistent voice, letting instinct take over. His senses hunted the man's unique scent and the beating of his heart.

Find him, he told the blade.

For long moments, Soulhunger remained silent, as if the blade was occupied in the search for its prey. The Hunter waited, taking in the world around him. He heard the sounds of the traffic below, smelled the fragrant odors of spiced meat and fresh bread. These sensations filled his mind, clearing it of thoughts that would distract Soulhunger from finding its prey.

Soulhunger jerked in its sheath, and the Hunter leapt in the direction he sensed it wanted him to go. He trusted the blade—and his own instincts—and he let them guide him across the rooftops of Lower Voramis.

Feed me, Soulhunger whispered in his mind, its resonance growing stronger with each step he took, *and revel in the power I will give you.*

Finally, the Hunter caught a flash of ragged grey.

I see you now, priest!

Just then, the Beggar Priest turned a corner into a small alley and disappeared from the Hunter's sight.

A flash of worry ran through the Hunter, but he shrugged it off. He had Soulhunger. With the blade to guide him, his quarry had no hope of escaping.

The Hunter scanned the streets below. They were empty, as was common at this late afternoon hour. He dropped from the roof, landing hard on the cobbled stones below. A stab of pain flashed through his knees as he climbed to his feet, but slowly it faded.

Now let's see how a Beggar Priest meets his god.

He moved toward the mouth of the alley, his eyes alert for any sign of danger. Soulhunger and his swordbreaker hung in sheaths at his hips; within easy reach should he need them. With a deep breath, the Hunter followed his prey into the narrow lane.

Pain blossomed in his chest as he turned the corner. His mind scrambled, shouting at him to escape, but his legs refused to move. Looking down, he saw the hilt of a dagger protruding from between his ribs.

The Hunter slumped to his knees, fighting to breathe. Dark red blood spilled down the front of his tunic.

The Beggar Priest stood a few paces away, a second dagger poised for throwing. The man watched the Hunter intently, as if waiting for him to die.

Unfortunately for you, the Hunter thought, struggling to remain conscious, *I'm not that easy to kill.*

It took every ounce of strength he possessed, but the Hunter slowly climbed to his feet. With a jerk and a grunt of pain, the Hunter ripped the knife from his chest. He dimly heard Soulhunger's lust pounding in his mind as the blade sensed fresh blood spilling from the wound.

"That hurt," he growled. He held the dagger up to examine it. "An excellent throw, I must admit."

The Beggar Priest gaped. The dagger in his hand remained motionless, his body frozen in disbelief.

"But you...I..." he stammered.

Confusion painted his face for a moment, then realization slowly dawned.

"Ah, of course. The Hunter." Not a question, but a statement of fact. The man showed no sign of surprise or fear upon seeing him.

"At your service," the Hunter replied, sweeping an expansive, mocking bow.

"I'm actually surprised it took the demon this long to send you after me," the priest said.

"Demon?" the Hunter asked, puzzled.

"You didn't think to ask your employer his identity?"

"Part of the job." The Hunter shrugged. "Secrets are always easier to keep when you don't know them."

"Spoken like a true tool," spat the priest, "unthinking, with no mind of its own, only fit to be used by the highest bidder." He studied the Hunter, taking in the dark brown cloak, the bloodied tunic, the scarred features. "To tell you the truth, Hunter, I've been expecting you to come after me for a long while now."

"Have you?" the Hunter asked, a hint of mockery in his tone.

"Yes," the priest replied simply. "Considering what you are, it seems only fit that *he'd* eventually recruit you to his ranks."

"Considering what I am? What in the hells does that mean?"

"You mean you don't know?" Genuine disbelief registered on the priest's face. "How could he not know?" he asked, as if speaking to himself.

The Hunter had no idea what the man was talking about, but he cared little. Soulhunger screamed its delight as the Hunter drew it, quivering in his hand.

"I have a contract to carry out, priest," he said, his voice harsh.

The priest's eyes widened. "You come armed with the relic," he said, his eyes locked on the dagger. "Did *he* give it to you?"

What nonsense is he babbling on about?

"Did who give me what? No one has given me anything, save gold as payment to deal with you."

"The blade," the priest gestured toward Soulhunger. "Where did you get the blade?"

Why does it matter?

Aloud, he said, "I have always had Soulhunger. It has never left my side."

"Soulhunger," the priest mused. "An apt name." His eyes scanned the Hunter's face, looking for...*what?* "Your reputation marks you as a man who knows how to use the weapon. Tell me, Hunter, have you bonded with the blade, yet?"

What in the burning hell is the fool talking about? The priest's words made no sense to the Hunter.

Ignore him, the voice in his head whispered. *We must feed.*

When the Hunter failed to respond, the Beggar Priest shrugged.

"No matter. Let us see if your reputation is earned, or if it is just the power of the blade that has made you what you are." He drew two short swords from a sheath hidden beneath his robes.

Watered steel glinted, light reflecting from edges honed to razor sharpness. The weapons were worn and the man held them with familiar ease, his grip loose, his stance relaxed, his weight on the balls of his feet.

Clearly, he knows how to use them.

"A priest with swords?" the Hunter mocked. "Will wonders never cease?"

"May the Fallen One have mercy on you, Bucelarii," the priest said, a sad smile spreading on his face. "You are more deserving of death than those who fall to your blade."

Bucelarii? This was the second time the Hunter had heard the name, but still he had no idea what it meant.

"You haven't killed me yet, priest. Now, do you plan to use those things, or are we going to stand here talking all day?"

The Hunter's eyes narrowed as he sized up his opponent. The Beggar Priest stalked toward the Hunter, approaching with wary caution. He moved with the grace of a master dancer, testing the ground with his toes before he placed his weight on the foot. The litter and refuse covering the muddy ground of the alley could cause a fatal misstep, yet the priest moved with confidence.

The Hunter realized he faced a man who knew how to use his weapons, and a flash of concern raced through him. Soulhunger alone stood no chance against the two longer blades. He slipped the heavy swordbreaker from its sheath, and the familiar weight of the knife comforted him.

He waited, blades held at the ready, and the priest obliged him by launching the first attack. It came faster than expected. The priest thrust his longer sword toward the Hunter's throat. The Hunter blocked it easily and returned with a blow of his own, which the man turned aside.

Each tested the other's guard with quick thrusts and cuts, parrying their opponent's blows with ease. They moved up and down the alley, the sounds of clashing steel and sloshing mud filling the air. Neither gained a clear advantage in their first exchange, and the priest retreated after a minute of trading blows.

"I see your reputation is well-earned, Hunter," he said, his voice full of confidence. His breath came easy and his stance was relaxed.

The Hunter gave him a mocking smile. "For a priest, you certainly know which end of a sword goes where."

"You mean *here!*" The priest's lightning thrust took the Hunter by surprise.

Pain raced along the Hunter's arm as the priest's blade pierced the muscle of his shoulder. Before he could retaliate, his opponent leapt back, out of reach of the Hunter's shorter blades.

"You'll need to move faster than that, if you want to carry out your contract, Hunter," the man taunted.

"Oh, aye," the Hunter said, his smile never wavering, "I believe you're right."

The wound stung, and blood trickled down the Hunter's arm. However, the injury, which would have rendered any other man's arm useless, simply hampered his movement for a few heartbeats. As he stared at the priest, he could feel his flesh knitting together. After a moment, he tested the shoulder and found it moved without pain.

"Ahh, much better."

The Beggar Priest's confident expression slipped. "So, it is as the rumors say."

"There are a lot of rumors, priest, but not all are true."

"They say your body can heal, that you can't be killed." The man pointed a finger at his chest. "I put a dagger in your heart and a sword in your shoulder, and yet here you stand."

The Hunter shrugged. "Many have tried to put an end to the Hunter, but the Long Keeper passes me by every time."

"We'll see about that," the priest said.

With a shout, he leapt forward, renewing his furious onslaught. His blows fell hard and fast, striking the Hunter from every angle.

The Hunter marveled at the priest's strength. Each blow jarred his arms, and he found himself pressed hard. He had to move fast to block or dodge the blows of the longer weapons, yet at the same time find a way to slip through the priest's guard or use the swordbreaker to disarm the man.

He ducked beneath a vicious slash, twisted out of the way of a thrust, and riposted with Soulhunger in his right hand. The sharp blade glanced along the priest's ribs before the man could fully dodge the blow. Soulhunger, tasting blood, screamed its pleasure.

The distraction nearly cost him an eye. The priest's sword sliced through the air toward his head, forcing the Hunter to backpedal. Stinging pain flared along his cheek, and touching his face, he found blood dripping from a shallow wound.

With a feral grin, the priest pressed the attack. He loosed a rapid succession of cuts at the Hunter's head and shoulders, adding occasional strikes at the Hunter's legs and midsection.

Smart man, thought the Hunter, parrying a cut to his knees. The blow would have hobbled him, or slowed him long enough for the priest to gain the upper hand.

"You're wasting your time, priest. You already put a knife in my heart, and I healed from that."

"Aye," rasped the man through gritted teeth, "but you may find it's not as easy to regrow your head once I take it off."

Their battle raged with a fierce intensity, each struggling to find the weakness in the other's guard. The Hunter had to marvel at the man's tenacity. The priest held his own, but the Hunter knew time was on his side. His opponent's breath came in ragged gasps, his movements slowing. Grim determination filled the Beggar Priest's face, but there was a hint of desperation in his attack.

The priest launched strikes seemingly at random, but careful study showed the Hunter the rhythm of the cleric's strikes.

A smile of satisfaction spread across his face. *Got you, you bastard.*

He sensed the low slash coming before the priest struck. When his opponent's sword dipped toward his knee, he was ready with the swordbreaker to block. He dodged an anticipated slash, and with a twist of the notched swordbreaker, he wrenched the priest's weapon from his hand.

The Beggar Priest managed to leap back, barely dodging the Hunter's follow-up slash—which would have opened his throat. The man stumbled backwards, staring in surprise at the Hunter.

"Of all the assassins they have sent after me," said the priest, wonder in his voice, "it is an irony that a creature like you would be the one to finish the job."

Creature?

"Careful, priest, or you might hurt my feelings," the Hunter said with a smirk.

He advanced on his opponent, looking for an opening in the priest's guard. The Hunter saw the grim determination on the man's face, and he had no choice but to admire the man's grit.

Courageous, even in the face of death. Certainly not the actions of a rapist.

The Hunter renewed his attack, his knives carving into his opponent. The Beggar Priest's sword moved with lightning speed to deflect the Hunter's onslaught, but the blades in the Hunter's hands flew faster than he could see.

Within the space of a dozen heartbeats, blood dripped from wounds in the priest's arms, legs, face, and chest. A deep gash in the cleric's wrist had sliced into the artery, and he struggled to grip his sword in weakening fingers. His uninjured hand clutched at the coils of his intestines spilling from a gaping wound in his abdomen.

"If only you knew what you've done, Hunter," the priest gasped. Pain flashed across his face, and he slumped to his knees. "Centuries of protecting Voramis and the people of Einan, and it ends like this."

The Hunter stared down at the dying man, his eyes devoid of mercy. "For a priest, you have a vaunted opinion of yourself. You are receiving the reward you have earned. *'An eye for an eye'*, your scriptures say, don't they? Your violation of an innocent young woman led to her death, and that is on your conscience."

"Violation? Innocent young woman?" Confusion flashed across the priest's face, followed by a slow, sad smile. "Is that the story *he* told you? Oh, poor foolish instrument in the hands of a master craftsman." A grimace of pain prevented him from speaking, and he swallowed hard.

Feed, whispered Soulhunger in the Hunter's mind. The weapon throbbed in his hand, eager for the man's blood.

The priest spoke again, his voice quiet. "If you knew what was good for you, Hunter, you would leave me to die. You have killed me, but there is no need for you to use that accursed blade." He thrust his chin toward the dagger in the Hunter's hand.

"My instructions were clear, priest," the Hunter said, shaking his head as he moved to stand over the dying man. The priest looked up at him with sorrow in his eyes.

"May all the gods take pity on you for what you are about to do this day," the man whispered. A smile touched his lips, and he closed his eyes.

The Hunter drove the blade deep into the man's chest, feeling the sharp edge slicing through flesh and muscle to find the priest's heart.

Soulhunger cried out in ecstasy, feeding, pulling the man's essence into itself. Bright light flared from the gem and burned the Hunter's eyes. Pain filled the Hunter's mind, and he dropped his swordbreaker to clutch at his head.

An inferno raged within the Hunter. His agony intensified with every passing second. Power raced in his veins, but it felt tainted, somehow unclean.

Something isn't right, his mind shrieked. *This can't be right.*

Soulhunger's howling voice overwhelmed his thoughts. *More,* it cried. *Give me blood. Satisfy my thirst.*

He struggled to open his eyes through the pain, staring down at the weapon pulsing in the priest's chest. Dark blood bubbled around the blade, and the light of Soulhunger's gem illuminated the street around him with its brilliance. Blood rushed through his veins, nausea swept over him, and numbness crept through his body. His head felt packed with wool, and his mind refused to clear. The pain in his body and mind felt eternal. Pressure built within him, shattering his ability to think clearly.

The words came to his numb limps unbidden. "May the Long Keeper take your body—your soul is forfeit."

The Hunter stumbled to his feet, moving without thought. He turned away from the priest's body and shuffled down the alleyway as quickly as his numb legs could carry him. Somehow, he had sufficient presence of mind to pull the hood over his face and hide his weapons from sight. His hands and legs moved as if detached from his mind, with a will all their own.

What in the icy hell just happened?

Lord Cyrannius' story raced through his mind, but it didn't fit with the man he had met. Somehow, he had been set up.

The bastard lied to me. But why? What is so special about this priest? Of all the lives Soulhunger has claimed, how is this one any different?

He struggled to corral his thoughts, but his mind refused to cooperate. He walked without purpose, directionless. He simply placed one foot in front of the other, not caring where he went. Power raced through him, both hot and cold at the same time, setting every muscle quivering. The contents of his stomach came up, and, staggering, he retched into a pile of refuse.

What did I just do? Why does this feel somehow…wrong?

The streets of Lower Voramis passed by in a blur, his eyes unseeing and his ears unhearing. People jostled him as they passed, yelled insults and curses at him. He paid them no heed, his body as insensible as his mind.

Something happened back there, something I don't understand. But what?

Chaos whirled in his mind. A single thought consumed him. *I have to find that bastard Cyrannius. I'll get answers from him, then I'll finish what that bloodbear started.*

"Spare a coin, sir?"

The voice of a beggar broke into his stupor, tearing him from his thoughts. He blinked, as if opening his tired eyes for the first time. The taverns and whorehouses of the Blackfall District surrounded him; somehow his insensate trudging had brought him here.

"A coin, sir?" the beggar asked again, his voice insistent.

"No, sorry."

He paid little attention to the approaching mendicant, hand extended in supplication. His thoughts were consumed by the pain racing through his body. A sinking uneasiness filled him. Somehow, he had done more than just kill an ordinary man. This was bigger than even he knew.

What have I done?

The Hunter failed to notice the beggar stepping in front of him, blocking his path. He bumped into the vagabond, and opened his mouth to yell an insult at the fool.

His words died in his throat as the beggar plunged a knife into his stomach.

Chapter Fifteen

Drip, drip, drip…

The insistent sound of dripping water grated on the Hunter's consciousness.

His head pounded in time with the falling drops.

Drip, drip, drip…

He struggled to open his eyes, and found them already wide open. Darkness filled his vision. He saw nothing, heard nothing save the persistent, irritating noise of water droplets hitting stone.

His thoughts came slowly, his mind a fog. *Where the fuck am I?*

Drip, drip, drip…

He tried to move, but his legs refused to function. Chains rattled in the darkness, the sound accompanied by the smell of stagnant water and thick dust. One of his eyes was crusted shut. A sharp pain in his ribs throbbed in time with the water droplets.

His arms were locked in place as well. He tested the reach of his bonds, and found them unyielding.

Drip, drip, drip…

No sounds of life. The Hunter strained to hear anything beyond his own heartbeat and the frustrating, eternal dripping. *I must be far below the street.*

His world remained in darkness for an eternity, the silence broken only by the sound of water.

Drip, drip, drip…

He remained motionless, his body drained and his muscles exhausted. Every part of him ached, but the pain of his body slowly healing was almost worse. Only the maddening echoes of water falling on stone marked the passage of time.

Mind-numbing fatigue clouded his mind, but he fought it, trying to corral his thoughts.

What happened? How did I get here?

The memory came back to him in a flash.

I killed the priest. I carried out the contract, but something went wrong.

He remembered the pain as he plunged Soulhunger deep into the man's chest.

Soulhunger!

He reached for the weapon where it should hang on his belt, forgetting the manacles on his wrist. Spikes set in the shackles dug into his flesh, sending waves of pain shooting up his arms. He tried to move his feet, but the chains pricked his flesh. Warm blood trickled down his ankles.

That's going to make it damned difficult to get out of here.

A heavy fog filled his mind. He shook his head in a vain effort to clear it. He struggled to recall what happened after he had killed the priest.

Soulhunger changed, he remembered, *became something different, something...dark, hungry.*

He sought the blade's voice, but his mind echoed the emptiness of the darkness around him.

He had a vague memory of walking the streets of Voramis in a haze, and the face of the beggar accosting him on the street.

Keeper's teats! And to think I didn't even have the presence of mind to defend myself. He growled his fury into the darkness.

A sound reached his ears, and he fell silent, straining to hear. Footsteps echoed somewhere in the distance.

Two pairs of feet, he thought. *Two distinct scents. Two men.*

One smelled of cheap whores, stale ale, and bloodied steel. The other's scent was heavy with leather, dried sweat, and rancid meat.

The footsteps approached, growing louder with each passing second before suddenly stopping. Panic filled the Hunter as the sound of dripping water filled his world once more. He feared the dripping would drive him insane.

He heaved an inward sigh of relief as a key rattled in the lock, and torchlight shone beneath a tiny crack in what the Hunter guessed to be a door. A heavy tumbler clicked into place, and the door swung open.

Light flared in the Hunter's vision, blinding him painfully. He squeezed his eyelids shut, tears streaming down his cheeks.

"Well, well," came a voice from beyond his closed eyes, "*this* is the legendary Hunter?"

Silence fell in the room for the space of a few heartbeats.

"I'd have to say," said the voice, sounding disappointed, "not a very impressive specimen when he's shackled and bound."

Heavy footfalls approached the Hunter, and he struggled to open his eyes. His vision, accustomed to the darkness, had yet to clear. He saw only a bright blur through his tears.

The voice came again. "Let's see if he's as tough as they say."

What felt like a brick wall slammed into the Hunter's stomach. The blow doubled him over. Blood trickled down his arms from the spikes piercing his wrists.

On the bright side, he thought, gasping for air, *at least my vision is returning.*

In the light of the smoking torch, the Hunter saw the most unremarkable man he had ever laid eyes on. He had a plain nose, mousy brown hair, scant facial hair, and eyes of a dull brown—features shared by thousands of commoners in Voramis. The man wore dun-colored clothing, the sort the Hunter wore when he wanted to remain unnoticed. He was the one who smelled of whores, ale, and bloody steel.

"Do you know who I am, Hunter?" the man asked. His voice, neither deep nor high, held no trace of accent. He had no scars on his hands or face, and his skin remained free of all tattoos and markings. The only thing marking him as anything but ordinary was the ring he wore on his index finger.

"Ahh," said the man, catching the Hunter's glance at his ring, "you see *this*, don't you, Hunter?" He removed it, held it up in front of the Hunter's eyes. "Now do you know who I am?"

The Hunter studied the simple ring. Made of silver, it bore only the engraving of a hand tipped with long, sharp claws.

The ring of The Bloody Hand, thought the Hunter. *Fuck me.*

The man smiled. He palmed the ring and slipped it back onto his index finger with ease.

"Allow me to introduce myself, Hunter. I am the Second, servant to the First of the Bloody Hand, true ruler of this city."

The Hunter said nothing, but his mind raced. He fought to recall everything he knew about the shadowy organization that held Voramis in its grip of terror, and the Five Fingers who served as the leaders.

The First was the absolute ruler, the Second his eyes and ears in the city. Looking at the man standing in front of him, the Hunter could see why. His innocuous appearance would allow him to travel anywhere in the city without suspicion.

The Third was said to be a hulking brute, able to break his enemies with nothing but his bare hands. He controlled the violent gangs of Voramis, extorting money from merchants with the threat of abuse and the promise of protection from his own gangs.

No one knew much about the Fourth, save that the man kept the brothels of Voramis stocked with flesh. None of those he had questioned had ever seen the Fourth's face.

Rumors held that the Fifth controlled the thieves' guilds of Voramis. Once a thief himself, or so the stories went, he was responsible for all of the drugs, spirits, and human trafficking that made the Blackfall District such a haven for vice.

And now I have fallen into the hands of the Second, he thought. *This could get ugly.*

The Hunter had made more than his fair share of enemies, and the Bloody Hand was not known for its forgiving nature.

The Second drew a dagger and tapped the flat of the blade against his pursed lips. "You are one of the few men—outside of The Hand itself, of course—who have seen my face and lived." He gave his shackled prisoner a vicious smile. "Though I may decide to change that soon."

He advanced on the Hunter, blade glinting in the torchlight, menace written on his face. He placed the tip of the dagger beneath the Hunter's right eyeball and applied gentle pressure. The Hunter's face twitched with the pain, but he remained silent. The tip of the dagger loomed dangerously close to his eye.

"I believe," said a voice from the door, "we are to wait until the First has decided what to do with him."

The Second, startled, whirled around, the edge of his blade scoring the Hunter's cheek. Blood trickled down the Hunter's face from the cut, but he ignored the pain.

He studied the man who had entered the room unnoticed. The man had arms thinner than the Hunter's wrists, a slight hunch in his shoulders, eyes sunken from years of malnourishment, and he moved with a limp. He stood no taller than the Second's shoulder. Twin knife belts crisscrossed his chest, holding nearly two dozen small throwing blades. A silver ring bearing the mark of the Hand sat on his little finger.

The Fifth shows his face, he thought, inhaling the man's scent. *Hinge grease. Cheap wine. Brass.*

"It is not *you* who commands here, thief." Venom dripped from the Second's words, and he stared down at the little man with a glare of mixed contempt and anger. "Have you forgotten your place?"

"I forget nothing," replied the Fifth, unperturbed by the vitriol in the Second's voice. "I am simply relaying a message to you." He reached into one of the myriad pouches hanging from his belt. "The master has spoken."

The Second's eyes widened upon seeing the gold ring clutched in the Fifth's bony fingers "The master sends word, does he?" He studied the ring, taking in the etching of the Bloody Hand. "Very well. We shall while away the time with a bit of entertainment, then." Turning to face the Hunter, he raised an eyebrow. "Brutus?"

Confusion flickered across the Hunter's face for a moment before a massive fist slammed into his kidney. The force of the blow bent him backward, and he would have fallen had not the chains held him upright. A groan escaped his lips.

The Second's face split into a wide grin. "Well done, Brutus!"

"Thank you, master," came the reply.

The Hunter caught movement out of the corner of his eye, but had no time to react as a blow rocked his head. A flash of pain ran up the side of his neck. The Hunter saw the man for the first time when the thug moved to stand in front of him.

If ever there is a man worthy of the name Brutus, he thought, *it is him.*

Brutus towered over him by a full head, and the diminutive Fifth barely came to the level of his chest. Impressive cords of muscle banded Brutus' arms, and his bald head shone bright in the torchlight. A thick nose sat beneath a sloping forehead, and dumb eyes stared at the Hunter.

His musculature would be impressive even on a statue of Balrid the Giant, thought the Hunter.

The scents of rancid meat and sweat-stained leather filled the Hunter's nostrils, accompanied by the smell of the wax giving Brutus' hairless pate its bright sheen.

"Hunter, meet Brutus," the Second spoke. "Brutus, I believe the Hunter needs some…administering to. He seems to have survived his capture without sufficient damage."

The behemoth's fist crashed into the Hunter's stomach with enough force to shatter a brick wall. He tensed in expectation of the blow, but it did little to dull the pain. Every breath hurt. His lungs refused to fill with air. He saw stars as he doubled over, heaving the contents of his stomach onto the floor.

"You are an impressive specimen, I must say, Hunter," the Second said. "Brutus has broken men's backs with that punch, and yet you still live." He paced in front of his captive, waving the dagger as he spoke. "Most men would have died from the wounds that knocked you unconscious. You know, it took nearly a dozen of my best men to take you down, even after the big brute here clubbed you over the head. They may have been a bit…zealous, but you can understand why."

The Hunter had no reply for his captor. He still struggled to stand upright, though he no longer fought for breath.

"There will be three weeping widows tonight," said the Second, turning to glare at him, "thanks to you and your…tools." The man strode to a table in one corner of the small room and whipped back the cloth covering it, revealing Soulhunger, the swordbreaker, and the daggers the Hunter had secreted beneath his clothing.

Soulhunger! The dagger's voice remained silent, but the Hunter felt its presence in the back of his mind. *If I can get my hands on one of those blades…*

A hungry look must have filled the Hunter's eyes, for the Second gave his prisoner a cruel, mocking smile and shook his head. "Not going to happen, Hunter. Those chains will hold even you. We can't have you getting free and hunting us down, though, I dare say, that's unlikely to happen, given your current state."

The Hunter turned his head to examine the chains holding him bound, ignoring the twinge of pain in his neck. His manacles were nearly as thick as Brutus' arms.

The Hand is certainly not taking any chances here.

Footsteps echoed in the passageway outside the cell, drawing the Hunter's attention toward the door.

"Ahh," said the Second, obviously hearing the sound as well, "the master has arrived."

A motley assortment of men of the muscle-bound variety filled the room, but it was the last man to enter that immediately arrested the Hunter's attention. The man had an aristocratic face, with an aquiline nose, thin lips, sharp cheekbones, an angled chin, and eyes that stared at the Hunter with haughty disdain. He wore the latest fashion in garments, a gold-handled sword hanging at his hip. The man's scent held traces of steel, an overwhelming amount of perfume, but a hint of something rancid beneath it all.

I've seen him somewhere, thought the Hunter. A memory of an evening of dancing and festivity flashed in his mind. *At Lord Dannaros' party. A minor noble, a Lord of something or another.*

The way everyone in the room looked to the man for command spoke volumes. He carried himself with utter confidence, and his mere presence electrified the air about him.

There is something terrifying about him, though what, I cannot say.

"Thank you," the man said in clipped tones, taking his gold ring from the Second's hand. He slipped it onto his finger with ease, and the Hunter knew for a certainty that he stared at none other than the First of the Bloody Hand, chief of the Five Fingers. This was the man in near-absolute control of Voramis' criminal underground, and through it, the entire city.

"So the Hunter has become the prey," said the First. The smile that spread on his lips failed to reach his eyes. "It is a distinct pleasure to make your acquaintance, though I have an uncanny feeling we may have met elsewhere."

The First stepped forward, stopping within easy reach of the Hunter's chained arms.

"The great Hunter of Voramis," he mused. "The man in the shadows. The legendary killer. The creature who single-handedly has every noble, merchant, and criminal in Voramis shitting in their breeches at the mention of his name." He gave the Hunter a wry smile. "That, my new friend, is a form of power I envy you."

"Your name is spoken with much less reverence, I assume?"

"He speaks!" The First clapped his hands in an exaggerated gesture of delight. "Not only do I have the Hunter at my disposal, but he is even inclined to have a chat. This is proving to be a singularly wonderful evening."

"However," said the First, his voice turning serious, "a bit of respect could go a long way in your current situation." Without turning to look at the hulking man, the First gestured. "Brutus."

The Hunter didn't see the blow coming, didn't have time to register the force of the impact. His head snapped to one side, his vision blurred, and his jaw popped out of its socket with a rush of pain. He fought to remain standing on sagging knees, the world around him spinning dizzily.

"That bruise will be there for quite a while, Hunter," the First said, stepping close and poking his injured face with an indelicate finger. "It will serve as a reminder that the odds are not in your favor, at the moment."

He stared at the Hunter as if expecting him to speak, but the

Hunter's jaw refused to move.

"Now, do you realize just how deep in it you have sunk?" the First crowed, his voice mocking. "You're up to your deep in shit, Hunter. You've been a naughty, naughty killer." He wagged an admonishing finger at his captive. "You've been operating in Voramis without the sanction of the Bloody Hand. That's not something we can allow without… repercussions."

The First paced around the room, arms clasped behind his back. "After all, if you were allowed to continue your work unchecked, we might find all sorts of freelancers cropping up around the city. Before you know it, Voramis would slip from the control we have worked so hard to achieve." He stepped close to the Hunter again, giving him a wicked smile. "I, for one, quite enjoy having the city's balls in my vise grip." The First clenched his fist in front of the Hunter's face, mimicking crushing a pair of testicles in his fingers.

"And so, my *new* friend," the First's mocking tirade continued, "you will serve as an object lesson to any in the city who would think about operating outside the purview of the Bloody Hand. It will not be a pretty lesson, I must say." He stared at the Hunter, measuring him for some unknown horrors. "By the time we're done with you, no one will think to take a shit in his own bed without first paying us handsomely for the privilege."

The Hunter struggled to speak, but his dislocated jaw prevented it. The First seemed to notice it for the first time.

"Where *are* my manners?" he asked, gesturing for the giant by his side. "Brutus, please restore the Hunter's ability to speak."

Brutus' fist plowed into the other side of the Hunter's face, leaving a matching purple bruise. The blow set the Hunter's head ringing and the stars spinning, but he found he could move his jaw again—albeit with significant discomfort.

"And what," he asked the First, slurring his words through bloody teeth, "do you have in mind?"

A wicked smile spread across the First's face. "Just a bit of fun testing out the Hunter's legendary immortality. I have heard you are damned difficult to kill. Oh, you hurt easily enough,"—as if to prove his point, he waved Brutus forward—"but killing you is proving nigh impossible."

Brutus plowed a massive fist into the Hunter's side. Through the pain, the Hunter heard one of his ribs crack.

"So," he coughed, a defiant glare on his face, "you're going to test out that theory, then?"

"Aye, that I will," replied the man, simply. "But before I do, I believe Brutus would like a bit of exercise, isn't that right, you big, dumb brute?"

The eagerness with which Brutus pounded the Hunter served as proof of the total control the First had over his men. Blood covered the bald giant's knuckles by the time his blows ceased, and he panted for breath. The big man looked at the First like an oversized puppy hoping for his master's eager nod of approval.

"Well done," the First said, giving Brutus a gracious smile. "Your reward awaits you at The Arms of Heaven. Tell the Mistress that Bichon is to be your treat for tonight, for all of your work in apprehending the Hunter."

A dumb grin split the big man's face, and he bowed in gratefulness before hurrying from the room. His features showed clearly his eagerness to receive the prize awaiting him at the brothel.

The Second sidled up to the First and whispered into his ear. At a nod from his leader, the Second followed the big man from the room. The assorted muscle trooped out as well, emptying the room of all save the First and a figure standing by the door.

He had not seen the woman enter, but his breath caught in his chest as he saw her for the first time.

Celicia?

Dark hair, dark eyes, full lips with a hint of mischief. Her clothing was far richer than the garments she had worn in The Iron Arms.

The First saw the Hunter's eyes fall on the woman, and he smiled grandly. "And of course you *must* remember my Fourth. Celicia, I believe she said her name was?"

A silver ring bearing the mark of The Bloody Hand sat on the fourth finger of the woman's right hand.

In the Five Fingers? The Hunter stared at the woman in disbelief.

A stab of pain ran through him, but it had nothing to do with the torment inflicted by the giant Brutus. Even though he had only met the woman once, for some inexplicable reason, he felt betrayed.

The First must have read his thoughts, for he broke out in a gleeful cackle. "Oh yes, she certainly *can* be a charmer, our Fourth." He moved to stand by the woman, caressing her face with long, graceful fingers. "They say," his voice dropped to little more than a whisper, "she can bring men to pleasure with nothing but a touch."

He turned his attention to the woman beneath his hands, giving her a lewd smile. "It is why she is the capable hand behind Voramis' houses of rapture. Perhaps you would like a sampling of what she can do, eh, Hunter?" He raised a mocking eyebrow at his captive.

The woman said nothing. Unmoving, her arms crossed and head held high, she met the Hunter's gaze, her eyes steely and unflinching.

"Another time, perhaps," the First said, releasing the woman and returning his attention to his captive. "Well, only if you live beyond this night—which I very much doubt."

At that moment, the door opened and the Second entered, pushing a wheeled cart before him. Upon the cart lay all manner of instruments of torture; knives, whips, garrotes, flaying tools, screws, pincers, and dozens more the Hunter had never seen. Torchlight glinted from the polished edges of the wicked steel implements.

"I believe my Second has a few…treats for you." The First's eyes—devoid of pity—filled with lust, and he licked his lips in anticipation.

The Second's hand hovered over the cart, as if weighing his options. He selected a small knife, and, testing its edge, smiled as it opened a shallow cut in his finger.

The Hunter's heart thundered as if trying to beat its way free of his chest, and a flash of fear raced through him. He stared in open horror at the tools on the tray.

"Let us begin the test of the Hunter's vaunted immortality," the First said, a depraved smile touching his lips.

The Second's blades sliced into the Hunter's skin with agonizing ease. The Hunter tried to remain silent, but pain caused a cry to escape his lips.

"Yes," the First laughed, a wicked sound that seemed to harmonize with the Hunter's suffering, "what fun we shall have tonight!"

The Hunter's screams grew louder as the Second grew more creative. The sounds of torment echoed in the quiet cell and filled the corridor beyond. As the agony intensified, one thing stood out in the Hunter's benumbed mind: Celicia—or whatever her name was—flinched with each fresh horror inflicted.

* * *

Silence filled the small underground cell, broken only by the insistent sound of water and the blood dripping from the Hunter's body.

He hung limp in his chains, the wicked spikes of his manacles digging into flesh long since numb from torment. Agony had filled his world for what felt like an eternity, though he guessed that only a few hours had passed.

The Second had taken a knife to his face, disfiguring his harsh features with every stroke. His shoulders, dislocated from repeated blows, throbbed painfully. The flesh of his chest and stomach burned, scorched by acid the Second had dabbed onto the exposed skin with careful precision. The smell of charred meat, hot steel, and blood—both fresh and dried—filled the room.

Pain stabbed into him with each breath. The Second had broken at least four of his ribs. The muscles of his arms and legs hung limp, the tendons carved by a razor stiletto. His knees had been shattered hours ago, but they had healed enough to allow him to stand.

"It seems," said the First, eyes glittering with delight, "you are as immortal as your legends proclaim, Hunter."

He cast an angry glare at the Second, displeased at the man's inability to break the stubborn captive. The Second seemed surprised that his ministrations had failed to have the desired effect. Blood covered his hands and clothing, and bright red streaked his face. Gore stained every instrument on his tray of horrors, a testament to the agony the Hunter had endured thus far.

"I must say," mused the First, "most men would have died hours ago under the Second's special…attentions. In fact, most men *have* died at his hands, but you seem to be the exception. How curious."

"The legends must be true, then," the Hunter rasped in a voice hoarse from hours of screaming.

"Indeed," said the First, pensively.

He moved to the table upon which lay the Hunter's weapons, and his fingers closed around the grip of the swordbreaker. His fingers caressed its edge as he strode toward the Hunter once more.

"But I wonder," he said, "how immortal are you really? Could you withstand, say, a knife to the heart?"

Fear flashed through the Hunter as the First lifted the notched blade high. The swordbreaker drove deep into his chest. He flopped weakly, numbness spreading through his limbs, blood spilling down his torso. His vision blurred, his consciousness slipping away.

Celicia's wide eyes were the last thing he saw before the world faded to a cold, empty black.

Chapter Sixteen

The Hunter floated in a silent void, darkness surrounding him. Here he felt no pain, no fear. All was still.

With a jolt, life filled his lungs. Ice-cold water splashed across his face, and he spluttered and coughed.

We cannot die, the voice in his head whispered. *We must live to kill another day. There are so many more who deserve to taste the agony of Soulhunger's blade.*

Agony coursed through every part of his body. His muscles struggled to support him, and his stubbornness warred with weakness. Opening his eyes took every shred of willpower he possessed, but he forced himself to stand.

"He awakens," the Second said, dropping an empty bucket.

Water dripped from the Hunter's naked chest. Looking down, he found that the cold water had washed away most of the blood. Only deep wounds and purpling bruises remained, but he could feel his body slowly knitting itself back together.

"So," the First spoke, a hint of wonder in his voice, "the great Hunter can survive a blade to the heart. You truly are as great as your legend describes. I suspected the rumors of your prowess were greatly exaggerated."

The Hunter, struggling to breathe, held his tongue.

"You may be harder to kill than I expected," the First continued, "but I dare say there is one weapon that could kill you." His eyes fell on Soulhunger, and hunger filled his eyes. As his fingers fondled the blade's handle, he inhaled sharply—the sound was almost orgasmic. For a moment, the man's features seemed to shift, but the Hunter dismissed it as a trick of the flickering torchlight.

The First stared at the blade for a long moment, his attention rapt.

Then, as if awaking from a dream, his face cleared and he regained his composure.

"Such a beautiful weapon," he breathed, his eyes never leaving the dagger. "Do you know of its origins, Hunter?"

Still the Hunter said nothing, but the First ignored his silence.

"I wish *I* knew from whence this blade came," he continued, "for it must have many fascinating stories to tell." He pulled his gaze away from the weapon with effort. "Tell me, Hunter, is it true that only your hand can wield it?"

"Try it and find out," the Hunter replied, grinning through his pain.

"Perhaps I will," the First said. His hand reached toward the blade, but hesitated for a moment, fingers hovering over the hilt. "Or perhaps not." His hand withdrew.

He turned to the Second. "Do you wish to try your hand at wielding the fabled blade of the Hunter?" he asked, gesturing at the dagger. When the Second remained silent, he turned to the thugs. "Any of you?" None moved. "I thought not."

At a gesture from his master, the Second hurried to replace the cloth covering Soulhunger and the swordbreaker—still stained with the Hunter's blood.

"What to do, what to do?" said the First, his gaze falling on the Hunter once more. He tapped his lips as if deep in thought. "I warn you, Hunter, I cannot allow you to continue operating freely in Voramis. The city is mine, and mine it shall stay."

His eyes glazed for a moment, as if lost in thought. "I shall give you this one chance to walk away, Hunter."

"Oh?" the Hunter asked.

"Yes," the First said with a calculating look, "I will allow you to walk away, and your past...*indiscretions* will be forgotten. All you need to do is swear your service to me, and you will leave here a free man."

"A free man, yet in service to the Bloody Hand?" The Hunter arched a bloodstained eyebrow.

"Yes," said the First, smiling. "I *do* see how the wording can be a tad confusing. Let me explain it thusly: you will be permitted to as usual, and I will even ensure the most lucrative contracts are sent your way. All you need do is make yourself available if and when I should require your services."

"That's it?"

"That is all." The First rewarded him with a gracious smile.

The Hunter pretended to weigh the offer for a moment, stalling to give his broken body time to heal.

"I must say," he said slowly, "your offer sounds good."

A smile broke out on the First's face. "So you accept?"

"No," retorted the Hunter. "Your offer *sounds* good. Which, of course, means it must be *too* good to be true."

The First's smile disappeared, and anger flashed in his eyes. "Look around you, Hunter," he said, his voice tight and controlled. "Look where you are." He accentuated his words by gesturing to the men filling the room. "There is no one to save you here. You will never walk out of here a free man unless you accept my offer. Consider your answer carefully."

The Hunter shook his head. "Then I must remain a prisoner, for I would rather die than submit to you." Anger filled his voice for the first time. "I am the Hunter, you coward. I am no man's slave, no man's errand boy." Rage flashed in his dark eyes, and those in the room flinched at the intensity filling his voice. "I will have no masters, especially not an arrogant pissant with a ridiculous name like The First of the Bloody Hand."

Only the First seemed unfazed by his tirade. "Are you certain, Hunter?"

For his answer, the Hunter remained silent, his gaze level.

With a sigh, the First shook his head. "So be it. By the gods, how I *wish* you had accepted my offer. I know that you, too, will soon come to regret your hasty decision to turn me down." He gave his second-in-command a curt nod, and the man stepped from the room.

When the Second returned, four men accompanied him—thugs who could have been Brutus' bigger, uglier cousins. Two sported fresh bruises on their face, and a third had gaps in his mouth where teeth should have been.

These must be some of the thugs who captured me earlier, he thought, grinning. *Glad to see I gave them plenty of trouble.*

"Unchain him," the Second commanded, "and don't bother being gentle with the bastard."

The thugs strode around the Hunter, giving him a wide berth His chains rattled, and he heard the *click* of a heavy padlock being opened.

With the shackles no longer holding him in place, his arms fell to his sides. He screamed as the weight of the chains dragged on his dislocated shoulders. He fought to stand on weak knees, his legs shaking with the effort.

Rough hands seized him, and a none-too-gentle kick forced him to his knees. He fought to move, but the muscled thugs held him firmly in place. Two loud *pops* echoed through the room, and he screamed once more.

At least my shoulders are back in place, he thought, still struggling against his captors.

The sharp edge of a knife against his throat stopped him. The Second glared down at him, pressing the blade against the soft skin of his neck.

"Twitch again, Hunter," the Second said, his voice low and menacing, "and I'll bleed you like a pig."

The Hunter ceased his struggles. He forced his face into a mask of calm, though his mind raced, searching for a way to break free.

The First stepped forward, bending low to stare into the Hunter's eyes. "And thus ends the legend of the Hunter," he said. His breath felt hot on the Hunter's face, and the cloying scent of too much perfume filled the Hunter's nostrils. "You will die, but not in some heroic, glorious manner.

No, you will die languishing in a cell until the end of your natural life—however long and miserable that may be."

The Hunter glared up at him, the anger in his dark eyes matching the intensity of the First's gaze. "The story has not yet been written," he spat, baring his teeth in a feral grin. "Until you find a way to kill me for good, I will always haunt your dreams."

A pitiless smile spread across the First's face. "I think not, dear Hunter. Where you're going, even light will soon become foreign to you. You will never again know the sound of another human's voice, and not even rats will be your companions."

The Hunter's face remained impassive, but the First continued. "It is a fate I would wish on few, but you are the one *fortunate* enough to receive it." He straightened, his voice rising with anger. "Thus to all who cross the Bloody Hand. You are fortunate that you have none to call friends, for their fate would be only marginally less horrifying than your own."

The Hunter paid the ravings of the First little heed, glad for the distraction. He gathered his last reserves of strength as the man spoke, waiting until the First had turned his back before making his move.

With a jerk of his arms, he ripped the chains from the grasp of the brutes holding them. Pain flashed through his healing shoulders, but the Hunter refused to allow it to slow him down. He spun to the left and slammed his fist deep into the stomach of one guard. The thug's breath whooshed from his lungs, and he doubled over, retching and gasping for air.

The Hunter's elbow connected with the nose of the guard holding the chain securing his right hand, and hot blood splashed his arm. His left hand swung around to strike the third guard in the windpipe. As the thug wheezed, the Hunter kicked out behind him. His foot struck the last guard under the chin, rocking the massive enforcer's head back. The chain holding the Hunter slipped from the thug's nerveless fingers.

The Hunter turned his glare on the First, rage filling his eyes. A rush of adrenaline supplanted the pain racking his healing body..

"You're next, you bastard," he snarled.

The First shrank back, but the Second stepped between the Hunter and his master, a dagger held at the ready. The Hunter whipped the heavy chain into the man's stomach. As the Second slumped to the floor, the Hunter pushed him aside to lunge for the First.

With a cry of fear, the First tried to retreat, but the Hunter's long, powerful fingers wrapped around his throat before the man could cry out. The stench of fear, mixed with the scent of his perfume, wafted from the First. He pounded his fists against the Hunter's arms, to no avail. The Hunter's depthless eyes held the First's gaze as he choked the life from him.

A hard punch to his spine made his legs wobble, and his death grip on the First loosened. Hands seized him from behind, dragging him off the wheezing First. The thugs wrestled him to the floor, fighting to regain their hold on the spiked chains. Breathing hard, the Hunter allowed himself to be restrained before the thugs were forced to break anything.

He stared up defiantly at the First. The man's face had turned an angry shade of red, and he gasped for air. The Second still fought for breath, clutching at his stomach and groaning. Through it all, Celicia had stood, unmoving, by the door, eyes wide.

"You bastard!" the First roared at the Hunter, his voice rasping. The man looked a sight, his elegant clothing torn and covered in blood. He strode to the Second's cart of torment and seized four slim daggers. With deft movements, he stabbed the blades deep into the Hunter's shoulders, slicing nerves. The Hunter's arms flopped by his side, numb and lifeless.

The First backhanded the Hunter, knocking him back. He followed up the blow with a vicious kick to his captive's groin. The Hunter doubled over in pain, but the thugs holding his arms wrenched him upright.

The First's face hovered a hand's width from his own. "You have earned what is coming next, you canker on the asshole of a leprous dog." Spittle flew from the man's lips, and the Hunter winced at the warm wetness on his face. "I would shove you up a dead horse's ass and have you drowned in the bay, but that would be a waste of a dead horse."

The Hunter's head rang—the First had struck him with surprising force—but he glared at his captors with an impassive stare.

"The fate you will suffer will be more horrible than you could imagine," the First thundered. "You will rot in a dark hole for as long as it takes for your flesh to fall from your bones. You will be fed, but not enough to stave off starvation and thirst. You will die a slow death as your body feeds on itself, and when you are dead, your bones will be cast into the Midden, where they will rot in the deepest, darkest hells for all of eternity."

"Then I shall prepare a place for you," the Hunter spat.

The First ignored his retort, instead nodding at the guards holding him in place. "Take him away. You know what to do."

Without a backward glance at the Hunter, he strode from the room. The Second gave the Hunter a sneer before following in his master's wake. A moment later, Celicia did likewise. He thought he had seen a flash of pity in her eyes, but he couldn't be certain.

The guards holding his arms dragged him to his feet, while the others used their fists to beat the Hunter into compliance. By the time they hauled him from the room, every bone in his upper body felt bruised and cracked. Blood streamed from his broken nose and myriad cuts on his face, and both of his eyes had swollen shut.

Through the pain, he clung to one small triumph: in his fingers, he clutched a fragment of cloth torn from the First's robe.

Chapter Seventeen

The Hunter caught glimpses of torchlight through the burlap sack covering his head. He was dragged through the streets for what felt like an eternity. That last beating hadn't done his already wounded, tortured body any favors.

Unable to see where he stepped, he found himself at the mercy of his captors. Manacles still shackled his wrists and ankles, and he knew any attempt to flee would meet a quick end. Sensation had yet to return to his arms, and he knew he would be unable to catch himself should he fall. He stumbled and would have fallen but for the strong hands holding him.

I wonder what fresh hell awaits me at the end of this journey, he thought.

His one consolation lay in the fact that one of the guards hauling him along struggled for each breath. The Hunter's sharp ears detected a wet gurgle in the man's inhalations, and he knew he had cracked a couple of ribs in the scuffle.

Better to bide my time, if I don't die from this gods-awful stench first.

The reek of dog shit filled his nostrils, causing him to gag. He had watched the Second fill the sack with offal before pulling it over his head. His lungs burned from breathing in the foul air, and it took all of his discipline to keep the meager contents of his stomach down.

He had no idea how long the journey lasted, but exhaustion gripped his muscles by the time his captors hurled him to the floor. His face slammed into the pavement, sending a fresh wave of pain through his body. The world around him whirled.

He struggled to stand, but was kicked mercilessly back down to his knees. Through the thin fabric of the canvas sack, he heard a murmured conversation in the distance. He strained in vain to hear what was being said.

After a long silence, rough hands gripped his arms and hauled him to his feet.

"Enjoy your new life, Hunter," a dull voice grated in his ear.

Someone shoved him forward, and he stumbled, falling to the cobblestones once more. Something hard—a boot, he guessed—slammed into his ribs, knocking the air from his lungs.

"Enough!" came another voice, this one edged with command. "You have received your payment. Now off with you before I remember what you really are, street scum."

"Any time, Captain," responded the first voice, which he guessed belonged to a Hand thug. "You know where to find me. Come on lads, let's go spend the King's coin in style."

"Fucking Hunter," spat another voice.

The Hunter heard coarse laughter and the voices of men discussing how they would squander their newfound wealth. The voices trailed off, leaving the Hunter in the company of his new captors.

Firm hands gripped his arm, and he struggled to rise to his knees. The sack was ripped from his head, but the scent of animal shit remained.

"Watcher's balls," cursed one of the figures standing over him. "He reeks!"

"Fucking Hand cunts," the commanding voice spoke.

The Hunter blinked in the torchlight, his eyes fighting to adjust to the brightness. He lifted his bound hands to his face in an effort to wipe away some of the stench, to no avail.

In the dim light of the street, he saw a pair of practical, worn boots in front of him. His eyes traveled upward, taking in the details of his captor: bright crimson red robes, a well-muscled body beneath worn steel armor, and a bearded face looking down at him sternly.

Heresiarchs. Fuck me.

"By the order of King Gavian of Voramis, and by writ of the Judiciars, I, Captain Erellos of the Heresiarchs, hereby place you under arrest."

The chains on his wrists rattled as one of the red-clad guards pulled the Hunter to his feet. The Heresiarch captain stared up at him, not a shred of pity in his dark eyes.

"I am ordered to transport you to the Hole," said the captain in a solemn voice, "where you will be incarcerated for the rest of your natural life. May the Watcher have mercy on you."

Chapter Eighteen

Darkness surrounded the Hunter on all sides, not a flicker of light in any direction. It seemed like an eternity since the Heresiarchs had thrown him in here. They had placed heavy manacles on his wrists and ankles—but not before brutally ripping the First's daggers from his shoulders. It could have been hours or days.

His body warred with fatigue and pain. He desperately wanted to sit, to lie down, to sleep, but the shackles were too short. He could only stand, forcing his exhausted legs to hold him upright. His head lolled on his shoulders. His mouth begged for water. Pain flashed through him at even the slightest movement, but he felt his body slowly knitting back together. He managed to find a somewhat comfortable position with his back against the cold stone wall. Leaning his head back, he closed his eyes from sheer exhaustion.

This is almost a worse form of torture. Alone in the dark, hungry, and parched. Nothing but the beating of my heart for company.

The darkness taunted him, holding out sleep before him yet ever pulling it away when he was on the verge of dozing. The pain in his arms, legs, chest, and head kept him from rest. He drifted in and out of a numb, unseeing haze, his world filled with nothing.

* * *

"Wake up, Hunter!"

Water splashed across his face and chest, shocking him with its chill. A hard slap snapped him into full consciousness. He opened his eyes and immediately regretted it. Torches flickered around him, casting dim light around the room.

He guessed he must have fallen asleep, though he felt as if he had been awake for weeks. His head throbbed, his eyes felt heavy, and every inch of his body ached. The air in the cell was dusty, pressing in on him.

What in the frozen hell…?

Jerking his arms, he found himself once again restrained by thick chains. His eyes traced their length to the ring set into the stone of the wall.

I'm no longer in the Hole. But this place feels all too familiar, he thought.

"We meet at last, Hunter."

Blinking away tears, the Hunter forced his eyes to focus on the source of the voice. The man before him stood below average height, with a slim physique and hands that had never seen a hard day's work. His nasal voice grated on the Hunter's ears. His slicked-back hair shone with enough wax to fill a candle mold. A hooked nose protruded above thin lips, and his eyes held the Hunter's own. They stared at him with a fierce, burning intelligence.

The man's scent filled the Hunter's nostrils.

Parchment, ink, and mold, with a hint of something else… He couldn't quite identify the scent, though it was familiar.

"I have heard much about you," the man said, his voice calm and polite, "but I scarcely dared hope we would meet—at least not without you coming after my head."

"I… am…at a disadvantage," said the Hunter, his tongue thick with thirst. "I…don't…know you." After what seemed like an eternity in his silent world, his voice sounded odd to his own ears, and his dried-up mouth made speaking difficult.

"My, you must be parched," the man said, seeing the Hunter attempting to lick his dry lips. "If you will allow me." He strode over to a small table on the side of the room, upon which lay a covered tray, a loaf of bread, and a pitcher and cup. Filling the cup, he brought it to the Hunter.

"Here you are," the slim man said, tipping it forward.

The Hunter gulped down the water, gasping at the delicious sensation of the fresh, clean liquid slipping down his throat.

"Much better," the man smiled up at him. "Would you like some food?"

At the Hunter's eager nod, the man ripped a chunk from the loaf.

"Good," said the man, smiling as he watched the Hunter devour the morsel. "Now, where are my manners? My name is Lord Jahel, though most in the city know me as Chief Justiciar." He bowed with a flourish.

The Right Hand of the Watcher. A sinking feeling rose in the pit of the Hunter's stomach.

The Voramis underworld whispered the name of Lord Jahel with fearful voices. As Chief Justiciar, he maintained law and order in the city—by whatever means necessary. He was commander of the Heresiarchs, and his word was law in the courts of the Justiciars. Criminals endeavored to escape the notice of the peacekeepers; those who attracted the attention of Lord

Jahel and his minions simply disappeared.

This is one of the most feared men in the city? The Hunter stared at the slight figure. *Not much to look at. Hard to believe he is the one responsible for the Dark Heresy.*

It was said the Dark Heresy—the secretive shadow arm of the Heresiarchs—served as spies, intelligence gatherers, and torturers, and they answered to one man only.

"The Demon of Voramis," the Hunter said.

Lord Jahel's face creased into a pleased smile. "Yes, that is one of the names I have been given, and to tell you the truth, I quite like it. It has a certain...*gravity* to it, don't you think?" When the Hunter said nothing, the man shrugged. "Fair enough. You may call me by whatever name you wish, but Lord Jahel will suffice for our conversation tonight."

"Conversation?" the Hunter asked, raising an eyebrow.

"Oh yes, Hunter," the man replied. "While you are in my keeping, I would learn more about you. I have to say, you have always interested me."

His eyes roamed the Hunter's muscled body, his long, dark hair, his now-healed and unblemished face, and dark, empty eyes. A slender finger traced the scars marking the Hunter's back and chest, sending a shudder of revulsion through the Hunter.

"I must say," Lord Jahel continued after a moment of silence, "you are a fascinating creature. The man who inspires almost as much terror as the Bloody Hand itself—or, to be immodest for a moment, the Demons of Voramis—is one to study. And study you I shall."

"So," the Hunter said, skepticism filling his voice, "you only wish to speak to me?"

"Of course not," the Chief Justiciar said, giving the Hunter a wry smile. "There will be much more involved. After all, I will need some answers from you before I throw you back into the Hole."

"You may not extract the information you seek as easily as you expect."

"Ah," Lord Jahel said with a knowing smile, "you must have experienced the tender...*ministrations* of the Second firsthand. Pardon the pun." He giggled at his own joke.

The Hunter stared at Lord Jahel, unsure of what to make of the man. *What an odd creature,* he thought.

"I assure you, Hunter," Lord Jahel said, growing serious, "the worst is yet to come. The Second may be something of an expert in the art of pain, but I have at my disposal men who would make him look like a child with a hammer." He spoke in a conspiratorial voice. "I myself studied under the Masters of Agony, and one of the Grand Masters has taken up residence here in the city upon my request. He can perform on the human body with the skill of a virtuoso playing his instrument of choice. The things he can do..."

The man's voice trailed off, and he seemed lost in his imagination for a minute.

"So," the Hunter said, "I can expect only torture and pain before a swift death?"

His words seemed to snap Lord Jahel from his private thoughts. "A swift death, you say?" The man looked surprised. "Oh, *no*, good Hunter," he said, shaking his head. "The Grand Master will take you beyond death, but I assure you he will bring you back—over and over and over again. When we are done with you, you will rot in the Hole or take your own life. I dare say, after suffering at the hands of Sha-Yun'Ti, you will be leaping into the darkness the minute your broken body has recovered enough to move."

"I see we are going to have a lot of fun," the Hunter muttered.

"That's the spirit!" Lord Jahel smiled. He moved to a small table—the single piece of furniture in the bare room—and pulled back one corner of a cloth to reveal Soulhunger.

His dagger lay unsheathed, and hope surged within the Hunter at the sight of the blade. The weapon's insistence throbbed far in the back of his mind, yet its voice seemed to change as Lord Jahel's hand hovered above it. Soulhunger sounded almost…eager.

"A marvelous weapon, this," Lord Jahel said, his voice filled with an odd longing. "I have heard much of what it can do."

"Perhaps you'd like a demonstration firsthand," the Hunter rasped.

Lord Jahel appeared mesmerized by the dagger, his fascination with its secrets written on his face. He stared at it for the space of a few heartbeats, then, shaking his head as if to clear it, he returned his attention to the Hunter.

"Well," he said, his gaze bright, a smile spreading on his face, "back to the business at hand. However, before I turn you over to Grand Master Sha-Yun'Ti, I have a few questions to ask you."

"Answer me a question first, Demon, and I will tell you anything you wish to know."

"Very well," sighed the Chief Justiciar, "what would you have of me?"

"You say you are the Chief Justiciar," the Hunter said, his words coming slowly, "and yet you do not carry out the King's Justice." Lord Jahel frowned at the Hunter's words, seeming puzzled. "The Bloody Hand turned me over to you, and yet you let their thugs walk away. How can you call yourself a man of law and order if you do not simply do away with the Hand once and for all?"

"Ah," Lord Jahel replied, comprehension dawning on his face, "I can understand the logic behind your question. After all, if I truly was the ruthless creature whispered about, why do I not simply wipe out every scum-sucking criminal in the Bloody Hand?"

The Hunter nodded.

"My good Hunter, you must understand that there is a certain… *necessity* that demands the Hand's continued existence."

The slim noble clasped his hands behind his back and began to pace the room.

"In essence, without one, the other would no longer be necessary."

Lord Jahel held out his hands, palms up, as if balancing a scale. "The Hand is the darkness in the city, and the Heresiarchs serve as the light of order, of justice. We of the Dark Heresy operate in the shadows between, and we only exist because of the Hand."

The Hunter remained silent, pondering Lord Jahel's words.

"The Bloody Hand is a sort of necessary evil," he explained in a patient tone. "Without the Hand, the citizens of Voramis would feel secure. They would cease depending upon the Heresiarchs and Justiciars for their continued safety, as there would be nothing threatening their peaceful way of life. They might begin to question our methods, the purpose for our very existence. The Heresiarchs—and the Dark Heresy by extension—would become the villains, the thing they promised to exterminate."

As he spoke, Lord Jahel strode over to the table. He pulled away the cloth to reveal the silver tray and its contents.

Next to Soulhunger lay a small device: a glass tube, fitted with a plunger at one end, and a long, sharp needle extending from the opposite end. The Hunter had seen the device before, used by physickers to draw blood.

His eyes roamed over the rest of the implements laid out on the tray. Some of the tools he recognized from his encounter with the Second, but many of them were new. All were sharp and wicked-looking, and judging by their appearance, they would inflict a gruesome torture indeed.

One tool in particular drew the Hunter's attention. It looked simpler, more primitive than the other items laid out on the tray. While the other implements had been polished to a bright sheen, this one was dull, showing hints of rust.

Iron. He tried to pull his eyes away from the tool, but it mesmerized him. Chills ran down his spine. His skin crawled, and icy tendrils of fear gripped his heart. *How did they know?*

"Have you ever wondered why Voramis has not been to war in centuries?" asked Lord Jahel, his voice snapping the Hunter from his thoughts. "Or why the city flourishes and prospers? The power of the Bloody Hand reaches no farther than the walls of the city, but the Dark Heresy's influence extends to every city on the face of Einan."

The Hunter studied the Chief Justiciar, searching for words but finding none. The urge to look at the tray of torture implements burned within him, but he fought to keep his eyes firmly fixed on Lord Jahel's face.

Lord Jahel picked up the slim metal tube, and his long, delicate fingers caressed it with care. "Now, I must beg your forgiveness," he said with a shrug and a wan smile, "but it is our custom."

The Hunter winced as the needle plunged through his skin, deep into his muscle. He felt an odd suction, and watched horrified as the glass tube filled with bright red blood—his blood. When Lord Jahel finally removed the needle, his arm throbbed from the puncture.

"Here in the Hole, we take a small sample of blood from each of the visitors passing through our humble halls. A ritual to the Watcher, you understand." He placed the device on the tray, covering it with a cloth before turning to face the Hunter once more. "I would ask you—"

Lord Jahel's words were interrupted midsentence by a dark figure slipping into the room. The man's clothing was cut in the style of the Heresiarch robes, but they were black rather than the bright crimson of the regular guard. The only sign of red—the color of the Heresiarchs—was a thin band hemming the robes.

A Dark Heresiarch, the Hunter thought.

The Chief Justiciar turned his attention to the man, who had sidled up to him and spoken in his ears. A whispered conversation ensued, their words too quiet for the Hunter to hear.

"You have your orders," Lord Jahel finally said, giving the man a commanding nod. The Dark Heresiarch saluted and slipped from the room as silently as he had entered.

"Your forgiveness, dear Hunter," said Lord Jahel, turning to face his captive once more, "but I must attend to an urgent matter. I trust you will be comfortable here for the time being. But, oh dear!" he exclaimed, raising an eyebrow, "you're bleeding. Allow me."

The Chief Justiciar removed a white handkerchief from the breast pocket of his dark robes. He gently dabbed at the spot where the needle had pricked the Hunter's arm, wiping away the trickle of blood.

"No sense wasting any of that blood of yours," he said, giving the Hunter a thin smile. "You'll need it all when you are visited by the Grand Master. Oh, what a treat it will be!" He accompanied his words with a delighted clap of his hands.

With careful movements, Lord Jahel draped the bloody cloth over Soulhunger.

"Now, if you will excuse me," he said, giving the Hunter a short bow, "I will return shortly." Turning, Lord Jahel strode from the room. The door *clicked* shut behind him, the sound of a deadbolt locking from the outside echoing through the heavy wooden panels.

The Hunter was once more alone.

Shit, the Hunter thought, his eyes flicking to the iron tool. *I can't let them use that on me.*

Panic welled up in his chest, threatening to overwhelm his rational mind. He had to break free before his captors returned. Would he have enough time?

In desperation, his eyes raced around the room, taking in its scant detail. The torches on the wall barely illuminated the large chamber, but his eyes had adjusted to the dim lighting. He took deep calming breaths, trying to force his mind to examine his predicament with cool logic.

The padlocks on the chains looked far too strong to break, and he had neither the skill to pick locks nor the tools to attempt it. He saw no key on the table, and even if his captors had carelessly left a key there, the table—and the items laid out upon it—lay well out of his reach.

He had only one option.

Let's see how strong these chains are.

He wasn't certain he could break the chains, but had to try. His eyes roved over every crack and crevice in the masonry, looking for a weakness.

Something caught his eye—could it be dust? He stooped to examine the ring holding his chains to the stone wall, and a smile crossed his face. He gripped the ring and tugged, feeling it give slightly.

Excellent.

He moved to the full length of his chains and pulled them taut. The thick muscles of his arms and shoulders corded, the veins in the Hunter's neck standing out as he hauled on the manacles with all his prodigious strength. His legs ached, his back arched, and the blood rushed through his body.

Something within the wall shifted. His ears detected the sound of metal grating on stone. A determined grin split his face, and he heaved once more, throwing his willpower and every ounce of force into his arms and legs. The place where the needle had pricked his arm still throbbed, but he ignored the pain.

With the eternal slowness of stone, the ring pulled free of the wall and clattered to the floor. The Hunter stumbled and fell forward, barely managing to catch himself. Without hesitation, he leapt to his feet and raced to examine the ring he had pulled free from the wall. Lifting it from the floor, he pushed the spike back into the masonry. It pulled free once more with a gentle tug.

Perfect, he thought.

Moving to the door, he strained to open it, but it refused to budge. He gave up the effort, knowing it was futile.

So how do I get out of here?

He had no way to break down the door, so his only choice was to wait until a guard returned.

Time to play the compliant prisoner once more.

The Hunter embedded the spike into the wall and resumed his original position—arms hanging by his side, shoulders slouched, his head drooping, and a mask of fatigue painting his face. With the patience of a hunter, he waited, adopting the demeanor of a compliant prisoner.

It seemed an eternity passed before he heard the *clang* of the heavy deadbolt being shot. He didn't look up as the door opened, but kept his eyes fixed on the floor. Heavy boots tramped into the room, and he knew immediately it was not the Chief Justiciar.

He raised his eyes, plastering a look of weary compliance on his face. The guard stared at him impassively, as if the Hunter was just another one of Lord Jahel's playthings.

The man stood nearly as tall as the Hunter, though with considerably thicker arms and neck. His hand toyed with the hilt of his sword, and his stance showed the casual ease of a man who knew which end went where. This guard wore the same red-trimmed black cloak as the man who had called Lord Jahel away.

"What is your name?" asked the Hunter, his voice low.

The guard said nothing, choosing to ignore him. He turned his back on the Hunter and strode to the table on the side of the room. The Dark Heresiarch held Soulhunger high, studying the multi-faceted gem set in its hilt in the light of the torch.

"What is your name, Heresiarch?" the Hunter repeated.

Still the guard ignored him.

"*Tell me*," menace filled the Hunter's voice, and he coiled his body in anticipation, "what name shall I give the Long Keeper when he comes for you?"

The Dark Heresiarch turned to growl at the Hunter, just in time to meet the end of a chain whipping at his face. At the end of the chain hung the thick metal spike that had been set into the wall. The guard's skull collapsed beneath the force of the impact, and brain matter splattered across the table and the wall behind him. His body wobbled for a moment before slumping to the ground, blood still pouring from where his nose had been.

He ripped the other chain from the wall and raced to the dead guard's side. Fumbling at the man's belt, he searched for the keys. His fingers closed around the hard metal of the key ring, and a triumphant laugh bubbled up from his chest. Within seconds, the chains fell from his arms and legs.

"Damn, but that feels good," he growled to the empty room, rubbing at his chafed wrists.

Soulhunger still lay clutched in the guard's lifeless fingers, and the Hunter stooped to retrieve the blade.

"Oh, how I have missed you," he said, relishing the feel of the worn leather clenched in his fist.

One more item caught his eye: the scrap of cloth Lord Jahel had used to wipe away his blood. He stuffed the bit of fabric into the pocket of his worn breeches and turned his attention to the door. It took a few moments of shuffling through the keys before he found the right one, and he quickly inserted it into the lock. The key turned with a satisfying *click*.

The Hunter threw open the door and it swung on silent hinges, revealing the darkened corridor beyond. He peered around the corner, wary of any guards, but only empty halls greeted him.

He moved like a wraith, bare feet padding silently along the stone floor of the passageway. Soulhunger pulsed in his hand, throbbing in time with his quickened pulse. He could only guess in which direction lay freedom, but he was just glad to be out of that cell. Armed with Soulhunger, he could fight his way free of the Hole.

Voices sounded from beyond an open door, and the Hunter shrank back into the darkness of the hall to listen.

"...have your orders," spoke a voice. "Go to these residences and collect anyone you find. They may give Lord Jahel the answers he wants. If not, they will be useful if our prisoner proves reticent."

"Of course, captain," replied a second voice. "I'll send a detachment to this house on Fishmonger's Street, and a second squad will join the men already outside the building behind Singwood Croft."

Fishmonger's Street, Singwood Croft. The Hunter's mind raced at the familiar street names.

"Good," the captain's voice rang out, "and make sure that you send two more squads to the Beggar's Quarter. He's got a huge place on Kadderly Row, and there are a lot of bodies to round up."

Kadderly Row, he thought. The Dark Heresiarchs were talking about his safe houses.

A sinking feeling rose in his gut, and the faces of Old Nan, Arlo, Ellinor, and the others flashed through his mind. *Bloody twisted hell. They wouldn't...*

"And don't hesitate to put down any of the filthy creatures that try to resist," the captain ordered.

"Aye, sir," spoke the second man.

The bastards! He gripped Soulhunger tighter, feeling the rage build within him.

Kill!

Yes. We will kill them, and anyone else who lays a hand on my friends.

Rage flooded him, and he charged into the room, eyes blazing, teeth bared in a snarl. The guards stared at him in horror, but neither had time to cry out before the Hunter reached them.

The Hunter wrapped an arm around the captain's neck even as Soulhunger opened the other guard's throat. The man's eyes bulged as fear seized his body. The Hunter twisted, and the Dark Heresiarch's spine snapped with an audible *crack*. The captain slumped to the floor, splashing in the puddle of blood leaking from his comrade's corpse.

Power coursed through the Hunter as Soulhunger drank its fill. He stalked from the room without a backward glance. His feet left bloody footprints on the cold stone floor, but he didn't care.

I can't let these bastards hurt anyone! He thought of the beggars living in his building, the outcasts he had come to call his friends. *I have to protect them.*

He sprinted down the hall, relishing the feeling of stretching his muscles again. An inferno of rage burned in his chest as he raced through the empty corridors of the Hole. He had no idea where to go, but simply ran, desperate to escape and save his friends.

The Mistress' own luck was with him. The twisting corridors led him to an exit, a single Heresiarch barring his escape. A snarl of rage burst from the Hunter's throat, and he raced toward the guard with every bit of speed he could summon. Soulhunger plunged into the man's gaping mouth, drinking deep.

The man died with a wordless scream, his lifeless eyes staring vacantly as the Hunter raced into the Voramian night.

Chapter Nineteen

The Hunter slipped across the rooftops of Lower Voramis, power coursing in his veins. The chill night air sent a shiver down his spine; the breeches he wore offered little protection from the wind whipping across the rooftops.

The stench of refuse that permeated the Beggar's Quarter drifted toward him. He scanned the building ahead for signs of life. No sound came from within, and he saw no movement. He closed his eyes and cast out his senses, letting his consciousness drift. Soulhunger pulsed in his hand, whispering its desire for blood.

The weapon had changed. It seemed more...*alive* since the death of the Beggar Priest. The blade had fed less than a half hour before, and yet it throbbed every time it came within a few feet of a living human being. The insistent demand for death had grown louder, and it was harder for the Hunter to ignore the voice in his mind.

No matter, he thought. *Tonight that will serve me well.*

He slid the door to his safe house open, taking pains to move in absolute silence. Darkness filled the rooms beyond, but Soulhunger's voice burned in the back of the Hunter's mind. The blade had found its prey.

There's someone here.

Soulhunger pulled him toward the nearby wall, sensing blood. *We must feed.*

Wait, the Hunter told the blade. *I need to be sure—*

He nearly slipped on something warm and sticky. The Hunter's sensitive nostrils filled with the scent of blood, and the skin of his bare feet crawled. He crouched, slowing his breathing and closing his eyes. Breathing deep, he filled his sensitive nostrils with the scents around him.

The foul, alcoholic stench of the rum Jak drank every time he got his hands on a few coins. The smell of rotting fish that wafted in with Harrn at the end of a day hanging around the docks. The scent of the flowers Filiana sold. After years of living with the beggars, the smells were as familiar to him as his hands.

The scents had already begun to fade, replaced by the foul reek of death from the unmoving bodies. The ones he had called his friends lay still and silent around him in the darkness. Sorrow washed over him, but the fires within him transformed the grief into a burning rage.

Derelana curse you, Lord Jahel. You, and every one of your accursed Dark Heresiarchs, will pay for this.

More scents filtered through the smell of death surrounding him. Dust from the streets. Steel whispering from a leather sheath. Sweat. Fear.

Men.

Men who deserve to pay for what they've done.

He moved without thought, his body responding beyond his control. Instinct took over, and the Hunter stalked through the darkness in silence.

His sensitive ears detected the sound of breathing from the other side of the wall, and he slithered through the shadows toward his prey. He had no need to see the man, for he felt the very beat of his heart. With a silent lunge, the Hunter clamped a hand over the man's mouth. The thug died before he knew what hit him, Soulhunger driving up through the base of his unprotected skull.

One down, thought the Hunter, lowering the man's corpse to the ground. His head spun as Soulhunger fed, power rushing through his body. He felt invigorated, invincible.

He sensed movement around the next corner, and he flowed toward the source of the sound. His foot lashed out, and he heard the sound of a shinbone splintering followed by a loud *thud* as a heavy body hit the floor. The fallen man gurgled for a moment, then lay still. Turning the body over, the Hunter found the man had fallen on his own blade.

Fool, he laughed silently to himself, pushing Soulhunger deep into the man's chest. Power burned in his veins. His heartbeat pounded in his ears.

"Frann?" a voice whispered from the darkness. The Hunter moved toward the sound, slipping a concealed blade from a stuffed eagle hanging on the wall. "Frann, can you hear me?" No answer came from his dead companion. "Shit! He's here! Get him."

Two pairs of feet thudded toward him, but the Hunter melted into the shadows of the room. Moonlight framed the heavy, scarred face of a man wearing dark colors, a bloody fist tattooed on his forehead.

The Bloody Hand.

With lightning speed, the Hunter hurled the blade in his hand. The weapon buried itself deep in the man's eye. The crimson gore gushing from his wound looked almost surreal in the pale moonlight.

Another figure loomed from the darkness, and the Hunter struck out with his free hand. The thug slumped to his knees, gasping and struggling to breathe, his windpipe crushed. Soulhunger's razor edge opened the wheezing man's throat with ease.

He watched with pitiless eyes as the man gasped out his final bloody breath.

Could the Bloody Hand already be aware of my escape? The thought of the Bloody Hand working with the Heresiarchs chilled him to the bone. His safe house had been discovered—whether by the Bloody Hand or the Dark Heresy, it made no difference—and he knew he had to leave quickly.

I have to put a stop to the Bloody Hand and the Dark Heresiarchs before they kill everyone I care about.

The Hunter ignored the blood soaking into the floor, stepping over the dead thugs as if they were nothing more than piles of refuse in the street. He strode to the armoire in the corner of the room, and his fingers probed the top of the furniture, searching for the trigger that would release the lock.

He smiled as it clicked open to reveal an assortment of sharp, bladed weapons.

Perfect.

The scent of his own clothing wafted up to him, and he nearly gagged.

I can't go around Voramis smelling like this.

His eyes turned to his bedroom, beyond which stood a bathing room and a bucket of—he hoped—clean water.

Chapter Twenty

The scent of leather, steel, and fear filled the Hunter's nostrils, mixed with the coppery tang of freshly-spilled blood.

"Fuck," he swore beneath his breath.

He had tried three other safe houses in the last hour, but they had all been filled with Hand thugs or black-clad Dark Heresiarchs. Death had visited each of his houses, every one of the corpses belonging to men and women he had considered friends.

Even the children...

The Hunter had clung to the vain hope that this—his last safe house—would be empty, but he could hear men moving around inside and see the light cast by the torches burning within his building. He sidled along the wall, letting the night hide him from watching eyes. He placed each foot with precision to avoid the puddles of filth dotting the Beggar's Quarter. The hood of his dark cloak obscured all but his glittering eyes from view.

His hand gripped the sword in its sheath on his back, testing it to be certain he could draw it with ease. A slow smile spread across his face, but the grin held no humor. Rage bubbled within his depthless eyes. His heart held only death.

Forsaking stealth, the Hunter raced through the streets leading to his home. With a wicked laugh, he spread his arms wide, as if daring those awaiting him to strike him down. A single crossbow bolt sped toward him, but the archer's poor aim sent the bolt clattering into the darkness.

"Come on, you bastards!"

"The Hunter!" shouted a voice from within the building. Fear tinged the cry, and the Hunter could smell terror on the night air. His fingers closed around the handle of the door, and the force of his anger ripped the flimsy wooden thing from its rusted hinges. He stepped into the room, and the smell of death greeted him—mixing with the scents of human excrement, mold, and refuse.

He took in the scene inside the room. Those he called friends huddled beneath the stern gazes and raised swords of the Dark Heresiarchs, who stared eagerly at the door as if expecting him. As he entered, the swords fell, and more corpses joined the pile of bodies on the floor.

Impotent rage bubbled within him as he saw the beggars slaughtered. Old Nan's empty eyes stared up at him from where she lay on the floor, accusation filling her lifeless stare. Twelve-Fingers Karrl clutched his chest, only three fingers sprouting from his blood-stained hands.

A cry came from the other side of the room. The Hunter's eyes darted toward the source of the sound. Arlo cried in his mother's arms, covered in the blood leaking from the gaping wound in Ellinor's head. The young girl sat dazed against the wall, staring helplessly as one of the Dark Heresiarchs raised his sword to cut off the child's terrified whimpers.

"No!" he cried, throwing himself forward. His sword crashed into the descending blade of the Dark Heresiarch. Soulhunger sank into the man's throat, drenching the Hunter in blood.

The Hunter ripped the blade free of the Dark Heresiarch's neck, turning to face the rest of the men crowding into the building. Soulhunger's pounding voice fueled his rage. Hatred twisted his lips into a snarl.

They are my friends, he thought, imposing himself between the Dark Heresiarchs and the pitiful figures of Ellinor and Arlo. *They are here under my roof, my protection. No more of mine will die this night.*

"Greet the Long Keeper for me, you bastards," he growled, just loud enough for the Dark Heresiarchs to hear.

One stepped forward, snarling. Larger than his companions, the man's bald head shone in the torchlight. A heavy beard covered his face, a large scar slashing through it. "Fucking Hunter," the man cursed, drawing a massive broad sword in ham-sized fists. The huge blade whistled through the air, the force of the blow enough to chop the Hunter in half.

The blade seemed to hang in the air, and he watched it hurtle toward him as if in slow motion. Contempt flooded the Hunter as the massive sword carved its deadly arc.

With fluid grace, he stepped aside. He moved like lightning, flowing across the floor and closing the distance to the huge Heresiarch. Too late, the man realized his error, and struggled to alter the direction of the strike. The Hunter didn't even bother to dodge as the huge sword whistled past his head. Inside the man's guard, the Hunter drove Soulhunger up beneath the bearded chin. The Dark Heresiarch's eyes widened in horror as the tip of the blade protruded from his skull. Blood gushed down the front of his uniform, soaking into the black cloth.

The Hunter bathed in the gore washing over him, letting it stoke the fires of his rage. With a vicious wrench, the Hunter ripped Soulhunger free. Dark blood dripped down his arm, and brain matter clung to the tip of the blade.

"Who's next?"

Two more Dark Heresiarchs charged, short swords flashing in the torchlight. The Hunter bared his teeth in a wordless snarl and swung his long blade with all the force he could muster. His blow knocked the Dark Heresiarchs' weapons aside, and the tip of his sword sliced through the soft flesh of their throats.

A fountain of blood cascaded over him, fueling his desire for revenge. He thrilled in the death around him—the death he brought this night. The fury in his eyes and the horrifying look on his face caused the next pair of guards to halt their advance. One of the men skidded in the slick blood on the floor, losing his footing. The heel of the Hunter's boot crushed his throat, and a quick thrust pierced the eyeball of his fellow.

Power and strength flooded the Hunter with every life Soulhunger took, adding fuel to the furnace of his anger. He offered the Dark Heresiarchs no mercy, ignoring the wounds inflicted by their swords. His blood mingled with the gore covering the floor in an ever-spreading puddle, and still the Hunter's rage demanded more.

The cramped space within the building forced the Dark Heresiarchs to attack him in twos and threes. Their numbers proved no match for his furious onslaught. The Hunter's long sword danced like lightning among the shorter blades of the Heresiarchs, laying open throats and piercing soft flesh. Soulhunger darted in to spill blood wherever an opening presented itself.

His eyes locked on the faces of the Heresiarchs before him, but he saw only the bodies piled on the floor. Beggars they may have been, but to the Hunter, they were the closest thing he had to friends.

As the world around him faded into a blood-soaked haze, his rage transformed once more into sorrow. A lump rose in his throat, and he swallowed hard, fighting back the tears that threatened at the corners of his eyes.

He had no time for sorrow.

The Dark Heresiarchs were well-trained, but tonight they faced the avatar of death. They fought for their lives, their souls. Soulhunger shrieked in the Hunter's mind as it fed him power, but he heard only the beating of his heart and the gentle voices of the friends he would never see again.

Then there were no more. The Hunter whirled around, searching for another victim for his rage-fueled vengeance. He didn't know how many of the Dark Heresiarchs he had killed, and he didn't care. He wanted to kill until the pain faded.

Only lifeless bodies greeted his eyes—the bodies of the Dark Heresiarchs lying atop the corpses of his friends. Rage burned in his chest, overwhelming his senses. Soulhunger pounded in his mind, lusting for more death.

A soft whimper sounded behind him, and he whirled, blade held at the ready. Arlo stood there, staring up at the Hunter, tears streaming down his blood-stained face. The toddler opened his mouth as if trying to speak, but nothing came out.

"Arlo!"

Ellinor struggled out from beneath the dead Heresiarch and raced to her child. She scooped him up in her arms, holding his head against her chest to hide the carnage around him.

The Hunter reached out to comfort her. "Are you—?"

"Stay away!" Ellinor shouted, backing away from him. Her eyes were wide in terror, but it had little to do with the corpses around her.

She was afraid of him.

"Ellinor," he started, "I—"

"Don't hurt us!" she cried, flinching back. "Please, just leave us alone!"

The words hit him like a slap in the face.

"But, I—"

"You're a monster!"

The Hunter looked down at his bloodstained clothes. Crimson gore covered his arms and hands, and dripped from his face.

"Please, Ellinor—" he begged.

With a cry of terror, the girl turned and fled into the night.

The Hunter felt as if a knife had been plunged into his stomach. He couldn't breathe, couldn't think. He watched the slim figure disappear into the darkness of Lower Voramis, at a loss for words.

Turning his back on the carnage, the Hunter stumbled toward the heart of the building, toward the place he called home. The bodies of his friends lay discarded on the floor behind him, but the Hunter couldn't look at them, not wanting to see the accusation in their unseeing eyes.

Where were you? He thought he could hear them asking. *Why didn't you protect us?*

He dimly heard the *click* of the lock opening, and the solid *thunk* of the deadbolt sliding into its housing. The heavy door swung open, and the Hunter pushed into the darkened room beyond. His apartments remained empty and undisturbed.

The scent of fresh blood filled his nose, and, looking down, he saw his dark grey robes covered in gore. It dripped down the front of his clothes, soaking into his pants, filling his boots.

He stripped quickly, casting the fouled garments into a corner of the room and throwing his bloodied weapons onto the room's lone table. He splashed cold water over his face to wash away the blood. The chill calmed his mind and dimmed the heat of his fury. The faces of the Heresiarchs flashed through his mind, the looks of horror as their lives slipped away at the end of his blade.

The Dark Heresiarchs deserve what is coming. They played a part in the death of innocents, on the orders of the accursed Lord Jahel. They will all pay, every Watcher damned one of them.

Numbness and fatigue stole over him, dulling the rage and clouding his mind. He couldn't think clearly. His eyelids drooped, and his limbs felt leaden.

His body moved of its own accord. Looking down, he found he had dressed himself. His boots were neatly tied, his weapons strapped around his waist. He was grateful that Soulhunger's voice remained silent in his mind, its lust for blood temporarily sated.

I need rest, he thought, feeling the weariness in his bones, *but not here.* Not among the bodies.

He no longer had safe houses to flee to—the Bloody Hand and the Dark Heresiarchs had seen to that. The blood of his friends still stained the floors of the places he had called home. He had no desire to look into the empty eyes of those he had wanted so badly to protect.

But where can I go?

He craved anything to distract his mind from the death of the beggars. From his failure to protect his friends. From the look in Ellinor's eyes before she had fled from him.

There has to be a place even the Heresiarchs and the Hand would never think to find me.

The face of Lady Damuria flashed in front of his eyes. It was a foolish idea, but he was desperate. She would be enough to distract him, for a while at least.

Chapter Twenty-One

The Hunter cursed as the sound of shattering crockery pulled Lady Damuria from sleep. She stared into the darkness, searching for the source of the noise..

"H-Hello?" she asked, a quaver in her voice. "Who's there?"

"It is I, my lady."

"L-Lord Anglion?" She pulled her covers close, as if to protect herself. Heavy curtains blocked all light from entering the tower chamber, hiding the Hunter from her sight. Only a sliver of moonlight penetrated the room, casting an ominous glow on the noblewoman's face.

"Yes, my lady," replied the Hunter.

"What brings you here at this hour, my lord?" Fear filled her voice, and she clutched at the thin blankets.

"I'm sorry, my lady, but I had nowhere else to run." The Hunter couldn't keep the deep fatigue from his voice, and it seemed Lady Damuria sensed his exhaustion.

"My dear Harrenth," she said, flinging aside the covers and leaping from her bed. "What has happened?"

She threw her arms around his neck, pressing her body into his. The Hunter felt himself stir in response, but exhaustion won out over desire.

"My-my father," whispered the Hunter, adopting a tone of stunned disbelief, "he's dead, killed by my brother."

"What?" exclaimed the woman in his arms. "Why?"

"My brother wants to take over the family business, and with it, the family fortune. He sent men to kill me as well, and I barely escaped with my life."

"Oh, you poor thing. But—by the gods!" she swore. He stepped forward into a patch of moonlight, and her eyes widened as she saw his face. "You are not Lord Anglion! You have his voice, but the face is different." She opened her mouth to cry out, but the Hunter clamped a hand over it.

"Hush, Giselle," he said, his voice quiet and soothing, "it is I, wearing a disguise."

Doubt filled her eyes as she stared up at him.

"My brother wants to kill me, so I had to adopt a disguise to hide from his assassins." The Hunter had rehearsed his lies as he crept through the shadows of Upper Voramis. "My face is different, but feel my hands and you will know that it is me."

He removed the hand covering her mouth. Hesitation flashed across her face as the Hunter intertwined his fingers with hers.

"Tell me you don't remember these hands caressing you, my lady."

At his gentle touch, she stilled.

"Oh my dear Harrenth, it really *is* you!" she cried. She wrapped her arms around his neck once more, holding him close. "It brings me such sorrow to hear of your dear father. You have my condolences, my lord."

"Thank you, my lady," the Hunter said, "but I must not weep now. I am so sorry to come to you like this, but I knew not where else I could find safety."

"Of course, my lord. You are always welcome here, at least until my husband returns. Can I offer you some wine and food?"

Relief flooded the Hunter and his anxiety drained away. Lady Damuria believed his story.

"Some wine would be wonderful, my lady," he said.

Releasing him, Lady Damuria moved to the thick iron-bound door of her chambers. "Barchai," she called, her voice echoing in the stone corridors beyond. From where the Hunter stood in the deep shadows of the room, he couldn't hear the instructions the lady gave her manservant.

When the well-dressed servant entered the room minutes later, he carried a large tray laden with bread, cheese, fruit, and a large brass pitcher. The manservant's sharp eyes darted around the room as if searching for something, but the Hunter remained hidden in the gloom.

"That will be all, Barchai," Lady Damuria commanded.

"My lady," the servant bowed and retreated. Only once the door had closed behind the man did the Hunter step from the shadows.

"Come, Harrenth, darling," Lady Damuria said, holding out an inviting hand to him. "Join me on the bed." She arranged her hair in a loose coiffure, using an elegant pin to hold it in place. A thin robe hung from the bedpost, and she reached for it. The Hunter watched her wrap it around her shapely form, marveling at how the silken fabric did little to hide her beauty.

"You look exhausted," she said, a smile crossing her face. She had caught him staring.

"To tell the truth, my lady," the Hunter answered, "I have not slept in what seems like weeks. I have been fleeing for my life, and this is the first time I have felt truly relaxed since my father's death."

He loosened his cloak and dropped it to the floor, taking care to wrap his sword belt and Soulhunger within its dark folds. Within moments, he had stripped down to his dark tunic and breeches, and sat beside Lady Damuria.

"Here, have some wine," she held a cup out to him, and he took it with a smile of thanks.

The wine cooled his dry throat, and he emptied the goblet in one long draught. She smiled as she served him more, and he drained it as quickly as he had the first.

"Forgive me my poor manners, my lady," he said with an apologetic smile.

She waved her hand in a dismissive gesture. "No matter, my lord. Given your circumstances, it is fully pardonable." She lay back on the bed with an inviting smile. "Come, lie with me and let me help ease your worries."

The wine had a pleasant warming effect, and heat spread through his body as Lady Damuria's robe fell open to reveal the soft skin beneath. He drained his third cup of wine before climbing into bed beside her.

His pain slipped away as she stroked his hair, placed gentle kisses on his neck, and whispered into his ear. The heat of her soft body drained away the tension of the night, and he allowed the fatigue to wash over him. Lady Damuria's warm, gentle hands massaged his shoulders, kneading the tired flesh.

Gods, that feels good, he thought.

She pushed him over onto his stomach, and climbed atop him. Her weight on his back felt wonderful. He relished the softness of her breasts pressing into him. His muscles relaxed, the pressure of her body stretching his spine. She pushed herself into a sitting position atop his back. He imagined he could feel the heat between her thighs, and his body sent blood rushing toward his groin.

The thrill of the kill overwhelmed him with desire, reminding him why he had come here. It was the distraction he needed, and he pushed all thoughts of death—and of Ellinor's horror-stricken face—from his mind.

Sudden agony flooded him, piercing the muscle and bone of his back. It rushed through him in overwhelming waves—a pain not even the First's dagger thrust to his heart could match.

"What in the fiery hell?"

The Hunter rolled onto his back, throwing Lady Damuria to the bed beside him. He struggled to stand, but his legs refused to obey his commands. The wine had dulled his senses, and the pain drowned out his thoughts.

He reached around, feeling for the weapon lodged in his upper back. It scraped across bone, and a cry of pain burst from his lips. He held the item up to his eyes, and realized with horror that it was the pin that had once held Lady Damuria's hair in place. Blood stained the pin's length—*his* blood.

Numbness radiated through his upper body. His shoulder screamed in pain, but slowly the sensation faded. He couldn't move his arm, and his whole back began to stiffen. His skin crawled, his hands burning from holding the pin.

By the Keeper, he thought, struggling for clarity, *the thing is made of iron. How did she…?*

The iron pin clattered to the floor. He followed it a moment later, his legs collapsing beneath him. The blood pumping in his veins slowed to a sluggish pace. With every beat of his heart, more iron coursed through him.

"How…?" he croaked. His throat tightened, every breath burning in his lungs.

"How did I know who you are, *Hunter?*" Lady Damuria spat the last word at him. "How did I know Lord Anglion never existed?"

She wrapped the robe tighter around her body, covering her nakedness. Stooping, she retrieved the bloody pin from the floor and wiped it on the Hunter's tunic. She straddled him, glaring triumphantly down at him, holding the pin like a weapon.

"My good friend *Lord Jahel* thought it was something I might like to know." She smiled at his look of stunned disbelief.

Her face swam before his eyes, and he struggled to focus. The iron coursing through his body felt like the pricks of a thousand red-hot needles. He fought for every ragged, agonizing breath.

"How dare you come here, after what you did?" Lady Damuria shouted. "You not only used the face of Lord Anglion to enter high society, but you came here and shared my bed after you killed my lord husband." Rage and hate burned on her face.

The Hunter tried to push her off, to stand, to move, but the iron flooding through his body left him weak. Lady Damuria lashed out with the pin. The wicked ornament sliced into his arms, his neck, and his torso. He struggled to cover his face with his arms, which grew number by the moment.

Pain lanced into his chest, penetrating the mind-numbing fog. Looking down, the Hunter saw Lady Damuria's pin embedded in his breast.

"They say you are immortal," she panted, her breath hot on his ear, "and yet here you lie in agony after being stabbed with a simple pin. It seems the great Hunter is not as mighty as the legends claim."

She pushed herself to her feet, and strode to the door. "Barchai," she called, "help me here."

The woman's voice seemed to come from far in the distance. Molten lead rushed through his limbs, setting his body on fire and immobilizing him. Numbness spread through his body, stealing his wits. He couldn't move for the agony.

Rough hands grabbed him by the shoulders, but he could do no more than grunt. The floor moved beneath him, and through his stupor, the Hunter felt his unresisting body being dragged. His ears registered the sound of the balcony doors opening. A cool breeze rushed across his face, the sensation set his skin aflame, intensifying his agony.

The Hunter heard a grunt of effort, felt his body lifted from the floor. Metal pulsed through his veins. Every beat of his heart sent fresh agony racing through him. Lady Damuria hovered over him, a wicked, vicious smile on her face.

"It is a delicious irony that a woman will be the one to kill the legendary Hunter." She grasped his tunic and pulled him close for a final kiss. "Farewell, and may the embrace of the Long Keeper take you away to the eternal torment you so richly deserve."

With a strength born of her anger, Lady Damuria pushed his unresisting body over the railing. He seemed to hang suspended in the air for a long moment, long enough to hear Lady Damuria's final curse.

"Fucking Hunter..."

Gravity took hold, and he began the long plunge to the unyielding cobblestones far below.

* * *

Broken and bleeding, the Hunter lay unmoving on the empty street.

Am...I...dead?

His chest rose and fell with effort, his breath bubbling in his chest. His arms and legs refused to move.

The iron...poison.

A familiar scent wafted toward him, penetrating the muddle in his dying brain.

Leather, steel, and lilies.

Delicate hands lifted him from the street. It seemed as if he drifted on a cloud. The world moved around him, but he felt nothing. His eyes simply stared unseeing into the starry night.

What...what's happening?

Soft light embraced him as the sun rose, clouds turning the morning sky a gloomy grey. He heard the distant rumble of thunder, tasted a storm on the air. The scent of rain filled his nostrils, but the gentle breeze flowing over his face carried with it that familiar smell once again.

Why do I know that scent?

A face flashed through his mind, a face locked away in his memories. *Her* face.

He remembered Her. He remembered her scent.

She smelled of rain.

Delicate drops fell on his face, their cool moisture soothing his mangled body and numb mind. The memory of his mystery woman's face faded as pain filled his world, and he slipped into unconsciousness.

Chapter Twenty-Two

The heavy, sickly-sweet smell of incense—the sort lit in the temples on Penance Day—filled the Hunter's nostrils. Darkness pressed in around him like a weight, but the Hunter's mind clawed its way through the pain, as if crawling through thick mud.

His head pounded with such force that it seemed an army waged war inside his skull. Every bone in his body clamored as he struggled to sit upright. Drained, devoid of strength, even the slightest motion required effort.

"Hush," said a quiet voice. A gentle hand pushed him back down. "Best not to try sitting up just yet."

He pried open eyelids heavy with fatigue. Vision swimming, he struggled to focus on the figure in front of him.

A lined, weathered face stared down at him. The scent of vellum, dust, and a smell the Hunter recognized as a soothing balm for aching joints emanated from the man, who looked to be almost as old as the temple itself. Liver spots dotted his skin and bald scalp, and the simple grey robe hung loose on his frame. His arthritic knuckles twisted his hands into grotesque shapes. Decades of hard work and constant stooping had left his back eternally hunched. A long white beard hung to the man's emaciated waist, and a sharp nose sat between thick eyebrows. His eyes, however, burned with a fierce intelligence that his age had not dimmed.

The Hunter tried to speak, but the priest held up a hand. "You had a nasty fall and barely escaped the Long Keeper's embrace. Might want to give yourself a bit of time to heal before you move."

The old man pulled back the Hunter's eyelids to stare into his eyes, measured his pulse at his neck, and probed the Hunter's ribs with an indelicate finger. His ministrations made the Hunter wince, but he had no strength to resist.

"It's a good thing you were brought here when you were," the man said, staring down at his unmoving patient. "You were a hair's breadth away from death, what with the iron in your blood and every bone in your body shattered. You heal quickly, but it was a close thing even so."

The Hunter struggled to speak, and this time managed to rasp out a few words. "Who…where…?" Even this small effort left him drained.

"Hmm," mused the man, "perhaps you need more time to heal." He disappeared from the Hunter's view for a moment, and when he returned, he held a delicate porcelain cup in his gnarled hands. Steam rose from the bitter, foul-smelling brew, which he poured down the Hunter's throat.

Gasping at the heat, the Hunter fought vainly to push the priest away. The old man had surprising strength in his arms, and the Hunter found himself unable to put up much of a fight.

"Enough," the old man said, his voice sharp. "Rest, and we will speak when you awake once more."

An unnatural lethargy stole over the Hunter's limbs. *The…tea,* he thought, tasting the bitter brew. *What…was…in…it?* Fear flashed through him.

He tried to stay awake, tried to hold off the effects of the tea, but slowly his mind calmed. His tension melted away, and with it his fear. He felt no need to escape, to run away. Though he had no idea where he was, it had the feel of a sanctuary, a place of peace.

A soothing warmth crept through his body, and he drifted in and out of fitful sleep, floating in a painless void.

* * *

He awoke, his eyes snapping open. The pounding in his head had subsided, the pain in his limbs fading. His side no longer ached when he breathed.

A candle burned low on the table, casting dancing shadows on the room's bare walls. Turning his head, the Hunter found his caretaker still sitting beside his bed, reclining in a comfortable chair. His twisted fingers gripped a tome that looked as ancient as the man himself.

The Hunter tried to sit up, but his body was still too weak. He slumped back, exhausted.

At the sound, the white-haired man turned to look at him. "Ah," he said, with a small smile, "you are awake. Wonderful."

With delicate care, he placed the ribbon in the book to mark his place and set the volume on the table. He groaned as he climbed to his feet, rubbing his back as he bent to examine the Hunter.

"Where am I?" rasped the Hunter. "Who are you?" He coughed, his throat dry.

"Forgive me, Hunter," said the man, "you must be parched."

Upon the table sat an ornamental blue teapot, which stood out as the single spot of color in the stark simplicity of the room. From it, the man poured steaming liquid into a small cup, which he brought to the Hunter.

The Hunter hesitated, unsure of what the tea contained. He sniffed, trying to detect the ingredients.

Seeing the Hunter's hesitant expression, the old man gave him a hard look. "Drink," he said. "It won't put you to sleep again. It's a healing tea that should have you back on your feet quickly."

The Hunter grimaced at the bitter taste of the dark tea, but emptied the cup. His eyes took in the room around him. There was little but the stone walls and a plain wooden door to look at, the room bare of furnishings save for his bed, the table, and the man's simple chair.

His eyes fell on Soulhunger, which lay on the table, still in its sheath. The dagger's voice whispered quietly in the back of his mind, anger emanating from the blade. His hand jerked of its own accord, as if to reach for his weapon.

"I wouldn't," said the old man, giving him a hard look. "You have a long way to go before you're up and about."

"Where am I?" the Hunter croaked, his voice weak.

"The House of Need."

The temple of the Beggar Priests. The Hunter's heart sank. His eyes flashed to the man standing over him, uneasiness filling him as he saw the simple grey robes—and the blue rings around his collar.

A priest. The three rings marked him as a high-ranking member of the Beggar God's clergy.

"By the look on your face," said the priest, lines of anger around his mouth, "you've realized the gravity of your situation." His eyes turned hard, and he clenched his jaw. "After what you did to Brother Securus..." He trailed off, letting the words hang in the air.

The Hunter's unease blossomed into panic, and his eyes flicked to Soulhunger on the table. He tensed, ready to leap out of bed at the first sign of danger.

"Fear not," the priest said, holding up a hand to forestall action. "If I was going to kill you, I'd simply have left you outside our door when *she* left you for dead."

The Hunter studied the old priest, trying to read his expression. The priest appeared to speak the truth, but the Hunter refused to let his guard down. Not here.

The voice in the Hunter's mind cried out in revulsion at being in the temple, but the pain of his injuries drowned it out. It faded to a dull, complaining whisper as he lay back, sipping the bitter tea. He studied the room around him with wary eyes, waiting in tense silence for the priest to speak.

"My name," said the cleric, "is Father Reverentus. As you have no doubt guessed, I am a servant of the Beggar God."

"What am I doing here?" the Hunter croaked, his throat dry.

"You were brought here to die," the priest replied. "The woman who brought you here said you fell from a high place."

"Woman?" the Hunter asked, curious. A memory of a familiar scent drifted through his mind. "Who was she?"

"Her face was covered, and she refused to give me a name," Reverentus said, shrugging. "She said you needed our help and left you here. It turns out that was the best thing she could have done."

"Why is that?" the Hunter asked.

"The sisters at The Sanctuary have been trained to deal with more mundane injuries. Given your...unique physiology, I dare say they would have been far out of their depth."

"Unique physiology?" the Hunter asked, confusion mixing with his anger at the priest's vague answers. "What in the Watcher's name does that mean?"

The priest stared at him for a moment, disbelief and skepticism written on his face. Then, slowly, realization dawned, and he nodded.

"Of course," replied the priest. "You don't know who you are. *What* you are." He seemed unsurprised at the Hunter's ignorance.

"Stop being cryptic, priest. What do you know about me?"

The priest lowered himself into the chair, his joints creaking. Leaning back, he steepled his fingers and stared at the Hunter.

"I know *everything* about you, Hunter," he said, his voice slow. "How much of that I will tell you remains to be seen. After what you've done…"

"I've done nothing more than what I was paid to do," snapped the Hunter. "Yes, I killed your priest. Is that what you want to hear? Do you expect an apology from me?"

"No," replied the old priest, anger flashing in his eyes. "I expect no apology from a creature like you. As you say, you were just doing what you were paid to do."

The Hunter tried to sit up, but his body refused to cooperate. Breathing hard, his strength fleeing, he fell back.

"Yes," said Reverentus, his voice hard, "you will be weak for days to come, unless drastic measures are taken to reverse the effects of the iron."

"And now that you have me in your clutches," snarled the Hunter, "you want to kill me in retribution for the death of your priest."

Anger flashed in the old cleric's eyes, and his gaze traveled to Soulhunger where it lay on the table. His gnarled fingers twitched, as if aching to reach out and grasp the blade.

"While you deserve death," said Father Reverentus, visibly struggling to control his anger, "let's just say that the situation demands we take a different approach. As a result of your actions, we find ourselves in need of your services."

The Hunter sat staring, his mouth agape. He struggled to find the words, but none came. After a long moment, laughter bubbled from his chest.

"The Beggar Priests," he chortled, "in need of an assassin!" His laugh turned to a cough, and a spasm of pain racked his body. When the agony passed, he studied the old priest, a sarcastic grin splitting his face. "Did someone take one of the temple's candlesticks?" he mocked. "Or run off with the collection plate?"

The priest failed to find humor in the Hunter's words, and sat with a mirthless expression on his face until the Hunter's laughter faded to weak chuckles.

"Had your fun?" the old man demanded. "Are you ready to hear why you still live, even after what you've done?"

"Tell me, old man," the Hunter said, his voice as hard as the glare on Reverentus's face.

"Then listen well, Hunter. Listen, and you may learn the truth of your past, as well as the reason we have brought you back from the Keeper's embrace."

The truth of my past? The Hunter's mind raced. Long had he wondered about the holes in his memory. *If this is a chance to find out more, it's worth letting the priest speak his piece.*

His eyes wandered once more to Soulhunger where it lay on the table. *I can always leave, if necessary.*

"To explain your part in all of this, I must tell you an ancient tale, one that few in Voramis—or the world, for that matter—have ever heard." The old man's voice rang out with a strength that belied his age. "In order to understand just what you are, Hunter, you must know whence you came."

Father Reverentus's voice changed as he spoke, growing strong and resonant.

"Our world has always been ruled by thirteen gods, among them the great Kharna—god of war. Einan was his proving ground, for he led the thirteen gods to victory over the ancient beings who once claimed this world as their own, in the time before time ever was. The other gods held him in high esteem, and none save Kiro, the Master, wielded more power in the Council of Gods."

The priest warmed to the topic, his face growing more animated as he spoke.

"By the side of Kharna stood his radiant goddess of devotion, love, and beauty, the fair Alzara. Together, these two gods stood for all of the virtues to which mankind aspires."

A smile wreathed the priest's face for a moment, but his expression darkened as he continued. "Then came the day Kharna no longer contented himself with being just one god among many. He sought to rule over *all* the gods, to replace the Master on his throne."

"He waged war on the other gods, a terrible war that shook the heavens and the earth. He summoned foul creatures from the depths of some unknown hell to serve as his minions, and to wreak death and havoc on the world. He transformed himself into the god of destruction and bloodlust."

The Hunter listened to the priest's story, though he was tempted to protest that he had heard the tales of the War of Gods—all of Voramis had.

"Humanity suffered greatly at the hands of the demons during the War of Gods, and the gods found themselves losing the battle. Only one god, the Swordsman, could stand against Kharna. He rallied the other gods in the fight against the Destroyer, and met Kharna in combat over the mountains of Pellean. Their struggle tore mountains apart, caused the sea to rise and swallow entire continents. While the Swordsman fought the Destroyer, Kharna's army of demons killed humans by the millions. The blood of the fallen fed the Destroyer, increasing his power until it seemed as if he would prevail over the Swordsman."

"Only thanks to the trickery of the Illusionist and the Watcher in the Dark did the gods manage to stop Kharna from destroying the world. The Swordsman sacrificed himself in order to stop the Destroyer. He held Kharna fast, even as the Destroyer's blade pierced his heart, giving the Watcher the opportunity to stab him with an iron blade. The iron poisoned Kharna, slowing him and allowing the Illusionist to create a spell to bind him."

"The eleven remaining gods, seeing what Kharna had done, knew they must combine their powers in order to stop him. They banished the Destroyer to the Hell from whence he had summoned the demons. His consort, the beautiful Alzara, wept for her lost lover. She wandered the heavens in search of his true spirit—the spirit of the Kharna that once was, the noble, valiant god of war. She became the Lonely Goddess, ever weeping for her lost love, the god who very nearly ended the world."

Father Reverentus paused to take a sip of his tea. When he spoke again, his words came more slowly, his voice contemplative.

"This is the tale of the War of Gods told by the priests to the people, but there is more to the story—much more that few today have ever been told." The old cleric shifted in his chair, trying to find a comfortable position.

The pause only served to rouse the Hunter's curiosity. "Go on, priest," he said, trying to hide his eagerness. Despite his mistrust of the priest, the tale fascinated the Hunter. He had heard the same legends as the rest of Einan, but the idea that there was more to it intrigued him.

"Patience," the old priest said with a smile. He seemed to find a comfortable position, and he studied the Hunter once more.

"In order to maintain the cosmic balance," Reverentus said, his voice solemn, "there must always be thirteen gods—or so the ancient texts say. While the blades of the Destroyer had killed the Swordsman's body, his spirit lived on. His corpse was interred deep in the ground beneath where his temple now stands.

"As for Kharna, the Destroyer, the gods knew he could not be destroyed without threatening the very fabric of the world. They entrapped his spirit in the deepest of the forgotten hells, but the shell of his flesh remained. The gods changed his body, transforming him from the glorious, noble Kharna he had once been into a broken creature. In an attempt to teach him humility, they gave him a name that would forever remind him of his place."

"The Beggar God?" the Hunter asked, incredulous. "The Beggar God was once the Destroyer?"

"Yes," the priest responded with a simple nod. "It is a hard thing to swallow, and few today would believe. And yet, there are those who know the undeniable truth. The Beggar God *was* created by the gods as most of Voramis believe, but he was created from the body of the banished Destroyer."

"Watcher's breath!" breathed the Hunter. His mind raced, and curiosity burned within him.

But if all this is true, how do I fit into it? He wanted to know more—to know how he was connected to it all—yet Father Reverentus seemed in no hurry to talk. The old cleric simply sat and sipped his tea, an enigmatic smile on his face.

"Keeper damn you, priest," the Hunter growled, his impatience mounting. "Finish your story, or I'll—"

"Do what?" demanded the priest, his eyes flashing again. "Leap from that bed and run your accursed dagger through me like you did Brother Securus? You'd steal my soul from my body as you did his?"

The Hunter's mouth hung open, his thoughts racing. *How does he know of Soulhunger, of what it can do? How much is he not telling me?*

Rage burned through the priest's mask of calm as he leapt to his feet and shouted, "I wish you would attempt it, Hunter." The man's glare pierced him like a hot knife. "I may not be as young as I once was, but you're too weak to do more than lie there. By the gods, it would be sweet justice for what you did to Brother Securus." The old man's hands flexed and relaxed, his chest heaving with rage as he stared at the Hunter.

The priest's outburst took the Hunter by surprise, and he gaped up at the fury in the old man's eyes. A tense silence filled the room as they stared at each other. Then, with a visible effort, the old priest unclenched his fists and took deep breaths, as if trying to calm himself. He sat back down, his expression carefully neutral.

"Enough of that," the priest said, his voice tight and clipped. "I will continue with my tale. But first, some tea."

Reverentus stood and poured tea into both cups, handing one to the Hunter before reaching for his own. The old priest dashed the now-tepid liquid down his throat. His knees popped as he sat once more, and, steepling his fingers, resumed speaking in a controlled voice.

"The gods had cast down the Destroyer, but when they turned their eyes to the world below, they saw it had been ruined. Death, destruction, and horror had been unleashed upon the world, and Kharna's demons still roamed free. The gods sought to cast out all of the demons summoned by the Destroyer, sending the creatures back to their hells. Now we come to the part of the tale that few alive today know."

The priest's tale mesmerized the Hunter, and he leaned forward, eager to hear more.

"After the fall of their god," Father Reverentus continued, "the demons discovered a way to hide from the faces of the gods. They took on mortal form, masquerading as humans and living among them. As long as they kept their true form hidden and never used their powers, the gods could not tell them apart from the humans.

"For long years, demons lived among mankind, evading the gaze of the gods. These demons-turned-humans discovered the pleasures of man, particularly the joys of intimacy between man and woman. In their human forms, they were able to reproduce. The offspring born of this unholy union were more than human, but not fully demon."

The Hunter's mind raced. *Could it be…?*

"Eventually," the priest continued, "the gods discovered their secret and cast them out of the world. They gathered together all of their half-human offspring, and debated what to do with them. After much counsel, the gods determined that these demonic progeny were a plague that needed to be eradicated. These creatures were greater than the humans with whom they shared the world, and would ever be a threat.

"The gods destroyed hundreds of thousands of the demonic offspring, but the Beggar God intervened. He pled for mercy, reasoning that the creatures were still half-human and thus deserved a chance to live. His arguments swayed the gods, who decided to let the last handful of them remain on Einan.

"However," Father Reverentus said, raising a finger as if lecturing a recalcitrant student, "not all the gods contented themselves with this judgment. Derelana, Lady of Vengeance and lover to the Swordsman, placed a curse on these half-demon progeny. 'Let them eternally wander the world lost and alone,' she proclaimed. The gods erased the creatures' memories and spread them across the face of Einan, never to find one another.

"Though the gods allowed these creatures to live, mankind never forgave them for the sins of their hellish fathers. The followers of the Lady of Vengeance, the Warrior Priests, hunted them to extinction in revenge for the death and destruction brought on the world by the demons. As far as we know, all of the Forgotten Ones have been killed—save one."

The priest stared at the Hunter, studying his expression.

"What?" asked the Hunter, impatient to hear the rest of the story.

"In the tongue of the Serenii, the 'Bucelarii' means 'forgotten ones'. The Bucelarii are the offspring of the demons, and only one of them remains living to this day."

Both Dannaros and the Beggar Priest called me by that name.

Realization dawned on him.

"I am that *one*. I am the last Bucelarii."

"Yes," the old priest nodded, "the last of a race all but wiped from the face of Einan. Though you remember little of your life, you have wandered our world for thousands of years."

The Hunter sat in stunned silence, struggling to take in the priest's revelation. His thoughts whirled in a chaotic jumble, yet relief mixed with the horror. He had finally found an answer to a question he had long pondered.

I am a Bucelarii, the thought repeated itself.

"So you're telling me," he said, his voice hesitant, "I am the immortal offspring of hellish creatures who roamed the world thousands of years ago, in the days of the gods?"

"In essence, yes." Father Reverentus said, nodding.

"And I'm the only one of my kind left?"

"As far as we know, yes," the priest replied. He seemed to see the confusion on the Hunter's face. "I know it's a lot to take in, so I'll give you a moment."

The old priest climbed slowly to his feet. His gnarled fingers gripped the handle of the teapot, and he walked toward the door.

"I'll be back in a few minutes," he said, his voice filled with understanding. "When I return, I will try to answer any questions you may have."

The old man's departure went all but unnoticed by the Hunter, who lay unmoving in his bed, his stomach roiling and his thoughts filled with confusion.

I am the descendant of demons.

His mind, fractured by the overwhelming information, struggled to absorb everything. Chills coursed through him, yet cold sweat rolled down his chest. His clammy hands began to shake, and blood pounded in his ears.

Half-demon. Bucelarii. Last of my race.

Despite the disbelief flooding him, he felt an odd sense of relief. It all made sense—his long life, his inability to die, the effects of iron.

It could fit.

Though it may not have been what he had expected, he finally had answers about who he was—*what* he was.

But a demon? It was hard for him to believe it, and yet the priest had said it with no hesitation in his voice. *Is it even possible?*

A memory flashed through his mind, of a tapestry he had seen years ago in the Temple of Heroes. It depicted horrible creatures of nightmare, ravaging the world of Einan as the gods waged war in the heavens above them. He had mocked the inhuman shapes, but the very idea of being related to the creatures appalled and filled him with revulsion.

Minutes passed in numb silence. Visions of terrifying demonic hordes rampaged through the Hunter's mind, and with increasing horror, he saw his face among the ranks of monsters. His heart thumped in his chest, his stomach churned, and he felt as if he would vomit.

The sound of the door opening broke him from his reverie. In one hand, Father Reverentus clasped a cloth-bound bundle to his breast, the teapot held in the other. The bundle clanked as the priest placed it on the table.

Reverentus filled the Hunter's cup with steaming tea, and, moving with care, passed it to his patient. In his stupor, the Hunter hardly noticed the scalding liquid burning his mouth.

"A bit much to take in, I see," said the old priest, nodding in understanding. "You'll want proof that I'm speaking the truth, won't you?"

The Hunter nodded again.

"Very well," Father Reverentus said. He rested ancient fingers on Soulhunger, which still lay in its sheath on the table.

The weapon still sat in its sheath, but…

"Soulhunger?" the Hunter asked, reaching out as if to touch the blade. The dagger whispered gently in the back of his mind, its words filling his mind. "That is your proof?"

"Soulhunger, you call the blade?" The priest mused on this for a moment. "A fitting name," he said, nodding, "given its purpose."

"Purpose?"

"Of course," the priest said, almost apologetically, "you wouldn't know the origin of the blade." He pulled it from its sheath, holding it up to the light of the candle "This," he said, an odd tightness in his voice, "is the last of the weapons forged by the Destroyer for his demonic army."

The old priest winced as he held the blade, and Soulhunger's voice protested, sounding angry in the Hunter's mind. As the Hunter watched, Father Reverentus seemed to age a decade in the space of a few heartbeats. It looked as if just gripping the blade required tremendous effort.

Slowly, the cleric sheathed Soulhunger, almost dropping it on the table. He sucked in deep breaths, leaning against the wall to steady himself.

"The blade," Reverentus said, his words slow, pain written on his face, "as with all demon-forged weapons, hungers for blood. It ever seeks to quench its thirst with the souls of its victims." The old priest turned blazing eyes to the Hunter. "In the tongue of demons, it is named Thanal Eth' Athaur. Loosely translated, the name means 'Gateway to Undying Decay'. These weapons fueled Kharna with power in his fight against the gods."

"That sounds a bit far-fetched, priest," the Hunter said. "It's just a weapon, after all."

"Is it?" Father Reverentus asked, his gaze piercing. "You've heard its voice in your mind, haven't you? Whispering for blood…" His voice trailed off, and his eyes glazed. Long moments passed with the priest lost in his thoughts.

"How did you know?" the Hunter asked. His words seemed to snap the cleric back to reality.

"That you can hear its voice in your mind?" Reverentus asked, and the Hunter nodded. "Because it tried to speak to me, too." The priest shuddered at the thought. "And because my order has been hunting this blade—and all like it—for thousands of years."

"Your order?" the Hunter questioned. "The Beggar Priests? Aren't you just a lot of do-gooders helping those in need?"

"Aye, many of us are," Father Reverentus nodded, his eyes flashing at the Hunter's mocking words. He hesitated, as if weighing the decision to reveal more.

"If you want my services," the Hunter said, "you'll need to tell me whatever it is that you're considering holding back."

"There are," the priest said in a reluctant voice, glaring at the Hunter, "a select number of Beggar Priests chosen, initiated into a secret order."

"Secret order?" the Hunter demanded.

"Yes," the priest replied. "We serve the Beggar God, and are charged with preventing the return of the Destroyer."

He stood tall, and his voice grew strong as he spoke. Pride filled the old priest's voice.

"We are the ones who hunt down the unseen threats, who protect mankind from the atrocities that would tear their minds apart with horror. We are the last line of defense against the darkness. We are the ones who forever watch, to prevent the return of demons to this world."

He gazed down at the Hunter, fire burning in his eyes.

"We are the Cambionari."

Chapter Twenty-Three

"Cambionari?" The Hunter echoed the unfamiliar name. Soulhunger's protests grew strident, and the pounding in his head rose to a painful crescendo. It seemed the dagger had heard it before, though the Hunter had no memory of it.

"Yes," said Reverentus, his voice somber. "You have not heard of us, but we are the only reason that the world as we know it still exists. We have killed creatures of nightmares, slain thousands of hellspawn, and hunted down Bucelarii. We have stopped the demons from returning to this world time and again."

That explained Soulhunger's anger at the presence of the priest. Something about Reverentus' words made the Hunter curious.

"Wait," he asked, disbelief filling his voice, "demons returning to the world? You speak madness, priest!"

"You don't believe me?"

"Demons are creatures of legend, of myth," the Hunter snorted. "They were sent back to the hells during the War of Gods."

"Can you truly believe that just because the demons were cast out by the gods of Einan, they would stay away forever? They terrorized this planet, feeding on the flesh of humans. They ruled this world under the Destroyer. Is it so hard to believe that they would do *anything* to rule once more?"

The Hunter nodded, acknowledging the priest's words. "But if they were cast out, is it even possible for them to return?"

"It is," said the priest, shuddering, "and the things they would do to achieve it will make your skin crawl and your blood freeze. I have seen what they do..." His voice trailed off, he stared at the Hunter with a look of horror filling his eyes. When he spoke again, his words held a chill.

"The creatures of the hells have long sought a way back to Einan, and there have been times when they very nearly succeeded. We have managed to block their passage to the world, but still they try."

"You say *we*, priest," the Hunter said, "but aren't you a bit old to be protecting anything?"

"There are many of us who have been given the burden of this secret task, including Brother Securus." The priest gave the Hunter a meaningful look.

"The priest I killed," the Hunter said, understanding dawning. "He was one of you. He was Cambionari."

"Aye," Reverentus replied.

"The rapist?" sneered the Hunter. "A Beggar Priest?"

"Rapist?" Father Reverentus asked, anger flaring in his eyes. "Is that what they told you when they hired you?" At the Hunter's nod, the cleric shook his head in disbelief. "Can you truly believe that a priest of the Beggar God is capable of doing something so horrible?"

"I've seen priests do far worse than raping the daughter of a nobleman," the Hunter said, his voice harsh. Fire flashed in the Hunter's eyes. Memories of watching priests lie with whores, girly-boys, and children twisted his stomach. "I know what priests are capable of."

"I'm certain you have seen horrible things," the priest replied, snarling, "but no doubt you've *done* things far worse as well." The two men locked eyes, and the Hunter saw genuine outrage written in the old priest's expression.

"I tell you this," Father Reverentus said, his voice solemn, "Brother Securus was innocent of any crime. He was a good, honest man, which is why the Beggar God chose him to carry out the task of hunting demons. Only those of pure, righteous blood are accepted into the Cambionari."

"I'll take your word for it," the Hunter replied, skeptical. Curiosity got the better of his temper, and he motioned for the priest to continue. "What were you saying about Brother Securus?"

The old priest swallowed hard and, visibly struggling, unclenched his gnarled fists. "He masqueraded as a minor priest in our order," Reverentus said. "This allowed him the freedom to focus on his real task: hunting down demons wherever they may be found."

"Demons? I thought you said you had *stopped* them from returning to the world?"

"So we thought," Reverentus replied, "but over the last few years we have received sporadic reports of demon sightings across Einan. Most have turned out false, but we could take no chances."

"So Securus was hunting down demons, and he believed he had found some in Voramis?"

The old priest nodded. "Aye, or so he told me when last we spoke."

The Hunter stared at the priest in expectation. "And?" he snapped when Reverentus remained silent. "Where did he find them?"

"He didn't say," the cleric said in a slow voice, "and I didn't press him. He was a very private man, Securus. All he said was that he believed demons had been living in Voramis for some time, beneath our very noses."

"So your demon-hunting priest failed to notice demons living in your own city," the Hunter mocked.

"Or maybe he had," retorted the priest, "which is why you"—the priest punctuated his words by stabbing a finger at the Hunter—"were hired to kill him."

"But why have me kill the priest?" he asked. "What would the death of just one Cambionari accomplish?"

Reverentus shook his head, his expression grave. "The Cambionari are spread throughout the world, each charged with their own task. Brother Securus was the only able-bodied member of the Cambionari in Voramis, the only one capable of fighting. With him out of the way, there are no more of us to hunt down and stop the demons."

"Us?" the Hunter asked. "You are Cambionari as well, I take it."

"Yes," the old priest said, "but what can *I* do?" He motioned to his frail, withered frame with his gnarled hands. "Look at me. My strength lies not in my skill at arms, but in the knowledge I have accumulated over my long life. The thought of my fighting demons is as ludicrous as it sounds."

The Hunter shrugged by way of agreement. He expected the priest to say more, but Father Reverentus remained silent. Instead, the old cleric hobbled over to the table to refill his cup with the fragrant, but now fully cooled tea.

Suddenly, the Hunter understood the meaning behind the priest's silence. "So, with all of the Cambionari gone and Brother Securus dead, you want *me* to hunt down the demons for you?"

The priest nodded, not looking at the Hunter. "Yes."

"And what makes you think that I would?" the Hunter asked. "Why would I do anything for you?"

Reverentus turned to the Hunter, his eyes flashing. "Because we saved you from death. It is thanks to our ministrations that you lie in that bed, not thrown in some unmarked grave."

"Isn't it the duty of all Beggar Priests? To minister to the needy, no matter who they are?"

"Aye," growled the priest, clenching his jaw, "our god commands us to give aid to those in need. But," he held up a warning finger, "remember who *we* are." His stare pierced the Hunter. "We are Cambionari, and you are demonspawn. We are sworn to wipe your kind from the face of Einan, and yet you still draw breath."

"So you *let* me live," snarled the Hunter. "How gracious of you. That isn't enough reason for me to agree to kill for you."

"You want a reason?" Reverentus demanded, his voice rising to a shout. "After we've brought you back from the brink of death, you ask for a reason?" The priest placed his face dangerously close to the Hunter's, fire burning in his eyes. His voice dropped to a harsh whisper. "You...*owe*...us."

"What?" the Hunter demanded, the timbre of his voice rising to match the priest's. "I owe you nothing!"

"You fool!" the priest retorted, unperturbed by the anger in the Hunter's eyes. "It is thanks to you that we are in this mess. You and your accursed dagger killed the one man who could stop this from happening. You do not need a reward or a reason to fight. It is atonement for your actions."

"Atonement," spat the Hunter. "I have killed hundreds of men, all far more important than some nameless priest of a weak god. I care nothing for atonement."

"So you would have the name of the Hunter forever reviled as the man who brought about the destruction of the world."

The priest's words hit the Hunter like a slap. He sat in stunned silence, at a loss for words.

"Aye, Hunter," Reverentus said, "your actions have undone thousands of years of protecting the world from the unknown. With a single thrust of your Kharna-accursed blade"—the priest stabbed a finger at Soulhunger—"you have become the cause of humanity's plummet toward extinction."

The priest's eyes hardened, and he spoke in a low, harsh voice. "You will do this thing—not because you carry a burden of guilt for killing a 'nameless priest', as you put it—but because somewhere inside that cold lump of stone you call a heart, you care."

"Care?" the Hunter snarled. "For you? For your foolish priests?"

"For those around you," the priest retorted. "For this city."

"This city?" demanded the Hunter. "What has Voramis ever done for me?"

"It has given you a home," Reverentus replied, his voice quiet. "It has given you purpose."

"Purpose? What purpose?"

"To protect those who cannot protect themselves," the priest said.

The Hunter opened his mouth to retort, but the priest spoke first.

"Farida."

The single word hit the Hunter like a blow, cutting off his protests. He stared wide-eyed at the priest.

"Aye," said Father Reverentus, "the child you brought to us so many years ago." Seeing the shock on the Hunter's face, he nodded. "We know it was you, and we know you still keep watch on her. You visit her often, always in disguise."

How did they know? The Hunter's mind raced. *So many years ago…*

As if reading his mind, Father Reverentus smiled. "We know much more than you'd think."

The Hunter stared into the priest's eyes, saw the cleric's stern glare soften.

"If you were the cold, callous killer you pretend to be," Reverentus said, "you would have left her to die in the cold, or abandoned her on our stairs. You would never have seen her again, and yet you continue to visit.

You care about her."

The Hunter tried to speak, but the lump rising in his throat stopped him.

"And the beggars with whom you share your home," the priest persisted. "Every one of them ignored—even reviled—by the world, yet you protect them."

"You've been watching me?" he demanded, his mind racing. *They know where I live? What else do they know?*

The old priest nodded. "It is our duty."

"For how long?"

"Not long," Reverentus admitted. "A few years, perhaps."

"And if you knew what I am," the Hunter asked, "why have I not yet shared the fate of the rest of my kind? Why not send Brother Securus to kill me?"

"Because he watched you, first." The priest's voice softened. "He saw you with those weak, helpless beggars, the outcasts of Voramis."

Sorrow welled within the Hunter at the thought of Old Nan, Jak, and the others he had offered the shelter of his home. They were dead, and the pain of their passing burned in his chest. What hurt even more, however, was the memory of the horror that had filled Ellinor's face as she'd stared at him. That terrified gaze would haunt him forever.

"He saw humanity, Hunter," Reverentus said. "That humanity is stronger than the demon within you, the thing driving you to kill."

"And that is the only reason I live?" the Hunter demanded.

"Yes," the priest said, nodding. "The others of your kind gave in to their demonic heritage, seeking power and wealth, bringing only death and destruction. You, Hunter, are the only Bucelarii who has proven to be more human than demon."

Something inside the Hunter snapped. His anger faded, leaving only heartache. Tears threatened to fall as he saw the lifeless faces of the men and women he called friends. He swallowed hard, struggling to hide the signs of what he considered weakness.

"They're all dead," he said, looking up at the priest.

"What?" the priest asked, his eyes wide. "What do you mean? Who is dead?"

"The beggars," the Hunter said, then corrected himself. "The people...the people who shared my home. They're dead."

"How?" the priest demanded. "What did you do?" Reverentus' eyes grew hard for a moment, as if expecting the Hunter to admit to killing the beggars as well. However, upon seeing the sorrow written on the Hunter's face, his expression softened. "What happened?" His voice was surprisingly gentle.

"The Bloody Hand is what happened!" snarled the Hunter. "And the Dark Heresy." Rage burned in his eyes as he stared up at the priest. "They killed every one of those innocent wretches." His voice cracked, but he refused to allow the tears to flow. "And for that, they will pay."

"But what about the demons?" the priest asked. "If you get yourself killed taking on the two most powerful organizations in Voramis, you will not be able to hunt them down."

"I have not agreed to help you find these demons," the Hunter retorted. "Besides, if, as you say, I am the spawn of these creatures, why would I hunt my own kind?"

"For the same reason you still live," the priest said, returning his hard stare. "Because if you do not, everyone you know and love will die at their hands."

"They are already dead!" shouted the Hunter.

"Not all of them," the priest said, his voice gentle. "There is still one person you can protect."

Farida.

"Is it not enough to protect a single child?" the priest asked. "Is that not sufficient reason to hunt down the demons?" His earnest, piercing expression drilled into the Hunter.

"I have yet to see evidence of these demons, priest," the Hunter said, changing the subject. He spoke quietly, still struggling to sublimate the sorrow threatening to overwhelm him. "You have told me much, but with little to corroborate your testimony."

"Here is your proof, Hunter," Father Reverentus said, reaching beneath his robes. He drew out a small knife, and before the Hunter could react, the priest grabbed his wrist. The strength of the old man's grip surprised the Hunter, and he tried to snatch away his arm. Anger had sapped his strength, and he could do nothing but stare wide-eyed at the dull, rusty weapon in the priest's hand.

Iron! The old bastard is trying to kill me.

"Watch," the priest said, his voice harsh as he raised the knife high, "and I will prove it."

Pain raced up his arm as the priest placed the knife's edge on his hand. The veins of his hand began to blacken upon contact with the metal.

"Enough!"

The old priest released his hand, and the Hunter jerked it back. The pain faded in an instant, but an angry welt had already formed on his skin.

"Now do you believe?" the priest demanded.

"What in the Keeper's name are you trying to do?" snarled the Hunter. Rage filled him as he stared up at the priest. "Is that how you convince me to do your bidding? Through torture? I can tell you, priest, I have endured far worse before."

"No torture," replied the priest, "just evidence that you will believe." He looked down at the Hunter's hand, and pointed to the welt, which had begun to fade. "The touch of iron is poison for you, is it not?"

The Hunter said nothing, but glared sullenly at Reverentus. His mind, however, was a seething maelstrom of conflicting thoughts.

Iron was poisonous to the Hunter, the only thing that could kill him. In the priest's story, iron swords had been used by the Watcher to trap the Destroyer long enough to imprison him.

"Why?" he demanded. "Why iron?"

"Iron is a pure metal, given to us by the gods as a means to drive the demons from the face of Einan. Its purity burns the demon blood in your veins."

"Given to you by the gods?" the Hunter snorted. "You and your foolish gods, priest."

"You do not believe in the Thirteen?" the priest asked. "Not surprising, I suppose. A man like you has no need for the gods."

"The gods are nothing more than the creations of humans needing something to blame for their problems," the Hunter scoffed.

The old man gave him a slow smile. "An interesting concept," he said, nodding his head, "and not entirely untrue."

This took the Hunter by surprise. He had expected the priest to answer with angry words, as had so many others. Instead, Father Reverentus had agreed with him, cutting off his argument.

"The gods are but aspects of an unknowable divine power. Humankind has given them faces and names in an attempt to understand the power, and thus we have created the gods as we now know them. What was once something vague and indefinable is now rationalized into a concept humans can grasp. In our worship of the various aspects of the gods, we have transformed those aspects into the gods themselves."

"Perhaps the Swordsman was not always the paragon of virtue and heroism, but by worshipping him as such, we have created that ideal of him, to which he is now bound. The Beggar God was once the great Kharna, but now he is the most despised of all the gods. The stories we tell are to help *us* comprehend the incomprehensible."

"So you're saying that *we* created the gods we now know?" the Hunter asked, his voice rife with skepticism.

"In essence, yes," Father Reverentus replied. "They existed before we knew them, but our worship has transformed them into the gods they now are. We use the gods as a higher power upon which we place blame for our misfortunes, but who also receive credit for the good in our lives."

"But the gods have no hand in either the good or the bad," the Hunter argued.

"To that, good Hunter," the elderly priest replied, "I must say that I agree. The simple man needs something beyond himself to blame and credit for the bad and the good. If we were to accept all the blame and credit upon ourselves, it would be more than we could bear. Looking back at the horrors perpetrated in the name of the gods, our minds would shatter. This way, with the gods, mankind has a way to ease its conscience."

The Hunter snorted in derision. "What a load of rot!"

"Aye," Reverentus replied, "but that is ever the way with religions. So few of us know the truth behind the façade. But, let me assure you, the gods are very real. Perhaps they do not play as prominent a role in our lives as the common man believes, but they are there."

"The gods we invented?"

"Yes, the very same." The priest gave him a smile. "I must point out, Hunter, that now is a good time to have these gods. For if they weren't created for a time like now, when the world could very well be facing an untimely end, why would they be needed at all?"

The Hunter could think of no reply, and Reverentus continued, his voice triumphant.

"I tell you this: It is difficult for many to understand the gods, but they are not meant to be understood. Humanity has given them faces and names, but they are indefinable. You cannot know the minds of the gods, cannot guess what they have planned for you. Some never see the hand of the gods in their lives at all. And yet," he said with a mysterious smile, holding up a crooked finger, "there are some in whom the gods take...*special* interest."

"Let me guess," said the Hunter in a voice heavy with sarcasm, "I am one of those."

The priest nodded, and the grin spreading across the old cleric's face only served to infuriate the Hunter.

"So you're saying," he spat, "the gods have some 'higher destiny' or 'fate' in store for me?"

"I will not waste my breath on empty words," Father Reverentus said, "for I know you have no desire to hear of either 'fate' or 'destiny'. What I will tell you is that there is a task that needs to be fulfilled, and right now you are the only one on the face of Einan in a position to carry it out."

"But why me?"

The old priest shrugged. "That is the question so many of us ask ourselves. Why have *I* been given this task when there are so many others to carry it out? Why me, gods, why me?" Reverentus stared down at him, his eyes softening. "It is not given to us to know the 'why', Hunter."

"I can't ask why I've been chosen by your gods for this?" the Hunter demanded.

"To be honest, I don't know if you *were* chosen." The priest gave him an infuriating smile. "What I *do* know is that your actions have brought us to this point, and you have been given a choice."

Reverentus' gaze pierced the Hunter, as if staring into his soul. "I have seen your heart," the priest said in a soft voice. "You are a killer, but that does not mean your heart is filled with evil. You will find there are many in your line of work that are there out of necessity, or because they know nothing else."

The Hunter struggled for words, but even as he did, his anger faded.

"You are at a crossroads, Hunter," Father Reverentus said. "You have a choice: hunt down the demons, or see the world as you know it come crashing down around you. You have no idea what these things can do..." He trailed off with a shudder.

The priest's words sent chills down the Hunter's spine. In his mind, he saw visions of death, destruction, and carnage. Things of unspeakable horror roamed the earth, burning, killing, and laying waste to villages, towns, and cities. Mighty armies fell before the onslaught of the terrible creatures, unable to stand against the ferocity of the demons of nightmare.

As he saw the visions in his mind's eye, Soulhunger's bloodthirsty whispers filled his thoughts. For a moment, the images seemed so real the Hunter nearly thought himself part of the horrors. It was as if he relived these events from memory, rather than just imagining them.

"For argument's sake," the Hunter said, hesitant, "let's say I *do* decide to help you. How would I find these demons?"

"You're the Hunter," Reverentus replied. "It's what you do, is it not?"

"Very helpful," snorted the Hunter.

Reverentus shrugged. "We have done our part in keeping you alive, Hunter. I wish I could offer more, but I trust that you will succeed."

"My thanks, priest," the Hunter replied with a sarcastic sneer.

The priest paused for a moment, seeming to debate something in his mind. "However," he said in a slow voice, "we may be able to offer you weapons to make the task easier."

"Oh? And what manner of weapons can be found in the temple of the Beggar God? Perhaps a holy collection plate or ensorcelled bandages?"

Reverentus glared down at him, saying nothing, but instead turned to the cloth-bound bundle he had deposited on the table next to Soulhunger. The priest's twisted hands unwrapped the ancient, ragged fabric with care, revealing a pair of beautiful blades.

"These are said to be made from the Swordsman's own sword," said the priest, running a loving hand over the weapons, "the only thing that could wound Kharna the Destroyer. They are the only thing we have that can kill demons."

The Hunter studied the blade in the priest's hand, taking in the details. The hilt was simple and unadorned, its leather-bound grip worn from use. The sturdy crossguard was notched, as if to catch a foe's weapon. Its blade, three fingers in width, was as long as a man's forearm, with a grooved central ridge. It tapered to a slim point, ideal for thrusting.

The perfect weapon, he thought, reaching out his hand to take it from the priest. *Practical, and meant only for killing.*

"They may not help you *find* the demons," Reverentus said, "but they will serve you well once you have located them."

His skin crawled the moment his fingers wrapped around the leather grip. The metal crossguard touched flesh, and he dropped the weapon as if burned. The priest cried out as the sacred blade clattered to the stone floor.

"Iron!" hissed the Hunter. The skin of his hand darkened, and he could almost feel the poison rushing through his weakened body. The voice in his mind screamed in agony at the contact with the metal. "You're going to give me *iron* blades, you old fool?"

"Aye, iron blades," replied the priest, stooping to retrieve the blade. He held it with reverence, his gnarled fingers curling awkwardly around the dagger's hilt.

"Iron is the only thing that can kill you," Reverentus said in a slow voice, pulling his eyes from the blades to stare down at the Hunter, "but it is also the only thing that will trap the soul of a demon inside the body of its host."

"Host?" the Hunter asked.

"Aye," the priest nodded. "Demons take the form of humans, nearly impossible to distinguish. They cannot die of sickness, and they live unnaturally long lives. But these blades"—he brandished the weapon with familiar ease—"are poison to the demon. Once the iron has weakened their flesh, they can be killed."

"One small flaw in your plan, priest," the Hunter sneered. "Just holding the blades will kill me before I leave the temple, much less carry out your precious mission to kill these demons. I would be better off without them."

"But without the Swordsman's blades, you will not be able to kill the demons. It is the only thing—"

"It will not work. You'll have to find some other fool to wield your precious blades." He tried to stand, but his body refused to cooperate. "And look at me," he snarled in frustration, "too weak to move, much less fight."

Reverentus stared down at him, remaining silent, his expression pensive. "What if I told you," he said in a slow voice, "that I had a way to heal you *and* allow you to carry the blades."

"You can stop the iron from poisoning me?" the Hunter asked, incredulous. "If so, how?"

"With the only thing able to combat the demon blood running through your veins," replied the priest, his eyes shining. "With the blood of the gods!"

The Hunter stared at the priest. "Blood of the…gods?" he asked, his expression making it clear he suspected the old man had lost his mind. "What in the frozen hell are you talking about?"

Reverentus rolled his eyes. "It's a symbolic name, you fool, not the actual blood of the gods." He pinched the bridge of his nose between forefinger and thumb, as if to massage away a headache.

"Well?" demanded the Hunter. "What is the name symbolic of, priest?"

The cleric regarded the Hunter, and when he spoke, his tone was that of a patient adult speaking to an infant. "There exists an ancient ritual, passed down through the millennia, which enables priests to sanctify themselves and purge their bodies of all evil. When the body has been purged thus, the blood is said to be 'as the gods'—pure, untainted, holy."

"And how will this ritual help me? I'm no priest."

"No," the cleric said in a flat voice, "you're not." He muttered something under his breath, which the Hunter chose to ignore.

"So, how will it help me if you purify *your* blood?" the Hunter asked.

"That is where this comes in handy." Father Reverentus drew

something from within his clothing, holding it up for the Hunter to see.

The thin, transparent tube was as long as the Hunter's arm, with a sharp, hollow needle on each end.

"And what in the name of the Illusionist's crooked rod is *that*?" The last time the Hunter had seen a hollow needle, Lord Jahel had used it to draw his blood.

"Nothing for a tough man like you to be afraid of," said the priest with a sarcastic smile.

The Hunter glared at him, and the priest's smile grew.

"This tube," Reverentus said, "allows me to pass blood from my body to yours."

"What?" the Hunter asked. "You're going to give me your blood?"

"It's the only way, Hunter."

"I haven't even agreed to do this, and already I'm regretting it." The Hunter leaned back in bed, crossing his arms over his chest.

"If it makes you feel better," offered the priest, "I've already used it on you."

"What?" The Hunter reflexively reached for the dagger at his side, but his hand found nothing but blankets. "What do you mean, you already used that thing?" He eyed the tube with distaste.

"This *thing* saved your life," retorted the priest. "When you were first brought in, I was forced to pass some of my blood to you. It was the only way to counteract the spread of iron through your veins. You came dangerously close to the Long Keeper's embrace, and only this"—he held up the tube again—"saved your life."

The Hunter stared at the things as if it would strike at him like a snake. Then the priest's words sank in.

"Wait," said the Hunter, "you gave me *your* blood?"

"At the time," said the priest, "it seemed like the right thing to do. Perhaps I made a mistake." He gave the Hunter a hard stare. "Perhaps we would have been better off letting you die. The only reason you still live, Hunter, is because you are the only man who can do what is necessary."

The Hunter stared hard at the old priest. *Would he really have let me die?* He saw hardness in Reverentus's eyes, and he knew without a doubt that the priest would have killed the Hunter himself had he perceived him to be a threat. *So either he trusts that I will accept his task, or else he knows that I can be killed another way.*

"The iron in your blood," said Father Reverentus, as if reading his mind, "could still kill you. We managed to stop it from spreading, but there is no telling how much damage it could do if left in your veins." He gave the Hunter a hard stare. "In truth, there is only one thing you can do."

Realization of what the priest had done dawned on the Hunter. "You gave me just enough of your blood to bring me back from the dead, but not enough to heal me completely." The priest remained silent, which confirmed the Hunter's suspicions. "You suspected I wouldn't comply, and thus you kept this as a means of persuasion."

Father Reverentus shrugged, turning his palms upward in a gesture of admission.

"Shrewd, priest," the Hunter said, a new respect for the old man growing within him. "I will remember this in all of our future dealings."

"If the gods will it," Father Reverentus said, "we will never lay eyes upon each other again." He rested his hands on the Swordsman's blades, but his eyes traveled to Soulhunger. "You are Bucelarii, and I am sworn to hunt your kind down. I may be old," he stared at the Hunter, and steel shone in his gaze, "but I am not yet dead and buried."

The intensity of the priest's words startled the Hunter, and he found himself once again at a loss for words.

"So, Hunter," Father Reverentus spoke, "what is your answer? Will you do what is needed, even if it means facing your own kind?"

His thoughts racing, the Hunter pondered the priest's question.

Should I do this? Is it truly my place to stop these demons from returning to the world? Do I even want *to stop their return?*

The faces of his dead friends floated before his eyes, and the vision of death and destruction flashed through his mind once more.

I cannot let the people I care for face such horrors. If it means I must put an end to these demons, and thereby 'save the world' as the priest says, so be it.

"I will do it," he said, his voice slow, "but know that I will not do it for you, priest."

"The reason *why* you do it matters not," the priest responded with a nod of his head, "so long as it is done."

"But," the Hunter spoke quickly, "is this 'blood of the gods' ritual the only thing that will cleanse the iron from my body?"

"If you wish to walk out of this temple, it is the only way. Besides, it will allow you to wield the Swordsman's blades. To kill the demons..." The priest trailed off.

Do I dare carry these blades that could lead to my own downfall—my own death? Is it worth the risk?

Farida's smiling face flashed through his mind. It was all he needed to make up his mind.

"Carry out your ritual, priest," he said.

"I will warn you, Hunter," Reverentus said, holding up a warning finger, "even with the purified blood, there will still be a great deal of discomfort from the iron."

"I am accustomed to pain, priest," the Hunter snarled.

"Good," said the cleric, nodding, "then it is settled."

The priest turned away, reaching for the Swordsman's blades and the tube on the table. "I must gather the others," he said, half to himself. "We must convene tonight."

He faced the Hunter once more. "I will return in a few hours, once the ceremony is complete."

"Not a Watcher-damned chance, priest," snarled the Hunter. "I'm going to attend this ritual to see exactly what you're doing."

The priest opened his mouth to protest, but the Hunter cut him off. "It may be your blood, but it's my body."

Father Reverentus pondered this for a moment. "The others will not be pleased, Hunter. There will be complaints—"

"They will have to accept it," the Hunter interrupted. "It is the only way I will do what you are asking of me."

Reverentus seemed to mull this over. A scowl grew on his face as he saw the stubborn look on the Hunter's face.

"There's no chance of talking you out of this, is there?" he asked.

"Not even if the Mistress herself offered to sit on my lap," the Hunter said, his tone resolute.

"Well, then," sighed the old priest, "let's get you out of that bed. We have much to prepare, and little time in which to do it."

The Hunter struggled to move his legs, refusing to admit his own weakness. Clinging to the bed for support, he rose to his feet.

"Lead on, priest," he said, his heart filled with dread.

Chapter Twenty-Four

"What in the name of the gods is *he* doing here?" The Beggar Priest's craggy face reddened with rage.

Anger clouded the sea of faces staring at the Hunter. The priests filling the small room were clearly less than pleased to see him, but he was too tired to care. He had barely managed to hobble the short distance to this chamber without leaning on Father Reverentus for support.

Bloody Minstrel, he thought, cursing inwardly. *I hope to never be this weak again.*

Exhausted, feeling every ache and pain, he slumped against the rigid granite, content to let Father Reverentus speak for him.

"He is here, Brother Paxus," replied Reverentus in a placating tone, "because it is the only way he will do what needs to be done."

To the Hunter's weary body, the hard stone bench beneath him felt wonderfully cool. The flickering torchlight made his head ache. Eyes closed, he inhaled the damp, musty air in the enclosed room, his ears taking in the vociferous protests of the Beggar Priests.

"Without his actions," snarled one, a heavy-set man with jowls that wobbled in his rage, "we wouldn't be in this precarious situation." The priest punctuated his protests by stabbing a finger at the Hunter, who lay slumped on the bench. "It is *his* fault we are here."

"And yet here we are," retorted Father Reverentus, steel in his voice. "We have no other choice in the matter. Would you really allow the demons to triumph, Brother Contritus, just because you are too short-sighted to see what must be done?"

Contritus shot a sullen glance at Father Reverentus, who, unperturbed, returned the glares of the priests filling the room with equal force. The mass of white-haired, wrinkled, long-bearded faces surrounding him remained locked in a struggle of wills for long, tense moments.

As he rested his head on the cool stone wall behind him, he studied the simple, sparse room. A row of benches ran around the circumference of the room. Water leaked from the stone walls, and he guessed they beneath the House of Tears. A simple altar stood in the heart of the chamber, but it looked like a relic from a time long past. Dust coated the floor in thick layers. The room appeared to have been unused for years. The shrine, however, had not a speck of dust on it.

What is this place? He wondered.

"But, Father," spoke another, cutting into the Hunter's thoughts, "the ritual has not been done in hundreds—nay, *thousands*—of years. Are you willing to risk its success just to cater to the whims of that creature?"

"The Hunter has agreed to help us, but *only* if we meet his conditions." Father Reverentus' stern glare cowed the priest who had spoken. "We all know what must be done."

"To give that *thing* our blood," spat Brother Contritus, his eyes burning with hatred. "It is an abomination before the gods. As is he!"

"He is a demon! A creature of the hells," cried another priest, this one rail-thin, with age spots dotting his skin. The other priests joined their voices in the protest, drowning out Father Reverentus' response.

"Demon blood flows through his veins," shouted Reverentus, trying to make himself heard, "but there is the blood of man as well."

At this, the priests fell quiet, though a few muttered sullen curses under their breaths.

"His humanity dilutes the evil within him," Father Reverentus said, his voice solemn, "or else Brother Securus would have killed him long ago."

"And Brother Securus lies dead at *his* hands!" shouted Contritus, the mention of their fallen comrade sparking his outrage once more. "His soul sent to the hells to feed the Destroyer. He—"

"Yes, I did," replied the Hunter, standing suddenly and interrupting the priest's tirade. "I did kill your priest, as I was paid to do." He stared at each one of them in turn. "No doubt you are all familiar with doing what needs to be done; carrying out the task you are given."

None of the priests met his gaze.

"You all carry regrets with you to this day," the Hunter continued, "because of your actions in the past. Mistakes are made by all—it is the way of life."

"Brother Securus is dead," Father Reverentus said, his voice hard. "He has met a horrible fate I would not wish upon any."

He is angry, the Hunter realized, hearing the anger in the old priest's tight, clipped tone, *but he knows the stakes. He knows what must be done.*

The priests muttered among themselves, but Father Reverentus ignored them.

"We all knew the risks we would face," he continued, "the day we spoke the oaths of the Cambionari." The old cleric's eyes drilled into the priests gathered in the room. "We knew the dangers, and yet we each took those oaths gladly."

He waggled an admonishing finger at the priests. "Yet were Brother Securus here, he would want us to do *whatever* needed to be done to stop the demons from returning." Reverentus gestured toward the Hunter, who had slumped back on the bench, his energy drained. "Securus would be the first to offer his blood if it meant the Hunter could put an end to the demons he believed plague this city. We are too old, too frail to fight, but we have a way to ensure the success of our endeavors."

Father Reverentus stared at the others, his eyes piercing. "Will you do it—not for the Hunter, not for yourselves, not even because I am asking you—but because it *must* be done? If we do not, our lives will have been spent in vain."

The Beggar Priests remained silent, sullen reluctance painted on their faces. Heartbeats dragged by as the Hunter waited, nothing but the sound of water trickling down bare stone walls to break the tense stillness.

"Aye," growled Brother Contritus, finding his voice at last, "we will do what must be done." He shot a glare at the Hunter. "But *he* had better hope the gods never allow our paths to cross again."

The threat rang hollow, but the Hunter resisted the urge to smile. Tangible resentment radiated from the priests. He knew their anger led them to curse him, but he didn't fault them for it.

"We are agreed," intoned Father Reverentus. "You have all followed my instructions to prepare for the ritual?"

The priests nodded old, white-haired heads in confirmation.

"Then let us commence," Father Reverentus said, "for we have no time to waste."

As if on an unspoken command, the priests slowly shuffled into a loose circle surrounding the stone altar in the heart of the chamber.

Father Reverentus' voice cut into his thoughts. "We are gathered here for the Ritual of Cleansing, as laid out in the Book of the Supplicant. There are twelve of us here, and, with the Hunter, we are thirteen. The number of the gods themselves."

This shocked the Hunter. He had expected to be a spectator in the ritual, not a participant. He opened his mouth to voice his complaint, but Father Reverentus's words drowned him out.

"The number thirteen holds much power. It is the power over life and death, and, if wrongly used, could break the world itself. However, with the sacred words written in the Book of the Supplicant, handed down to us by the first Beggar Priests, there is potential for great things. The Ritual of Cleansing will purify us; make us as clean as the gods themselves."

From within their cloaks, the priest drew forth stilettos. The slim blades gleamed ominously in the torchlight, the bright metal at odds with the stark simplicity of the room.

"Let blood be spilled in the names of the gods," said Father Reverentus. As one, razor sharp blades slashed into pale, parchment-thin skin. A slim trickle of blood rolled down the priests' forearms from the shallow wound left by the knives.

"Speak the names of the gods, and let your blood be the sacrifice that turns their face toward us this night." Father Reverentus' voice seemed distorted, somehow richer than would be expected coming from such a frail old man.

"Garridos," said Brother Contritus.

"Derelana," echoed another priest.

"Kiro," a third intoned.

In turn, the priests around the circle named the gods, each priest spilling a single drop of blood onto the stone altar.

"The Maiden."

"The Illusionist."

"The Watcher in the Dark."

"Bright Lady."

"The Long Keeper."

"The Mistress."

"Bloody Minstrel."

"Fair Alzara."

"The Beggar," said Father Reverentus, completing the circle. The twelve drops of blood atop the altar stood out in stark contrast to the white granite. The shrine had seemed so simple and plain moments ago, but now power throbbed in the back of the Hunter's mind.

Turning slightly, Father Reverentus motioned for the Hunter to speak. The Hunter wanted to protest, but a force beyond his control pulled the words from within him.

"The Swordsman."

Something warm and wet flowed down his arm, and looking down, he saw one of his wounds had reopened. A single drop of blood trickled from his limp hand to the dusty stone floor.

For a moment, nothing happened. The priests remained motionless, their eyes closed as they gathered around the stone altar. Without realizing it, the Hunter held his breath, expecting…*What?*

His eyes remained fixed on the bright crimson drop. It seemed to shudder, as if the floor beneath it shook.

What in the Keeper's name?

With agonizing slowness, the blood oozed across the dusty floor. The Hunter's mouth hung open as the droplet flowed of its own accord toward the stones set in the heart of the room. It crawled up the side of the altar, finally coming to rest atop the shrine.

Thirteen drops of blood. The ring was complete.

"The thirteen names have been spoken," the voice of Father Reverentus echoed loud and commanding in the room, "blood has been spilled. The gods turn their faces toward us; let us beseech them for their cleansing."

"Sanctify us, purify us, make us clean," Brother Contritus intoned.

"Sanctify us, purify us, make us clean," the priest next to him echoed.

"Sanctify us, purify us, make us clean," a third priest took up the chant.

One by one, the priests around the room spoke the words. Their voices joined in harmony, blending in a chorus that reverberated throughout the small room.

The Hunter more than heard the words...he felt them. Something primal within his mind shouted profanities at the priest's chant. A shudder coursed through him—millions of tiny legs seemed to crawl across his skin. He felt hot and cold all at once, and his heart pounded faster and faster in time with the chanting.

"Sanctify us, purify us, make us clean." Father Reverentus added his voice to the chant.

As the cleric spoke, pain ripped through the Hunter's mind. The voice within him cried out in terror, begging, pleading for him to make it stop. A pressure built in his ears, pounding in his head. The Hunter felt as if he would explode from the force of the power in the room. He clung to the stone bench for his very life, and stone cracked beneath the strength of his grip. Through bleeding eyes, the Hunter saw Father Reverentus open his mouth and speak.

Words of power ripped into his ears, searing his eardrums. Blood poured from his nose, steaming and bubbling as it flowed down his chest. He fought in vain to stanch the bleeding. It was as if countless needles buried into his eyes, and he heard a cry of agony through the pain. Some dark corner of his brain told him that the screams were his. He beat the back of his head against the wall in an attempt to relieve the mounting stress in his head.

He abandoned his sanity to the merciful embrace of momentary unconsciousness, welcoming the darkness as it washed over him.

Chapter Twenty-Five

A gentle hand shook his shoulder, pulling him from the insensate world where no agony existed. Warmth spread over his forehead and something wet trickled down his cheeks and into his mouth. He swallowed the tepid water, welcoming anything to wash the dust and dried blood from his parched throat.

"He lives."

The Hunter heard relief in the shaky voice of an old man, though the voice echoed, as if from far away. Piercing blue eyes stared down at him with genuine concern as he struggled to keep his eyelids open.

"Who…?" he asked, disoriented and confused.

"Give it a minute," said the man, pushing the Hunter back down on the cold stone floor with surprising strength. "The ritual seems to have affected you more profoundly than I had expected."

Ritual? Fog still filled the Hunter's mind. He was so tired…he just wanted to sleep. *What ritual? Where—?*

The old man's wrinkled face seemed familiar, and for a moment he couldn't place it. Then, with a rush, memories clicked into place.

"F-Father? Wh-what happened?" The Hunter's tongue felt swollen, and his voice was thick and heavy.

"You know where you are?" Father Reverentus asked.

"In the House of Need," the Hunter replied.

"Good," the old cleric said, nodding. He pushed off his knees with his hands, climbing to his feet with ponderous slowness.

"What happened?" the Hunter asked again.

"The ritual worked, it seems," Father Reverentus said. He offered a hand, but the Hunter brushed it aside as he climbed to his feet on his own.

"Feeling better?"

The Hunter flexed his arms and legs and found his weakness of earlier had gone. Only his head throbbed, but already the pain was receding. The voice in his mind, usually so insistent, had quieted to a whisper. He rolled his shoulders and tilted his head to the side, cracking his neck. "Much," he said with a smile.

"Thank the gods," said the priest. "I can see now that letting you in the room while the ritual was taking place was folly. I believe the demon within you rejected the purifying of the gods, and it very nearly killed you. Had I known you would react so strongly, I would have insisted you remain outside."

"Next time," the Hunter said, giving the priest a weary smile, "I'll be sure to steer well clear." Looking down, he saw the floor stained with bright red blood—his blood, far more than his body should hold.

"It was a close thing," said the old cleric, "but we gave you our pure blood, all that we could spare."

The Hunter followed the priest's gaze and saw the hollow, needle-tipped tube on the stone bench. Blood still leaked from the sharp points on both ends. For the first time the Hunter noticed how wan and pallid the cleric's aging skin looked. His eyes had sunken deeper, and his bony cheeks protruded at a sharp angle. Compared to the authoritative priest who had led the ritual earlier, the man in front of him seemed drained and hollow.

"Will you be well?" the Hunter asked, unsure as to why he felt concern for the wellbeing of the old priest.

"Aye," the cleric said with a tired nod, "the ritual took more out of us than we had imagined. The power of the gods is not something the human frame can handle easily, and it very nearly killed a few of us."

He turned his gaze to one side of the room, where the rest of the Beggar Priests surrounded two of their brothers on the floor. One looked to be sleeping, but the second seemed more corpse than man. The priest's skin was a sickly ashen grey, and the Hunter guessed the man walked close to the Long Keeper's embrace.

"He will be well," Father Reverentus said in a soft voice, "though he will not be moving around much for the next few weeks."

Nodding, the Hunter turned to face the old cleric once again. "And my weapons?"

"They are being brought here even now. Brother Mendicatus will deliver them to you, but first..." Father Reverentus drew the twin daggers from beneath his cloak and held them out to the Hunter. "We must put the ritual to the test."

A knot formed in the Hunter's stomach, but he ignored it. Gritting his teeth, he gripped the worn leather hilts of the twin blades. Heat raced along his fingers and palms where skin touched metal.

"It...is...tolerable," he said, his jaw clenched through the pain.

The Hunter tested the blades, moving them through a few simple sword forms in order to evaluate their weight, balance, and heft. Designed for stabbing and slashing, the weight of the blades rested near the hilt. They could block a sword, and the length of the daggers made them ideal for fighting up close, but he knew the iron would shatter beneath the blow of a steel weapon.

As he moved, the pain faded to a dull ache, present but not enough to interfere with his ability to wield them. His hands felt stiff and awkward, and his fingers grew white as he forced them to grip the blades despite the agony.

"They will suffice," he told the priest, handing him the twin weapons. He grunted in pain as his burning hands released their death grip on the leather-wrapped hilts. The fire died, and his fingers tingled as fresh blood repaired the injury.

"It will have to be enough, for it is all we can do." Father Reverentus said. "You will live up to your end of the agreement, Hunter?"

Doubt and worry filled the priest's eyes. With the iron purged from the Hunter's blood and his wounds healed, the priest no longer held any power over him, and thus no way to ensure he would do as he had promised.

"It will be done, Father," the Hunter replied in a solemn voice. "You have my word."

Skepticism flashed across the old cleric's face for a moment, but he stifled it. "Good."

He opened his mouth to speak, but just then a cough sounded from behind the Hunter. He turned to see Brother Contritus.

"Yes, brother?" Father Reverentus asked.

"We'll be off, father," Contritus said. The priest stared at the father, making a point to avoid looking at the Hunter.

"Very well," nodded Reverentus. "Do be quick about it, though, brother, and hurry back. The evening prayers will be held in a few hours."

"Yes, father."

With a bow to the old priest and a poorly concealed glare for the Hunter, Brother Contritus scurried away. As he left the room, the other clergymen followed him until only the two unconscious figures on the floor remained.

"Where are they going?" the Hunter asked, raising an inquisitive eyebrow.

"To sin," Father Reverentus said.

"What?" asked the Hunter, shocked. "I thought you priests were supposed to be holy."

"That, dear Hunter, is a misconception," the old cleric gave the Hunter an enigmatic smile. "Priests are meant to pass on the word of the gods, minister to the poor, and provide the services offered by their temples. No one said anything about being holy. Not even the gods are truly holy."

The Hunter found this new information hard to digest. In his mind, he had always believed priests held one goal: to emulate their gods. If that meant living a life of starvation, deprivation, and suffering, they would do it. And yet…

"So they're just going to go and sin because they can?" the Hunter's voice held disbelief.

"Not because they can," replied Reverentus, his grin wide, "but because they *must.*"

"What?" the Hunter asked. "Explain, priest."

"The ritual we have carried out this night purifies the priest's blood. That purified blood holds an immense amount of power, but should it fall into the wrong hands, it could be used to bring death and destruction."

Realization dawned. "You mean," the Hunter asked, incredulous, "they sin to *pollute* the pure blood in their bodies?"

"Yes," Father Reverentus replied, "the stain of sin taints them, and the power is banished. It is the one time the gods smile on committing unholy acts."

An image flashed through the Hunter's mind: a fat priest, wearing the rust-colored robes of a Minstrel Cleric, lounged among the women at the Arms of Heaven. Wine rolled down florid, laughing cheeks as the cleric pawed at a bawdy woman wearing little in the way of clothing.

The rest of the time, he thought, *they sin just because it brings them pleasure.*

He opened his mouth to speak, but at that moment, another priest entered the room. This one looked to be on the far side of middle years, with a balding head, a thick nose, red cheeks, and a paunchy waist that stood in sharp contrast to the slim form of the ancient Reverentus. The smell of oil, wax, and wood rose from the man.

"Ahh, Brother Mendicatus," Father Reverentus said, nodding at the cleric.

"The weapons you requested, Father," the pudgy priest proclaimed. Fat fingers clutched the Hunter's sword belt, along with a small bulging satchel. Brother Mendicatus turned to the Hunter, making no effort to hide his disdain. "Here," he said, holding out the bag.

"Thank you," the Hunter replied with a nod.

Mendicatus handed him the weapons, and the Hunter reached for them eagerly. Father Reverentus had insisted Soulhunger remain in the room where the Hunter had convalesced, but having the familiar weight of steel in his hand comforted him. The blade throbbed at his side, its voice pounding in his mind—though without its former overwhelming intensity.

"Here," said Brother Mendicatus, "these belong to the Swordsman's blades." In his hands, he held two simple wooden sheaths, bound with plain leather. The Hunter buckled the scabbards onto the back of his belt and slid the twin blades home. He tested their draw, satisfied to find the daggers slipped free of the sheaths with ease.

"Good," he nodded. The iron made his skin crawl, but he ignored the sensation. "Is there anything I need to know about slaying these demons?"

"Thrust one blade into the demon, and the iron blade will weaken it," the fat priest blurted out. "The second blade will slay the creature—a thrust straight to the heart should do the trick." Mendicatus failed to notice he had butted in before Father Reverentus could speak, and the older cleric's glare was lost on him as well.

"And how will I tell these demons apart from any other humans?" the Hunter asked. "If, as you say, they can possess human hosts, won't they be indistinguishable from those around them?"

"The eyes," said Father Reverentus, gesturing toward the Hunter's own. "They are empty orbs of blackness. A glimpse into the endless void of the hells."

"So you're telling me I'll have to get close enough to look one in the eyes?" the Hunter asked. "Not a very easy task you're giving me, is it, Father?"

"If it were easy," retorted Reverentus, "you would not be here. You are the last creature on Einan we would choose to hunt down demons. But here we are…"

The Hunter knew Father Reverentus had purposely left out the "because of you", and for a moment, something akin to remorse flashed through him.

"Father," he said in solemn tones, "for what it's worth, I truly am sorry for the death of your priest."

Father Reverentus looked as if the Hunter had just slapped him. His mouth hung slightly agape, and he struggled to maintain his composure.

"He was a brave man, and a true fighter," the Hunter continued. "He died a worthy death, befitting a man of valor."

"Then do not let his death be in vain, Hunter," Father Reverentus said, his voice tight with suppressed anger. "Atone for your actions."

The Hunter nodded. "It will be done, Father."

"And quickly," the old priest spoke. "Something tells me that you will not have long to stop whatever the demons are planning. With the full moon just two days off…"

His ominous warning trailed off, and the Hunter nodded.

"As you say, Father." Turning to Brother Mendicatus, he said, "If you could show me the way out."

"A warning, Hunter," Father Reverentus said, placing a hand on the Hunter's arm and turning him to stare into his eyes with a burning intensity. For a moment, the Hunter thought the old cleric peered into his very soul.

"Beware the demon blade, Soulhunger," Reverentus said, his eyes flicking to the sheath on the Hunter's belt. "It will whisper into your ear, demanding to be used to kill. The power it feeds you will give you strength, but that same strength will feed the demons as well. The blood we have given you should prevent the blade from overpowering your mind, but you will need a strong will to resist the temptations of the weapon."

"I'll keep your words in mind, priest," the Hunter said, nodding. "However, I may have need of the blade, regardless of the consequences."

With a sigh of resignation, Father Reverentus released the Hunter's arm. "So be it. You undertake a task few on this world are able to carry out, and I fear even you will be unable to defeat the foe you are about to face.

However, you are the only hope for Voramis, so may the gods take pity on you. Farewell."

Nodding to Father Reverentus, the Hunter followed Brother Mendicatus out of the room, the old priest's baleful words ringing in his ears.

Chapter Twenty-Six

The Hunter followed the chubby priest through the maze of corridors. Only the flickering of the torch in Brother Mendicatus' hand broke the darkness of the passages beneath the House of Need. The smoky, pitch-laden scent of the torch filled the tunnels, mixing with the smell of centuries-old dust.

How odd that I find myself helping the people who have hunted my kind for millennia, the Hunter thought. *It is a bizarre twist of fate that has led me here, yet here I am.*

He felt the temptation to simply walk away from his task, to leave Voramis forever.

It would be so easy to leave everything behind. With all those I cared for now dead, there is nothing holding me here.

A child's face flashed through his mind.

Not everyone. There is still one person keeping me in Voramis.

His decision was made for him. There was no question whether or not he would protect her.

I will do what I have promised and hunt down these demons. For Farida's sake, if not for my own.

The thought of atonement seemed oddly tempting to him. He had never felt guilty for bringing death to those he was paid to kill, and yet he felt a twinge of shame for the death of Brother Securus.

If I can atone for what I have done, it will be well. If not…

If not, what? What would he do, knowing he had brought about the return of the demons to the world?

If I cannot atone for my sins, at the very least I can avenge the deaths of those I swore to protect.

It would have to be enough.

The Hunter's attention returned to his surroundings, and as he followed Brother Mendicatus through the twisting corridors, he noticed strange symbols etched into the stone walls. The markings looked as ancient and arcane as the temple itself, written in a language the Hunter had never encountered before.

"What do the walls say?" the Hunter asked.

The priest reached out a chubby hand and ran thick fingers along the engravings in the stone. "Truth be told, no one knows what these marks mean. They date back to the days of the Serenii, during the War of Gods."

"The Serenii?" The Hunter had heard Father Reverentus speak the name upstairs. "What in the twisted hell is a Serenii?"

"Not a 'what', sir Hunter, but a 'who'." Brother Mendicatus turned to face the Hunter. "Not much is known of the creatures, as there are few records that mention them. However, what we do know is that they were a race of demi-humans who populated Einan in the days when mankind was still young."

The Hunter, hearing the lecturing tone in the priest's voice, rolled his eyes. The cleric continued his oration without noticing the Hunter's expression of dismay.

"It is said," Mendicatus said, his voice filling with excitement, "that the Serenii had technology far beyond the primitive tools used by humans. They wielded vast power, but kept to themselves within the massive walls of their cities."

His voice echoed through the tunnels, rising in pitch as he warmed to the topic.

"During the War of Gods, when the Destroyer unleashed the demons onto the planet, the Serenii simply disappeared. What happened to them, no one knows. But their cities were destroyed in the war, and only the foundations remain."

He stopped, turned to face the Hunter, and gesticulated around him with sweeping motions. "Did you know," he asked the Hunter, "the city we now know as Voramis is built on the ruins of an ancient city of the Serenii? If you know where to look, you'll find passages beneath the city that run miles deep."

"I've never heard of any passages beneath Voramis," the Hunter said, surprised.

Mendicatus motioned for the Hunter to continue, but his voice never slowed as he walked on. "Few know of the existence of the underground ways of the Serenii, but some have undertaken the effort to chart the myriad paths and tunnels wending their way beneath Voramis."

"And these passages," the Hunter asked, tucking the information in the back of his mind, "where can they be found? Is there a map?"

The priest shrugged. "History was Brother Securus' area of expertise, but unfortunately he is not here to pass on the details of the Serenii catacombs."

Anger filled the priest's voice. The Hunter fell silent, unsure of what to say, and the quiet stretched on for long moments.

"Did he mention anything that could be of use?" he asked, attempting to break the tension.

"Well," said Brother Mendicatus, his words clipped, "I do remember him saying something about the Hidden Circle."

Another name the Hunter had never heard. "The Hidden Circle? Who are they?"

"Alchemists," Mendicatus replied, "practicing their craft outside the strictures of the Secret Keepers." The clerics of the Mistress had learned the ways of alchemy centuries ago, and they protected their secrets with a fierce ruthlessness.

"Why would *alchemists* know anything about secret passages built by a race long dead? The Secret Keepers deal in poisons, alchemical cures, and ridiculous love potions."

"Most of them, yes," Brother Mendicatus replied with a nod, "but a few of the Hidden Circle deal in information rather than elixirs. Many people would pay good coin for information, making it a trade far more lucrative than philter-mongering."

The Hunter knew this to be true. In his work, he had come across all manner of private information his targets would rather have kept hidden from the public eye. He had stolen and sold a few secrets himself, and there was a great deal of profit, if you could find the right buyer.

"Should you find a member of this Hidden Circle," the pudgy clergyman said, breaking into his thoughts, "you may be able to find what you're looking for."

Smiling at the priest, the Hunter nodded, "I believe I may know just the person to talk to." Someone to whom he had sold information in the past.

They rounded a corner in the passageway, and at the end of the corridor stood a heavy wooden door. Brother Mendicatus drew a large brass key from within his robe, inserted it into the lock, and strained to twist it. After a moment of effort, the ancient lock clicked open with the sound of heavy mechanisms. The priest swung one thick door open, revealing the last fading rays of daylight beyond.

"Go with the Beggar God, Hunter," Brother Mendicatus said, his voice abrupt, as if eager to get rid of the Hunter.

"Priest," the Hunter replied with a curt nod. He turned away, but Brother Mendicatus' sausage fingers gripped his forearm.

"A favor, Hunter," the priest said.

The Hunter saw worry etched into the lines of the cleric's thick cheeks. "I make no promise," he replied, "but you may ask."

"It's about Farida."

"What about her?" the Hunter snapped, his voice harsher than intended.

"I have not seen her since morning vespers, though she should have returned after the noon bell. It is not the first time she has arrived late, but still I worry for her. Perhaps you could keep a watch out for her in your travels?" His hopeful expression showed genuine concern for the child.

The Hunter tried to keep his face calm, but fear stabbed through him.

Farida? Missing?

His mind raced through horrifying scenarios, worry nagging at his mind.

No, he tried to tell himself, *she is fine. Someone has taken pity on her and offered her a decent meal.* While not common, he knew it did happen on occasion. *Yes,* he insisted, *that's it. Still, I had best search for her before the night is through. After what happened with the others...*

"I will find her, brother," the Hunter replied. "You have my word that I will bring her back safe."

"My thanks, Hunter." Brother Mendicatus released his hold on the Hunter's arm. "Be blessed in your endeavors."

Nodding, surprised to hear genuine compassion in the chubby priest's voice, the Hunter turned his back on Mendicatus and hurried away.

The temple gate clanged shut behind him with an ominous ring of finality. He had felt an odd sense of safety while in the House of Need, but now it fled, and the night pressed in around him. The growing darkness around him seemed empty, hollow once more. He pulled his cloak tighter around himself, shivering though no chill hung in the air.

The sensation of being alone overwhelmed him. Even the voice in his mind remained barely a whisper. He felt the dull ache of loneliness, but pushed it to the back of his mind. He had much to accomplish before the dawn's light greeted Voramis.

It was going to be a busy night.

Chapter Twenty-Seven

Night descended upon Voramis as the sun sank beneath the ocean. Evening brought with it a chill wind that blew away the smells permeating the city, until only the scent of imminent rain hung in the air. Citizens of Voramis hustled through the streets, coats clutched around their bodies to ward off the cold and gloom.

In a small shop in a forgotten corner of Lower Voramis, near the Beggar's Quarter, a balding figure sat hunched over a desk. His hairless pate glistened in the candlelight, and an eager sweat dripped from his cheeks as he squinted at the illegible handwriting filling the pages of the book beneath his plump fingers. The only sound in the room was his heavy breathing and the accompanying *scritch, scritch* of a feather pen scribbling on cheap parchment.

Next to the man's arm sat a bowl of food, long forgotten in his fascination with the tome's contents. A small lamp lit the cramped room, the flame within the glass bulb flickering from some hidden draft. Rickety shelves lined the room, stretching from floor to ceiling. Wood creaked beneath the ponderous weight of hundreds of books, scrolls, and parchments.

The man paused his writing to remove his fogged spectacles and wipe them with the dirty hem of his robe. He studied them and, satisfied that they were as clean as they would ever be, replaced them on the bridge of his nose before reassuming his uncomfortable position—his face far too close to the book.

"Good evening, Graeme," came a harsh voice from the darkness behind him.

The bespectacled man let out a screech of fright, his feather quill falling from his hand. He leapt from the hard wooden stool, sending it clattering as his thigh slammed into the underside of the table. Graeme's chubby hand snatched at the tilting inkwell just in time to stop it falling. The heavyset man breathed hard at the exertion, and turned a baleful glare on the Hunter in the shadows.

"Illusionist confound it!" Graeme cursed, groaning at the pain in his leg. "You know how I hate it when you do that!"

"And yet," the Hunter said, his face spreading into a wide smile, "seeing you like this is just so damn enjoyable, Graeme." The smell of ink, dried sweat, and the stench of chemical mixtures—Graeme's unique scent—pained the Hunter's sensitive nostrils.

"Go suck goat balls, Hunter," Graeme snarled. The man turned back to his work, and a moan of dismay escaped his lips at sight of the large ink stain spread from the nib of the pen. He attempted to prevent the ink stain spreading by dabbing it at with old paper, but his face fell as he saw his parchment was ruined.

"Look what you've done," he railed, rounding on the Hunter. "All of my work copying Taivoro's plays gone, thanks to you! What in the name of torment do you want?"

"Is that any way to talk to your best customer, Graeme?" the Hunter asked, his smile growing.

The fat man snorted in derision. "I would *hardly* call you my best customer. Yes," he said, waving his hand in a dismissive gesture as he turned to the messy worktable, "you *do* pay handsomely for the argam, but you buy quantities large enough to get me hanged in any city on Einan."

For a moment, Graeme's search for a fresh parchment absorbed his attention. When he finally located an unsoiled sheet among the mess, he held it up to the light, examining it. With a grin of triumph, he slapped the paper down in front of the book.

"Don't tell me you've already run out of the stuff," he asked, turning to glare at the Hunter. "You can't possibly have used it all up *this* quickly."

"No," the Hunter replied, "I still have more than enough."

"And your alchemical masks?"

"Intact."

"Bandages and poultices for the lad?"

A twinge of sorrow raced through the Hunter at mention of Arlo, but he swallowed the lump in his throat and shook his head.

"So, you've come for another reason?" the fat man asked. At the Hunter's nod, he threw up his hands and scowled. "Oh, gods, this can't possibly be good."

"Not a very positive attitude," the Hunter pointed out, the twisted smile on his scarred face growing even larger. "Especially not when I give you more than enough to cover any…*incidentals* that could arise as a result of this favor."

Graeme's eyes widened in mock horror. "So it's a *favor* now? Gods be good! The Hunter is going to ask for a favor. What has this world come to?" He stooped to right the stool, sitting heavily and turning his back on the figure in the shadows.

"Graeme," the Hunter said, anger flaring across his face, "I will have you know that my patience will wear thin soon enough. You may be the best argam-maker in Voramis, but you're not the *only* one."

He stepped forward, and the light of the room fell on his harsh features as he pulled back his hood. Thick bands of scars crossed his face, twisting his nose and lips into a wicked grimace. Eyes so brown they looked near black stared down at Graeme, but the alchemist didn't bother to face him. The Hunter's glare failed to instill proper terror in the fat man.

"Please, Hunter," the man said with a derisive snort. "This isn't the first time you've threatened me."

"Don't make it the last," the Hunter snapped.

Graeme finally turned to face him, a look of long-suffering patience stamped on his face. "Well, this *has* been a pleasant chat, Hunter," the fat man beamed up at the Hunter. "Now, either tell me what you want, or leave me alone with my Taivoro." He held up the book in pudgy fingers, showing it to the Hunter. "It's the real deal, you know." His voice dropped to a whisper. "All of his best plays, which were believed to be lost."

"And I'm sure the erotic works of the mad playwright are guaranteed to thrill on a night like this," the Hunter mocked, "but it's going to have to wait."

"Fine," he said, with a sigh. The alchemist ran his fingers lovingly over the moldering leather cover of the book one final time before dropping it on the table. "Come with me into the back."

The fat man strode to the nearby bookshelf and reached for a thick book.

"A Treatise on the History of Fungal Development in the Emperor's Concubines," the Hunter read the title aloud as Graeme's fat fingers closed around it. "Must be a stirring read, that one."

Graeme said nothing, but cast a skewering glare over his shoulder. He pulled on the book, and a hidden mechanism tripped with an audible *click*. The bookcase swung back to reveal an opening.

The Hunter followed Graeme into the ample back room, marveling at the tidiness of the workspace. In their years of acquaintance, the Hunter had never seen the room so orderly.

"Forgive the order," the man said, "but the new assistant has a nasty habit of putting things back where they belong. Makes it damn difficult to find anything."

"I see business at The Angry Goblin Bookstore is flourishing, Graeme," the Hunter noted. The clutter filling the room had an expensive look to it. Instead of the usual collection of withered skulls, dried bones, and pouches of herbs and spices hanging on the walls, jars filled with all manner of exotic miscellany sat on the new shelves lining the room. "I'm surprised people still buy books from you."

"Yes, because *that's* my main stock and trade," Graeme rolled his eyes and snorted. "Books! As if people were educated enough. Did you know," he turned to the Hunter, raising his voice in anger, "that less than one in a thousand Voramians have ever learned to read? And that's counting the nobility! What is the world coming to? Such ignorance!"

With a shake of his head, Graeme turned to rummage among a stack of books. "So," he asked the Hunter, "what do you need now?"

"First, I'll take a few of those blue bottles you know I love." The Hunter held up a warning finger. "The *good ones*, mind you, not the ones filled with that gods-awful liquid you sell as 'love potion'."

Graeme, a heavy book clutched in his pudgy fingers, turned back to the Hunter with a grin. "Ah, yes," he chortled, "the 'love potions'. They certainly *do* work, though not quite in the way most customers expect. I do so love those adorable little heart-shaped scars—a nasty side effect."

"Plus," the Hunter added with a nasty grin, "the accursed potions tend to make people forget where they bought the damn things. Makes it easier than having to deal with a stampede of irate customers with scarred faces."

"Anyone who needs to use a love potion has no business in love, I always say." Graeme grinned at his own witticism, but the Hunter just rolled his eyes.

"Says the man who sits alone in a gloomy, dusty room reading Taivoro."

"Go get fucked by a horse," the fat man replied with a scowl. He hated to be reminded of the fact he had yet to meet the woman—any woman, really, he wasn't choosy—to fill the position of Missus Graeme. "Now, tell me what you want so I can give it to you and you can leave me alone." He eyed the Hunter, expectant.

"The Serenii catacombs."

The fat man's face turned a fascinating color—a combination of sickly green, bloodless pale, and terrified white the Hunter had never seen outside a tavern cesspool. "Wh-wh-what do you want with the catacombs?"

The Hunter gave the man a nasty smile, "So you've heard of them, I see. Don't even think of shaking your head, Graeme," he warned the man, who had opened his mouth to protest. "I can see by that look on your face that you know exactly what I'm talking about, so there's no use lying to me."

"But- but..." Graeme's mouth hung open. For long moments, nothing but unintelligible sounds came out. The alchemist gaped, trying hard to form words but with little success. Finally, it seemed his wits returned, and he managed to utter a curse. "Fuck me with a thornbush," he breathed. The alchemist seemed to deflate, slumping onto the canvas stool behind him.

The Hunter winced as the cloth stool creaked beneath Graeme's bulk. He expected the flimsy-looking seat to collapse, but the wooden frame held.

"The catacombs, Graeme," he urged.

Graeme stared up at the Hunter, fear filling his eyes. "I'm sorry, but you don't know what you're asking me, Hunter. You don't know what it would mean for me if I gave you what you wanted."

"Oh?" the Hunter asked, raising an eyebrow. His pitiless eyes bored into the fat man.

"You must understand," Graeme pleaded, cringing beneath the Hunter's stern gaze, "the Serenii catacombs are a secret that we have guarded for nearly a thousand years."

"'We' being the Hidden Circle, of course."

"Oh, Keeper take you," Graeme cursed. "Is nothing in this city kept hidden?" He studied the Hunter, narrowing his eyes in suspicion. "Why do you ask about the catacombs?"

The Hunter debated how much to tell the man. "I must travel around the city unseen," he said. "These passages beneath the city will allow me to do so."

He chose to leave out the fact that he was hunting demons, and that he planned to take down the Bloody Hand and the Dark Heresy. He trusted Graeme as much as he trusted anyone, but couldn't be certain the alchemist wasn't working for either organization. Informants could be found everywhere in Voramis, from the highest circles of society to the lowest dregs of humanity.

"No," said Graeme, his voice firm. "None but the Hidden Circle know of the tunnels."

"And now *I* know of them," the Hunter replied with a shrug. "My contract is no ordinary assignment, and the only way I will be able to carry it out is if I can move about without my enemies finding me."

Graeme stared at the Hunter with questions written on his face. "I heard about the murders in the Beggar Quarter," the alchemist said. "Did you have anything to do with that?"

"No," lied the Hunter. When he failed to volunteer more information, the alchemist's expression changed to one of stubborn refusal.

"Graeme," said the Hunter in a solemn voice, cutting off the alchemist's protest, "I would not ask if it were not important. I need your help. At least tell me about the catacombs." The Hunter gave Graeme an encouraging smile—the sort of smile a cat gives a trapped mouse.

Moments passed in silence. Graeme's expressions flitted between stubborn refusal and fear of the Hunter, and he seemed to be waging an internal war.

"I guess I can tell you a little of what you want to know," the alchemist finally said, resignation filling his voice. "What can *they* do to me? They have no way of finding out what I'm telling you."

Now that he had begun, the words poured from Graeme's mouth in a torrent.

"The Serenii tunnels are a mystery even we of the Hidden Circle have failed to uncover fully. We have spent years—nay, centuries—exploring the tunnels beneath the city, and yet have only mapped a small portion of the endless passages. We have gone farther into the earth than you could imagine, and yet we fail to even come close to discovering the breadth and depth of the catacombs."

"There are things down there..." The fat alchemist's eyes took on a faraway look, and he shuddered as some horrible memory played across his mind. "Hunter, we have kept the tunnels a secret for a reason, for there are things down there even more terrible than you."

"Why, thank you, Graeme," the Hunter said, smiling at the shuddering man.

"I make no jest, Hunter." Graeme's face remained fearful. "Stories have been passed down through the centuries, telling of things terrible and monstrous. Thankfully," he said, his expression filled with relief, "the lower passages of the catacombs have been sealed. Only the tunnels immediately beneath Voramis remain open, and none but the Hidden Circle know of their presence. And yet..." he trailed off again, his face scrunching up in pensive contemplation.

"And yet what, Graeme?" the Hunter pressed.

The alchemist snapped back to reality with a jerk of his head. He stared up at the looming figure of the Hunter.

"I might have been hearing things," he said, musing aloud, "but I would almost swear I heard faraway voices in the tunnels when last I passed through them."

This surprised the Hunter. *It would explain how he wanders in and out of the store without being seeing.*

"You use them often, Graeme?" he asked aloud.

"That's neither here nor there, Hunter," the alchemist snapped. "What matters is that the tunnels should be completely empty, and yet they are not."

The Hunter opened his mouth to press further, but Graeme continued, seemingly oblivious.

"Of course, when I tried to follow the voices," the alchemist said, as if talking to himself, "all I found were miles of empty tunnels. The dust was undisturbed, and there were no signs of life."

"Perhaps your wits are deserting you in your old age," the Hunter mocked. "Plus, there's all that agor you drink." The alchemist brewed his own agor, a foul drink made from a collection of the most potent herbs and spices Graeme could find to ferment.

"I have often thought that myself," the fat man nodded in agreement, "but I cannot be certain that the voices I heard were not real. Could someone else have learned of the presence of the tunnels?" He asked the question aloud, not really expecting an answer.

"Who else knows of the catacombs' existence?" the Hunter pressed.

"Aside from the Hidden Circle, no one," Graeme said, his expression earnest. "Or so I thought." The alchemist held up a hand as the Hunter opened his mouth to speak. "Stop right there! I will not tell you the names of the other members, no matter what you do to me."

The Hunter shrugged, holding his hands up in a gesture of assent. "Fair enough. You must have your secrets, Graeme..."

"As you have yours, Hunter," the fat alchemist replied. "However, something comes to mind. One of our members recently died under somewhat...mysterious circumstances."

"Mysterious circumstances?" the Hunter questioned, raising an eyebrow.

"Found in his home, floating in a bathtub filled with his own blood. Not a bad way to go, from what I hear," Graeme mused, "but certainly not what I'd expect from a man like him. Far more likely to hang himself than cut his wrists. All the blood was just too...messy for the prim, proper fellow."

"I heard nothing of any death."

"No, you wouldn't have," Graeme replied with a shake of his head. "The man was nothing if not ordinary, and his death would rate little attention from the world at large. However," he said, growing pensive, "I've heard whispers among my fellow Circle members that it was the work of the Bloody Hand. They didn't leave their mark on the victim, but we believe it to be their work nonetheless. And with what was taken..."

Graeme trailed off, his expression guarded, as if he had just said too much.

"So," the Hunter asked, leaning forward to loom over the sitting alchemist, "you think the Hand might have learned the secrets of the Serenii catacombs?"

Graeme hesitated, weighing his reply. "I'm not saying I believe the rumors that it was the Hand, mind you. It's very possible that his death was a suicide—an inordinately messy one, given the man in question. However, it is almost too much of a coincidence for my tastes. But," he held up a finger, "if it was the Hand, why else would they kill someone so apparently unimportant?" The fat man stroked his double chin as he thought. "I'm almost convinced they killed him for those maps."

Maps? The Hunter wondered if Graeme had meant to let that slip just as the alchemist winced in realization of what he had said.

The Hunter nodded. "You have convinced me, Graeme," he said with a smile hovering somewhere between friendly and menacing. "And now we come to the part of the evening where you tell me where I can find those maps."

"But," the fat alchemist protested, "if the Hidden Circle—"

"The Hidden Circle is far away, Graeme," the Hunter said, a hint of threat in his voice. "I'm right here. Weigh your options well, alchemist."

Graeme refused to cringe beneath the Hunter's withering glare. "I will never tell you the locations of the tunnels, Hunter." The fat man matched the Hunter's gaze in intensity. "We of the Hidden Circle have sworn to keep it a secret from the rest of the world. No matter how painful the torture or how cruel the punishment you inflict, the words you want to hear will never pass my lips."

The Hunter's hand dropped to Soulhunger's worn leather hilt. "Graeme," he shook his head in sorrow, "you know I hate to have to do th—"

"However," Graeme interrupted him, a sly smile playing across his features, "if I was to be bound, gagged, and knocked unconscious, I would certainly be unable to stop my assailant from searching through my personal items. Perhaps said assailant might chance to look in that file cabinet over there."

The alchemist nodded toward the heavy wooden cabinet at the far end of the room, and the Hunter stepped closer to examine it. It looked as decrepit as the rest of the furniture, but upon closer inspection, he found a complex locking mechanism sealing it shut.

Not an easy lock to break, even for a master thief, he thought.

"Of course," the fat man continued, "my assailant might search through that shelf"—his eyes flicked toward the shelf blocking the entrance to the hidden room—"and accidentally find a book labeled 'The Drunken Goddess and Her Monkey King'. If he were to open it, he may very well find the key for the cabinet. In my unconscious state, I could do nothing to prevent him from searching through the contents and finding a map labeled 'Catacombs'."

"Perhaps a few serious-looking flesh wounds would help to convince certain acquaintances that the assault was genuine," the Hunter said. His hand closed around the hilt of a dagger, and a wicked grin split his face.

"Absolutely not!" the alchemist snapped, his eyes growing wide. "Knocked unconscious should be more than enough to—"

"Graeme," the Hunter wheedled, "I'm only thinking of your safety."

The fat man scowled at the Hunter, and opened his mouth to retort.

"Perhaps," the Hunter interjected before the alchemist could protest, "if said assailant happened to leave a *very* hefty purse in its place, it could aid in your convalescence?"

Graeme considered this, and his eyes narrowed. "Nothing serious, Hunter." He held up a warning finger. "Flesh wounds, no more."

"My friend," the Hunter said, feigning insult, "you wound me with your mistrust, after all these years."

"Trust?" snorted the alchemist. "Our relationship is built entirely on mutual profit, Hunter. It has little to do with trust."

"How jaded you are, Graeme," the Hunter said with an exaggerated sigh of mock sorrow.

The alchemist rolled his eyes. "Let's get this over with, Hunter," he said, impatience in his voice. "You will have what you came for."

"Of course," the Hunter said, nodding and pulling the swordbreaker from its sheath.

The alchemist's eyes widened at the rasp of steel on leather, but his fear turned to understanding as the Hunter flipped the dagger in his hand to hold it pommel-down.

As the Hunter approached, Graeme's expression suddenly grew serious. "I don't know why," he said, "but somehow I get the feeling that what you're doing this night is of the utmost importance. Gods speed, my friend."

"My thanks, Graeme," the Hunter replied, surprised at the genuine warmth in his voice. He had few people to call his friends, fewer still who would call him 'friend' in return. He swallowed hard, plastering a wicked grin on his face. "Now, if you don't mind..."

"Of course," Graeme said, turning his back on the Hunter.

The Hunter struck quickly, the blade's rounded pommel slamming into the fat man's temple. Graeme sagged like a sack of grain. The Hunter winced as the alchemist's body hit the ground hard.

Good, he thought, checking Graeme's pulse and finding it steady, *his head will certainly be protesting for the next few days, but he'll live. Plus*—he studied the myriad bottles on the shelves—*he has all these alchemical potions to deal with the pain. Time to make this look like a real assault.*

The swordbreaker's tip left deep gouges in the fat alchemist's body, but the Hunter took care to avoid serious wounds. A gash to the man's head, a stab in his shoulder, a vicious-looking but harmless leg wound, and a few smaller cuts to his stomach, chest, and arms would convince any that Graeme truly had been the victim of an assault.

He'll have to see a physicker, but he'll be no worse for the wear. He rolled Graeme onto his face. The pressure of his weight would stanch the flow of blood from the more serious wounds. A thought made him smile. *Perhaps a few scars will toughen up his appearance, give him a better chance with the women he meets.*

The Hunter turned his attention to the bookshelf, scanning the titles to find the book Graeme had mentioned. Locating it, he flipped through the pages. The hollow center of the book held a small key, which the Hunter inserted into the complex locking mechanism. He slid open the top drawer and pawed through the myriad papers within.

Most of the papers filling the drawer appeared to be written in a crabbed, illegible script—which the Hunter guessed was the secret language of the Hidden Circle. They would be useless to any but Graeme, so he simply put them aside to continue his search.

After a few minutes of searching, the Hunter found it: a large map detailing the layout of what were clearly underground passages. The word "Catacombs" was inscribed neatly across the top of the page.

The Hunter spread them out over Graeme's worktable, studying them in the torchlight. He marveled at the extensive network of passages honeycombing the earth.

According to these markings, they stretch for miles outside the city. By the Watcher, it's going to take forever to find the bastards.

He rolled up the map and slid it into an empty tube he found discarded in the corner. He would take the maps to his home in the Beggar's Quarter, where he could take his time to examine them and learn the layout of the tunnels.

With a nod of satisfaction, the Hunter secured the map beneath his cloak, drawing a purse from within his robes. The bag jingled as he placed it in the drawer, and the heft of the bag told the Hunter it would more than cover the cost of the map—not to mention the blue bottles the Hunter had purchased.

The fat bastard should have little to complain about next time I come to visit him, save a pounding head, perhaps.

The Hunter knelt over Graeme once again. The fat man still breathed, and the flow of blood from his wounds had stopped.

Rest well, friend Graeme, the Hunter thought, nodding at the sleeping alchemist.

The secret bookshelf swung silently shut behind the Hunter as he entered the darkened front room of The Angry Goblin Bookstore. Ignoring the front door, he slipped out the window through which he had entered.

A breeze whipped at his cloak—nights in Voramis grew cool at this time of year. The chill sent a shiver down his spine, but he forced himself to ignore the cold. He flexed his arms, rolled his shoulders, and stretched his back. It felt wonderful to move without pain once more.

Thank the gods the bastard Second only used tools of steel, or else things could have been a lot worse.

With a shudder, he remembered the iron blade Lord Jahel had planned to use on him. He reached around to touch the spot on his back where Lady Damuria's iron pin had pierced him. While still tender, the skin had healed enough to allow him freedom of movement.

That blood of the priests' seems to have done some good.

Boxes and debris filled the alley behind The Angry Goblin, but what appeared to be a confused tangle of garbage was actually a neatly-stacked pathway to the neighboring rooftop. With a quick glance to ensure no one was watching, the Hunter quickly leapt up the precarious walkway.

Chilly gusts of late night air whipped across the rooftops of Voramis, but the Hunter ignored the cold. The urge to run, to fly free, flooded him. He began a slow jog across the shingles of the crumbling building, placing each foot with care. He felt no pain as he ran, so he pushed his body to move faster, leaping from roof to roof with glee. He laughed aloud, a rumbling sound that carried through the stillness of the night. It felt good to run once more.

The rooftops of the Beggar's Quarter flashed beneath him, and he left the foul scents of refuse and offal behind as he outpaced the wind. He leapt across a narrow alleyway, his body suspended in the air for the span of a heartbeat.

For one long moment, peace filled his world.

Then the scent hit him. A simple smell—roses, dirt, and temple incense.

Farida's scent. His feet skidded on loose tiles as the Hunter ground to a stop.

A primal, earthy scent filled the Hunter's nostrils: the smell of fear. It drowned out the clean, innocent scent of the child.

She is somewhere nearby.

His stomach twisted, worry flashing through his mind. He forced himself to close his eyes and draw in a deep breath, willing his sensitive nostrils to find her scent. He could almost taste it on his tongue, could almost feel it around him, though the smells of passing horses, vendors, and pedestrians threatened to drown it out. His eyes snapped open.

I have to find her.

The Hunter's feet dug into the tiles beneath him as he hurtled through the air. He ignored the protests of his knees and feet as he landed hard, scrabbling for a purchase on the slanted roof. With all the speed he could muster, he raced through the night toward the scent he knew so well.

The Hunter's heart pounded in time with his feet, adrenaline surging through his body. His powerful legs propelled him across the shingles, tiles, and thatched roofs of the Beggar's Quarter. One misstep could send him plummeting through a weakened section of roof, but Farida's safety was more important. He had to trust his instincts to guide him.

I have to keep her safe.

He saw the pale faces of Old Nan, Jak, Karrl, Filiana, and the others. They stared at him with empty, accusing eyes. Their deaths were on his head.

I can't let that happen to her.

Coming to a busy intersection, the Hunter crouched low in the darkness, breathing hard. Soulhunger pounded in his mind, filling his head with a dull ache. He tried to calm himself, to cast out his senses again, searching for any hint of the child.

There! Coming from the other side of the Temple Market.

Something about Farida's scent changed—the smell of roses and dirt drowned out by an acrid harshness. The animal within the Hunter roared to life as he recognized the scent of vomit mixed with the coppery tang of blood.

Feed, Soulhunger begged.

Fear flooded through him, drowning out the insistent voice in his head. His terror spurred him to move faster, and he sprinted through the night, heedless of his own safety. He raced across rooftops, leaping across gaps he would never have dared attempt. Pigeons scattered in his wake, and clay tiles shattered beneath his feet. A pair of lovers screamed and hurled curses at his fleeing back.

There's something wrong. He wasn't sure how or why he sensed it. He just knew. *If I lose her now, I may never find her again.*

The Voramis skyline flew beneath his feet, and suddenly the Hunter found himself in the middle of the Temple Market. The overwhelming scents of spices and cooking food obscured Farida's scent, but he detected it once more—this time tinged with the foul odors of the Midden.

The Hunter leapt to the street below, preferring the flat ground for speed. The impact jarred his knees, but he limped onward. His body would heal. He couldn't lose Farida's scent, couldn't let her disappear. He had almost found her, but something was horribly wrong.

Please don't let me be too late.

He ignored the protest in his legs and broke into a run once more. His breath burned in his lungs, but the gnawing pain of fear in his chest and clenching in his stomach propelled him to greater speeds.

She's close.

Then he saw her, and his knees sagged beneath him.

A little body lay on the lip of the Midden, broken and bleeding. Dark blood dripped down the walls of the Midden, Farida's life slowly trickling away. It was as if the child had been discarded, like refuse to be thrown into the gaping chasm.

The Hunter stumbled toward her, weaving like a drunk. He fell to his knees, heedless of the filth staining his clothes. With frantic efforts, he scrambled to pull the limp figure away from the edge of the void. His fingers searched for a pulse, but found only a weak flutter.

His eyes widened in horror as he stared down at the little body in his arms. She had been tortured first; the flesh of her chest and stomach sliced to ribbons, and deep incisions had been carved into her body. The cuts had jagged edges—the mark of a dull blade wielded by a strong hand.

Feed, the voice in his head begged. *Let me feed.*

"No!" He shook the small figure.

He nearly gagged at the horror on her neck. Burned into the delicate white skin, the claw-tipped insignia of the Bloody Hand glared up at him. The Hunter saw an image in his mind's eye: *the First heating his ring over a torch, pressing it into her skin to brand her.* A deliberate act of cruelty, one that made his stomach twist in revulsion and rage.

He pressed a hand to the massive hole in her chest, fighting in vain to stanch the flow of blood. Her pulse felt weak beneath his fingers. The pale cast of her skin told him she was not far from the Long Keeper's embrace. Worst of all, he could do nothing to stop it.

Farida's eyes fluttered open, and she stared up at the Hunter. She struggled to move her head, but lacked the strength.

"H…" she fought to speak.

"No, Farida," he whispered, his voice cracking. "You can't..."

An icy pit opened in his stomach. He felt an overwhelming sense of emptiness, as if his heart had just been ripped out. His stomach roiled, and his breath quickened in his throat. He shivered, a cold sweat breaking out on his body.

Her eyes focused on his face. "Wh…" she whispered.

The Hunter bent low, struggling to hear the weak words from her lips.

"Who…are…you?"

It was as if a knife had been plunged into his chest. He sat in stunned silence, holding the little figure close. He could do nothing but watch, powerless, as the light in the child's eyes dimmed. Slowly, silently, with only a small gasp of pain, her life slipped away.

"No!" he raged. "Don't leave me alone!"

He refused to accept that she was gone. She was just sleeping, he told himself, attempting vainly to shake her awake. He pounded her chest, trying in desperation to force her heart to beat once more. Even as he did, he knew it was useless.

Farida remained silent, motionless in his arms.

As the Hunter watched the only thing he had left in life being torn from him, something within him snapped. A roar ripped from his throat, the primal, animalistic sound of an enraged monster. His howl of agony rose into the night. Dogs joined their voices in chorus. He screamed his anger into the lonely darkness around him, filling the night air with his anguish.

Then his voice broke, and for the first time in his memory, the Hunter wept. He clutched the bloodied, mangled body in his arms, squeezing the limp form to his chest. His tears splashed hot on Farida's cold, clammy skin. They fell until his cries grew hoarse. Sobs racked his body, shaking his shoulders in sorrow.

It seemed the moment stretched on for an eternity as the assassin cradled the lifeless form in his arms, weeping like a child clutching a broken doll.

But soon the tears dried up, and sorrow gave way to rage.

Why did she have to die? She had no part in this. She is...was...innocent. The Bloody Hand thinks this will stop me. They've made a horrible mistake.

Cold rage surged within him, churning within his thoughts like a furnace. He stood, gathering Farida's body in his arms. Mind numb with fury and grief, he placed one foot in front of the other, uncaring of where he went. A red haze swam before his eyes, dark thoughts coursing through his mind.

Every one of those bastards will pay.

It seemed a lifetime passed in an agonized heartbeat, and his feet moved of their own accord. He walked and walked, carrying the lifeless body in his arms.

His unthinking steps led him to the House of Need. It seemed an odd choice, but fitting.

He laid the child's body on the front steps of the temple. Farida looked as if she was sleeping, but the blood staining her body belied her peaceful face. He stared into her lifeless eyes, hoping to see a flicker of light—but he hoped in vain. She lay as silent and unmoving as she had when he had found her, lying upon the edge of the Midden.

His rough hand gently closed her eyes, his other hand resting on her heart. "May the Long Keeper take your soul," he said, his voice cracking. Swallowing hard, he continued his simple prayer for the departed. "May you feel the loving embrace of the gods." His voice hardened. "And may the bastards who did this to you rot in the darkest corners of the hells."

He pounded on the heavy doors of the temple with the pommel of his dagger, but slipped away before anyone emerged.

They'll find the body, he thought. *She'll be buried with the rest of the Beggared.*

He turned his steps toward the Beggars Quarter. The familiar embrace of the shadows welcomed him, and he slipped into the night. He had a mission of his own: to hunt down the ones who had done this.

The Bloody Hand. The Dark Heresy. They will pay for what they have done.

The priest's mission would have to wait. Tonight, the Hunter sought vengeance for the deaths of the innocent.

Chapter Twenty-Eight

The Hunter had never felt so alone as he did now, walking through the empty, darkened building he called home. His ears kept searching for sounds of life—the sounds of Jak, Ellinor, Old Nan, Karrl, and all the others—but none came. He had grown accustomed to the noise, and now the silence was oppressive. Only his footsteps echoed in the darkness, an eerie sound that mocked him with every step.

Rounding the corner, his eyes fell upon the corpses that had once been his friends. The bodies lay as they had the previous night, their empty eyes staring back at him. Their faces—Tonn, Erik, Willem, Narine, Old Nan, and the others—reminded him of his failure once again.

At least they won't suffer in the winter's chill, some dim corner of his mind told him.

Tears blurred his vision, and the Hunter turned away before the sorrow overwhelmed him. He had dreaded seeing the bodies lying lifeless and discarded on the floor, as abandoned as he now felt. Loneliness washed over him. He would never see their faces again. Shame flooded him; shame at his inability to protect his friends, to protect Farida. He felt as hollow as the building around him.

His fingers moved across the mechanisms of his door lock by rote, and he hurried into his rooms, desperate to escape the horrors behind him. He slammed the door shut, leaning against it as if to stop the ghosts of his dead friends from entering.

Phantom faces floated before his eyes. He saw those he had killed, the victims who had died by his hands. The faces of his friends were also there, and Farida's lifeless features flashed in front of his eyes once again. Pain roiled through him and he sagged to the floor, wrapping his arms around his knees.

I'm sorry, my friends, he thought, sorrow welling up within him. *I'm sorry I couldn't protect you.*

Her weak voice asked the question that had ripped his heart to pieces. "Who..are...you?" Tears streamed down his scarred cheeks.

She never knew the real me, only the lie. Lies he had told himself so many times that they had become a part of his reality. The death of the child reminded him of who he really was: faceless...nameless...nothing.

There is no one to know the Hunter, not even the child I thought I cared for. In the end, I am once again alone. The bastard offspring of some hellspawn. I deserve to be alone, for I am nothing more than a killer.

Misery threatened to overwhelm him, but he refused to wallow in his grief. He had to find a way to distract himself. He knew one thing sure to take his mind off his sorrow.

Lord Jahel took my friends from me, and the First took Farida away. By all the gods of Voramis, they will pay for what they have done.

Climbing to his feet, the Hunter fumbled in the darkness, searching for a match. The flickering candle cast eerie shadows around the room, but the light would suffice for the Hunter's ritual. The first rays of false dawn showed above the rooftops of Voramis. Day would break before long.

He fumbled within his clothing for the two small pieces of cloth he had hidden. One belonged to the First, the small fragment ripped from the man's robes as the Hunter's hands grasped his neck. He had managed to hang onto it during his torture and imprisonment in the Hole. The other had come from the Hole—the cloth Lord Jahel had used to wipe the Hunter's arm after drawing his blood.

He placed the cloths on the floor and lowered himself to sit in front of the candle. The dancing light beckoned him, pulling him toward it with an enchanting solemnity. He stared into its fiery depths, mesmerized by its movements. He poured every shred of rage and fury into the flame. His anger flowed out of him—replaced by a cold, furious calm. He was ready.

Soulhunger throbbed in his mind, crying out in eager anticipation as he drew the enchanted dagger. He held the bright steel up to the candlelight, watching the flicker of light on the blade. It held his attention rapt, grounding him and giving his mind a focal point.

Without conscious thought, his hand strayed to the fabric he had retrieved from Lord Jahel's torture table. A quick slash of the knife and the Hunter's blood dripped onto the material. His fingers ran the cloth gently over the blade, and he closed his eyes.

Soulhunger pounded in his mind. It searched for its target, its throbbing rising in intensity. He cast out his senses, seeking the man to whom the cloth belonged: Lord Jahel, commander of the Dark Heresiarchs.

Nothing happened. Soulhunger's pounding quieted, but no heartbeat echoed in his mind. No scent filled his nostrils.

Something is not right, whispered the voice in his head. *There is no scent. How is this possible?*

The Hunter repeated the ritual, struggling to focus. Once again, his efforts proved futile. He sensed little more than a vague hint of Lord Jahel's existence.

This has never happened before.

Frustration mounting, the Hunter went through the rite's motions again. Only the memory of the man echoed in his head.

It's as if Lord Jahel has found a way to hide from my senses.

The Hunter tried with the cloth he had torn from the First's robe, again closing his eyes and casting out his mind.

Nothing but the lifeless face of Farida filled his eyes. The vision of the child's pale cheeks, empty eyes, and bloodied chest swam before him, breaking his concentration.

"Fuck," he cursed aloud. "Gods damn it!"

He hurled the cloth aside, but it only fluttered a few feet away, which only served to enrage him further. His anger returned in full force, building within him until it threatened to burst from his chest in a wave of destruction.

I need something to kill, or else I'm going to go mad.

Never in his memory had he experienced the emotions running through him—the sorrow, the emptiness, the fury. The feelings melded with the voice in his head, goading him into a furious bloodlust.

He stared at the antique weaponry hanging on the wall, the plush furniture, the elegance of his apartments. The wealth he had accumulated over the years had served him well, and he had lived well. He had even had enough to give to the poor wretches who lived outside his front doors, though never directly. Whenever the beggars discovered mysterious bundles of food and clothing, it had been the Hunter's money spent.

Now, he wanted nothing more than to leave it all behind. It all seemed so empty, useless. The things he had gathered in his desire for luxury and comfort felt like cheap trinkets now that he had no one with whom to share them. Voramis had felt like home for so long, but how he realized it had little to do with the city.

They were my home. Farida, Old Nan, Ellinor, Jak, and the others. They were my home, and now they're gone. The ones responsible must pay.

Climbing to his feet, the Hunter strode to the cabinet at the far end of the room. He threw open the heavy wooden doors, and a smile touched his face as the candlelight revealed the wicked assortment of weapons.

"You may be able to hide from my ritual," the Hunter growled, his voice low as he spoke into the darkness, "but let's see if you can escape me."

He drew out the map from within his tunic, spreading it out over the table once more. He had all day to commit it to memory.

It is as Brother Mendicatus said. I should have no trouble traversing Voramis unseen.

Soulhunger whispered in his thoughts, begging to be fed. He stared at his sword hanging on its wooden peg, his fingers itching. When darkness fell, he would go hunting the old-fashioned way.

The voice in his mind crowed its delight, adding its echoing cries to his grim thoughts. A mirthless, predatory smile touched his lips.

Today, I am the Hand of the Watcher. I will *bring justice for the forgotten.*

Chapter Twenty-Nine

The wind whistled through the empty streets of the Merchant's Quarter, an eerie sound that set nerves on edge and caused grown men to jump at sounds in the darkness. No moon hung in the sky this night. The scant light of the twinkling stars did little to dispel the shadows.

"Keeper's taint," muttered Fillip, "I hate nights like this."

"Shut it," his companion, Reder, retorted, "and keep your eyes on the street."

The two men lounged outside a building that looked like any other in Lower Voramis, with walls made of brick and mortar, a sloping roof set with flimsy tiles, and a sagging foundation that made the building tilt precariously.

Closer inspection, however, would reveal a solid oak door set on sturdy iron hinges, barred from within. Should anyone be foolish enough to attempt to break into a gathering house of the Bloody Hand, the door would withstand an assault with ease.

"It's not like anything's coming this way," Fillip complained. "None but us know what's really going on inside."

"Yes," Reder agreed, "but the Third said we'd be beaten if he caught us sleeping on guard duty. I'd prefer to suffer this wind and avoid the lash, if it's all the same to you."

"But—" Fillip began.

"No buts," Reder interrupted, turning to face his friend.

He fully intended to continue berating his complaining friend, but his words died on his tongue. A knife handle protruded from his friend's eyeball. Blood dripped down Filip's dumbfounded face, trickling into his gaping mouth. The light slowly faded from his other eye, and he collapsed to the floor without a sound.

Reder sucked in a breath to shout, but a deep shadow flowed toward him and clamped a hard hand over his mouth, cutting off his cry. A dagger pressed into his stomach.

"One word," growled the shadow, "and I gut you like a pig. Got it?"

Ever the pragmatist, Reder nodded.

"Good," came the harsh voice. "If I remove my hand, will you be stupid enough to cry out?"

Reder shook his head.

"Then let's take a walk." The figure removed his hand from Reder's mouth, but the dagger remained where it was, poking into the soft flesh of his side.

Reder stumbled down the steps, his mind racing as he walked. *Where in the twisted hell is he taking me? And who is he?*

"There." The hooded figure pushed Reder toward a door a few houses down.

Reder's hand shook as he reached for the door latch. Finding it unlocked, he pushed it open and stepped inside. Darkness greeted him, and a stab of panic flashed through his mind.

"All right," he said, turning to face the dark form behind him, "I've done what you asked. What—?"

A blow to his jaw sent him staggering, setting his head spinning and his knees wobbling. Strong hands pulled him into a chair. Thick ropes tightened painfully around Reder's wrists.

Dizzy, struggling to clear the ringing in his ears, he watched the figure lighting the flickering candle. A handsome face turned to regard him, with a sharp chin, strong cheekbones, and a well-proportioned nose. But the pitiless eyes looking down at Reder sent shivers down his spine.

Darkness, he thought, staring mesmerized into the empty, depthless orbs. *Like the pits of hell. Gods above, it's the fucking Hunter!*

A rasping of steel on leather snapped his attention away from the face. "Now," said the Hunter, a mirthless smile touching his lips, "I think it's time you and I had a chat." The assassin's fingers ran lovingly over the grip of a heavy notched blade.

"I have nothing to say to you, bastard," Reder spat. He eyed the dagger's edge, honed to razor keenness. His false bravado was nothing more than a desperate act.

The Hunter moved with such speed Reder didn't see the punch coming. It rocked his head back, sending pain shooting through his neck. Blood trickled from his lip and dripped onto his tunic.

"Let's try that again," the Hunter growled, menace filling his voice. "Next time, I'll use the blade." Lightning fast, he slashed a long, shallow cut across Reder's forehead.

Reder cried out, more from fear than from pain. Blood dripped into his eyes, blinding him. He struggled with his bonds, trying to pull his hands free, but the ropes held fast.

"Watcher curse you, Hunter," he snarled, his struggles ceasing. "What do you want from me?"

A smile split the Hunter's face, but there was no mirth in the grin. "Tell me everything you know about the Fifth…"

* * *

Darkness shrouded the Port of Voramis in a misty blanket, sending chills through the girls lined up outside the stuffy container that had been their home for the last month. A few whimpered, but most remained silent—too tired to do more than remain upright.

A group of rough-looking men surrounded them, their eyes eager as they watched the barely-clad young women. Smoky torches illuminated the dark night, but the flickering flames offered little warmth. The sound of chattering teeth echoed in the silence.

"Girls," said a man, striding into the circle of torchlight, "welcome to Voramis, your new home."

The shadows of the dock accentuated his emaciated body and his death's head skull of a face. A silver ring glinted on his pinky finger.

"Who I am is not important, but what is important is that you are all going to find work in the city. I will not lie and tell you that it's going to be a pleasant life you'll lead," he gave the girls a nasty smile, "but I *will* tell you—"

A cry echoed from the darkness, interrupting his words. The scream held raw terror. A shiver ran down the man's spine, and it had nothing to do with the cold.

"What the fuck was that?" he asked, whirling around and peering into the darkness beyond the circle of torches.

"Sounded like Binnty, sir," said one of the torch-bearing thugs.

"Go check it out," the thin man yelled. He pointed to another of the guards. "And take Plarno with you."

The two men rushed off into the night, heavy clubs clutched tightly in hands clammy with sweat. One carried a torch, but the flickering flame did little to illuminate the misty night. Silence fell as they disappeared from view—a silence that seemed to stretch on forever. The remaining thugs gripped their weapons with whitening knuckles. Sweat broke out on their faces as they stared nervously into the night.

Two more screams rang out, just as horrible as the first. Death had come for the Bloody Hand tonight.

* * *

The midnight bell rang as the Heresiarchal night patrol strolled through the docks. They were in no hurry to march past the container they had received a generous bribe to ignore. The Bloody Hand supplied the guards with wine, whores, and warm clothing to keep out the chill, so the Heresiarchs were more than happy to turn a blind eye, on occasion.

As they approached the container, nothing but silence and the sound of the waves crashing on the shore greeted their ears.

"They must be done already," said Sergeant Alum, a heavy-set man with a bristling moustache and graying whiskers.

"Bloody Hand scum," muttered one of the guards, peering into the darkness for any signs of life.

"Enough," barked the sergeant. "At least now we can finish our rounds and get back to the guard house. I've still got a few good cards left to play, so don't go thinking you'll clean me out tonight."

"Admit it, sarge," another guard spoke up, "you're going to—" He never finished his sentence.

The Heresiarchs gaped at the gruesome sight before them. Seven bodies, twisting slowly in the breeze, hung suspended from a hitching post. Blood dripped from their crotches, and the flesh beneath was a grisly, horribly mangled sight. A ghastly puddle of gore crept outward, reaching crimson fingers toward the guards' feet.

One of the guards retched loudly. Sergeant Alum found himself fighting to keep his own meal down. "Gods above," he whispered.

An emaciated man hung from a nearby pole, his empty eyes staring unseeing into the night. While the other thugs had been strung up by hempen rope, this man's noose was a far more grisly one: his own intestines. A silver ring bearing the symbol of the Bloody Hand sat on his pinky finger.

"Sarge, look," his corporal spoke.

With effort, he turned his face away from the horrifying sight. He followed the corporal's pointing finger, and his stomach lurched as he saw the bloody writing on the floor.

The Hunter cometh.

"Let's get the hell out of here, lads," the sergeant whispered, a shiver flashing down his spine. "Let someone else find this horror."

To a man, the Heresiarchs turned and fled. They only stopped running when they had barred the heavy door of the guardhouse behind them.

* * *

Dariel watched from the shadows as his whores plied their trade. The three young women—girls, really—stood beside the main thoroughfare running through the Blackfall District, a street known as the Lusty Stroll. Flimsy garments barely covered their thin, adolescent bodies, showing off their wares to those passing.

"How about the night of your life?" Fanira—his top earner—called out to a figure wearing the robes of a merchant. "One drake gets you anything and everything."

The merchant, stepping close, pulled back his hood to reveal the tonsured pate of a priest of the Master. He stared at the women with lust in his eyes, but, seeing the girl's youth, hustled away. Farther up the street, the cleric stopped to whisper into the ear of a doxy old enough to be his mother.

"You're going to have to do better than that if you want to meet the Fourth's quota for the night," Dariel growled. He strode toward the young girl, barely old enough to be considered a woman. She flinched as he raised his hand, but he only stroked her cheek.

No sense ruining the merchandise, he thought.

"Be a good girl and turn your tricks, or else you're out on your ear."

"Yes, daddy," she replied, cowed.

He returned to his shadowy perch, out of sight of the desperate men walking down the streets, examining the dozens of harlots unfortunate enough to be out tonight. The competition was stiff, but—

All thoughts flew from his mind as a noose dropped around his shoulders. Before he could react, the rope yanked tight, pulling him from his feet and into the air. He clutched at the rope around his neck, his legs kicking in desperation. His lungs refused to draw in air, and his neck protested at the strain.

A face loomed before him, hidden within the shadows of a deep hood. He could see little more than the eyes—their color a depthless black. There was no pity in those eyes, only naked hatred for the man dangling from his rope.

As he fought to draw even a single desperate breath, a harsh voice whispered in his ear.

"Give me the Fourth."

Chapter Thirty

The Hunter strolled from the deep shadows of the Lusty Stroll, pulling the hood forward to hide his face.

"Ladies," he said, nodding a greeting to the young girls shivering in the cold.

He ignored the curious glances of the too-young whores behind him. His cloak hid the pimp's blood, which stained the front of his tunic. No one would find the body until it started to smell, which would be at least a day or two, given the chill. The Hunter had covered the corpse with refuse; a miserable burial for a miserable creature.

He ducked into an alley a few houses down the street. A rope hung in the darkness, allowing him to climb to the roof of the single-story building. A chill breeze gusted across Voramis, but the Hunter ignored its bite. It helped to cool the fire burning within him.

The Blackfall District is a pox on the face of my city. It's time to rid Voramis of this disease once and for all.

His shadow blended with the darkness of false dawn as he moved across the rooftops with the grace of a stalking predator. Power rushed through him, fueling his rage. He thought killing would help to dim the anger burning in his chest, but it only served to stoke the furnace.

Soulhunger whispered in his ear. The dagger had fed well, but it wanted more. It always wanted more.

Tonight, he wanted more as well. He *needed* more.

He would cleanse the city of the Bloody Hand and the Dark Heresy. He would kill to avenge the deaths of his friends. It didn't matter how many had to die—all that mattered was that Farida's murder would not go unanswered.

Only after justice had been served would he turn his attention toward hunting down the demons.

* * *

Men and women crowded the common room of The Arms of Heaven, lounging on couches in various stages of inebriation. The women wore little clothing, their lithe bodies tantalizing the men who had paid good coin for the pleasure.

Elaborate tapestries depicted erotic scenes to enhanced the sexual atmosphere of the room. Nude servants scurried in and out of the room, arms laden with food, wine, pipes, opiates, and other substances both powerful and illegal.

A large lamp hung from the ceiling, but even its light failed to penetrate the thick smoke hanging in the air. Smaller lamps illuminated a hexagonal table and the three men sitting around it.

"A half drake," said one of the men, pushing a coin forward into the growing pile in the center of the fabric-covered table. His free hand ran up and down the soft thigh of the half-naked woman draped over his shoulder. "What do you think?" he asked, showing the woman his cards. She giggled, and he squeezed her ample bottom.

"I've got nothing, Pristo," sighed a second player, throwing his cards to the table in disgust. "Did you hear about Lady Damuria?"

"What about her?" asked Pristo, the first man. He turned to glare at the third man, who was studying his cards. "You're up, Manchego."

Lord Manchego ignored the impatient glare of his friend. "A moment, Pristo," he said, sipping his drink calmly. "I want to hear about Lady Damuria before I take your money."

"They found her body on the street outside her house, the body of her manservant lying next to her."

"What?" Arkadis, the second player, gasped.

"Aye," Pristo nodded, "it is said she slipped from her balcony, but I heard whispers of foul play. She was so horribly mutilated that her body was barely recognizable, and not all of the damage came from the fall." He emphasized his point by running a finger across his throat.

"How horrible!" shuddered Arkadis. "And to such a beautiful creature." He turned to the woman stroking his hair and neck. "Though her beauty could never come close to yours, my dear."

"I heard she was having an affair while Lord Damuria was away," Manchego interjected. He studied his cards for a moment before dropping three silver coins into the pile.

"Didn't you hear? He's dead," Arkadis said, lowering his voice. "They found his body at the bottom of Dead Man's Cliff. The Hunter's handiwork." His voice held a note of fearful reverence.

"You're such a gossip," Manchego snorted at his friend. "You're just as bad as my lady wife."

"No talk of your wife 'ere, my lord," the woman at his shoulder spoke. Her voice held a thick, exotic accent, which only added to her foreign beauty. She had skin far darker than any Voramian, eyes the blue of a brilliant sky, and red, full lips men fought to pay for.

"My apologies, Galette, my beauty," Lord Manchego said, kissing her dusky-skinned hand. His eyes roamed up her swarthy body, staring at the salacious curves of her breasts and hips. His gaze rested for a moment on her dark nipples before traveling downward to the gauzy cloth covering her delicate lips.

"One imperial. You're up, Manchego," Pristo said, his gold coin clinking on the pile of glittering silver and copper. "You'll have time to enjoy Galette later, but for now, I need to take your money." He ran a hand down the back of his companion, a well-formed creature with long blond hair, heavy breasts, and bright pink nipples.

Sighing, Lord Manchego turned his attention back to the table. "Fine, one imperial it is."

"I trust my lords are enjoying themselves?" a smoky voice drifted toward them, accompanied by the full figure and pale skin of the Madame of The Arms of Heaven.

"Absolutely, Mistress Croquembouche," Pristo smiled at the approaching woman.

"Madame," Manchego said, inclining his head respectfully, "so wonderful to see you this evening."

None would have dared called the Madame '*old*', though her prime years had long passed. Something about the way she carried herself still arrested the attention of every man in the room, and clearly she knew it.

"I take it that Carac, Galette, and Mille-Feuille here are taking good care of you?" A knowing smile touched her lips as she spoke.

"Mistress, I could never complain when I am in the hands of the magical Mille-Feuille here," Arkadis said, stroking the soft skin of the woman standing next to him. Where the other two women had full figures, Mille-Feuille had a hard body, pert breasts, and slim hips. Long, arrow-straight black hair hung down past her waist. Her gaze was haughty as she stared at the simpering women on the other side of the table.

"Yes," Mistress Croquembouche replied, "I know how she does that thing with her tongue—"

Her words cut short as a servant rushed into the room.

"Fire!"

Stunned silence filled The Arms of Heaven, and all movement stopped.

"Out, now!" Mistress Croquembouche yelled. Her shout galvanized the room into action. Thick smoke filled the air as the assorted men and women stampeded through the heavy doors.

Within moments, an inferno raged where The Arms of Heaven had once stood. The scorching heat of the flames seemed unnatural, consuming the building in a pillar of fire.

"The bastard who did this will pay!" cursed Mistress Croquembouche, her pale face turning red from rage and the heat of the fire.

A crowd gathered on the street, and not all of those standing there had come from within the pleasure house. The women clutched at their scant garments, attempting in vain to cover themselves. Few had eyes for the sparsely clothed women. For most, their attention remained firmly fixed on the fire in front of the whorehouse.

It shouldn't have been possible, but somehow the stones of the street burned. Fiery letters blazed on the cobblestones, and the words written in tongues of fire sent shivers down the spines of every man and woman watching the conflagration.

Ware the Hunter.

* * *

The four red-robed Heresiarchs marched in silence, only the '*tromp, tromp*' of their boots on the cobblestones breaking the unnatural quiet of the evening. Watchful eyes scanned the night for signs of life; the streets of Lower Voramis were empty tonight.

Their pace quickened as they saw the light beaming from their small watch station. The warmth of the guardhouse beckoned, and they all wanted to escape the whipping wind and its eerie moaning.

"Halt!" Corporal Anders shouted, raising a gauntleted fist.

The four men stopped in unison, marching with a precision the Legion of Heroes would envy. Corporal Anders took pride in his service in the Heresiarchal Guard, and he had trained his squad to be the city's finest. He and the three men in his command undertook missions his Heresiarchal commanders—those not named Lord Jahel—knew nothing about.

"Well done, men," he said, nodding to Frollin, Paytr, and Derrin. "We'll do the rounds again at the sound of the fourth bell."

The three men swore under their breath, but not loud enough for their corporal to hear. They wanted nothing more than to spend their nights in the warm guardhouse, and the thought of trudging the streets of Voramis held little appeal—particularly on a night like this.

Derrin's huge hand pushed the door open so hard that it crashed against the wall.

Every damned time, Anders thought. *That man is too strong for his own good, and dumber than a hitching post.*

"By the Swordsman, Derrin," he cursed aloud. "Watch what you're doing!"

"Sorry, Corporal," the huge man mumbled.

"Every time, Derrin," Paytr snickered at the big man. Derrin's opposite in every way, he came no higher than the man's shoulder. "One day you'll pull the door right off its hinges."

The fire within the guardhouse had burned low, casting deep shadows in the room. For a moment, Corporal Anders thought he saw something move in the darkness, but shrugged it off as a trick of his imagination.

He strode to the fireplace, and stabbed at the last burning log with the iron poker.

"Hand me another log, will you, Derrin?" Anders held out a hand without turning his head.

An odd sound fell on his ears. It sounded almost like a sword being…

"What the—?" Paytr shouted, alarm and fear filling his voice.

A meaty '*thunk*' sounded behind Anders, followed by a horrifying gurgling sound. He whirled around in time to see Paytr clutching his throat, blood bubbling from between his fingers and splashing from his mouth. Derrin slumped to the floor next, his screams loud and horrifying. The big Heresiarch clutched at the stump where his right hand had once been.

Frollin was the last man through the door, and he now stood alone against the Hunter. He stared wide-eyed at the Hunter, struggling to draw his blade. The assassin moved with unnatural speed, and Anders watched in helpless horror as the Hunter's blade sliced through the bone, gristle, and flesh of Frollin's neck. Frollin's head flew through the air, rolling to a stop between Anders' feet. When the corporal looked up from the grisly trophy on the floor, the Hunter's baleful glare greeted him.

"And then there was one," the Hunter said, his voice a menacing growl.

"Back, I warn you," Corporal Anders said, waving the poker in front of him.

"Lord Jahel," the Hunter said, his eyes fixed on the iron implement in Anders' hand, "tell me everything about him. I warn you, though, you don't need your hands to talk."

The dark eyes flicked to Anders' face, and the Dark Heresiarch saw the pitiless depths. They looked insane with bloodlust. A quiet fury burned in his merciless eyes. He knew he wasn't going to leave here alive.

"Never!" the corporal yelled, dropping the poker and drawing his sword.

The Hunter's face creased into a wicked smile, which never reached his eyes. "That was a mistake you won't live long enough to regret."

Corporal Anders raised his sword, but the Hunter was a blur in the shadows as he moved toward the Dark Heresiarch. The corporal's slashing cut went wide, and he staggered. Agony flooded his hands. Looking down, he saw the Hunter's blade buried in the leather grip of his own sword. The corporal's fingers fell to the floor, his Heresiarchal sword clattering beside it.

Anders screamed and wept, pain racing up his arm. He stared in wide-eyed horror at his ruined right hand. The Hunter kicked the sword to the other side of the room. What the corporal saw in the dark, empty eyes terrified him.

"About Lord Jahel," the Hunter snarled, placing his face dangerously close, "there are a few things I'd like to know…"

Chapter Thirty-One

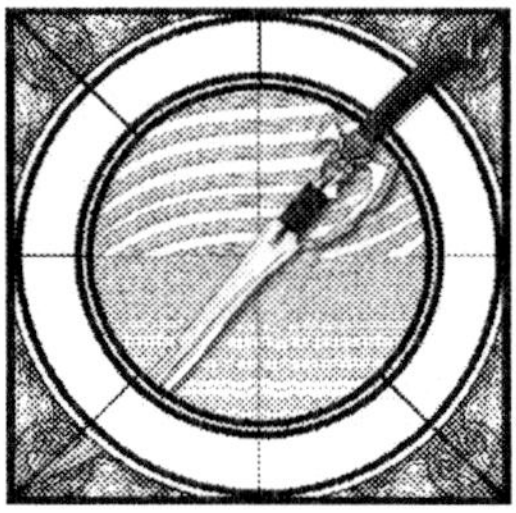

"No, please!" cried the merchant struggling in the vice grip of Alden and Erlick, two of the Third's favorite strong-arms. "I already paid for protection this month."

"Well, looks like you di'n't quite pay enough," Grom, the Third's second-in-command, spat back at him. "If you had've, there'd be someone here protectin' you from the likes of us, wouldn't there?"

He buried his meaty fist into the merchant's stomach, the force of the blow folding the man in half. Grom watched the pathetic creature heave his dinner onto the cobblestones, and nodded to the two thugs holding the merchant's arms.

Alden and Erlick heaved the man through the front window of his shop in the heart of the Merchant's Quarter. Glass shattered, and Grom heard the sound of wooden furniture crunching.

There was an odd whistling sound, followed by two '*thunks*' in quick succession. Grom turned, and his mouth hung open as Erlick fell to his knees. The wicked tip of a crossbow bolt protruded from the front of his comrade's throat, spilling blood onto the cobbled stones of the street. Another bolt had buried itself deep in his spine, and the big thug flopped to the floor like a fish, blood pooling beneath him.

A figure leapt from the darkness toward Grom and Alden. The cloaked figure held no weapons, but he moved with a confidence that shook Grom to the core.

"Get him," he shouted.

Alden rushed toward the dark form, lowering his head and preparing to ram the smaller man in the stomach. The man in the hood sprang to the side with an agility Alden couldn't match, and the big man sprawled to the floor. The dark figure crunched a heavy boot down on the back of Alden's head before the thug could recover. From where he stood, Grom heard the loud '*crack*' of Alden's neck.

The man in the hood turned to face Grom. "I'm going to ask you a few questions about the Third," he said in a voice heavy with fury, "but I'll keep them simple so your tiny brain can understand them."

With a loud roar of rage, Grom charged his assailant. Yet something made him stop a few paces away. An air of menace radiated from the figure in the dark hood. A voice in the back of Grom's mind shrieked a warning to flee.

The figure pulled back his hood, revealing a handsome face and glittering eyes the color of night.

The Hunter, Grom thought, a twinge of fear running through his dull mind. *I get to kill the Watcher-damned Hunter!*

The Hunter removed his cloak, dropping it to the street behind him. He rolled his shoulders and neck as if to loosen up, and, with a wicked grin, beckoned the big man to attack.

Grom led with powerful swings of his meaty fists. The force of his blows had shattered doors and windows, but he found it much harder to break something that never stopped moving. The Hunter ducked, dodged, and sidestepped each of Grom's wild strikes. The assassin's punches landed in Grom's ribs, elbows, and throat, with far more force than the big man anticipated. He fell beneath a flurry of blows to his solar plexus, gagging and retching.

Strong hands closed around Grom's wrists. Pain ripped through his shoulders as the Hunter wrenched his arms from their sockets. He fell to the street, his face splashing into the sickeningly warm pool of his own vomit.

A knee dug into his spine, but it was the Hunter's soft growl in his ear that terrified Grom to his core. When the big thug finally spoke, his words flowed freely, and he told the Hunter everything he wanted to know.

* * *

Opium smoke hung thick in the gambling house, floating from the mouths of the men puffing on water pipes. No pictures hung on the walls, no feminine décor adorned the shelves around the edge of the room. Women had never stepped foot within the hallowed halls of this all-male establishment, a place where wealthy men from around the city could smoke and gamble in peace.

A heavy table dominated the center of the room, laden with an ever-growing pile of papers, wooden chits, and assorted valuables. Six men sat around the table, the highest-ranked members of the Bloody Hand outside of the Five Fingers. The men gambled not with money, but with deeds for mansions, chits representing controlled territories, and stolen jewelry.

"Handel, if you want to stay in the game," grated one man, a stocky thug with the scarred knuckles of a bruiser, "you're at least going to have to match Arris's bet."

"Shut up and let me think, Kelnon." Handel glared at Kelnon with open distaste. Far smaller than his opponent, Handel's small build and agile fingers made him an adept thief, second only to the Fifth in skill. His larger companions often pushed him around—verbally and physically—leaving him with a foul temper and a quick blade hand.

The thief inspected his cards, struggling to make up his mind. He studied his companions as if trying to read their thoughts.

He shrugged. "I will wager the region between Borthwick Street and the Palisade." He pushed wooden chits into the growing pile in the center of the table.

Kelnon's face creased into a wide grin. "Ooh, gambling big are we? You think you have a winning hand?"

"Kelnon seems pretty confident, Handel," a third, Arris, spoke up. He held a perfumed handkerchief to his nose in an attempt to block out the intoxicating smoke hanging in the air. "You sure you want to do that?"

"Aye," the little thief growled at the dandified Arris. "Now shut up and show your cards."

Arris turned over his cards, revealing two suns and a jester. "The Fool's Run," he said with a smile. "What do you have, Kelnon?"

"Two swords and a sun," the stocky man said, grinning as Arris' face fell. "You, Handel?"

"Nothing more than a pair of Queen's Courtiers and a Spectacle." The little thief laughed as Kelnon's face purpled with rage. "And you thought I had nothing!" He reached forward to pull the pile in the center of the table toward him, but Kelnon's meaty hand stopped him.

"You fucking ass-licker, Handel," Kelnon growled, dangerously close to the thief's face. "How in the Keeper's name could you possibly have that hand twice in a row?"

A fourth player rested a restraining hand on Kelnon's massive forearm. "You're just angry because you've lost every hand tonight, Kelnon."

"And how is that possible, Balddin?" Kelnon asked, turning his fierce glare on the man. Balddin jerked his hand back as if burned. "There's no possible way I can lose every hand. You ever read Modan's *Principles of Probability*? It says that everything averages out, meaning I *have* to win at least once in a while."

"Where the twisted hell do you find the time to read dusty old schoolbooks, Kelnon?" the fifth player at the table, Prios, asked. While not as heavyset as Kelnon, he outweighed the other five.

"What else am I supposed to do while sitting and listening to you cunts prattle on about your takings on Sunrise Row?" Kelnon shot a glare toward Prios. Prios seemed unperturbed by Kelnon's anger, and he simply smiled back at the bigger man.

Kelnon sought a new target for his anger. "And you," he growled, rounding on the little thief, "I could swear you're cheating, but I just can't figure out how."

"Why you…!" Handel exclaimed, struggling to stand. Finding he could not break Kelnon's grip, his free hand reached toward the knife on his belt. Before he could draw it, however, a hand far larger than Kelnon's clamped down on his shoulder.

"Careful, Handel," said the man to whom the hand belonged. "You know the Third's rules: no steel in the gambling house. You want to fight, you take it outside."

The giant stood a full head taller than Kelnon, and came close to twice as wide, with heavy muscle covering his huge body. The massive hand on Handel's shoulder didn't squeeze, but the thief knew there was enough force in Kad's grip to shatter bone.

"Sorry, Kad," Handel said, swallowing hard. He released his hold on the knife and quickly sat back down.

Kad turned his glare on Kelnon, who quickly let go of Handel's forearm. The little thief snatched back his arm, nursing his wrist as he pulled the pile of chits and markers toward his corner of the table.

"Hand's up, lads," Arris said, throwing the cards across the table. "Get 'em while they're hot."

The six figures sat in silence, each studying their cards—save for Kelnon and Handel, who exchanged angry glares over the tops of their cards. The opium smoke seemed to press in around them, the gloom narrowing their world to nothing but the table around which they sat.

Arris coughed, covering his mouth with his handkerchief. "Is it just me, or is the smoke thicker than usual?"

Kelnon opened his mouth to retort, but the heavy smoke filled his lungs. He turned to shout at the guard. "Damn it, Kad, why doesn't someone open a—"

His words cut off as Kad slumped to the floor, his huge face reddening as he struggled to breathe. Horrified, Kelnon watched the giant's face turned purple, then blue. Blood vessels burst in Kad's eyes.

"Fuck!" Kelnon gasped. "Poison!" Coughing fits gripped the others in the room, and his lungs burned with every breath.

He managed to find his feet, though he had to support himself on the table just to stay upright. His comrades had slumped forward or fallen to the floor, their faces twisted in horrible grimaces as the thick smoke smothered them.

The door seemed miles away as Kelnon fought to put one foot in front of the other. Nightmarish hallucinations—caused by both the opiate and whatever poison floated through the room—swam in his vision. The handkerchief covering his mouth felt far too heavy for his arms, which suddenly seemed made of lead.

He fell forward, but by pure chance, his hand landed on the latch. With his remaining strength, he pushed, and the door swung silently open. Cool night air wafted past him, but already his vision had begun to dim. The last thing he saw was the sign nailed to the door of the gambling house.

The Hunter will have his due.

Chapter Thirty-Two

Sweat dripped from Fraid's bald head, mingling with the soot staining his face. The heavy door shuddered beneath the onslaught of his meaty, heavily scarred fists.

"Open the door, quickly," he panted. Even as he beat at the door, his eyes flashed in all directions, fear filling his face. His legs burned from running across the Blackfall District, and he rested his hands on his knees to take in huge gulps of air.

"What is it?" came a dull voice matching the thickness of the ironbound door.

"Open the damn door, Oden," Fraid bellowed.

The man on the other side of the door seemed in no hurry. A small panel slid back, revealing a single red-rimmed eyeball. "What's the password?" Oden drawled.

"Fuck you and the password, Oden. I have to speak to the Second, now!" Urgency filled Fraid's voice, a tone lost on the thug within.

"Password," Oden replied, "or go fuck off."

"Fine!" Fraid gasped in frustration. "'Abruxil's hairy balls'. Happy now?" He swallowed an insult; Oden tended to be tetchy, and the last thing he wanted was to offend the only man who would open the door for him.

I have to see the Second, he thought, his mind filling with panic.

Locks, latches, deadbolts, and chains rattled, then, with agonizing lethargy, the ponderous door swung open.

"Damn you, Oden," he cursed at the guard opening the heavy door. "Don't you know what's going on out there tonight?"

"What?" asked Oden, his voice dull and heavy with sleep. "What's going on? What happened to you?"

But Fraid had already pushed past the guard, knocking him aside in his hurry. He sprinted toward the lighted room at the end of the long hall. Within the room, four men lounged on comfortable chairs. One sat sharpening a dagger. Two more muttered over a pack of playing cards, and snores rose from the man dozing in the corner.

"Where is he?" Fraid demanded as he entered the room.

The one sharpening his dagger looked up, taking in Fraid's dirty appearance. He seemed not to care, but simply jerked his head in the direction of the door at the far side of the room.

"In the back room," the man said, not pausing in his task. "I wouldn't go in, if I were you. He's…busy."

Fraid strode toward the door, ignoring the warning. "He's going to want to hear this."

He pushed the door open and burst into the room beyond. His eyes noticed the candles around the room a fraction of a second before his ears registered the moans of pleasure. A woman lay naked on the Second's desk, the man himself standing between her legs. The Second's hands gripped her arms, pulling her toward him as he pushed deeper into her. Her breasts sagged to either side of her sweaty chest, and her stomach wobbled with each thrust of the Second's hips.

For a moment, the two failed to notice the thug standing by the closed door. When the Second finally did see Fraid, rage filled his face.

"What in the name of the Long Keeper's shriveled gonads do you want, Fraid?" he snarled, not pausing in his thrusting. The whore on the table continued her moans of pleasure—though, to Fraid's ears, they sounded contrived.

"Uh…" he stammered, unsure of how to respond in this delicate situation. Everyone knew the Second had a mean temper. He had killed men for less.

"Speak up, you dullard son of a pox-ridden donkey," the Second repeated. "Why the fuck are you disturbing me? And why isn't that door locked?"

"Sorry, sir," muttered Fraid, ducking his head as he turned to lock the door in place. The deadbolt shot home with a '*thunk*', and he turned to face the outraged Second once more. "It's the Hunter, sir, he's-"

Something cut him off mid-sentence. Pain blossomed in his throat, and his breath bubbled in his lungs. He felt no pain as his knees hit the hard wooden floor, felt nothing but the warmth rushing down the front of his tunic.

* * *

The Hunter watched the thug slump to the floor. Life fled from the dying man's eyes as blood leaked from the wound in his throat. The haft of his throwing dagger protruded from the man's neck—a perfect throw, even by his standards.

Satisfied that he had neutralized the secondary threat, the Hunter snapped his gaze to the figures on the table. The Second, already shaken by the surprising entry of the thug, now lay frozen in place atop the squirming whore.

The woman tried to wriggle out from beneath him but, finding his hands held her firmly in place, gave up trying to break free. Instead, she screamed, a sound that echoed through the small room.

The Hunter covered the distance to the table with a single leap, his sword singing through the air. The Second somehow found his senses in time to throw himself backward, pulling out of the woman. He stumbled backward, his ankles catching in his breeches, and he fell hard. The fall saved his life, but not his face. The Hunter's sword carved a chunk out of his cheek, eliciting a yelp of pain.

The Hunter slammed the pommel of his sword into the whore's temple, and her cries fell silent.

Can't have her getting in the way.

His eyes sought the Second in the dim light of the room, and found the man hastening to tie a knot in his breeches.

"I've been expecting you," the Second said, glaring.

"Obviously not, or you would have been less...vulnerable," the Hunter replied with a sardonic smile. The Second reddened at being caught with his guard down, which only caused the Hunter's smile to widen. The Hunter nodded at the thick door. "No doubt there are a handful of your best cutters sitting right outside."

"Of course," said the Second, shrugging. "How you got in here without their noticing I don't know, but it's definitely a mistake on your part, *Hunter.*" The Second spat the last word.

"Let me guess," mocked the Hunter, "you think *you'll* be the man to kill the Hunter?"

"I guess we'll find out tonight!" With sudden speed, the Second reached into the desk and drew a brace of daggers. "Time to put your skills to the test, Hunter," he snarled.

"The last man who said that now sits beside the Long Keeper." With an exaggerated flourish and a bow, the Hunter attacked.

His long sword slashed through the air, forcing the Second to twist out of the way. His swordbreaker caught a thrust of the Second's long knife, turning it aside and opening the man's guard for a return stroke of the sword.

The Second, anticipating the blow, stepped inside the Hunter's guard and lashed out with a foot. The Hunter twisted aside, dodging the powerful kick aimed at his chin. He grunted as the man's boot struck his shoulder.

"I have to admit," he said, with a grudging smile of admiration, "you're far better than any other I've faced in a long time, Second."

The man took this as encouragement, and renewed his attack with a fury that surprised the Hunter. His vicious skill proved he had earned his place in the Bloody Hand, and the Hunter found himself hard-pressed. The

Second carved intricate patterns in the air with his blades. Even the added reach of the Hunter's long sword seemed useless in the face of the Second's attacks.

The Second fought like a man possessed; whirling, spinning, ducking, cutting, and stabbing at every opening. He launched kicks, threw elbows and knees, and used every dirty trick he knew. Had he faced anyone else, the fight would have been over in seconds.

But he faced the Hunter this night.

The Hunter's sword moved like the flicking tongue of a serpent, darting in to strike the Second and slipping away before the man could block. Within the space of half a minute, the Second bled from a dozen places. While not mortal wounds, the painful cuts would sap his strength. Grim determination filled the man's expression, but the Hunter could see panic at the corner of his eyes.

The Second stooped to cut at the Hunter's exposed legs, but the Hunter's sword traced a red line across the man's forehead as he dodged the blow. Blood dripped down the panting Second's face, mixing with sweat. The Second winced and wiped his eyes, and the Hunter seized the momentary advantage. He sliced the swordbreaker's razor edge across the knuckles of first one hand, then the other, leaving deep gashes. Fear flashed across the Second's face as his bloody fingers struggled to grip the daggers.

Pain raced up the Hunter's arm, and he staggered to one side. Looking down, he found a deep gash in his left bicep, a wound he had not noticed during the lightning flurry of blows. Sticky black tar mixed with the bright blood soaking into his cloak.

Argam.

"Room beginning to spin, Hunter?" the Second asked, confidence filling his voice.

The poison seeped into the Hunter's arm, and the swordbreaker clattered to the floor. He leaned on the table for support.

"Like I said," the Second's face split into a mocking grin, "I knew you were coming."

The Hunter wobbled and sagged, the point of his sword resting on the floor for a moment as he sought to hold himself upright. He stumbled backward, off balance, and with renewed vigor, the Second pressed the attack. Eyes filled with triumph, he lunged forward to impale the Hunter on his blade.

But the Hunter had only feigned weakness. He blocked the Second's thrust with contemptuous ease, and the swordbreaker in the Hunter's left hand crunched down on the Second's fingers. The Hunter's right hand came up hard and fast. The blade set into the sword's crossguard slammed into the Second's throat.

Blood spurted over the Hunter's knuckles as the little blade cut deep. The Second clutched at his throat in a vain effort to stanch the torrent, but the wound gushed with every labored breath. The room filled with the coppery tang of fresh blood and the foul stench of the Second's bowels loosening in terror.

The Second slumped to his knees, still fighting to stop the gore pumping from his throat.

"Many have tried to kill me before," the Hunter whispered into the man's ear, "better men than you, Second. And all have failed. Join them now."

With his free hand, the Hunter drew Soulhunger from its sheath. The Second's eyes widened at the sight of the blade. He tried to scream, but only a horrible gurgling punctuated the silence.

With a howl of rage, the Hunter drove the point of the dagger deep into the Second's chest. "May your soul rot in whatever hell it has gone to," he cursed, watching life fade from the man's eyes.

Power flooded him, and Soulhunger screamed in ululating ecstasy as it drank deep of the Second's lifeblood. The Hunter stumbled backward, clutching at his head to drown out the horrible cried echoing through his mind. The scars on his chest burned, and a new mark joined those etched into his skin.

But the pain didn't bother him. Vengeance had been served.

* * *

"Get that damn door open, Kuritts," Oden yelled.

They had all heard the screams from within the Second's room, and the clash of steel on steel had been unmistakable.

The four thugs battered at the heavy door, but the bloodwood refused to yield. Long minutes passed before the Hand cutters forced the door open, but by that time, the sounds from the room beyond had died. The carnage within showed the futility of their efforts

"Keeper!" Oden cursed as he surveyed the carnage in the room. Blood dripped from the forehead of the naked whore splayed over the top of the Second's desk, pooling in a foul-smelling puddle at the center of the room.

The body of the Second hung naked and bleeding, pinioned to the wall by his own daggers. From where he stood, Oden could see something carved into the corpse's chest. Stepping closer, he squinted in an effort to read the bloody words.

The Hunter is inexorable.

Fire blossomed in his face as an explosion filled the small room.

* * *

Grim satisfaction flooded the Hunter as the detonation shook the tunnel around him.

Thank you, Graeme, for your little blue bottles of alchemical fire!

He basked in the cool darkness of the Serenii passages, slipping through the shadows without a sound.

A twinge of fear raced through him as dust and debris rained down from the roof. For a moment, he worried the weight of the crumbling building might trigger a collapse in the tunnels. He was immune to most wounds, but he doubted even he could survive being buried under a mountain of stone. But only a few loose chunks tore free before the rumbling overhead died down. The Serenii had built their tunnels well.

These secret passages truly are marvelous. The Serenii tunnels had allowed him to enter the Second's room unseen and unheard, and he had used them to escape the building before the alchemical bombs exploded. *Now let's see if they lead me to where the First is hiding.*

A wave of nausea flooded him, forcing him to stop and lean on the wall for support. Breathing hard, he struggled to stay upright as the smell of the argam in his veins overwhelmed his senses.

Derelana damn that Second and his fucking poison. Cowardly bastard. He recognized the irony of his anger.

The weakness passed, and the Hunter continued his trek through the darkness. He knew his body would flush out the poison within a few hours—more than enough time for him to track down the remaining members of the Hand.

After tonight, Voramis will be free of the burden of the Bloody Hand, and I can turn my attention to the demons.

He pictured the First's smug grin and relished the thought of wiping it from the man's face with the edge of his sword.

I'm coming for you, you bastard.

The First would pay for his sins. He could not outrun the Hunter.

Chapter Thirty-Three

The little pickpocket crept through the darkened Serenii tunnels beneath Voramis. His eyes darted nervously around and his hands shook with fear, setting the shuttered lamp he carried rattling.

Just out of reach of the meager lamplight, the Hunter smiled, his eyes tracking the jumpy pickpocket. The smooth floors of the tunnel made it easy for him to move without fear of stumbling, and the soft leather of his boots muffled his footsteps. He ghosted along in pursuit, ever just out of sight.

"Watcher damn the Hunter," the thief muttered. He pivoted his head from side to side, and he stopped periodically to check for signs of pursuit.

"Lead me to your master," the Hunter whispered softly into the darkness. "Your time will come, little thief." His voice carried through the tunnel, reverberating until it seemed to echo from every direction.

The thief jumped and spun around. "What?" he called, his voice trembling. Holding the lamp high, he peered into the shadows around him. "Wh-who's there?"

Nothing but silence greeted him.

"Damned tunnels!" he cursed, turning and picking up his pace. "Creepy bloody things. It's all in yer head, McCreedy."

The Hunter stifled his laughter as he followed the pickpocket, who walked at a near-run, his breath coming in gasps. The thief reeked of terror, the smell overwhelming his natural unwashed fragrance.

Let's see where the little bastard scurries to now.

The Hunter had laid waste to every place the Bloody Hand could hide. He had killed their men, frightened away their customers, and burned their primary source of income to the ground. He was certain the thief would lead him right to the First—one of the final loose ends to tie up. Once he had ended the Bloody Hand's leader, he could hunt down the Third—whoever he was—and Celicia.

A stab of anger ran through him at the thought of the woman who had called herself Celicia. She had played him, and for some reason that stung far worse than any pain caused by the Second's implements of torture.

She was just doing her job, he told himself. He wasn't certain why he was so angry at her betrayal, but it hurt nonetheless.

He would also have to eventually deal with Lord Jahel, as well. Dozens of the Dark Heresy had died tonight, but it wasn't enough to dim the Hunter's rage.

Even if I have to tear apart the Palace of Justice, I will *find the place where he skulks.* The days of the Dark Heresy were numbered.

His promise to Father Reverentus echoed in his mind. The weight of his vow pressed on him, but he pushed those thoughts aside. It would have to wait—first, he needed to put an end to the Hand once and for all.

Instinct told him that the thief headed in the direction of a large, open cavern—a location marked clearly in a script he had been unable to decipher. The cavern would be a good place for the First to lie in wait. It had enough space to hold a small army—or however many of the Bloody Hand remained alive.

He consulted Graeme's map, which he had committed to memory. If it was correct, he should reach the cavern in a few minutes. A thrill of anticipation coursed through the Hunter, and his heart pounded in excitement. The First was so close; he could all but feel the man's presence.

The pickpocket fairly sprinted through the tunnel in his fear, his lamp rattling and bouncing as his heavy boots echoed in the corridor. He turned a corner in the tunnel, disappearing from view.

The Hunter moved quickly to catch up with the man, and rounded the bend in the passage in time to see the thief disappear through a small opening a few dozen paces away. Light shone from beyond, and the Hunter heard the sound of voices.

The little pickpocket was speaking, his voice filled with fear. "Sorry, boss, but it was time for me to get back here. There's no sign of anything anyways, just those bloody creepy tunnels." The thief's voice echoed, as if he stood in a wide-open space. Immediately, the Hunter knew he had found the cavern.

Uncertain of what to expect, the Hunter peered around the edge of the opening. Torches flickered in the room beyond, illuminating the cavern. An eerie wind whistled through the high-vaulted space. From where he stood, the Hunter could see gaping darkness at the edge of the room.

His mind took in the details without conscious thought. He had eyes only for the figure in the center of the cavern.

Found you, you bastard!

The First cut an imposing figure in his elegant garments, towering over the small thief. His clothes were as colorful and ostentatious as the day he had tortured the Hunter, and he stood as the single bright spot of color in the massive, empty cavern. The scent of his perfume wafted toward the Hunter's hiding place. Beneath it, the Hunter detected a sickly sweet odor of decay.

That smell...

It was an odd scent, one he had encountered before. It teased at his mind, but it was a puzzle he couldn't solve...yet.

He pushed the frustrating thought aside and quickly scanned the room, his eyes searching the shadows for the First's army. Surprisingly, the man was alone. No heavily-armed thugs flanked him—a testament to his overconfidence.

He has no fear that I will find him here, the Hunter thought. *Time to put the fear of the gods into him.*

The Hunter stepped from the shadows and threw back his dark hood. "Your time has come, First," he said, his voice solemn. "The Hunter always finds his prey, and tonight you will suffer the same fate as your men."

The little thief leapt into the air, squeaking in fright. He turned to face the Hunter, and his mouth fell open. The pickpocket squirmed beneath the Hunter's glare, looking as if his bladder was a heartbeat away from emptying itself. His hands shook as they reached for the pitiful dagger at his belt.

The First, however, showed no sign of fear, but calmly turned to face the Hunter.

"By the gods," he said, a smile spreading across his face, "if it isn't the Hunter himself." He swept a courtly bow. "What a pleasant surprise! Well, perhaps not quite a surprise. To tell you the truth, I've been expecting you."

Instinct screamed in the Hunter's mind a heartbeat before his sensitive nostrils detected the coppery scent of dried blood and cold steel. He felt movement behind him, and without thinking, threw himself to the floor. That instinct saved him, for a heavy fist whooshed over his head, missing him by a hair's breadth.

He lashed out and heard a grunt of pain as his kick connected. His boot struck a massive shinbone instead of the man's knee, as he had intended. He rolled away, seeking to place distance between himself and the huge hands reaching for him—the same hands that had gripped the handles of Lord Cyrannius' wheeled chair.

Tane stared at the Hunter with a dark expression, his heavy brows knitted in frustration. The Hunter's hand flashed toward his sword belt, but Tane moved with a speed that should have been impossible for his size. He spread his massive arms wide, attempting to encircle the Hunter in a bear hug powerful enough to crush ribs. A grin of triumph spread on his face.

But this time, instead of retreating the Hunter stepped forward, moving between Tane's arms. His fists pummeled the big man's solar plexus, kidneys, and throat. He slammed the knife-edge of his hand into the bunched muscles on the side of the Tane's neck, and his elbow shot upward to strike the underside of the huge man's chin. Tane gasped for breath, his arms dropping.

The Hunter risked a glance over his shoulder. The First had not moved, but his hand rested calmly on his sword. Unwilling to chance a surprise attack from the rear, the Hunter danced to the side, placing both of his enemies within his field of vision.

"You're going to have to do better than that, Hunter," Tane rasped, rolling his huge shoulders, "if you want to take me down." He shook his arms as if to loosen the muscles before settling into a weaponless fighting stance. Hands empty, fingers spread, knees bent, eyes watching the Hunter's every move.

While the Hunter had trained in unarmed combat, he preferred to fight with weapons in his hands. He slipped his sword from its sheath with a ring of steel on leather. The blade felt comfortable in his hands, filling him with confidence.

He stepped forward to launch his attack, but his body betrayed him. The effects of the argam still lingered, slowing his movements and causing his legs to wobble. His knees sagged for a heartbeat, but it was all Tane needed. The huge man leapt forward with inhuman speed and plowed his fist into the Hunter's stomach.

The blow knocked the breath from his lungs and doubled him over. With lightning quickness, Tane's arms snaked around him. One huge bicep crushed the Hunter's throat, cutting off his breath, while the other arm wrenched his right arm behind his back, nearly twisting it from its socket. Tane wrapped his legs around the Hunter's midsection, and the man's prodigious weight pulled the Hunter off balance. He fell backward, his arms and legs splayed.

Panic flashed through him as he fought desperately to break free from Tane's vise-grip, but the arms wrapped around him yielded not an inch.

"Hunter, Hunter, Hunter," the First said, shaking his head in mock sorrow. "Always so *predictable.*"

Struggling for breath, the Hunter stared up at the First, defiance in his eyes.

"He could kill you right now, you know," the First said, still standing and calmly watching the struggle. "Our Third here has killed dozens of men with his bare hands. Even you can be broken."

Third?

The Hunter's mind raced, struggling to put the pieces of the puzzle together even as Tane's massive fingers choked the life out of him. He tried to breathe, tried to speak, but nothing came out.

Fear flashed through him. *Not like this,* he thought. *This can't be how I die.*

He tried to struggle, but the lack of oxygen left his limbs weak. Slowly, his vision blurred, darkness creeping in.

"Don't kill him just yet," someone said. The voice seemed a long way off, barely audible as the Hunter drifted into a warm, soothing haze.

This is the end. The Hunter felt his body go slack, his struggles weakening. *Let it end.*

The pressure around his throat suddenly eased, and the Hunter gasped and filled his lungs with air. He coughed, sending pain flashing through his body. It hurt to breathe, to move, even to think.

He felt himself being dragged along the ground, but he had no fight left in him. It required all of his will just to remain conscious. He was roughly hauled to his feet, but when the hands released him, his legs refused to hold him upright.

A hard slap rocked his head to one side, startling him from his daze. He opened his eyes, but a wave of nausea washed over him. The room whirled around him. Swallowing hard, he closed his eyes until the spinning stopped.

"You might have been a bit too eager," the First said. Tane's only response was a grunt.

The Hunter cracked an eyelid, and to his relief, the room no longer spun. Opening the other eye, he found himself staring into the smiling face of the First. Tane stood scowling behind his master, his expression wary as he watched the Hunter.

Cool stone pressed against the Hunter's back, and thick ropes held him fast. Try as he might, he could not break free of his bonds. Thankfully, they offered some support, holding him upright as his shaky legs regained their strength. He clenched his fists, feeling his hands grow cold as the tightness of his bonds cut off the flow of blood.

The First had called Tane "Third"—the missing Finger. The Hunter found it odd that such a high-ranking Hand member would pose as servant to Lord Cyrannius. He couldn't figure out how it fit, and his inability to solve the mystery frustrated him.

It just doesn't make sense!

Even as his mind searched for answers, his eyes took in the details of the room around him. An eerie wind moaned through the high-vaulted stone ceiling of the cavern, carrying with it a horrifying smell of decay and rot—the foul odors of the Midden. Dust lay thick on the floor, and every step the First took kicked up small clouds of ancient debris.

His hands jerked instinctively toward his weapons, but they no longer hung at his side. A momentary stab of panic flashed through him; he felt naked without them. His eyes darted around the room in search of his sword belt. He found it—on the floor, between the feet of the towering Tane.

His heart sank. Perhaps if he could break free, there was a chance he could reach them. He knew it would be next to impossible, but he had to try.

The First stooped over the Hunter's weapons, and his hand closed around Soulhunger's grip. For a moment, the First simply stood staring at the dagger, caressing the blade with delicate fingers, seemingly lost in thought. There was reverence in the way he handled the weapon. Soulhunger pounded in the Hunter's mind, yet it seemed somehow...off. The blade whispered in a voice filled with eager blood thirst, but there was something else he couldn't quite explain.

"I know what you must be thinking, Hunter," the First said, turning suddenly to stride toward the Hunter. A sardonic smile spread on the man's face. "You find yourself tied up and at my mercy once again."

His mocking laughter infuriated the Hunter, who strained at his ropes in a vain attempt to break free. Tane stood like a massive statue in the background, his wary eyes watching the Hunter's every twitch. The First, however, paid no attention to his struggles. He had eyes only for the ornate dagger in his hands. His fingers played with the blade's sheath, turning it over.

"Forgive me for the restraints," he said, his voice almost apologetic, "but you can see why I found it necessary. Once I explain myself, I believe you may come to see things in a...different light."

The Hunter, breathing hard from exertion, ceased his struggles.

"First of all," said the First, his gaze lingering on the blade, "I must thank you, Hunter. You have done me a favor this night."

"A favor?" the Hunter asked. "I've just killed most of your gang of thugs. By the time I'm done, the Hand will never be heard of again."

The First seemed to take little notice of the triumph in the Hunter's voice. "Ah yes," he said, waving his hand in a dismissive gesture, "The Hand. The Bloody Hand. I have to tell you, Hunter, it did give me a feeling of power to control the city from behind the scenes." A tone of excitement filled his voice, but his eyes remained empty. "The crime, the vice, the horrors, quite the little thrill."

Bile rose in the Hunter's throat. "A little thrill? You've ruined countless lives, filled the city with chaos and death. And all for entertainment?" Of all the horrors he had witnessed in his years, the man's callous dismissal of human life seemed the worst.

"And don't you just *love* it?" the First asked, spreading his arms wide. "All of these horrors make the perfect niche for a man like you to claim as his own. With the chaos of the Bloody Hand, one man must rise to bring justice and righteousness to the city. I can see it now: the Hunter, the hero Voramis deserves."

"There are no heroes here," the Hunter said, his voice quiet.

"Ah, so the Hunter is truly nothing more than a killer for hire, earning a living doing dirty work. The people whisper, 'Is he the true power behind Voramis? Who is this mysterious creature?' Tell me Hunter, who are you?"

"A killer, plain and simple," the Hunter replied. "But at least I'm not bottom-feeding scum like you and the rest of the Hand. Profiting off misery and chaos. I tell you now, First, by the end of this night, the Bloody Hand will cease to exist."

"Why of course!" the First said, stabbing a finger at the Hunter. "And it's all thanks to the unlikely hero of Voramis: the feared Hunter!" He laughed, mocking the Hunter.

Soulhunger pounded eagerly in the Hunter's mind as he watched the First toying with the dagger. Something about the blade's voice unnerved the Hunter.

"I applaud the theatrics, by the way," the First said. He assumed the pose of an actor on a theater stage. "The grand gesture, the startling reveal, the warning of death and doom! It definitely made for a spectacle, my friend."

The Hunter said nothing, and the First continued. "I, too, understand the value of sending a message." The grin on his face turned feral, ugly. "I assume you received my 'little message'?"

Rage burned in the Hunter's chest. He threw himself against the ropes, but his fury proved useless.

"She had nothing to do with this! She didn't deserve to suffer like that!" The man stood just out of reach, tempting the Hunter, mocking him with his proximity. Once more, he strained at his bonds, but to no avail.

The First shrugged. "Of course, she didn't *deserve* to die, but it had to happen.But tell me true, Hunter, would you have waged this private war on the most powerful organization in Voramis had she not met her grisly end? It was her death which pushed you over the edge—exactly where I needed you to be."

He talks about her death as if it was just one more move in a game of Nizaa. The pain of his loss surged through him, fanning the fire of his rage. But instead of wasting his fury on the ropes that held him fast, he silently stoked the flame within, waiting for his opportunity.

The First seemed to take the Hunter's look as one of incomprehension, for he continued his gloating speech.

"Let me help you to understand exactly how you have unknowingly played a central role in the success of tonight's endeavors." He stepped closer to the Hunter. "Do you recognize me?"

"You are the First of the Bloody Hand," the Hunter replied.

"No, not my face. Do you recognize my scent?"

How does he know? The Hunter thought. *No one else can know of my abilities.*

"Breathe deep, Hunter," the First said, his face uncomfortably close to the Hunter, "and see what your senses tell you."

The Hunter inhaled deeply, filling his nostrils with the man's scent. He smelled perfume and lace, but beneath it all, a hint of rot and decay tinged the First's essence.

That scent of death is familiar, almost as if...

Something snapped into place in the Hunter's mind.

"It can't be," he breathed, disbelief flooding him. He had smelled it before. *Could he be...?*

"Oh, yes, Hunter," the First said, throwing back his head and laughing.

"Impossible!"

"It's a talent I have," the First replied, stepping back. "Let's just say it's *in my blood...*"

The torchlight flickered for a moment, casting shadows on the man's face. There was nothing extraordinary about the First's features, nothing to indicate he was anything other than what he appeared to be. Then the face shifted. Muscle and bone moved, twisted, contorted, like maggots crawling across a carcass. The aquiline nose, sharp cheekbones, and thin lips of the First seemed to melt, and moments later, the hook nose and high forehead of Lord Jahel stared back at him.

Stunned, the Hunter looked at the face of the leader of the Dark Heresy.

"Quite a useful skill, isn't it?" Lord Jahel asked, giving the Hunter a thin-lipped smile of contempt.

He wore the bright robes of the First, but the face no longer belonged to the leader of the Bloody Hand. Even his voice had changed, though the scent of rot and decay still permeated the room. Dark intelligence burned within the man's eyes—empty pools of darkness mirroring the Hunter's own.

The demon!

"You!" the Hunter choked out.

His thoughts were a jumble as he stared at the man, and confusion warred in his mind. *The demon is Lord Jahel* and *the First?*

"I see you remember me." Lord Jahel gave him a wan smile. "I trust memory of the Hole still burns bright in your mind."

"It does," the Hunter said, suppressing a shudder. "I also remember how easy it was to escape your fabled prison."

"Of course!" said Lord Jahel. "Silly me." His patronizing voice held a mocking edge. "You were *so* valiant, wrenching that chain from the wall and making a heroic escape into the night. An almost picture-perfect ending, if you don't mind me saying."

"Did you really think you could hold me there?" the Hunter asked. "Better men than you have tried to imprison me, and they all lie dead now."

"No doubt," Lord Jahel said, shrugging. "The Hunter is a creature of legend, and rightly so. But let me ask you this," he raised an eyebrow. "Do you *really* think Lord Jahel, the feared Demon of Voramis, would allow the chains of his dungeon to weaken sufficiently to the point that they could be ripped free?" Lord Jahel's voice rose to a feverish pitch of excitement. "Could it be just a coincidence that you were locked in the one set of shackles that would allow you to escape?"

This revelation felt like a slap to the Hunter's face. He had been certain his strength and will had allowed him to escape, but it had all been a ruse.

"So you wanted me to escape," he said, trying to hide the doubt in his voice, "but you had no idea I would hunt you down. After all, you are a member of the Heresiarchs, as well as commander of the Dark Heresy. To kill you would set the Palace of Justice on my heels, essentially signing my death warrant. That would be a fight even *I* would not relish."

"Of course," Lord Jahel said, nodding his head. "You're far too smart to take revenge on someone as important as Lord Jahel. Which is why I needed a bit of…assistance. Enter, the First of the Bloody Hand. A villain the likes of which Voramis has never seen."

The torchlight played across Lord Jahel's shifting features as bone and gristle morphed. The Hunter didn't even try to hide his revulsion, but watched the transformation in dumbfounded amazement. In seconds, the face of the First stared back at him.

"You see this face?" the First asked. "*This* is the face you needed to hate in order to set tonight's events in motion. You had to want to destroy the Bloody Hand, and we gave you a reason when we captured and tortured you." He patted the Hunter on the arm. "Nothing gets the blood up like a bit of agony."

The Hunter fought to gather his thoughts, to spit the First's words back in his face. "You wanted to make me angry," he growled, "wanted me to 'break free' and attack you."

"Of course!" said the First with a smile. "I needed you to track me down, after all."

A sudden sinking feeling seized the Hunter. "Which is why Lord Jahel—you—left that scrap of cloth on the table." His stomach roiled, and he felt the urge to vomit. How could he have been so blind?

"Convenient, wasn't it? With that cloth, the bit torn from the First's robe, and the purse Lord Cyrannius gave you, you had everything you needed to find us. Or should I say me?"

The Hunter remembered the twisted, scarred cripple in the wheeled chair. The man who had hired him to kill the priest had reeked of decay, but the Hunter had attributed it to his age and deformity. He now realized why the scent had been so familiar.

"You were Lord Cyrannius as well," he said. It explained why Tane—the Third—had posed as bondservant.

"Full marks, Hunter!" Lord Jahel said with a patronizing smile. "It was an act worthy of the greatest stage in Voramis."

He gave the Hunter a theatrical bow, one foot forward and his hands spread wide. He dipped low, and when he stood, the wrinkles, age spots, and disfiguring scars of old Lord Cyrannius stared back at the Hunter.

"I must say," Lord Cyrannius said, his voice thick with the effort of speaking through twisted lips, "hunching over in that wheelchair was extremely uncomfortable. Definitely one of my least favorite guises, but I believe I pulled it off with aplomb. Don't you agree, Hunter?"

"You were Cyrannius." Disbelief warred with the evidence in front of him. "Why?"

"Think about it," the First said. "Why would I adopt the guise of an old man?"

The Hunter pondered for a moment and cursed himself for a fool. "To make me think my employer was harmless. That way I wouldn't expect the ambush."

The First smiled and gave the Hunter a theatrical bow.

"Bastard," the Hunter growled. The Hand thugs had caught him off guard, and it had been far too easy for them to capture him.

"I must thank you, by the way, for carrying out that contract for me."

"The priest?" the Hunter asked.

"Yes," Lord Jahel said, his features shifting back to the aristocratic face of the First once more. "A necessary part of this charade."

"You knew the truth of Brother Securus?" the Hunter asked.

"The Cambionari have hunted my kind for millennia," the First replied. "I have made it my business to learn everything about these Beggar Priests." He spat in contempt.

"But why did you need me to kill the priest?" the Hunter said. "Why not simply kill him yourself?"

"Aside from the delicious irony of it all?" the First asked. "You have no idea how many assassins we have wasted on that one priest. The bastard was good, I must admit." He spoke with grudging respect in his voice.

"You hoped I would be the one to kill him where all of your men had failed."

"I do love a bit of senseless death for death's sake," the First said, giving the Hunter a malicious smile, "but I found myself short on assassins to send to their death. I knew if anyone could do it, it would be you."

"It seems your plan worked," the Hunter said, feeling anger rising within him.

"Like it wafted from the gods' own assholes!" the First exclaimed. "You not only eliminated the *one* threat to our plans, but you then delivered yourself right into our hands."

The Hunter's stomach sank. "The ambush, the torture. What was the purpose of it all?"

"We needed you angry," the First said casually, shrugging, "angry enough to look for someone to hurt. We needed you out for blood, but it seemed that torturing you wasn't quite enough to…motivate you."

"Your man plunged a knife into my heart!" the Hunter shouted.

"I knew it wouldn't kill you," the First replied, waving his hand in a gesture of dismissal. "I am familiar with your kind. After all, we do share the same blood."

"That may be," spat the Hunter, disgust flooding him at the First's familiar tone, "but we are nothing alike."

"Don't be too certain, Hunter," the First replied, his voice clipped. "You may have human blood running through your veins, but you are still the offspring of the Abiarazi." For the first time, a hint of anger showed through the man's calm façade.

"Abiarazi?" the Hunter asked. He had never heard the word before. "Is that what you demons call yourselves?"

The First winced as if the Hunter had slapped him. "Demon," he snarled the word. "Such a crude term. You humans use it as a curse, but you have no idea the true power of an Abiarazi." The First's voice filled with something akin to ecstasy, and his eyes took on a faraway look. "If only you could have seen it, Hunter. They called it the War of Gods, but it was our war to conquer this world for our own."

He stared at the Hunter, his expression rapt. "When the Great Destroyer summoned us to this world, man had not yet spread across Einan like a plague. They were few in number, living such deliciously short lives." He licked his lips in an obscene gesture of delight, setting the Hunter's skin crawling.

"A fragile race, indeed. I ruled this world with my brothers, and, by Kharna, the slaughter we wreaked! The humans fell before us like wheat, and we fed on your bloated corpses. The power, oh the power!"

A shudder of pleasure ran through the First, and his features wriggled once again. For a long moment, the demon said nothing, seeming to relive some memory of a forgotten era. When he finally recovered it was with visible effort, and his shifting features solidified into the aquiline nose and sharp cheekbones of the First.

"But then that cowardly Swordsman defeated the Great Destroyer," the First snarled, "and our mighty ruler's essence was sentenced to the forgotten hells. Worse still, his body walked the heavens in the guise of a filthy beggar."

Rage twisted his features. "We were hunted nearly to extinction, and those of us who survived were forced into hiding. If only you could understand the frustration of being as powerful as the gods one moment, and the next having only a fraction of that power. Being forced to conceal who you are to avoid destruction."

"I may know more about that than you think," the Hunter said, his voice quiet.

"Of course you do!" the First said. "But do you know what it's like to have your children ripped away from you, never to be seen again?"

Pain flashed as he remembered the lifeless face of Farida, and a lump rose in his throat. A sense of loss overwhelmed him, just as it had when he'd placed her body on the steps of the House of Need.

"Your *children*," the Hunter said. "You mean the Bucelarii. You mean me."

"Oh yes, Hunter," the First said, and for the first time a look akin to compassion filled the man's eyes. "My child was torn from my hands, taken away, and put to death. Their names—their true names were forgotten. The Serenii called them Bucelarii, the Forgotten Ones, and that is the only name they have known since." His eyes filled with pain as he relived the memory. For a moment, the Hunter actually felt sympathy for the man.

Then the moment passed, and the First's features hardened. He once again became the cold, haughty First of the Bloody Hand, with empty eyes and sneering lips. When he spoke, his voice was lifeless, flat.

"If you spoke to the accursed Beggar Priests, they must have told you the true story of the War of Gods. No doubt they told you that the gods cast the Great Destroyer into the darkest hell."

The Hunter nodded, and the First continued.

"But what you don't know," said the First, "is that a fragment of the almighty Kharna remained in the mind of the Beggar God. That piece of the Destroyer's mind has twisted and warped the frail Beggar to suit his needs."

This revelation shocked the Hunter. *The Beggar Priests are worshipping the very god they are trying to stop.* The thought sent a chill through him.

"When the gods planned to kill the Bucelarii," the First continued, "it was the Beggar God who stopped it. He pled for their lives, not because they were innocent, but because he had his own plans for them. He needed them to one day regain his full power."

This puzzled the Hunter. "I don't understand. How could *we* bring back the Destroyer?"

The First looked down at Soulhunger still clasped in his long, thin fingers. He caressed the tooled sheath of the blade. "Have you ever wondered where you found such a blade as Thanal Eth' Athaur?" he asked, his voice slow.

"How did you know its name?" the Hunter asked, surprised.

"I know this blade because it was forged by my brothers. One like it was given to every Bucelarii." The First ripped open the Hunter's shirt, revealing the myriad scars crisscrossing the Hunter's chest. "See here, Hunter," he said, triumph in his voice, "the blade has marked you with the proof that you are worthy to serve by our side. Thanal Eth' Athaur is linked to you, to the blood in your veins. The power of the blade makes you who you are, and yet it serves a greater purpose."

Dread filled the Hunter at these words. "Greater purpose?" he asked, raising an eyebrow.

"See this gem?" The First ran a finger along the contours of the jewel set in Soulhunger's hilt. "It links you to the source of your power, the essence of the Great Destroyer."

The Hunter's stomach churned in disgust as he realized what the demon meant.

"Every time I spill blood with this weapon…" He trailed off, unable to speak the words.

"You feed the heart of Kharna," nodded the First. "You, Hunter, are bringing the Great Destroyer back to life."

Chapter Thirty-Four

An icy chill ran down the Hunter's spine. Acid burned in the back of his throat, his stomach twisting.

"You have felt the rush of power after you take a life with Thanal Eth' Athaur, haven't you? That thrill you feel is a fraction of the power that comes from spilled blood, a fraction of what is channeled into the heart of the Great Destroyer with every death."

Betrayal stung him as the realization of what he had done flooded through his mind. *Every man and woman that I have killed, it has all been to feed the Destroyer's power.* Hundreds of faces swam before the Hunter's eyes, every one of them belonging to those who had died at the end of Soulhunger's blade.

"We gave these weapons to you, Bucelarii, in order to feed the Destroyer the power he needs to break free of his chains. But the gods killed so many of you..." Sorrow flashed across his face, slowly transforming into naked hatred. "And the accursed Cambionari are ever vigilant. They have hunted our children down and slaughtered them all. Save for you." A fiery intensity burned in his eyes.

A feeling of profound sadness washed over the Hunter at these words. With it came aching realization.

I am the last of my kind. I truly am alone in the world. Despondence dimmed the fire of his anger.

"You, Bucelarii, were meant for great things," the First said. His fingers toyed with Soulhunger's grip, caressing the blade as he would a lover. "You were to bring back the Destroyer, and join us in serving him as masters of this world. But you were the only one left to feed the Great One."

A look of disappointment and frustration crossed the First's face. "You fed him far too slowly," the demon said. "A death here and there is nowhere near enough power for what we do here this night, much less bring back our god. Thus, you have forced my hand."

He began to pace, his voice filling with the excitement of a master strategist laying out a brilliant plan. "First," he said, "we had to start with something small, something that would set things in motion."

"Lord Dannaros," the Hunter said, remembering the seal of the Bloody Hand in the man's office. "He worked for you."

The First nodded. "His death gave me the necessary leverage to turn the Hand against you."

"But before you could turn the hounds loose, you needed me to kill Brother Securus," the Hunter said. "How did you know that he would be the only Cambionari in Voramis?"

A sly smile broke out on the First's face. "For years we have spread rumors of Abiarazi sightings around the continent. Not enough to make the bastards actually send out a full force, but sufficient to compel them to investigate. One by one, we have drawn the Cambionari away from Voramis, until only one man remained. Only *he* had the power to stop us." His eyes flicked toward the Hunter's sword belt, and a momentary shiver of fear and loathing seized the First as he stared at the Swordsman's iron blades.

"He was the only one capable of wielding those blades," the Hunter said, "but I disposed of him for you."

"Yes," the First said, gloating, "it was truly a marvelous plan. After that, it was easy to goad you into a fury just by killing off a few of those pitiful beggars who shared your home."

The faces of Old Nan, Jak, Karrl, and the others flashed through the Hunter's mind, and his stomach twisted with sorrow.

"Once we had you angry and spoiling for blood," the First continued with a gleeful grin, "we did the one thing that would make you do exactly what we wanted."

"You killed Farida," the Hunter said, his voice lifeless. He tried to push away the sense of loss, fought to ignore the pain flooding him, but a memory of the child's face haunted him. A lump rose in his throat, and he blinked, angry at the tears that threatened at the corner of his eyes.

The First smiled at the pain written on the Hunter's face. "Oh, yes!" he leered. "It was a delicious act, I must say." He stepped close to the Hunter, whispering in his ear. "Her blood will feed the ritual tonight, though perhaps we could have done without. It was just a simply wonderful happenstance that an innocent had to die. Such pure blood always tastes marvelous." The man licked his lips, an obscene gesture clearly meant to goad the Hunter into a rage.

The Hunter fought the revulsion and fury within, but it exploded from him in an animal roar. He threw himself forward, muscles cording, straining against his bonds. The sinews in his arms nearly burst in his struggle to break free.

I will kill you! His mind raged, Soulhunger adding its fury to his own. The demon side of him wanted nothing more than to rip out the man's throat, to taste his blood, to feel the rush of power as he took the First's life. Tane stepped forward, tensing his muscles in anticipation of a fight.

"Let him storm," the First said, holding up a hand and calmly stepping back. His laugh echoed in the cavern, infuriating the Hunter further. "It will be good for him to let it out."

The Hunter's back arched, his chest heaved with the effort, and his powerful legs pushed against the ground. He threw every ounce of strength into his effort. But the stone was hard and unyielding, his bonds thick. Try as he might, he couldn't break free.

Something within the Hunter broke, and strength failed him. He slumped back, exhaustion threatening to steal his consciousness. Blood pounded in his ears, and his muscles ached with the effort.

A sob broke from his chest, a weak, pitiful sound filled with defeat. His head hung down, his eyes on the stone floor beneath his feet. He fell against the ropes, leaning on them heavily. They were the only thing holding him upright; all he wanted to do was curl into a ball to escape the pain flooding him. Every shred of his willpower fought to hold back the tears threatening to fall.

"It had to be done," said the First. He sounded almost apologetic. "Your rampage of death and destruction tonight was necessary, and now, thanks to you, we have enough power to accomplish what has not been done in thousands of years."

The Hunter stared at the demon in incomprehension.

"All this is possible because of *you*, Hunter!" Triumph rang in the First's voice. He gestured around him. "What we do here, it is thanks to you and your hubris!"

The Hunter had never felt so defeated. He could find nothing to say.

"You were the Bucelarii we needed you to be, the willing pawn in our game. You even followed my men here, to this glorious place where our destiny will become manifest once again."

"What do you mean, 'followed' your men here'?" the Hunter asked. A tiny spark of anger still burned within him, and the First's mocking words fanned it into an ember.

"*Please*, Hunter," the First mocked, "you think you 'tracked' me tonight? Following the *one* idiot thief creeping through the Serenii tunnels?" He shook his head, as if disbelieving anyone could be so naïve. "I have dozens of men 'wandering' these tunnels, waiting for you to 'find' them."

"You meant for them to lead me here."

"Yes," crowed the First, a triumphant smile wreathing his face, "and here you are, right where I want you." He walked around the Hunter, placing a hand on the smooth stone obelisk. "Look here, to this glorious altar to which you are bound. It was on these stones that the Serenii sacrificed their victims, their blood drained for the Great Destroyer."

"This city," the First gestured around him, "all of this was built by the Serenii, given the name 'Hohnin'—Sanctuary. They once took it upon themselves to protect mankind, to guide you in your evolution."

The First's eyes glittered darkly as he stared at the Hunter. "But then came the day the Mighty Kharna declared war on the gods," he said, and the way he told it almost sounded like he had been there. "He attempted to enlist the Serenii in his ranks, but the cowards refused to fight directly. Yet they were the ones who opened the portal to our worlds. Right here," he pointed to the ground at his feet, "we Abiarazi emerged to rule the world!"

"Look into my eyes." The First strode around to stand in front of the Hunter. "Look at me and see the endless depths of the Hells, our realm eternal."

For a moment, the Hunter thought he stared into a mirror. The eyes gazing back at him matched his own—pools of endless liquid darkness, empty of life and light. He shrank back from the intensity in the First's expression, which caused the demon's smile to widen.

"We wielded power immense, and we will wield it once more," shouted the First, his arms raised. The void behind the Hunter seemed to echo the First's words, ringing with triumph. "On this altar blood was spilled to release us, and here blood shall be spilled once more. We needed you to unleash your rage on the Bloody Hand. The deaths of those fools will provide the power to fuel our ritual tonight!"

He turned to face the Hunter, stabbing a finger at him. "Thanks to you, Hunter," he intoned, "tonight we open the way for the Abiarazi to return. We will bring death to this world once again, and with the help of my brothers, we will gather the power to free the Destroyer. Your blood and your blade made it possible for the way to be opened."

His fist closed around Soulhunger's worn leather grip, and a smile played on his lips. The throbbing in the back of the Hunter's mind intensified as the dagger slipped free of its sheath.

"Thanal Eth' Athaur," the man whispered. "How I have missed thee, my brother." Rapture filled the First's eyes, and for the first time, the Hunter saw the demon within.

There is nothing human about that thing. He wears the face and adopts the guise of a human, but beneath the flesh there is only a creature of darkness and death.

Emotions warred within the Hunter as he watched the First caress the sharp edge of Soulhunger's blade.

Is that what I have been doing all along? I have worn hundreds of faces, adopted hundreds of disguises. Have they all been an attempt to deny who and what I really am?

The First looked up, locking gazes with the Hunter. "You have seen what I am, Hunter, what hides within me. I know what hides within you, what drives you to kill. You have the weakness of humankind in you, yet you possess the strength of an Abiarazi. What you have done this night proves that you are worthy to take your place as a true Bucelarii."

Pride filled the First's eyes as he spoke, his voice passionate. "You have the chance to join us now, to fulfill your destiny. Imagine being able to show the world what you really are, rather than hiding behind pitiful masks. Abandon the humans that have shunned you, hunted you, and killed your kindred. You alone of your kind remain, but there is no need for you to be alone."

The First's expression turned sorrowful. "The burden of a long life takes its toll as you watch those around you wither, age, and die. But join us, and you will never be alone again. Once the Abiarazi have dominion over the earth again, we will breed thousands of Bucelarii to rule beneath us. You will lead your kin in the conquest of this world, and you will have all the power you can dream of."

The First extended a hand to the Hunter, his expression earnest. "Unleash the demon within you, and claim your rightful place. You are a descendant of greatness, a creature destined to rule the world with us. Become the thing you were meant to be. Embrace your kinship with power, and together we can conquer. "

The Hunter's instincts told him to spit the man's offer back in his face.

How could he think I'd join him after what he's done? He killed my friends—even tortured Farida to death—all to get me to do his bidding. He is a demon!

And yet, something deep within him wanted nothing more than to accept the First's offer. The word *kinship* had struck the Hunter like a punch to the gut, and he could not ignore the overwhelming sense of loneliness.

For as long as he could remember, he had been alone. Few had seen his true face, and those who had always flinched when staring into his depthless eyes. They only saw the demon, never the man. But to be among his own kind once more…

Why shouldn't I accept his offer? We share the same blood. He has seen the truth behind who and what I am, and welcomed me when everyone else in the world fears and wants to kill me. Could I finally find the place where I belong? If I am like them, should I not join them? Where else will I be accepted as I am?

His stomach twisted in revulsion. *I am half-demon, the offspring of creatures of nightmare. I will never find my place in the world of man, for I am the last of the Bucelarii.*

There was no one else on earth like him, no one who would ever understand him. How could anyone know was it was like to have the driving urge to kill warring within—an urge that could only be satiated with blood? Who could ever accept him knowing all the horrible, monstrous things he had done?

The First's words rang in his thoughts. *"Become what you were meant to be." I am meant for greatness. I wield the power that can awaken a god from eternal death.*

Soulhunger echoed the demon's promises, whispering of power in a voice eager for blood. It wanted to feed…it wanted blood.

He tried to push the whispers aside, tried to clear his head. He tried to think why he should resist, why he should fight back, yet he could find none.

This world is filthy, disgusting, filled with sin.

Priests committing murder. Righteous men doing horrible things because of their lustful nature. Children stealing and killing. Women forced to sell their bodies for the pleasures of men. Beggars fighting over scraps of food.

Humans have done that to one another, forcing some to live in poverty while others live in mansions. Humanity is the cause of its own suffering. Why shouldn't this world be cleansed?

Yet he was torn. His human half protested, screaming for him to deny the demon.

Can I really consign all of humanity to their deaths? Do I have the strength to accept the burden of millions of lives lost just to satisfy my need to belong? Am I selfish enough to do that?

Farida's face floated through his thoughts; her pale, lifeless skin, unseeing eyes, and bloodied clothes.

She died because of me.

Then he saw her as she had been: smiling, laughing, her face covered with sticky syrup. He could still smell the roses, dirt, and incense as her chubby arms gripped him around the waist, hugging him tight. He heard her exclamation as he presented her with a cloth doll, her laughter as she plucked a treat from his hand.

How could I allow this to happen to her? An innocent child who never hurt a soul, killed just to push me over the edge. Could I ever truly find my place among creatures who would so casually perpetrate these horrors?

The agony of loss ripped through his heart, but instead of pushing the pain away, he reveled in it. It washed over him like a tidal wave, and pressure built within him, threatening to shatter his mind.

Suddenly, he no longer stood in the torch-lit cavern beneath Voramis. He seemed to be in another place...another time. Images of death and destruction flashed in front of his eyes, almost as if they were a memory.

Storm clouds roiled in the sky, the sound of thunder joining flashes of lightning as the gods warred in the heavens. Massive creatures walked, slithered, and crawled across the face of the earth, leaving only havoc and carnage in their wake.

A weeping child clung to her mother. The woman screamed for the husband being dragged away by the horrible monsters of nightmare. Blood spattered the mother's dress as talons slashed across her throat, pouring down onto the child and staining her final moments in horror. A huge fist crushed the child's skull, crustacean-like claws snatching up the body and devouring it whole.

The voice within the Hunter shouted as he watched, helpless, horrified.

Two children, a boy and a girl, raced through the burning streets of a village. Snarling demons pursued them, shouting curses and screaming their hunger. A huge spear flew through the night, piercing the boy and pinning him to the ground. The little girl could only watch in mute horror as the demons surrounded her. Her voice lifted in horrifying screams as talons and claws raked the skin from her bones.

Graves filled with hundreds—nay, thousands—of bodies, mountains of skulls and bones. Demons feasted on the carcasses of women and children. Men were tortured to a slow death.

Atop the pile of corpses, the lifeless body of Farida turned empty, accusing eyes toward him. "You did this," her stare seemed to say.

Whether it was a memory or simply a hallucination, the Hunter couldn't tell. The pain of loss, however, was all too real.

How many more like her will die? Could I ever live with myself knowing I had harmed a child like this?

The demon within him howled, but his human half fought it back.

I cannot allow this to happen. I have found a home among these humans, and it is a home I will fight to protect, even from my own kind.

No, screamed the voice in his mind—a voice he now realized belonged to the demon within him. *We must rule the world again.*

It is not who I am, the human half of the Hunter thundered. *I refuse to stand by and do nothing. I refuse to let any more die needlessly.*

The war within his mind raged, tearing him apart. His two halves fought to overpower each other, but something in him snapped. Suddenly, with startling clarity, the Hunter knew neither side could be allowed to win.

I am both *man and demon, but that is what makes me who I am. It is what makes me the Hunter.*

With realization, came acceptance. As much as he hated it, that voice within him—that demon half—would always be a part of him.

His internal struggle came to a sudden, shuddering conclusion, and an odd sense of peace flooded him.

The vision of horrors dissipated. He found himself once again in the Serenii catacombs. Ropes bound him to the stone upon which thousands had died, and before him stood a demon wearing the face of the First of the Bloody Hand.

"So," the First asked, "what is your answer? Will you become what you were meant to be?"

Swallowing the lump in his throat, the Hunter struggled to speak. "No." The word cut through the silence like a knife.

"What?" The First seemed taken aback by this answer. "You're rejecting your own kind, your own blood?"

"Yes."

"Even though you are the last of your kind? Help us, and we can make thousands more like you! Isn't that what you want? Aren't you tired of being alone?"

"More than you could possibly know," said the Hunter. "Yet even though it is what I want, I could not live with the consequences. Mankind—"

"Cares nothing for you!" the First raged, cutting off the Hunter's words. "They have hunted you down, killed your family, and made you an outsider. You will never be one of them. Should they discover who you are, they will fear you, hate you."

"Then that is the burden I must bear," the Hunter replied. "I may never be fully accepted by humankind, but I cannot permit them to be slaughtered for the sake of power. There will always be that part of me that belongs to your kind, but I choose humanity." His mind no longer raced, and for the first time in his memory, he was at peace.

The First glared at him, but the anger on his face gave way to an expression of resignation. "You have made your choice," he said, sighing, "but at least you will not have long to live with it!" He raised Soulhunger high, and the blade's thirsty edge glinted in the firelight.

The Hunter's eyes widened in horror, and his arms jerked reflexively. Fear replaced his momentary calm. Icy dread froze him in place. He knew what happened to the dagger's victims, had seen the effects firsthand. The thought of the same happening to him filled him with terror, yet he could do nothing to stop it.

With a wicked smile of triumph, the First plunged Soulhunger into the Hunter's leg.

Agony flooded the Hunter—a pain he had never dreamed could exist—and his screams filled the cavern. Soulhunger's voice cried in ecstasy as it fed on his blood, absorbing the power running through his veins. Every fiber in his body burned, yet the horrifying chill of death stole the strength from his muscles. He couldn't move, couldn't think—nothing but torment filled his world.

You will not have me!

The war raging within burned with an intensity that pulled on the very essence of his being. The blade sought to steal his soul, and he fought it with every shred of willpower he possessed.

An eternity passed in a heartbeat, and then the blade was ripped from his thigh. With agonizing slowness, the suffering receded and the pressure within him diminished. Tears of pain streamed down the Hunter's face. His throat ached from screaming.

The First held the blade up to the Hunter's face, watching the dagger absorb the blood. "We won't need all your blood, just yet," the First said. "For the moment, a few drops will do. We can always use the rest up later."

A few drops?

To the Hunter, it felt like he had just lived a lifetime of pain in a few short moments. The blade had torn at his soul, and it left him feeling hollow, empty. Drained of strength and too weak to stand, he slumped. The ropes supported his sagging frame, but the exhaustion was more than just physical. He had never felt so defeated and helpless.

There's nothing I can do to stop this from happening, he thought, despair flooding him. *It's over. They win.*

The First gestured Tane forward, handing the big man the dagger before turning to the Hunter. "With your blood, Hunter, and the power of Thanal Eth' Athaur," he shouted, excitement filling his voice, "a new age of power will begin. Your blood opens the way for the legions of Abiarazi, and with them, the Destroyer will be released from his imprisonment!"

The moaning wind from the Midden whipped at the Hunter's clothing and hair, filling his nostrils with the stench of decay—the same scent emanating from the First. Soulhunger screamed in its mind, sensing the power coursing almost tangibly through the cavern.

"Tonight, Hunter," said the First, "you witness something the likes of which has not been seen on this world for an age!"

Tane walked toward the edge of the Midden, holding the dagger in his hands with reverence. Just within the Hunter's line of sight stood a pedestal, a groove in the center of its smooth top. Tane inserted the dagger with care, but the Hunter's stomach lurched as the blade sunk deep into the stone.

It was as if he could feel the blood draining from the weapon, drawn into the heart of the cliff by an immense force. He almost tasted the power flowing around him; sensed it being pulled far, far down, reaching tendrils deep into the core of the earth.

An enormous heartbeat echoed in his mind, thumping with enough force to shatter mountains. The Hunter shuddered in terror, yet he couldn't help feeling a sense of overwhelming awe.

The heart of the Destroyer.

Words poured from the mouth of the huge Third, spoken in a horrible language that sliced through the Hunter's core. Yet the words were familiar, almost comforting. His two halves warred within him—the demon screaming to be released, the human fighting for control. The inhuman sounds pouring from the Third's throat carried through the hurricane winds, the cascade of guttural words echoing loud over the pounding in the Hunter's ears. A voice screamed with delight, its cries of joy ringing in the Hunter's mind.

Something tugged at him, pulling him toward the Midden and its yawning void. Had he not been bound to the obelisk by heavy ropes, he had no doubt he would have been sucked into the maelstrom whipping through the cavern.

The air around him seemed to coalesce. It flowed toward the empty space above the gaping abyss of the Midden. Shadow seemed to solidify, becoming thick, viscous. Reality itself appeared to bend and twist, buckling with the force of the incantation.

Darkness formed into black light, expanding rapidly as a fiery hole rent the night. Demonic flames burned bright, yet they seemed to absorb the torchlight, casting horrific shadows. Waves of heat emanated from the portal, drenching his tunic with sweat. A foul wind blew through the cavern, and the Hunter gagged as the fetid stench of eternal damnation washed over him.

With a smile of triumph, the First turned to the Hunter. "Let us call forth the others," he shouted over the sound of the wind, "and we will once more rule this world as we were meant to!"

The thick darkness was replaced by brilliant, hellish light that blinded the Hunter and sent waves of agony rippling through his head. Reality screamed as a demonic form pushed into the world of man, and the Hunter screamed with it.

A terrifying roar burst from an inhuman throat, shaking the Hunter to the core. His subconscious mind recoiled from the horror around him, sealing itself off from the torment of reality ripping apart. Pressure mounted in his head, and his ears pounded until they felt they would burst.

"Behold," the First cried into the storm, "the first of my kin have returned to Einan. Welcome, my brother. Welcome, Abiarazi!"

Chapter Thirty-Five

Brilliant light leaked from the portal, and the Hunter, unable to shield his eyes, could do nothing but stare in horror at the monstrosity pushing its way into his world.

The thing towered twice the height of a man, its body seemingly carved from living stone. Arms far too long hung to the creature's knees, with razor claws sprouting from many-jointed fingers. It stood on paws instead of feet. Massive spikes protruded from the creature's back, and a serpentine tail trailed behind the thing as it emerged fully into the world of man.

The demon's eyes—pools of liquid darkness—stared around, taking in the cavern and its occupants. When it finally saw the Hunter, still bound to the obelisk, a horrible rictus grin spread across the thing's serpentine face, revealing row upon row of razor sharp teeth. The foul creature drooled, its spittle falling to the floor with a loud sizzling sound. Its forked tongue flicked in and out in a horrifying display of hunger.

Uncontrollable terror flashed through the Hunter. His legs sagged, and he felt as if his bowels would empty of their own accord. Panic overwhelmed his mind. He could do nothing but stare at the demon before him. This was fear like he had never experienced.

"Brother!" cried the First, shouting to make himself heard over the hellish winds whipping through the cavern. "Welcome back, Shem-zith-el, mighty warrior of the Fallen Host!"

The demon threw back its head and roared, a rumbling, crashing sound that slammed into the Hunter with the force of a thunderclap. The human half of his mind cried out in terror. The other half—his demon half—howled its delight.

Brother!

He fought to suppress the panic flooding him, willing his legs to hold him upright. The demon's roar faded, but still his heart thundered.

I cannot let this end here. He was so close to fulfilling his promise to the priests, so close to getting vengeance for Farida. *I have to fight.*

The Hunter want to curl up into a ball and disappear, yet he fought to control the fear coursing through his body like poison.

No! I am the Hunter, he thought. *I am the one to be feared.*

He threw himself against his bonds. Desperation and fear lent strength to his arms and legs. With a thrill, he heard the ropes creak; in his rage, he had stretched his bonds enough to slip his arms free. His hands fumbled at the knots that held him bound to the obelisk, his eyes never leaving the demon.

If I can just...

The ropes fell away, and immediately hope replaced terror. Without hesitation, the Hunter sprinted towards the First, scooping up a rock from the cavern floor. He had eyes only for the man who had so callously ordered the death of his friends.

Tane was the first to notice him. The big man's eyes widened in surprise, but he reacted quickly, leaping into the Hunter's path in order to prevent him from reaching the First.

A smile touched the Hunter's lips. Instead of throwing himself at the Third, he dove in the opposite direction. Before Tane could react, the Hunter threw himself into a forward roll. His hands closed around the hilts of the Swordsman's twin blades, and the motion of his body slid them from their sheaths. Contact with the iron weapons sent waves of pain down his arms, pain he fought to ignore.

Another roar ripped through the cavern, echoing off the stone and sending fear coursing through the Hunter once more. Swallowing his terror, he turned to face the demon leering down at him.

"Come on, you bastard," shouted the Hunter, hefting the iron blades.

"You fool!" cried the First, finally noticing the Hunter. "Your heroics are useless. If you face him"—he stabbed a finger toward the huge creature—"you will be torn to shreds."

"I made a promise," the Hunter retorted, "one I intend to keep." Raising the Swordsman's blades high, he charged. He had no time for fear.

The monster swiped at him with a huge clawed hand, forcing the Hunter to throw himself beneath the massive fist. The blow missed him by less than a hand's breadth. He dashed between the thing's legs, striking out with the iron blades.

The creature roared in pain at the touch of iron. A momentary thrill of triumph flashed through the Hunter, but his heart sank as he saw that he hadn't even scratched the thing's hide. Only two small black spots marked the place where he had struck.

By the Swordsman, he cursed. *How in the twisted hell can I kill that thing if these blades won't even hurt it?*

The demon turned to pursue him, but its movements suddenly grew erratic, jerky. It seemed to convulse, shuddering as the fire within it flared to a blinding intensity. Covering his eyes, the Hunter retreated until he felt the wind of the Midden whipping at his clothing. Looking down, he saw his heel hanging over the edge of the precipice—nothing but an empty, gaping void behind him.

Shit!

He expected the demon to give chase, to hunt him down and tear him limb from limb, but instead he found the nightmare creature engulfed by flames. Heat singed the Hunter's face and hands, but he had nowhere to retreat, nowhere to hide from the blaze. The demon screamed as the living stone of its flesh burned, filling the cavern with the foul smell of sulfur.

"No!" cried the First, panic filling his voice.

The demon's convulsions ground to a halt, its voice dying. The flames consuming the creature whipped into a towering inferno, and a blinding light flashed through the cavern. Then, it faded into nothing. Nothing but flickering torches and the foul portal into the hells illuminated the room. Not a sound could be heard—even the wind fell eerily quiet.

The Hunter stared in amazement at the place where the demon had once stood. A shapeless mound of stone stood in its place, the only thing marking the creature's existence. The fear that had overwhelmed him at its presence diminished.

How...?

"No!" the First cried again. "It's not possible!"

Did I kill it? The Hunter looked at the blades in his hand. *I couldn't have.*

"How in the frozen hell...?" the First screamed. He rounded on Tane, anger flashing in his eyes. "What did you do?" His features shifted to those of Lord Jahel.

The big man's eyes were still wide in shock, but he raised his hands in a gesture of protest. "I'm certain I said the right words." He fell silent for a moment, then his eyes darted to the Hunter.

"You," he growled. "How did you do that? How did you kill him?"

The Hunter tried to find the words to respond, but in truth he had no idea what had happened. One moment the demon had been about to kill him; in the next, the thing had turned to lifeless stone.

He stared at the mound where the demon had once stood, and watched open-mouthed as it crumbled into dust.

A thought struck the Hunter. *A blood ritual.* The First needed his blood. *But what if...?*

Hope surged within him.

It's not over yet.

"Maybe the blood itself caused the rite to fail," the Hunter offered. A sardonic expression spread across his face.

"It can't be!" shouted Lord Jahel, his frustration mounting. His features shifted in a sickening wave of meat and bone until he once more wore the face of the First. "You are the last of the Bucelarii, last descendant of Abiarazi blood."

"That may be true," the Hunter said, nodding, "but my blood is not entirely my own."

"What in the name of *Zhr-zha-aurz* does that mean?" the First cursed. Realization dawned, and his mouth fell open in disbelief. "You don't mean...the Beggar Priests?"

Smiling, the Hunter said nothing, content to watch the First's face purple with rage.

"Those thrice-damned priests. Of *course* they would have to find a way to ruin our plans once again." He stormed around the cavern, gesticulating wildly. "When I'm done here, I will storm that dung heap they call a temple and rip them limb from limb. I'll..."

He proceeded to give a vivid, complete description of the pain and suffering he would visit upon the priests. Even the Hunter's ears burned at the graphic imagery.

"...fuck their empty eye holes and piss on the pieces of their bodies."

Panting, his face red with exertion, the First finally finished his rant. His features morphed, shifting between the faces of Lord Cyrannius, Lord Jahel, and another face the Hunter had never seen, before finally settling into that of the First once more.

"Keeper take you, Hunter," the man snarled. "You will suffer for this! You will be thrown into the Hole once more, this time into a cell from which there is no escape. When your body has purged itself of the taint of the gods, we will attempt the ritual once again."

The Hunter hefted the iron blades. "You'll have to capture me first," he snarled, "a task you will *not* find easy."

The First stared at him, and for a moment, a proud grin touched his face. "You, Bucelarii, never fail to impress," he said, clapping his hands in appreciation of the Hunter's defiance. "If only there were more of you, we would once again rule the world!" He shook his head in sorrow. "Unfortunately, I have had to make do with mortal instruments."

"The Dark Heresy," the Hunter said, stepping away from the obelisk. "More pawns in your demonic game."

"What a beautiful trick to pull on the foolish humans," the First mocked. "Heresiarchs—the followers of the Heresy. The Heresy of Kharna Reborn, the Destroyer returned to Einan. Long have they furthered the aims of the Abiarazi without even realizing it. Only those of the Dark Heresy knew what they did, and what pleasure they took in their efforts!"

"They, too, will receive their justice this night, but not before you!" the Hunter growled.

"Please," the First retorted, rolling his eyes, "your bravado is wasted."

Turning to Tane, he waved his hand toward the Hunter in a

contemptuous gesture. "Take him."

"Alive?" Tane asked, flexing his hands in eager anticipation.

"Yes," nodded the First. "We need his blood."

He turned to face the Hunter, who glared back in defiance. "Break every bone in his body, if you must," the First said, speaking to Tane without ever taking his eyes off the Hunter, "but take him alive."

"You coward!" snarled the Hunter. "Face me like a man!"

"Fool!" retorted the First. "Your theatrics are meaningless to me. You may have thwarted my plans here, but I will return stronger than ever. Voramis is *my* city, and nothing you can do will stop me. I do not fear those foolish blades"—his eyes flicked to the Swordsman's daggers—"for you will never come close enough to touch me with them."

Turning away from the Hunter, he placed a hand on Tane's shoulder. "Break him," he snarled, "and bring him to me!"

He strode toward the mouth of the tunnel, his pace unhurried and calm.

"I will find you!" shouted the Hunter. "By the gods, demon, I will hunt you down for what you have done!"

The First didn't look back as he disappeared into the darkness of the passages.

"It's just you and me," Tane growled, a vicious smile crossing his face. The big man had drawn Soulhunger from its pedestal. The long blade seemed puny in his massive hands. His dark eyes tracked the Hunter's movements, wary and expectant. He shifted on the balls of his feet, carrying himself with the confidence of a dancer.

Soulhunger pounded in the Hunter's mind, lusting for blood. *His* blood. The dagger had had a taste, and it wanted more. The thought sickened the Hunter.

"Come on, then," the Hunter snarled.

He saw nothing but confidence in Tane's eyes; the Third stared at him as a predator would its prey. With deliberate slowness, the big man tucked Soulhunger into his belt, as if taunting the Hunter to "*come and get it*". He turned his back contemptuously on the Hunter, striding to the nearby wall. A staff nearly as tall as the man himself leaned against the stone, but Tane gripped it easily despite its length and thickness.

Shit, thought the Hunter, marveling at the grace of the huge man. He watched the pole whistling through the air as Tane swung it with quick, powerful movements. A twinge of fear ran through him—his opponent might very well outmatch him—but pushed it out of his mind.

Nothing I can do about that.

Besides, he had no time to waste; he couldn't let the First escape.

The Hunter lunged forward, thrusting the iron blades in a quick feint toward Tane's midsection. The huge Third swung his staff in an overhand blow powerful enough to crush the Hunter's skull. The Hunter managed to leap out of the way, then stepped inside Tane's guard, his swords slashing for the Third's throat.

Tane proved faster than the Hunter expected. The Third managed to evade the Hunter's thrust and even launch a counter of his own, his staff whistling through the air toward the Hunter's left temple. Ducking, the Hunter leapt to the side, out of range of the spinning staff.

The big Third pressed him hard. He whirled and struck from all angles. The Hunter dodged where possible, but found himself forced to block with both of the Swordsman's blades. The force of Tane's blows jarred his arms and shoulders.

By the Swordsman, he thought, cursing inwardly as he struggled to stay out of the reach of Tane's weapon. *That staff weighs far more than it should.*

Tane wielded his long weapon with deceptive ease, but the Hunter feared its weight more than its speed. He guessed the pole had a steel core—it probably weighed more than he did.

"This staff has broken men far larger and stronger than you," the Third snarled. The man reeked of confidence, a musky odor that blended with his scent of dried blood and cold steel. "It will break you as well."

"Only..." the Hunter growled between panting breaths, "if...it...can...*hit*...me."

A newfound respect for the Third filled the Hunter, along with a nagging worry. Tane's heavy staff not only had the longer reach, but could shatter his iron daggers with ease. The Hunter knew the Swordsman's blades wouldn't survive too many blows from the staff. He could only deflect the strikes he could not dodge.

Reflex took over, and animal instinct alone kept the Hunter alive as he evaded the ferocious swings. Sweat dripped down his face, stinging his eyes and forcing him to retreat. Wiping his forehead, he felt the moisture soften the leather grips of the ancient Swordsman's blades.

"It's a shame you have refused to join us." The voice coming from Tane's mouth startled the Hunter. It was guttural, somehow less than human. "You could have been a useful ally."

The Hunter gaped. "What are you—?"Empty blackness stared back at him from Tane's eyes, mirroring the depthless void of his own.

Fuck! The Hunter cursed inwardly. *One demon was bad enough, but two?*

"You, too?"

Startled, the Hunter lost concentration for a moment, long enough for Tane to slam the butt end of the staff into his stomach. He rolled with the force of the blow, allowing it to knock him back. When he found his feet, however, his breath wheezed in his lungs, and he fought the urge to vomit.

I have to end this before the First escapes. He couldn't let that happen.

Tane lunged again, his staff whirling above his head with blinding speed. The Hunter's forearms ached from the repeated battering. His arms, shoulders, and neck complained every time Tane's whirring staff slammed into his blades, but he had begun to find the pattern in the Third's strikes.

A quick step to the left sold the Hunter's feint, and Tane brought his staff in a cross-body blow meant to shatter the Hunter's knee. The Hunter, however, leapt to the right, avoiding contact. Committed to his strike, Tane could not block the Hunter's lightning slash in time.

"Argghh!" the Third screamed. Iron seeped into his blood from the deep gash in his forearm. Spider veins blackened on his arms as the metal coursed through him. Pain showed on the big man's face, but he gripped the staff tighter in shaking hands.

Tane unleashed a barrage of quick strikes in an attempt to end the fight, but the Hunter had learned his lesson. Dodging another heavy swipe of the staff, he leapt inside Tane's guard to slice another shallow cut on the man's leg. The Hunter stepped back, out of the reach of Tane's staff, his teeth bared in a grin. The wound wouldn't be fatal, but it would slow down the huge Third.

Tane limped in pursuit, favoring his wounded knee. There was a second of hesitation, and in that moment, the Hunter saw a glimpse of fear—mingled with respect—in the Third's depthless eyes. Tane had expected the fight to be over in seconds, but the Hunter's speed and the effects of the iron blades had left him vulnerable.

Time to finish it, you bastard.

The Hunter moved before the big man could react, lunging forward and thrusting his sword toward Tane's throat. Tane blocked and struck back with a blow that jarred the Hunter's right arm.

The force of the contact threw the Hunter to the ground, but he twisted his body as he fell and rolled around behind the Third. The iron blade in the Hunter's uninjured hand lashed out, slicing through sinew at the back of Tane's right ankle. The giant's calf muscle rolled up, and he screamed in pain. The Hunter slashed the blade across the back of Tane's left knee, severing ligaments and tendons before grinding against bone. Tane fell to his knees, screaming in agony as more iron flooded his veins.

The Hunter scrambled to his feet. His shoulder throbbed; had he broken it?

"Hurts like a mule kick in the berries, doesn't it?" he asked, his voice mocking.

Tane fought to retain his grip on the huge staff, using it as a support to hold his body upright. The veins in his forearms had blackened, crawling up his arms like horrible spiders. His thick fingers had puffed up, and the effort of clutching the staff left his hands shaking.

The Hunter lashed out with a flurry of savage kicks, shattering Tane's wrists. He completed his brutal assault with a spinning heel kick that splayed the Third's nose across his face.

"Time to end this, you bastard!" the Hunter shouted. He raised his uninjured arm, the Swordsman's long iron blade held high for the kill.

"No!" cried Tane, real fear flashing through his eyes.

The Hunter drove the blade deep into Tane's gut, slicing through thick muscle and skin. Blood gushed over the Hunter's hand as he buried the dagger to the hilt. Tane's eyes widened in terror, and he screamed—a horrible, inhuman sound—as the iron spread through his body. Tane writhed on the floor in agony, his huge fingers curling around the iron blade in his guts.

The Hunter released the worn leather grip of the dagger, watching Tane flop limply. Satisfaction flooded him at the stench of Tane's loosening bowels. He watched with pitiless eyes as Tane's movement stilled, until the massive chest no longer rose and fell.

It is done, he thought, stooping to retrieve Soulhunger still tucked in the massive man's belt. A mixture of relief and satisfaction flooded him as his fingers closed around the hilt of his dagger. *The demon is dead. Only one left...*

Tane's eyelids snapped open, fire blazing in the empty blackness of his eyes as he bared his teeth in a wordless snarl. His huge hand shot out and thick fingers closed in a vise-grip around the Hunter's wrist.

The Hunter felt himself pulled forward, and before he could react, Tane kicked his chest with a heavy boot, propelling the Hunter through the air. The Hunter slammed against the hard stone wall of the tunnel, the impact knocking the breath from his lungs.

Gasping, he climbed to his feet, staring numbly in open-mouthed horror at the figure before him. Tane's face convulsed in agony, his teeth gritted tight against the pain. His fingers closed around the iron blade embedded in his stomach, and with a superhuman effort, pulled it free.

"But..." the Hunter stammered, at a loss for words, "the...iron..."

"Hurt like nothing you've ever felt," the Third said, clasping his hand to his stomach in an attempt to stop the bleeding. A spasm shook his huge frame, and there was pain in the big man's voice. "But when you spend an eternity being tormented in the deepest recesses of a nameless hell, you develop a certain...tolerance for pain."

The Hunter's mind raced. *The priests said to use two iron blades, but it seems to just slow him down. I need a more...permanent solution.*

His eyes fell on Soulhunger, still tucked in the Third's belt. The blood leaking from Tane's gut stained the blade, and the dagger cried its pleasure—absorbing the gore dripping from the gaping wound.

Tane followed the Hunter's gaze, and a slow smile spread across his face. "Thanal Eth' Athaur." He drew it, his huge hands dwarfing its long blade. "A truly blessed weapon you wield, Hunter, one you have proven you do not deserve."

Tane stalked forward, his movements slower and more precise. He advanced on the Hunter, who, in a flash of panic, realized he only held one of the Swordsman's iron blades. The other lay discarded on the cave floor, still stained with Tane's blood.

Damn, he cursed. *I can't face him with just this...*

He searched the cave, and a surge of hope raced through him as his eyes fell on his sword belt.

There!

He sprinted toward the sword as fast as his aching body would carry him. The sound of Tane's booted feet rang out behind him, but the Hunter ignored the fear coursing through him. His fingers closed around its hilt and, without hesitation, he yanked the sword free of its sheath. He spun just in time to block a vicious thrust that would have buried Soulhunger deep in his gut. The attack left him off balance, forcing him to backpedal as the huge Third attacked.

The Hunter found himself forced to keep his distance from Tane, to avoid the wicked edge of his own blade. Tane lunged forward—too fast for the Hunter to block. Somehow, the Hunter managed to twist out of the way of the attack, though Tane's elbow slammed into his ribs. He scraped the Swordsman's blade across Tane's forearm, hard enough to lay it open to the bone. The Hunter slammed his knee into the big man's gut, once, twice, three times. The pain must have been overwhelming, but still Tane refused to yield. The big man clutched Soulhunger in fingers the Hunter knew were growing weaker with every second.

The Hunter kicked out, his boot connecting with Tane's hand. Bones crunched. Soulhunger spun from the big man's grip. Tane screamed in pain and clutched his mangled fingers to his chest. Blood still leaked from the wound in his gut, slowing him down as he tried to grasp at his opponent. The Hunter leapt backward, and, turning, sprinted toward Soulhunger. He reached down to grasp the fallen blade, but something struck him hard in the back of the head.

Darkness filled his vision for a heartbeat, and the world around him spun. When he finally opened his eyes, he found himself lying on the floor. Blood leaked from a wound on the back of his head, and his face ached from the impact with the hard stone floor. Soulhunger was only a few paces away, just out of the Hunter's reach. Beside the blade lay a rock stained red with his own blood.

If I can just—

Even as he tried to stand, a huge hand clamped down on the back of his neck.

"You cannot win," snarled Tane, far too close for comfort. The Third lifted the Hunter and held him as he would a doll.

A blow to the Hunter's stomach folded him over, gasping for breath and fighting the urge to vomit. He struck out at Tane with his sword, but the big man's fingers closed around his wrist. Tane squeezed hard, snapping the Hunter's wrist like a twig. The Hunter screamed. With disdain, Tane threw him to the floor.

"You see, Hunter," Tane said, his laughter echoing loud in the cavern as he stared down at the Hunter gagging and struggling to breathe. "You may be a Bucelarii, but I am Abiarazi. I am forced to wear human flesh, but I am more than strong enough to rip you apart, even in my current state." His right hand gestured to his limp left arm. "Damage my flesh all you want, but you will find it harder to kill my true form."

Even as he exulted, pain flashed across Tane's face. He clutched at the wound in his gut, holding his injured forearm close to his chest. The Hunter guessed the iron still spread through his veins, and he saw the flesh of Tane's arm had begun to blacken and fester.

"I may take time to heal," the Third said, noticing his gaze, "but I will have time aplenty once you're out of the way. There will be no one to stop us, and Voramis will be ours once again. I will rebuild the Bloody Hand to be stronger and better than it ever was!"

"Even after your cowardly master has deserted you here?"

"Master?" the Third snarled. "That urrzad b'th *calls* himself my master, and it suits my purpose to allow him to do so. However, by the end of this night, I will have proven which of us is worthy to rule this filthy planet."

"By the end of this night," the Hunter growled in response, "you and your fellow demon will be sent back to the hells from which you came."

"Even if you stop us," Tane shouted, "we will never stop trying. You have no idea how many of us walk this world, Hunter. We may look mortal, but we are far more powerful than even you could imagine. We are legion, and we *will* rule the world. You'll never destroy us all!"

"I'll settle with putting an end to you tonight." With effort, the Hunter climbed to his feet, cradling his shattered left hand. "You, and that creature you call the First."

"You realize what you're doing, Hunter?" Tane asked. "You understand that you are killing the only things on earth just like you? By killing us, you ensure that you will be forever alone in this world."

"We do what we must," the Hunter said with a careless shrug. "Your time has passed, demon. This world belongs to humankind now. Even if it means I am the only one of my kind left, I *will* stop you Abiarazi from returning."

He dove forward and threw himself into a roll. His hands closed around Soulhunger's grip, and though he gasped in pain when his shoulder collided with the stone floor, he managed to find his feet. He thrust the blade forward, intending to drive it deep into Tane's gut.

Tane's foot slammed into his face, snapping his head back and lifting him from his feet. Pain exploded through him. His mouth filled with the coppery taste of the blood gushing from his broken nose. He fell backward, his head ringing, unable to stand from the dizziness washing over him.

"You fool," snarled Tane. The big man towered over him, his eyes devoid of all pity as he stared down at the Hunter. "You never know when to quit."

Tane stamped down hard. His massive foot shattered the Hunter's right leg, sending agony ripping through him. The Hunter tried to crawl away, but an immense weight pressed his left leg to the floor. Tears streamed down his face, and he could do nothing but lie helpless, screaming in torment, as Tane slowly applied pressure to the bone until it too snapped with a loud crack.

"We need you alive, and that is the only reason I do not kill you right here and now. It is over, Hunter." Tane's breath was hot and vile as he leaned close and wrapped his fingers, still slick with his own blood, around the Hunter's throat.

The Hunter's lungs burned, his head pounded, and agony raced through his legs. He tried to speak, but the blood filling his mouth turned his words to a mumble.

"What's that?" Tane asked, trying to make sense of the words. "Did you say—?"

The Hunter retorted with a wordless snarl, spitting blood into Tane's face. Tane flinched, and his grip on the Hunter's throat weakened for a heartbeat. Even as the Hunter filled his lungs with air, his right hand closed around Soulhunger's hilt. In desperation, he struck out blindly at the huge man towering over him.

The blade sliced through windpipe and vocal cords, driving deep into his neck. The big man's mouth opened and closed soundlessly as he fought to breathe, to speak. Only a horrible bubbling sound emerged.

Blood dripped down Tane's massive chest, washing over the Hunter, soaking him in gore. Tane released his death grip on the Hunter's throat. He tried to claw at the blade embedded in his neck, to break the Hunter's hold on it. His legs wobbled and sagged. His struggles grew weaker, but still the stubborn demon fought.

As Tane fell to the floor, the Hunter collapsed atop him. The pain of his shattered legs washed over him, nearly stealing his consciousness. He fought back the pain, refused to give in to it. He had one thought.

Finish him!

The Hunter released Soulhunger and reached for the iron blade lying on the floor beside him. Pain flashed through his hands as he gripped the weapon, but he welcomed it. It kept him conscious, distracted him from the agony racing through his shattered legs.

Tane lay on the cold stone floor, his eyes wide in horror and surprise. Slowly, painfully, the Hunter dragged himself atop the Third. The big man's stomach rose and fell in agonized gasps, his face twisted with fury.

The Hunter drove the iron blade into Tane's throat. Blood sprayed in a fountain, washing over the Hunter's face. With a jerk, he ripped Soulhunger from the Third's neck. Tane shuddered in pain, but lacked even the strength to lift his hands to stop the blood pouring from the wound.

"Give your brothers my greetings, you hell-spawned bastard!" shouted the Hunter, raising Soulhunger high.

Down plunged the dagger, driving deep into the heavy muscles of the big man's chest, piercing flesh, and finally slipping between the cavernous ribs. Soulhunger's wicked tip searched for the man's heart, the blade screaming with pleasure as it fed.

Dark blood spurted from the wound in Tane's chest, covering the Hunter's hand and the hilt of the dagger with gore. It mixed with the dust on the floor, coursing in a slow, thick stream toward the gaping void of the Midden.

A bellow tore from the Third's mouth, an inhuman, horrible sound. The Hunter fought to blink away the tears of pain, staring in horror at the creature beneath him. Flesh and hair burned away from Tane's face, revealing the demon's true features. A face of nightmares stared back at the Hunter. Screams poured from a mouth filled with far too many jagged teeth, and a serpentine tongue panted for breath. Horn-like protuberances sprouted around the thing's face, and the deadened eyes filled with inky blackness.

The demon's true form, thought the Hunter, a chill racing down his spine. His nostrils filled with the scent of charred meat, rot, and decay.

Then came the pain.

Never before had the Hunter experienced an agony so intense, so all-consuming. He felt pain when Soulhunger took a life, but now every fiber of his body screamed with the torment. Soulhunger's gemstone blazed with a fierce light, shining with such force that the crimson brilliance nearly blinded him. The Hunter struggled to move his hands, to shield his face from the power filling the cavern as the accursed blade fed on the demon's lifeblood. Agony blossomed on his chest—a new mark etched into his skin.

With the pain came an overwhelming rush of power. It flooded his body, knitting flesh and shattered bone together. This power felt different…foul and unclean. He wanted to vomit, to purge himself of its taint, but he could not. Tears streamed down his face. He lay on the cold stone floor, immobilized by pain. The thrill of the Third's death rushed through him, and Soulhunger added its voice to the din in his mind.

His cries of anguish echoed loud in the hollow cavern. He writhed on the floor, his body twitching as wave after wave of agony racked him. It threatened to steal his mind and shatter his consciousness.

Have…to…stay…awake!

The demon's body thrashed in its death throes before finally lying still. The Hunter's fingers curled around Soulhunger's blood-covered grip, and with a mighty heave, he wrenched it from the dead demon's chest. The blade drank eagerly, and within seconds, the light of the gem had faded.

The wind howled around him, carrying the sounds of screaming from beyond the still-open portal into the fiery hell. The scent of sulfur and charred meat wafted toward him, and he fought the urge to gag. The portal writhed and twisted. The breach in reality collapsed inward, and the world seemed to bend around him, shrinking to a tiny point and exploding outward faster than his mind could comprehend.

A concussive force washed over the Hunter, throwing him through the air. He slammed hard against the ground. Dark spots swam in his vision, and he struggled to breathe. He could do no more than lie on the ground, fighting to remain conscious.

The demon's life force must have anchored the portal, his mind thought dimly. *When Soulhunger took his life, it severed the connection.*

"Keeper-cursed demons," he spat, his voice weak and faint.

Slowly, with great effort, the Hunter rolled onto his stomach. Climbing to his feet seemed to be an impossible task, and yet somehow he managed. His legs still ached, but they had healed sufficiently to allow him to move.

Have…to…find…the First, he thought, gritting his teeth through the pain.

He lurched toward the tunnel into which the First had disappeared, pausing only long enough to retrieve the Swordsman's iron blades and his sword belt. Vision swimming, his stomach lurched when he bent over. He swallowed his gorge and stumbled on.

Rumbling sounded high above his head. He looked up in time to see a massive boulder crumble and fall from the roof of the cavern. The ground beneath the Hunter echoed the ominous grumbling of the roof, and stone rained down around him.

Shit!

He tried to hurry, but his legs refused to cooperate. They sagged beneath him, sending him stumbling. He fell hard, then scrambled to his feet once more, determined to keep staggering toward the tunnel with all the speed he could muster. Something slammed into his shoulder and hurled him to the ground.

One arm in front of the other, he thought. If he could not walk, he would crawl. The distance to the mouth of the tunnel seemed endless. Another chunk of rock struck the back of his neck, and his vision blurred.

Move, move, move!

A gigantic stalactite broke free of the roof with a deafening '*crack*'. The enormous shard of stone plunged toward him, tons of debris and loose stone accompanying its descent. A curse flashed through his mind as the roof collapsed, burying him beneath a mountain of rubble.

Chapter Thirty-Six

Am I dead?

He felt nothing, saw only darkness. He floated, drifting through the empty void around him.

If so, the afterlife is supremely boring.

As conscious thought returned, pain whispered its way back into his limbs. An immense weight pressed on his spine, crushing him and rendering him immobile..

What in the frozen hell?

Dazed and confused, he tried to focus through the throbbing in his head. He remembered crawling away from the body of the Third, fighting to escape before…

The roof of the cavern collapsed.

His ribs creaked painfully, and pulling air into his lungs seemed impossible. Dust filled his mouth and nose, setting him coughing. More pain.

I must be buried beneath the rubble.

For long moments, he struggled to move his arms, his legs, his head, even his fingers. Nothing. Nothing but pain.

No! I have to get out of here.

Darkness pressed in around him, paralyzing him with its immense weight. He tried to move, threw every ounce of strength into the struggle, but his muscles failed. Fear rippled through him as he fought for breath. The oppressing blackness trapped more than his body; his very soul felt crushed beneath the burden.

It's hopeless, he thought, panic seizing his mind. *I can't get out of here. I'm going to die buried alive.*

His head spun and his stomach twisted, threatening to empty itself in his fear. Sweat trickled down his face. His heart beat so fast it felt as if it would rip free of his chest. His breath came fast and hard, and his limbs jerked violently. The faint sound of clattering stone reached his ears, but only darkness greeted his eyes.

For the first time in memory, the Hunter truly feared death. He had faced ghastly odds before, but nothing like this. There was no one to kill, no one to hunt. There was only him and the mountain of rock and stone over his head. Visions of his crushed, buried body raced through his mind.

Not like this, the animal side of him howled in panic, *not alone and trapped far beneath the earth!*

Another wave of terror flooded him, and his limbs twitched in a paroxysm of fear. The hopelessness of his situation overwhelmed his animal instinct. Despair filled him. He had no way of escape.

Accept it, he told himself. *Accept that you cannot escape, and surrender to the darkness. It can all be over. The pain, the suffering, it can all end.*

Tears filled his eyes. Something within him broke, a dam holding back the pain, and emotion burst from within his chest. Salty wetness flooded down his cheeks as he wept.

I've tried to ignore the pain my whole life, tried to distract myself from feeling the desolation of being alone in the world.

He relaxed muscles, his heartbeat slowing. He no longer fought for breath, but simply lay there, acceptant of his fate.

Let it be over, he thought. *I'm tired of being alone, being an outcast, being rejected.*

No, something within him whispered. *Never truly an outcast, never completely rejected. Never alone.*

Faces floated in the darkness. Old Nan. Jak the Thumb. Ellinor. Little Arlo. They had accepted him, even welcomed him.

But they are gone now.

He had always kept his emotions bottled up, telling himself they were a sign of weakness. Now he wept freely. He wept for himself, letting the emotion wash through him as hot tears streamed down his dust-stained face.

Don't lose control, screamed the demon in his head, howling with rage. *To lose control is death.*

He had always considered his animal instinct a gift, the thing that made him the killer he was. He had listened to it, had used it to make him a peerless hunter…*The* Hunter. But now, with a sinking in his gut, he realized what that other half of him truly was.

The demon within.

He had fought to control his urges, his desire to kill, but the demon had always won. Every time he killed, he had given more of himself to the demon. With every death, his humanity had died a little more.

No longer, he vowed. *With my death, the demon will be silenced once and for all. It will never again be able to harm another human being. The time of the Hunter must end.*

With acceptance came peace. His pain seemed to fade into the darkness around him. He floated, weightless, numb. Emptiness filled his mind, and he closed his eyes.

It is the end.

A new face materialized—a happy face, with chubby cheeks, long eyelashes, and a smile so infectious it had always brought a grin to his own face.

Farida.

Her smile dimmed, and her skin turned cold, lifeless. Once again, the Hunter saw the empty, unseeing eyes and slack expression on the child's face as he had laid her on the steps of the House of Need. He couldn't look into those eyes, couldn't see the accusation written there.

I'm so sorry, child. I'm so sorry.

A fresh wave of sorrow flooded him, and tears fell anew.

It is all my fault, he thought. *I allowed this to happen to her. It is because of me that this innocent child was killed.*

Farida's features rippled, morphing once more into the happy, smiling face of the child he had seen so many times. She stared back at him through eyes bright with life. She saw him now—the real him, without disguise.

It's not your fault, she seemed to say. *It may have been because of you, but it is not your fault.*

But I allowed it to happen, his mind screamed at her. *I let you die!*

No, the vision responded, *you gave me life all those years ago when you brought me to the House of Need. Death is inevitable, but it is thanks to you that I lived as long as I did. You saved me.*

A wave of emotion flooded him, joy mingling with his sorrow. The pain of loss at Farida's death remained, but happiness washed over him as he realized that he truly had saved her all those years ago.

Were it to end like this, your death would be meaningless, she told him. *Your life had meaning to at least one little flower girl. Is that not enough for you to keep living?*

End it all, the demon within him whispered. The darkness around him beckoned. He wanted nothing more than to accept the peaceful embrace of death.

Get up, Farida's face seemed to say. *Fight, Hunter.*

With a final haunting smile, her face slowly faded from his thoughts, leaving his mind empty. Only empty blackness filled his vision as he was once more left alone.

It is over, his demon half said.

No. I cannot let the First escape. I cannot let him out into the world once more, where he will disappear forever.

Embrace the comfort of death, the demon whispered, its voice soothing, *and we will join our brothers once more.*

NO! I WILL NOT YIELD!

The voice murmured promises of an end to his suffering, offering him peace, but the Hunter had found his will to live.

I will *escape,* he thought, *and I* will *fight. The First still walks free, but he will pay for what he has done.*

Pain flooded him once more, the pressure of the rubble above him threatening to break him in half. Agony filled every corner of his body. His ribs felt as if they would shatter at any moment. Yet the pain only strengthened his resolve.

It will not end here. I am the Hunter, and I will not *die trapped like a worm.*

The Hunter heaved, his muscles straining. Pain flared along his chest and back with the effort. Every bone in his body protested, yet the mountain refused to move. Willing his body to work harder, the Hunter fought to arch his back, to bend his elbows, to bring his knees to his chest. He threw every ounce of his strength into his muscles, his will alone forcing his body to keep pushing though his sinews quaked with the effort.

I can't be far from the surface, he thought.

The debris covering his right arm shifted. He heard the clatter of rubble, and hope surged through him at the sound. He pulled his hand toward him, trying to free it from the crushing mountain atop him. A muffled scream tore from his lips as blood rushed into his wrist and the nerves came back to life in his crushed fingers. He nearly collapsed from the agony of returning sensation. Yet he poured the pain into the fire of his will, using it to fan the flame and feed his rage.

I WILL NOT YIELD!

With agonizing slowness, the heavy stones above him shifted. He heaved upwards, struggling to free his body from the debris burying him.

But the strain was too much, the weight too heavy. His strength fled. Exhausted, his muscles drained, he fell back to his face and hands. The stones above him threatened to crush him beneath their weight.

Yet he refused to give up.

No! It will not end here!

A soft breeze wafted across his face, beckoning him. He fought toward it, crawling one painful pace at a time. Rocks carved deep grooves into his back, and blood trickled down his sides, but still he struggled. Hand over hand, he pulled himself toward the pinprick of light in the distance.

Almost there…

With a final tremendous effort, the Hunter dragged his body free of the rubble. He flopped to the stone floor and sucking in huge gulps of air. The mountain collapsed behind him, burying the small cavity in a shower of dust and stone.

For long moments he lay there, panting for breath, sensation washing over his body. Blood coursed through his arms and legs. He was weak, but alive. Agony permeated every nerve and muscle in his body, yet he refused to let it steal his consciousness. The pain served to remind him that he had escaped death once more.

Something hard pressed into his back, and relief flooded him as he touched the hilts of the iron blades. His left hand still gripped Soulhunger. Already the shattered bones had begun to re-knit, hardening with every passing second. Soulhunger remained silent, but the Hunter could sense its consciousness slowly returning. His head throbbed, both from his injuries and from the dagger's presence in his mind.

Slowly, the agony in his fingers subsided. They felt thick and clumsy, but he could move them without too much pain. His vision wavered when he tried to stand. Another wave of pain swept over him, forcing him to lean against the wall for support. His knees threatened to give out—his legs had not yet fully healed.

"Bloody Minstrel," he cursed. "Let's hope I don't run into anyone on my way out." He realized he was speaking aloud. "Great, and now I'm talking to myself." Talking into the empty silence of the tunnels felt oddly comforting. It made him feel less alone.

Dust showered from the ceiling, along with a few chunks of loose stone. A rumble echoed through the cavern. Somehow, the Hunter found the will to move. Though it required all of his resolve, he forced himself to take slow, pain-filled steps down the tunnel. Fear of the tunnel's collapse propelled him forward. He had already climbed his way free of one mountain of debris, and had no desire to do so again.

I'm coming for you, you bastard. A smile touched his lips. He visualized the suffering he would visit on the First in vengeance for what he had done.

"Fucking demon!" he cursed aloud.

He filled his lungs with the stale air, ignoring the ache in his ribs. If he could find the First's scent, he could—

A smile touched his lips, a grim, wolfish snarl of rage.

I've got you now.

Fighting to ignore the pain in every step, the Hunter hobbled down the empty Serenii tunnels. He followed the demon's trail through the darkness, his eyes ever alert for danger. The scent of decay, faint as it was, led him unerringly toward his prey.

Chapter Thirty-Seven

It seemed like hours had passed, but the Hunter guessed he had walked for no more than half an hour. The sound of his boots scuffing on the stone floor echoed loudly in the silence of the dark passages. His hands no longer throbbed, and his legs only complained with every other step. The pain had gone, but exhaustion threatened to overwhelm him. He wanted nothing more than to collapse, to close his eyes, to sleep on the cold stone floor. The echoes of the tunnels crumbling behind him forced him onward.

Light flickered ahead, beckoning him and yet filling him with a sense of dread. Light could only come from torches, meaning people. His sensitive nostrils detected the scents of steel, leather, and stale sweat. Armed men, undoubtedly left there by the First to kill him.

The Hunter peered around the corner, and cursed silently. Five men stood in the circle of torchlight, wearing the crimson-trimmed black robes of the Dark Heresy, heavy swords strapped to their waists. He wondered if he should find another way, but the First's trail led through the group of men. He had no choice but to fight.

Fuck, he thought, *this is* not *going to be fun.*

The fingers of his left hand had not yet healed sufficiently to wield the long sword. Instead, he drew one of the Swordsman's iron blades and gripped Soulhunger in his weaker hand.

Here goes nothing.

With all the speed he could muster, the Hunter dashed around the corner of the passage and charged toward the Dark Heresiarchs. His soft boots made no sound on the tunnel floor, and he whispered a silent blessing on the cobbler who had made them.

Soulhunger throbbed weakly in his mind, and the voice in his head and the weight of the dagger in his hand comforted him. He just needed to get close enough to sink the blade into one of the Dark Heresiarchs…

The Hunter waited until he was within a dozen paces of the Dark Heresiarchs before hurling the Swordsman's blade. Even as he released it, he knew the cast had been poor, but it was enough. The crossguard slammed into the face of one Heresiarch, and the man dropped, clutching at his broken nose.

Before the other Heresiarchs knew what was happening, the Hunter was upon them. He lashed out with Soulhunger, and the dagger's tip sunk deep into the back of the nearest guard. The blade slid through the man's ribs and sliced the smooth muscle of the heart. The Dark Heresiarch died with a blood-curdling scream.

Power rushed through the Hunter, flooding him with strength and vitality. As the first Dark Heresiarch slumped, the Hunter's right hand—now fully healed—tugged his sword free of its sheath.

"The Hunter!" one of the Dark Heresiarchs gasped, his eyes going wide.

"Stop him!" shouted another guard. The Heresiarch had more courage than good sense, for he lunged forward to cross swords with the Hunter without waiting for his companions to join him. He died in seconds, blood spurting from a gaping wound in his neck.

Two more guards found their nerve, and, drawing heavy swords, rushed the Hunter. He easily fended off their attacks, waiting for an opening. But when he saw a third man struggling to clear his blade from its sheath, he knew it was time to change tactics. The last thing he wanted was a long, drawn out struggle; he could not allow the First to escape.

The Hunter leapt forward, sword held high, a growl of rage bursting from his lips. One of the Dark Heresiarchs' swords slipped past the Hunter's guard, slicing a deep gash in his stomach. The Hunter's shout of pain blended with the guard's wet gurgle as the Hunter buried his sword in the man's throat. The other Heresiarch swung high, and the Hunter thrust Soulhunger between his ribs. The two Dark Heresiarchs slumped to the floor in unison.

Fear filled the faces of the last two Dark Heresiarchs, but the Hunter gave them no time to flee. He laid open the thick artery in the arm of the first guard, who screamed and clutched at the wound in a vain effort to stanch the torrent of blood.

The last Heresiarch proved more proficient with the sword than his companions; he managed to hold off the Hunter's strikes for a few moments, even landing a lucky blow across the Hunter's forehead. A contemptuous slash of the Hunter's sword sent the guard's blade wide, and Soulhunger thrust in for the kill.

The Hunter watched with pitiless eyes as the guard slumped to the floor. The weight of his falling body wrenched the bloody dagger free of his chest. Soulhunger's voice returned as it drank deep of the man's lifeblood, the blade throbbing in the back of the Hunter's mind.

Breathing deeply, he let the thrill of battle wash over him. But instead of exulting in the rush of death, the Hunter felt sick. He remembered that overwhelming force that had drawn the power in Soulhunger's blade downward. Once again, he heard the *thump, thump* of an immense heart beating.

The First said that every life taken feeds Kharna, he thought with a shudder, *the god who would rule the world or destroy it. I am the blade of the Destroyer, and I wield the weapon that will bring about his return.*

He took deep, shuddering breaths, fighting down the desire to vomit.

How many more have to die before the Destroyer returns? Can I refrain from using Soulhunger to kill, and thereby prevent his return?

No, I cannot, he told himself. *I do what I must.*

Though his justification rang hollow, he ignored the nagging guilt in his mind. He needed the power the blade offered if he was to put an end to the First, the Bloody Hand, and the Dark Heresy once and for all.

I do this for Farida. I will stop once I have avenged her death.

He stepped over the lifeless forms of the Dark Heresiarchs who had dared to stop him. Their blood stained the stone floor in an ever-widening pool of red, and his boots left grim prints in the dust. He only paused long enough to retrieve the Swordsman's blade from the ground before striding into the darkness of the tunnels.

I will finish this, no matter how long it takes to hunt down the demon.

Chapter Thirty-Eight

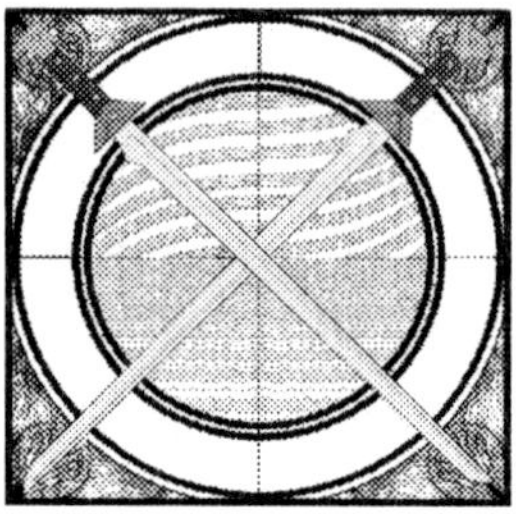

"How many more of you are there?" the Hunter shouted, slamming the hilt of his sword into the Dark Heresiarch's gore-covered face.

The man cried out in pain, but refused to speak. Blood stained his robes from a deep wound in his side and trickled down his heavy bearded face from a split lip. His left eye had already swollen beneath the Hunter's abuse.

"Tell me what I need to know," the Hunter said, cutting off the man's cries with another blow, "and I may spare you the fate of your companions."

Four dead bodies littered the room, still bleeding and dying in the wake of the Hunter's violent onslaught. The Hunter had come upon this second Dark Heresiarch patrol as he tracked the escaping First. All lay dead save for the man bleeding on the floor.

"Now, are you going to tell me," the Hunter snarled, "or do I have to cut it out of you? No doubt you know what this can do?" He held Soulhunger up before the man's eyes.

The blade glinted in the flickering torchlight, and the Dark Heresiarch's eyes widened as he saw it. "No," begged the man, "please don't…!" The acrid stench of urine wafted up from the floor, mixing with the stench of sweat-soaked terror emanating from the man.

"Not so tough, are you?" the Hunter mocked. "Can't blame you there, knowing what Soulhunger can do." He placed the tip of the dagger beneath the man's eyeball and pressed it into the skin—hard enough to draw blood. The Dark Heresiarch's cries of pain echoed loudly through the tunnel as Soulhunger drank.

"Now," the Hunter shouted, "you were saying?"

"All right," the Dark Heresiarch pleaded, his voice filled with fear. "Just take that damn blade away!"

"There," said the Hunter, sheathing Soulhunger, "now talk, or I will be forced to use the dagger on you. How many more of you are there?"

The Dark Heresiarch coughed, a wet sound that brought up flecks of blood. "A dozen," he said. "A dozen in the tunnels, plus another few spread around the city."

"That's it?" the Hunter asked, surprised. "I'd have thought the dreaded Dark Heresy had more than a handful of idiots working for them."

"Fuck you, Hunter," the Dark Heresiarch spat through blood-stained teeth.

"That's not very polite, is it?" the Hunter asked, a vicious grin spreading across his face. "Don't make me angry. When I get angry, bad things happen."

Soulhunger slipped from its sheath with a whisper of pleasure, and the Hunter pressed the blade's tip into the Dark Heresiarch's kidney.

"You'll never stop us all!" the guard managed to shout between cries of agony. "You can kill us, but the Demon will just gather more to his side."

The Hunter slipped the blade from the man's side and stared down at the pitiful, bleeding figure. "Your Demon is dead," he said, a vicious grin on his face, "or he soon will be."

"Dead?" the Dark Heresiarch asked, shock registering in his face. "But, you can't…"

"But I will!" the Hunter snarled, cutting him off. He raised Soulhunger high, and the Heresiarch's eyes widened in fear.

"But you p—"

The man's words were drowned out by screams of agony as the Hunter thrust Soulhunger into his chest. Those screams faded and soon died altogether.

A feral grin touched the Hunter's lips. "I lied."

* * *

Hours had passed in his relentless pursuit of the First, but the Hunter sensed he was finally getting close.

Once the First has met his end, there will be none seeking to return the demon horde to this world.

Tane's words flashed through his mind.

'You have no idea how many of us walk this world,' he said. How many demons are there on the face of Einan?

He pushed that thought aside, returning his mind to the hunt for the First. He would have to track Celicia down as well, along with any remnants of the Bloody Hand still living. They deserved the justice he was meting out this night.

The Hunter raced through the tunnels, his sensitive nostrils searching for the scent of decay that marked the First's escape route. He consulted the map in his head, charting the First's route in an attempt to figure out where the demon would exit the tunnels. He had a pretty good idea where the First would try to escape into the night. He was determined to be there before the demon could disappear.

As he ran, he basked in the power coursing through his body. His pain was gone and his injuries had healed. His strength had returned with every life Soulhunger had taken, and he felt stronger than he had in a long time.

He ground to a halt at an intersection, his feet skidding on the smooth stone floor. He filled his lungs with air, inhaling through his nostrils in an attempt to pick up the smell again. A cross breeze from one of the tunnels brought him the barest hint of the First's scent.

There! The odor, while faint, held a distinctive smell of decay. *Found you, you bastard.*

Smiling, he raced up the tunnel. The smell grew stronger with each step, and he knew his quarry was close. Footfalls echoed through the empty corridors. He hastened onward, running without a sound—save for the gentle clanking of his weapons in their well-wrapped sheaths.

The light of a torch far in the distance cast eerie shadows along the tunnel walls.

There he is!

The Hunter sprinted through the darkened tunnels, heedless of his surroundings. He had eyes only for the light ahead, and the man carrying the torch.

I've got you now, you bastard!

He drew Soulhunger, but the blade remained silent—sated by the lives it had consumed. Moonlight shone at the far end of the tunnel. The Hunter was determined to cut off the First's escape.

So close, you coward, and yet so far!

Something caused the First to glance over his shoulder, and his eyes widened in shock at sight of the Hunter. He dropped the torch and fumbled for the elaborate sword at his side. As the sword whispered from its sheath, his expression changed from astonishment—and a hint of fear—to calm confidence. The demon held the blade with familiar ease, his stance relaxed.

"You're not getting away that easily," the Hunter snarled. Dried blood still coated his face and clothes, but he didn't care. He had only one thought in his mind: to kill the man—no, the *creature*—before him.

"So," the First said, a note of surprise in his voice, "you killed Tane." The demon eyed Soulhunger with wary eyes, and regarded the gore-covered Hunter with an expression of haughty disdain.

"You may have killed him, but you can't possibly expect to kill *me*, Hunter," mocked the First. "For every year you have lived, I have lived a dozen. For every life you have taken, I have killed thousands. You have no idea how many have died at my hands." He bared his teeth in a predatory snarl of rage. "Would you be one more?"

"You slaughtered humans like sheep," the Hunter spat. "You killed my friends."

"Those filthy creatures should mean nothing to you. *We* are family. You are not human," the First said, a tone of pride in his voice, "you are something much more. You are the spawn of the greatest race ever to walk this pitiful earth. Embrace who you are."

"My blood may be accursed," the Hunter said, slowly, "but I will not be manipulated by a...*creature* like you." His spittle landed in the dirt between the First's feet.

"So the great Hunter turns his back on who he is," the First mocked. "He disowns his blood to play the hero, the protector."

The Hunter gritted his teeth. "I am no protector, demon," he snarled, pounding his chest with bestial ferocity. "I am the Hunter, and tonight, you are my prey."

"Brave words, Hunter," the First snarled, "but once again you choose poorly. I will relish feeding your blood to my blade, as yours has fed on so many before."

For the first time, the Hunter truly looked at the sword in the First's hands. Steel burned bright in the flickering torchlight. The graceful blade seemed almost alive in the demon's hand. Symbols in a language the Hunter had never seen were etched clearly into the steel. He stared at the markings, his skin crawling.

Soulhunger pulsed in the Hunter's hand, screaming of desire. The sword echoed the dagger's whispers. With a horrified sinking in his gut, the Hunter realized the sword was as alive as his own blade. The two blades joined their murderous voices as one, and the din threatened to overwhelm the Hunter's senses.

"I see fear in your eyes, Hunter," the First said, smiling. "Before Thanal Eth' Athaur ever was, this blade had drunk the blood of thousands. It is older than this world, and its power is beyond your comprehension."

The Hunter, fighting to pull his gaze away from the blade, locked eyes with the First. He drew one of the Swordsman's blades, passing Soulhunger to his offhand. The pain of the iron distracted him from the pounding voices in his head.

"Your sword hasn't done you any good," the Hunter growled. "After all, your precious Destroyer has yet to return."

"Perhaps not," the First said calmly, "but all that changes now that I have found you. Your blood is all we need to restore the Destroyer to this world."

"You'll have to take me first, Demon," the Hunter snarled.

"I always loved that name," the First mused. "The 'Demon of Voramis' they called me. Perhaps a bit on the nose, but apt." He gave the Hunter a condescending smile and a salute of the demonic blade. "Farewell, Hunter. You have been a valuable tool, but your usefulness has run out this night."

The First attacked, striking so quickly that the Hunter found himself retreating before he could raise a defense. He twisted away from the First's lightning thrust to his midsection and nearly slipped as he ducked beneath a blow that would have opened his throat.

He counterattacked with Soulhunger, slipping it between the First's guard, striking for soft tissue and vital organs. The First interposed his own blade, batting the dagger aside and opening the Hunter's guard for a riposte. Only the Hunter's reflexes saved him. He barely managed to raise the iron blade in time to turn away a strike meant to pierce his eye.

The First stared at his sword in disbelief. Smoke rose from the blade where the Swordsman's dagger had touched it. The iron corroded the accursed sword with every contact.

"You may just find me harder to kill than you had expected, *demon.*" The Hunter spat the last word as an insult, but the First only grinned.

"Beware hubris, Hunter," he said, "for that is what has led you here in the first place."

When the First renewed his attack, the Hunter realized he had only been measuring his skill. The Hunter found it harder to keep his distance from the First's whirling blade. The demon moved with precision, his strikes increasing in speed.

I barely managed to survive Tane, the Hunter thought, blocking a vicious slash aimed at his throat. A flash of fear raced through him. *Can I survive again?*

Their swords clashed in a flurry of steel and iron. The ringing of their blades echoed loudly through the empty passages. The Hunter retreated, barely able to stay out of reach of the First's longer blade. His chances of winning were slim, but he was determined to fight on.

The iron blade in his offhand lent him both an advantage and disadvantage. It would break under a direct blow from the First's long sword, but the accursed steel smoked every time the Swordsman's blade touched it. He defended with Soulhunger, using the iron blade solely as an offensive weapon.

In desperation, he changed tactics. He leapt backward, well out of the First's reach. He quickly sheathed Soulhunger, passed the iron blade to his left hand, and drew his sword.

Confidence flooded him at the familiar feel of the sword, and he launched a storm of steel, striking at the First with blows faster than the eye could follow. For a moment, the Hunter saw fear on the demon's face as the iron blade whistled close to his face, the tip narrowly missing his eye. But the First recovered quickly, and the Hunter was forced back once more.

The slim sword in the First's hand hummed in the air, carving deadly arcs around the Hunter. The demon moved with the grace of a fencing master, but fought with the savagery of a warrior. Only the Hunter's desperate speed saved him from the demon's blade. After long minutes of furious struggle, the combatants finally broke apart.

"My my," panted the First, "it seems you are determined to die here."

"I will not die," retorted the Hunter, his lungs burning, "not until I have repaid you for what you did to my friends."

Not willing to allow the First a moment to recover, the Hunter attacked again with a roar of rage. Every muscle in his body ached, but anger stoked the fires within him. His sword sang as he slashed at the First with a series of concerted strikes that pushed the demon against the tunnel wall.

Real fear flashed in the First's eyes as the Hunter battered his guard. The Swordsman's iron dagger slammed over and over into the demonic sword. The accursed blade smoked and withered, yet it refused to break. The First desperately tried to protect himself, but the fury of the Hunter's sword overpowered him.

The Hunter finally broke through the First's guard with a lightning thrust that pierced the demon's eye and sliced into his brain. The impact slammed the demon's head against the stone wall and his body flopped limply—the nerves in his brain severed. The accursed sword dropped from insensate fingers.

Panting, his face twisted with rage, the Hunter stared down at the unmoving figure at his feet. He raised the Swordsman's blade, preparing to drive it deep into the man's other eye before he could recover. He would have justice for Farida and the others.

"Heal from this, you bastard," the Hunter said.

Pain shot up his spine. His body suddenly jerked, going rigid. His knees buckled and he fell hard. He slammed into the stone floor of the tunnel, unable to arrest his fall. He couldn't feel his arms or legs. A cold numbness slowly seeped through his entire body.

The Hunter screamed as the blade was wrenched from his back. His body twitched, but there was no response from his limbs.

A familiar scent wafted from behind him. Leather. Steel. Lilies.

The voice accompanying the scent was harsh and cold.

"Fucking Hunter," snarled Celicia, Fourth of the Bloody Hand.

Chapter Thirty-Nine

Celicia's steel-toed boot slammed into his face. Blood trickled from his lips, mingling with the gore staining his face. A vicious kick to his ribs knocked the wind from him. He willed his limbs to respond, but nothing happened. Celicia's blade had sliced through his spine.

"You bastard!" Celicia shouted. "You've killed him!"

Strong hands gripped his right arm and turned him over. He stared up into the rage-filled face of the Fourth.

"You've destroyed everything!" she shouted.

He tried to speak, but his swollen lips and bloody mouth made it difficult.

"You'll pay for what you've done!" Celicia said, spittle flying from her mouth. She gripped a dagger in her right hand, the blade covered with the Hunter's blood.

She kicked him hard, this time between the legs. Agony coursed through the Hunter, but the pain signaled that his spine was healing—albeit slowly. He felt the urge to vomit, and tried to curl up in a protective ball.

"Wait," mumbled the Hunter, his words mumbling through swollen lips.

"No," she growled. "You die *now*!"

"Hold," came another voice, this one belonging to the First.

The voice froze Celicia, and surprise showed plainly on her face as she stared at her master. She made no move as the First slowly climbed to his feet—the Hunter's sword still embedded in his eye.

"Damn," the First said, his voice thick and clumsy. He pulled the blade free and threw it to the ground with a scowl of contempt. "That actually hurt."

Blood leaked from the demon's eyeball, trickling down his cheek, but the man seemed not to care. He casually dabbed at the seeping blood with a handkerchief. In open-mouthed horror, the Hunter and Celicia watched as the demon's eye slowly re-knitted. The eyeball rolled around loose in its socket for a moment before coming to rest on Celicia, who still knelt atop the Hunter's chest.

"Thank you for the assistance, my dear," he said, nodding to her and extending his hand. Celicia cringed away from him, still staring open-mouthed. She tried to speak, but seemed too shocked for words. Only a strangled choking sound came out.

He sighed and rolled his eyes. "I suppose you had to find out the truth at some point," he said, his voice resigned.

This surprised the Hunter.

She didn't know?

He found it hard to believe, but couldn't let the opportunity slip to drive a wedge between the Fourth and her master.

"He is a demon, Celicia," shouted the Hunter, spitting blood. "Your master is a demon. Think about that!"

Celicia's expression remained one of stunned disbelief, though she managed to close her mouth. "Yes," said the First, rolling his eyes, "I am a demon, as are you, Hunter."

Celicia's amazement doubled as she stared down at the Hunter. He could see her mind working, struggling to accept the truth of what she had seen. It was a lot to grasp, but he had to hope that she would come to the right conclusion.

"D-Demons…?" she managed to speak. "B-But…"

"Demons are no more than legends?" the First asked. He spoke in the patient voice of an adult addressing a child. "Not quite true, I'm afraid."

The First stepped forward, and though Celicia flinched away from him, he took her hands in his.

"Look at me, Celicia," he said, towering over her. "Look at my face. Feel my hands. You know me."

"B-but…" she stammered.

"Listen to me," the First said, his voice forceful. "I am the First of the Bloody Hand, and you are my Fourth. You once swore to serve me to the death. Do you remember your oath?"

She stared up at him, her eyes fixed on his face. "Y-yes," she finally managed to say. She swallowed, and when she spoke again, her voice was strong and clear. "Yes. I am the Fourth, and you are the First. I serve you, to the death."

"Good," nodded the First, squeezing her hand in a reassuring gesture. "That's good. Now, bring me that dagger." He pointed to Soulhunger, still tucked into the Hunter's belt.

Celicia looked as if she wanted to say more, but something in the First's eyes stopped her. She swallowed her question and walked over to the Hunter. Stooping, she reached for the knife in his belt, and the Hunter seized the moment to strike. He grabbed her wrist and pulled her atop him, slipping his left arm around her throat. The First seemed poised to step forward, but the Hunter glared at him and only squeezed tighter.

"Don't do it, demon," the Hunter snarled. "One step and I'll snap her neck."

The Hunter tightened his stranglehold on Celicia's neck until she cried out in pain. She struggled to break free, but he wrapped his legs around her waist, locking her in place.

Hesitation warred on the First's face, as if he was unsure if the Hunter would keep his word. Then, hesitation gave way to contempt.

"*Please*, Hunter," the First said with a cold, calculating sneer, "you think I care what happens to her? She is just one more pawn in my game. Her death means nothing to me, and it will not stop me from breaking you."

Heedless of Celicia's choked cries, the demon stepped forward and reached down to retrieve his demonic blade. The Hunter felt her struggle in his arms, but her strength was no match for his.

"If she dies here," the First said, "it matters little. She is only human, after all." He stared down at her, his eyes devoid of pity. "I'm truly sorry, my dear. This is not how I wanted it to end, but sacrifices must be made." He strode toward the Hunter and raised his demonic blade high to strike.

Celicia jerked in the Hunter's arms, her body stiffening in fear. For some reason, the Hunter felt a flash of pity for the woman in his arms. She was being betrayed by someone she had trusted—a sentiment all too familiar.

With all the strength he could muster, the Hunter her out of the path of the descending blade. She slammed against the nearby wall of the cavern and lay still.

At the same time, he rolled in the other direction. The First's blade missed him by less than a finger's breadth, and the horrible voice whispered in his mind as it sparked off the stone floor. He kept rolling in an attempt to put distance between himself and the First's long sword. Ignoring the weakness in his legs, he struggled to his feet. Pain raced along his spine, and though his knees wobbled, they held him upright. He forced his stiff, numb fingers to grip Soulhunger's hilt firmly.

"Shame that," the First said in a voice filled with disdain, glancing at Celicia's unmoving form. "She was useful, though she refused to work as a back-bedder." His admiring gaze ran over her body, sending a shudder of revulsion down the Hunter's spine. "She would have been good at it, no doubt."

His eyes returned to the Hunter, who had drawn the Swordsman's second blade and now gripped it in a shaky left hand.

"Look at you, Hunter," said the First, shaking his head in exasperation. "You can hardly stand, and yet you want to fight? Just surrender now, and when I have finished with you, your death will be quick and painless. It is the best you could hope for under the circumstances."

The Hunter, trying to hide the weakness in his legs, said nothing. He stared into the empty eyes of the First, wary of any sudden moves.

"Very well," the First said with a sigh. Then his face creased into a feral grin, and with a snarl of rage, the demon attacked.

The First pressed the Hunter hard, and the Hunter found himself forced to retreat before the First's slim sword. He moved sluggishly, and it took every shred of skill to stop the demon's blade from touching him. Even a small wound would sap his strength; he could hardly stand as it was. The sword's voice echoed in his thoughts, crying out for his blood.

Driven back by the flurry of blows, the Hunter sensed the tunnel wall immediately behind him. With nowhere to retreat, he launched himself forward, striking out with a powerful blow that caught the demon by surprise. The iron blade in his left hand lashed out at an opening in the First's guard, and he slashed Soulhunger at the demon's face. Somehow, the First managed to twist out of the way, though only barely. His slim sword whistled through the air, forcing the Hunter to duck and step back.

His momentum checked, the Hunter again fought a desperate defensive battle. The First's long sword seemed to be everywhere at once. He knew he would not quickly recover from the wounds left by the demon's sword. While his body could heal, the blade fed on the very essence of his being. Too many wounds, and the Hunter would have no strength or will to fight.

The back of his heel struck something solid—the prone, unmoving form of Celicia—but before he could recover, the First slammed into him. He fell hard, the wind whooshing from his lungs, the back of his head striking the ground with enough force to make him see stars. Blackness filled his vision, and he heard the distant clatter of steel on the stony floor. His fingers scrabbled in the dirt for his weapons, only to find them out of reach.

"It is over, Hunter," the First said, his voice sounding distant through the aching in the Hunter's head. "Yield or die."

Shaking his head to clear his vision, the Hunter saw the First standing over him. The tip of the demonic blade rested against his throat. He saw no pity in the endless void within the demon's eyes. There was no question about what would happen to him if he yielded.

"It's not over yet, demon!"

He kicked out, striking the back of the First's knees with enough force to throw the demon off balance. In that heartbeat when the First wobbled, the Hunter rolled out of reach of the accursed sword. He leapt for the Swordsman's iron blade, closing his fingers around it and launching himself to his feet. Moving with all the speed he could coax from his tired body, he thrust the iron blade toward the demon's throat.

Before he even came close, the First whipped his sword across his body in an elegant movement that blocked and cut in synchronous motion. The Hunter, his upper body extended in the thrust, had no time to avoid the blow. Pain flared in his neck. Blood dripped down his chest, soaking into the front of his tunic.

"*Please*, Hunter," the First said, contempt filling his voice. "You think something so elementary would work? I walked this earth long before you were spawned. My true form is more powerful than you could ever hope to be, and even in this frail human form I am more than a match for your skill."

The Hunter fought to speak, but his lungs refused to fill with air. He coughed, a wet cough that spattered the First's boots with blood.

It…can't…end…like…this! I…will…not…let…him…win.

He struggled to retain his grip on the iron blade, but it slipped from nerveless fingers. He couldn't feel his legs. Soulhunger seemed to sense the Hunter's heart slowing, and the blade screamed in his mind, thirsting for his blood.

Feed me, it whispered.

The First seized the Hunter's hair and violently jerked his head back, exposing the gaping wound in his neck. The Hunter clasped his hands to the tear in his throat in an attempt to quench the torrent of blood. He struggled to breathe, fighting to retain consciousness even as his life ebbed away.

Farida's face flashed before him, her eyes filled with pity for him. Even as darkness filled his vision, his eyes remained locked on the child's face.

I'm sorry, he told her. *I'm sorry I failed you.*

Suddenly, the hand holding his head released him, and he slumped to the floor. A scream echoed from somewhere in the distance, but dimly the Hunter realized it was not his own. Raising his head, he saw the demon's face contort into a mask of agony, bone and flesh rippling in a horrible wave. An iron blade protruded from the thing's neck. The creature's face matched the horror of his depthless eyes, his breath as foul as the stench that had wafted from the portal to hell.

"You bitch!" the demon gurgled, blood staining his teeth. "What are you doing?"

The thing that had once been the First stared at Celicia, who leaned dizzily against the wall of the cavern. The veins of the First's neck had begun to blacken, and smoke bubbled from the wound. A horrible odor filled the tunnel. When the creature reached up to grip the iron blade, the skin of its fingers withered. With a horrifying shriek of pain, the demon pulled the blade from his neck. Blood spurted from the wound, but the flesh began to slowly knit itself back together.

"Bastard!" snarled Celicia. She pressed one hand to her head, and gripped a dagger in the other. "You tried to kill me!"

"And now I'll finish the job," the First shouted, lunging toward her.

Celicia's dagger carved the demon's flesh with ruthless efficiency. But even as she sank her blade to the hilt in the First's chest, her eyes went wide in horror. Her mouth hung open, and she coughed weakly.

"Traitorous back-bedder," the First snarled, blood-tinged spittle flying into Celicia's face as she slumped to the ground. When the demon stepped back, the Hunter saw the Swordsman's iron blade buried in her side. Though the First clutched his scorched and withered hand to his chest in visible agony, he stared down at the gasping Celicia without a trace of pity.

He watched with remorseless eyes as her movement slowed, then stopped altogether.

Something within the Hunter snapped, just as it had when he cradled Farida's dying body in his arms.

Celicia may not have meant to help him—certainly she only meant to enact revenge on the First for trying to kill her—but inadvertently she had. And now she was going to die because of it.

Whatever you touch dies a horrible death, whispered the voice in his head. *You are death to all around you, Hunter.*

She is no innocent, but she didn't deserve to die.

Celicia coughed. It was weak, but she still lived. He could save her. He had failed Fari and the others, but perhaps there was time to do something for her.

The Hunter's arms and legs felt too heavy to move, but he climbed to his feet despite the pain. Slowly he stooped to retrieve Soulhunger and the Swordsman's blade from the ground. The First turned at the sound and stared at the Hunter with a look of disbelief.

"Give it up, you fool," the demon said in exasperation. "I can do this all night, and you're barely able to stand."

Yet the Hunter sensed that his words were a pretense. Black blood oozed from the wound in the First's neck. The demon had somehow managed to retrieve his accursed sword, but its point rested on the floor as the thing visibly struggled to stand.

He's just as weak as I am, he thought. *It's now or never.*

Forcing his feet to move, he lurched at the First with a lunge that felt far too slow. The demon knocked Soulhunger aside, but the Hunter struck out with the iron blade. Its razor edge bit deep into the First's knee, severing the tendons, muscles, and striking bone. The First's face registered disbelief, dumbfounded confusion, and pain.

Just then, the Hunter's legs gave out, but as he fell to his knees, he ripped the sword from the First's leg. Unable to support his weight on the leg, the First slumped to the floor. The Hunter twisted the dagger in his hand, placing its pommel against the cavern's stone floor and pointing the tip of the iron blade upward. The First's full weight collapsed onto the Swordsman's blade, and it sank deep into his groin.

A cry of agony ripped from the demon's mouth, a hellish sound of nightmares. It echoed around the massive cavern, increasing in volume as it reverberated from the hard stone walls. Blood gushed from the wound in his groin, spilling over the Hunter and sizzling as it flowed down the iron dagger. A horrid stench of charred flesh filled the Hunter's nostrils. The demon fell forward, collapsing atop the Hunter and knocking him to his back.

The Hunter shoved the First from atop him, rolling away from the pool of blood spreading beneath the fallen demon. Pushing himself to his elbows, he stared at the screaming, writhing creature beside him.

"Stings, doesn't it?" he asked with a mocking smile. More blood spurted from his throat, and he clamped his hand over the wound. With effort, he struggled to his knees. A chill stole over his limbs, robbing them of strength and sensation. His left hand, weakening, fell away from the wound in his neck, slumping lifeless by his side. His legs refused to hold him up, so he crawled, supporting his weight on his right arm.

The First's screams rang out, and real fear filled the demon's eyes.

"I...don't need...iron...to kill you," the Hunter choked out, his voice wet with his own blood.

Soulhunger screamed in his mind, throbbing with such force that it ripped through the numbness filling his limbs. It begged for blood; his blood, the First's blood, any blood.

Feed me, it pleaded.

The Hunter forced his back to straighten and his head to remain upright though he wanted nothing more than to collapse. Blood trickled down the front of his tunic. He couldn't feel his left arm, but he gripped Soulhunger tightly in his right hand. The familiar weight of the dagger strengthened his resolve.

This is for you, Fari, he thought.

"Wait," begged the First, his expression fearful, his eyes locked onto the dagger's razor edge gleaming in the flickering torchlight. "I'll—"

"Choke on this, you bastard," the Hunter growled.

Rage lent strength to his arm as he rammed the dagger deep into the First's eye. The blade passed through soft tissue with ease, its tip striking the bone at the back of the First's skull, but the Hunter pushed until the weapon's hilt slammed against the demon's cheekbone.

The First's remaining eye went wide in shock and horror. The Hunter twisted the blade, and the demon screamed. Blood poured down the First's face, and the Hunter shouted in triumph as Soulhunger drank deep of the demon's essence. A scar etched itself deep into the flesh of his back, eliciting a cry of pain.

Power flooded the Hunter, rushing through his veins with such force that it set every fiber of his being afire. Flesh and bone re knit, but the pain of his healing body immobilized him. His lungs burned, and his heart beat far too fast. Agony overwhelmed his mind and ripped his consciousness into tiny fragments. Molten metal raced through his veins, burning through him with wave after wave of torment. He squeezed his eyelids shut in an effort to block out the pain, but it was no use.

Through eyes blurred with tears, he watched the flesh of the First's face blacken and scorch. Skin burned away to reveal the demon's horned, scaled face. The thing screamed up at him, grasping for him with twisting fingers. It clawed at his face, his chest, its cries of agony threatening to shatter his ears.

He slumped atop the body. His body writhed and twitched with the torment racking every muscle and bone. He fought to remain conscious, refusing to give in to the weakness. Blood pounded in his ears, and he feared his heart would explode, until its beating gradually slowed and the pain coursing through him retreated.

The demon shouted in a horrible guttural language. Its empty, depthless eyes stared up into his own, and fear filled the creature's face as its struggles weakened. With a final, horrendous gasp, it shuddered and lay still.

He lay still for long moments, listening to his frantic heartbeat and his labored breathing. Yet when he finally tried to sit upright, he could move without pain. His head felt clear. Vigor raced through his veins, and though blood still stained the front of his tunic, only thick scar tissue remained where the wound in his neck had been.

The scent of lilies reached him, accompanied by the smell of iron and leather. Opening his eyes, he saw the form of Celicia lying on the floor. He moved to kneel beside her. A pool of blood spread beneath her, yet the way she glared at him told him she would live.

"You're hurt badly," he said, speaking in a calm, quiet voice, "but it's nothing a physicker can't deal with." He guessed the dagger had missed the major organs, and the wound, though painful, didn't appear to be fatal.

"Bastard!" Celicia snarled weakly, blood tingeing the flecks of spittle on her lips. "Kill me now and get it over with." Pain filled her face, but her eyes were clear as she stared up at him—the hatred in her expression plain.

"No," the Hunter replied. "Now hold still."

He ripped a length of cloth from the First's brightly-colored robes and pressed it to her side.

"Here, take this," he said, placing her blood-stained hands on the cloth. "Apply pressure, and you should be able to stop the bleeding."

"What do you care?" Celicia snarled. "You killed everyone else, so why save me?"

The Beggar Priest's words flashed through the Hunter's mind. *You are given over to a life of crime,* the aging voice said, *but that does not mean your heart is filled with evil. You will find there are many in your line of work that are simply there out of necessity, or because they know nothing else.*

"Some deserve death," the Hunter said, "but others deserve a second chance at life."

"So you save my life, and I fall into your arms?" she asked, anger lending strength to her voice. "You think that because I'm a woman I will be grateful for your assistance?"

"No," the Hunter replied, "this has nothing to do with your being a woman."

"So what then?" Celicia demanded. "Why save me and none of the others?"

"I owe you my life. Twice now."

She fell silent at this.

"It was you who brought me to the Beggar Priests, wasn't it?" He remembered her scent that night as he lay on the cobblestones of Upper Voramis.

She said nothing, and he took her silence as confirmation.

"I don't know why you did it," the Hunter said, "but I owe you my life for that. And for helping me stop the First."

"You owe me nothing for that!" Celicia snarled. "The whorespawn tried to kill me, and I simply repaid him in kind."

"Fair enough."

Turning his back on Celicia, he ripped more of the First's robes for bandages. She winced when he wrapped the cloth around her midsection, but made no protest.

When he had finished, he climbed to his feet. "Consider my debt repaid, Celicia. If that is even your name…"

Turning away from her, he collected his weapons from the cavern floor. Soulhunger's voice remained silent in his mind. He winced as he touched the iron blades, but the pain faded once he slipped them into their sheaths on his back. The weight of his sword on his back comforted him.

As he reached for the First's sword, it whispered to him, enticing him to wield it, offering to serve him. With an effort, he shoved the voice to the back of his mind. Unwilling to touch the blade, he wrapped it in the First's robe before tucking it into his belt.

"So what now?" Celicia called out. The Hunter turned to see her struggling into a sitting position. "You just walk away, and life goes on?"

"Yes," said the Hunter with a shrug.

"And you expect me to let you go? What will stop me from hunting you down in vengeance for what you have done tonight?"

"The Bloody Hand is no more. Their reign of terror has come to an end. What you do with yourself is of no concern to me. Hunt me down, and I will not hesitate to end you."

Celicia tried to keep her expression neutral, but fear flashed in her eyes. She flinched beneath the menace in the Hunter's voice, and finally looked away. Her eyes rested on the First's twisted body.

"You killed him," she asked, "yet he said you're one of them. Is that true?"

"Yes and no," he replied. "Their blood may run through my veins, but that doesn't make me like them. I am only half-demon; the other half is as human as you are."

"You're a murderer. You deserve to die."

"Perhaps," the Hunter said, nodding his head, "but I have been given a second chance. Now, you have been given one as well. Do with it what you will."

"And you're just going to leave me here to die?" she snarled at him.

"The bleeding has stopped," the Hunter replied. "You will live."

"Will I? You've destroyed everything I worked hard to build, so what do you expect me to do now? Work at The Arms of Heaven?"

"If you must," the Hunter shrugged.

Anger flashed in Celicia's eyes. "I will never—!"

"I don't care what you do," the Hunter said, cutting off her words. "But know that if you *ever* harm an innocent, I will finish what was started here tonight."

Celicia looked as though she had just been slapped. "What *he* did," she said, her eyes flicking toward the First's corpse, "it was…inhuman." She shuddered.

A vision of Farida's lifeless body flashed before the Hunter's eyes, and his face darkened at the memory.

Celicia must have seen the anger in his face, for she held up a weak hand. "I had nothing to do with it," she said, "I swear!"

Silence fell between them as the Hunter studied her face.

"I believe you," he said at last, "and that is the only reason that you still live. I loved that little girl, and *he* took her from me." He swallowed hard and dashed away a tear. "I killed him because of what he did, but that doesn't mean you have to die."

She remained silent.

"You're not like the others that surrounded you, are you? You have no real desire to kill me. You *never* wanted to kill."

He stared into her eyes, but she avoided his gaze.

"You feel the weight of guilt for every life you have taken, don't you?" She said nothing. "You may have forgotten who you once were, but buried somewhere deep, it is still there. You still know right from wrong, and that is why you live."

He knelt beside her. "Look at me, Celicia."

Slowly, she turned her face toward him.

"Tell me," he said quietly, "what do you see when you look into my eyes?"

Celicia looked into his eyes. "Darkness," she gasped, recoiling in horror. "Emptiness."

"I am forced to live with this evil every day, but you are not. You don't have to hide who you are. Fear and shame need not rule your life. Go, live your life the way it was meant to be, and leave behind this disguise you wear."

Uncertainty, hesitation, doubt, and fear collided in her expression, but he could see his words taking effect.

"Here lies the Fourth of the Bloody Hand," he intoned, "killed alongside her men. From this tunnel emerges a new woman, one who will choose her own path in life."

The Hunter slowly stood, feeling every muscle and bone of his body protest. Blood stained his face and his clothes hung ripped on his frame, but his heart felt somehow light, unburdened.

He extended his hand to her, and she took it. Her hand was soft and warm in his, yet her grip was strong. "You are free, Celicia."

"And you?" she asked in a quiet voice. "Are you free, Hunter?" Her face had seemed to change as well. Where she once stared at him with naked hatred, now there was something akin to pity in her eyes.

"No," he replied, shaking his head. "I was born to be the Hunter, and it is who I am and will always be."

"Can you not choose a different path?"

He shook his head. "I wish I could, but it is not meant to be. I have tried to ignore the voice within me telling me to bring death, but in the end, that demon within will always win."

Celicia reached out to place a gentle hand on his cheek. "You say you have seen the real me, Hunter, but I have seen into your heart this night as well. You claim to be less than human, but your actions prove that you are more than just a man."

He tried to think of something to say, but no words came out.

"I have to say, I like this face much better than the one you wore that night in The Iron Arms." Her eyes took in his features, and a smile played at the corners of her lips. "Why do you wear the disguises, Hunter?"

He fought for an answer. "To protect my identity from those around me who would seek retribution."

"That may be," Celicia said, thoughtful, "but have you ever considered that they only serve to hide you from the world around you?"

He had no reply to this.

"If you truly are immortal, as the rumors say," the woman continued, "could those masks not be your way of keeping the world out? A shield against pain? If no one ever sees the real you, there is no risk of anyone growing close. With no one to care for, there is no risk of loss."

Something within the Hunter threatened to burst, and a lump grew in his throat.

"What a lonely existence it must be to have no one to share your life with." There was sorrow in Celicia's words. "I can relate to that, Hunter, for I, too, have worn a mask all these years. Thanks to you, I am free of mine. Perhaps you should seek freedom from yours as well."

She placed her other hand on his cheek, pulling his face close to hers. "Don't hide from the world, Hunter. Find someone to share your world with and you will never need to fear being alone again."

A single tear trickled down his cheek, and she smiled up at him.

"Perhaps there is more to you than you suspect," she continued. "Perhaps you were meant to be something more than just an assassin-for-hire. Search your soul, and you may find your true purpose."

She pulled him forward, pressing her lips to his. The kiss lasted for several seconds, and a thrill coursed through his body. It was a sensation he had never experienced with Lady Damuria or the other women he had taken to his bed.

When Celicia finally released him, she gave him a weak grin. "Farewell, Hunter. May the gods smile on you wherever you go."

With a nod of farewell, the Hunter turned and strode toward the end of the tunnel. He had walked only a few paces before he turned around.

No! protested the voice in his head. *We must feed. You cannot let her get away.*

Silence, he thundered inwardly. *I know what you are, demon, and you will no longer control me.*

"One question," he said, fighting to swallow the lump in his throat.

Celicia stared up at him, arching an eyebrow in response.

"What is your real name?" he asked.

Smiling, she responded in a quiet voice. "Kiara. My name is Kiara."

With a nod, he turned and walked into the darkness of the Serenii tunnels. A single torch flickered on the floor behind him, casting eerie shadows on the walls within its small circle of illumination. Celicia lay within its circle of light, a small figure blending with the night.

The Hunter's heart thundered in the silence of the empty passages. Yet it didn't beat with fear or rage. He was alone, but for the first time in his memory, the Hunter no longer felt lonely.

Epilogue

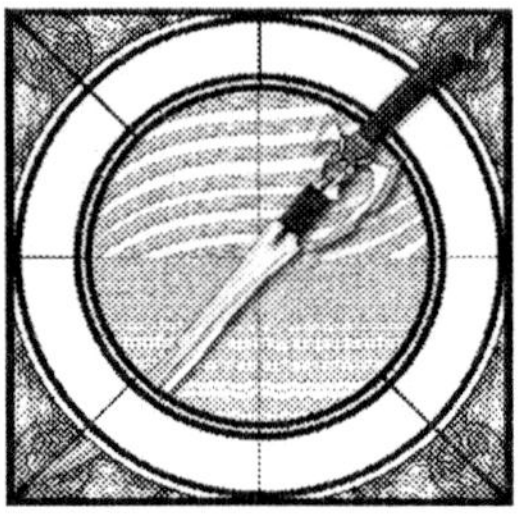

The first rays of morning sunlight peeked over the eastern horizon, illuminating the beautiful terrain surrounding the city. The sounds of commerce had yet to rise to the heavens, and the city remained silent and peaceful. His body ached from the exertion of climbing, and fire still raced through the scars on his back and chest, yet he felt an odd sense of peace. Soulhunger pounded in his mind, but its voice had grown quiet since feeding on the lifeblood of the demon.

From his perch atop the Palace of Justice, the tallest building in Voramis, the Hunter looked down on the sprawling metropolis below. A cool dawn breeze blew across the Hunter's face, and he reveled in the morning's chill. The wind carried the scents of the city to him. The fragrance of flowers and Snowblossom trees from the Maiden's Fields. The odor of incense from the Temple District. The smell of filth from the Beggar's Quarter. The aroma of the myriad goods sold in the Merchant's Quarter.

My city, he thought.

He had lived in Voramis for nearly half a century and had come to call it home. Now, he realized he had merely forced himself to believe he had a place in the city.

The desire to kill is overwhelming, and yielding to it helps to silence that aching emptiness for a time. But no matter how many lives I take, I can never dull the pain of that yawning abyss within.

He thought of Lady Damuria, and the countless others like her with whom he had shared a bed. They had helped to drown out the murderous voices in his head, providing a temporary distraction. Yet, as he remembered the feelings of disdain, he knew in truth it was disgust for himself that had overwhelmed him.

Farida's smiling face flashed through his mind, causing his heart to ache. Sorrow flooded him, and tears fell from his eyes. Instead of brushing them away, however, he let them flow. They burst from him in great heaving sobs, and he wept into the dawn.

For a short time, she had filled that hole in her own way. What little of the Hunter she did see, she had never rejected. When he was with her, he had felt somehow… complete.

The pain diminished, but the hollow feeling remained. *She will always be a part of me, but I have to let her go.*

Her face faded, blown away by the gentle breeze.

Goodbye, Farida. You are gone, but never forgotten.

For long moments he remained motionless, his mind an empty void. He closed his eyes, letting his senses bask in the new morning.

Voramis had been cleansed. The Bloody Hand was no more, the Dark Heresy a thing of the past.

So now what? What does my future hold?

He stared out over the city where he had lived for so many years, but saw only an unfamiliar jungle of buildings and streets. Something beyond the horizon beckoned to him, a pull he could not resist.

Voramis is no longer my home; of that much I am certain.

It had ceased being his home the moment Farida died. He knew he needed to find answers, but something told him he would not find them in Voramis.

He needed to know more about who he was—what he was. He needed answers about the creature within him. He had escaped death, but still the demon raged in his mind. Soulhunger added its voice to the tumult in his head.

The events of the night flashed before his eyes. He had taken dozens of lives, and now he saw their faces, felt the pain of their deaths etched into his body. He recalled the temptation of death, a longing for the cessation of pain. It would have been so easy to give up, and yet he had chosen to live.

The demon's words played through his mind. "Embrace who you are," the creature had said.

I am the last of my kind, the last Bucelarii, but I refuse to accept the 'destiny' the First spoke of.

The Hunter knelt and unwrapped the clothbound bundle he had carried here. The First's accursed sword stared up at him, whispering in his mind.

Wield me, it told him, *and I will give you power beyond your wildest dreams. You will conquer the world, and together we—*

The voice intensified the moment his fingers closed around its hilt, and it filled him with revulsion. He held it out at arm's length as he walked toward the center of the roof, unwilling to let it any nearer his body than necessary.

Wait! The blade's tone turned begging. *You cannot cast me off. I am—*

You are nothing, the Hunter thought, steeling his mind and shutting out the sword's pleas. *You are the last relic of a civilization long past. You are a curse, one I will put an end to now.*

He placed the blade on the tiles of the roof, covering it with the blanket.

No one will ever find you. As long as you remain here, the world will be safe.

Rising to his feet, the Hunter turned and, without a backward glance, strode away. The action felt paramount to turning his back on his kind, but he was at peace with his decision.

As he neared the edge of the rooftop, he was seized by an overwhelming urge to throw Soulhunger from the roof of the Palace. He wanted nothing more than to rid himself of the dagger, to be free of the whispers that incited him to kill. Yet something stopped his hand. He could not part with the blade, for it was his only link to his past. He somehow knew it would play an important role in discovering the truth.

I may have been created to serve Kharna, he thought, *but I will be the blade of the Destroyer no longer. I will fight it with every breath! By the gods, I swear I will find a way to undo what my actions have set in motion.*

"Gods damn you, Destroyer," the Hunter cursed aloud. He raised his arms high, his voice growling into the quiet dawn. "I will be a pawn in your game no longer!"

Without warning, a bolt of lightning shot from the cloudless sky. Crackling tendrils of power surged toward the Hunter, striking his upraised arms in twin concussions. Agony ripped through him, and every fiber of his being sizzled with the force of the strike. He felt himself pulled into the air, floating, weightless. His body burned with the energy coursing through him, and he screamed into the rushing wind. He fell for an eternity, his body battered by the gale around him.

Then he stood once more on the rooftop, his arms raised to the heavens. The sky remained clear, the morning breeze gentle and cool.

What in the Watcher's name was that? The memory of the agony remained, but no pain coursed through him. Had it even truly happened?

His hands trembled, and the skin of his chest tingled. He ripped open his shirt, and his eyes went wide in shock as he saw the smooth skin.

The scars! They're gone!

For as long as he could remember, the marks had been the price he paid for every life he took. They served as a reminder of what he was, but they had also reminded him of his humanity. When he stared at them, the faces of his victims appeared. He bore a burden of remorse over their deaths, though he tried to ignore it.

And now they were gone. The marks etched into his skin had disappeared, all save one scar immediately over his heart.

How is this possible?

It is redemption of a sort, the humanity within him whispered. *A chance to start again.*

Freedom.

Something within his mind seemed to shift, to click into place. A rush of memories flooded him, driving him to his knees with their overwhelming force.

An elusive scent from out of his forgotten past filled his nostrils. The smell of jasmine and honey, cinnamon and berries.

Her scent.

The shape of a woman hung in the pre-dawn air.

A sapphire necklace accentuates the soft curves of her neck, the ridges of her collarbones. Golden hair falls in perfect ringlets on her pale skin. Soft flesh in my hands as I run them along her spine, the curvature of her waist, the swell of her breasts.

His hands tingled as they remembered the feeling of warm skin. The ache in his heart returned, and the memory of the face before him nearly overwhelmed him with sorrow.

I can almost touch her.

His hand reached out of its own accord, but it found only empty air. A lump rose in his throat as he stared at the figure from his past. The agony of loss—a pain all too familiar to the Hunter—coursed through him.

The woman faded from before his eyes, but her presence had opened the floodgates in his mind. Memories rushed through his head faster than his mind could comprehend, scenes from his past flitting before him in a torrent of images, scents, and sensations.

I remember...

Then they were gone, locked away once more. Only the memory of the woman remained.

He felt empty, hollow once more. Yet the memory of the woman's face, of her scent, had filled a fraction of the void within him.

Who is she?

The Hunter could put no name to the familiar face, but he didn't care. If he remembered her, would she remember him? Could this woman help him piece together the fragments of his past?

Another thought flashed through his mind.

Am I truly alone?

He breathed deep, relishing the scent of the fresh morning breeze. His chest felt as if it would burst, yet his heart was filled not with sorrow, but with hope. For the first time in his memory, he had a purpose beyond bringing death and destruction.

I have to find her.

He wanted—no, needed—answers. He had been given a fresh start, but what would he do with it?

My life is my own, and I will allow no one to control me. What do I choose to do?

Never had the sunrise seemed so beautiful. The bright morning light warmed him to his very core, the rising sun beating down with an intensity that sent a shiver down his spine. Smiling, the Hunter stared out over the city of Voramis for the final time.

"The hunt always beckons," he whispered.

* * *

City of Voramis Map

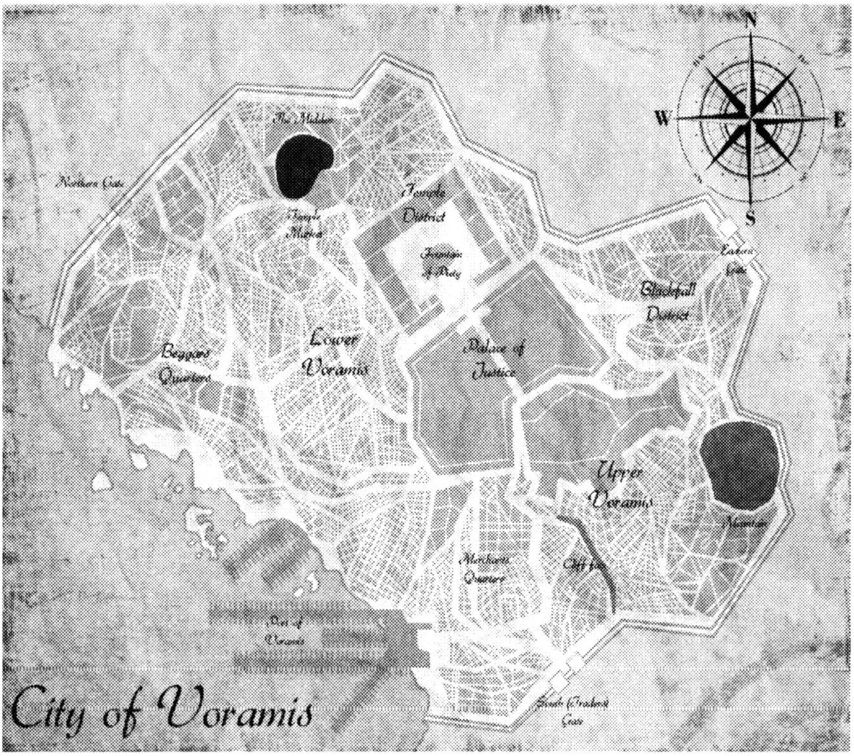

If you enjoyed this book, please consider writing a short review and posting it on Amazon, Goodreads and/or Barnes and Noble. Reviews are very helpful to other readers and are greatly appreciated by authors, especially me. When you post a review, drop me an email and let me know and I may feature part of it on my blog/site. Thank you. ~ Andy (andy.peloquin@gmail.com)

Here is a sneak-peek at The Last Bucelarii (Book 2):

Lament of the Fallen

The Hunter is alone.

Voramis is far behind, with nothing but the empty road ahead. Though his future is uncertain, of one thing he is convinced: he has to find *Her*, the mystery woman who plagues his dreams and haunts his memories. She is calling to him, drawing him ever northward.

When the Hunter stumbles upon a pair of bandits attacking a group of travelers, something within urges him to help. Yet he discovers that even the best intentions can lead a man astray, putting him in the path of those given the task to hunt down his kind: the Cambionari.

Wounded, his body failing, the Hunter finds himself in the beautiful city of Malandria, where he is inexorably drawn into direct conflict with the Order of Midas, the faceless, nameless power in the city.

From feared assassin of Voramis to outcast of Malandria, the Hunter's journey leads him to truths about his forgotten past, the Bucelarii, and the Abiarazi he has pledged to hunt. Yet these discoveries may shed light on who he really is—the demon and the man.

* * *

About the Author

Andy Peloquin has loved to read since before he can remember. *Sherlock Holmes*, the *Phantom of the Opera*, and *Father Brown* are just a few of the books that ensnared his imagination as a child.

When he discovered science fiction and fantasy through the pages of writers like Edgar Rice Burroughs, J.R.R Tolkien, and Orson Scott Card, he was immediately hooked and hasn't looked back since.

Andy's first attempt at writing produced *In the Days: A Tale of the Forgotten Continent.* He has learned from the mistakes he made and used the experience to produce *Blade of the Destroyer*, a book of which he is very proud.

Reading—and now writing—is his favorite escape, and it provides him with an outlet for his innate creativity. He is an artist; words are his palette.

Let's Get Social!

Be My Friend:
https://www.facebook.com/andrew.peloquin.1
Facebook Author Page: https://www.facebook.com/andyqpeloquin
Twitter: https://twitter.com/AndyPeloquin
Google+:
https://plus.google.com/100885994638914122147/about